THE
COTILLION
BRIGADE

A Novel of the Civil War and the
Most Famous Female Militia in American History

GLEN CRANEY

BRIGID'S FIRE PRESS

Published in the United States

FIRST EDITION

Library of Congress Cataloging-in-Publication Data
Craney, Glen
The cotillion brigade: a novel of the civil war and the most famous female militia in american history / Glen Craney — 1st ed.

ISBN 978-0-9961541-1-6

1. The Nancy Harts—Fiction, 1861-1865 2. Civil War—Fiction. 3. Georgia—History—Civil War, 1861-1865—Fiction. 4. Oscar H. LaGrange—Fiction, 1861-1865. 5. Plantation Life—Fiction. 6. Women—Civil War, 1861-1865—Fiction.
7. United States—History—Civil War 1861-1865—Campaigns. 8. Confederate States of America, 1861-1865—Fiction. 9. Women's Militia—History—Fiction.

Brigid's Fire Press
www.brigidsfire.com

A few passages in this novel contain offensive language common to the time. Those who write about the Civil War era confront a dilemma: Preserve the authenticity of such usage, or risk diluting the hatefulness of the speaker by expunging the word and substituting an anachronism. The author has attempted to err on the side of sensitivity while still fulfilling the duty of the historical novelist to present the past with all of its faults and prejudices.

"But when Cleomenes, king of the Spartans, having slain many Argives … proceeded against the city, an impulsive daring, divinely inspired, came to the younger women to try, for their country's sake, to hold off the enemy. Under the lead of Telesilla they took up arms, and, taking their stand by the battlements, manned the walls all round, so that the enemy were amazed."

— Plutarch, *The Women of Argos*

PRINCIPAL CHARACTERS

The South

The Nancy Harts Militia

Nancy "Nannie" Colquitt Hill Morgan.............................*Captain*

Mary Cade Alford Heard........*First Lieutenant and Nancy Hill's classmate*

Caroline Ware Poythress........*Third Corporal and Dr. Augustus Ware's sister*

Martha "Pack" Beall.........*Second Sergeant and Mary Heard's sister-in-law*

Leila Pullen...*First Corporal*

Augusta Hill............................*First Sergeant and Nancy Hill's sister*

Aley Smith..*Second Lieutenant*

Andelia Bull.......................... *Third Lieutenant and Sallie Bull's sister*

Sallie Bull.........................*Second Corporal and Andelia Bull's sister*

Ella Kay...*Treasurer*

Dr. Augustus Ware...........*Caroline Poythress's brother and Nancy Hill's cousin*

Jeremiah Brown Morgan..*LaGrange lawyer*

Benjamin Harvey Hill......................*Politician and Nancy Hill's distant cousin*

Sallie Fannie Reid......................*Popular belle from Sunny Villa, West Point*

Sarah Potts....................................*Sallie Fannie Reid's younger friend*

Marie Harrison.......................................*Poythress family house slave*

Lizzie Andrews.......................................*Daughter of a Macon planter*

Lieutenant John Gay.................................*Fourth Georgia Infantry*

Eugenius Ware..........*Fourth Georgia officer, brother of Augustus and Caroline*

Joseph Ware...............*Fourth Georgia officer, brother of Augustus and Caroline*

Joseph Hill.............................*Fourth Georgia officer and brother of Nancy*

Miles Hill...............................*Fourth Georgia officer and brother of Nancy*

General Joseph Wheeler....................*Cavalry commander, Army of Tennessee*

Duff Green Reed..............................*Adjutant for General Joseph Wheeler*

Colonel William Jeffers..............................*Eighth Missouri Cavalry*

General Robert Tyler...........................*Infantry officer, Army of Tennessee*

General William Hardee...............*First Corps commander, Army of Tennessee*

General Alfred Colquitt..........*Brigade commander, Army of Northern Virginia*
Captain William Grant.................*Officer serving with Nathan Bedford Forrest*
Dr. George Todd...........*Confederate physician and Mary Todd Lincoln's brother*
Captain Celestino Gonzales...*First Florida Infantry*
Major Rutledge Parham.............................*Twenty-Fourth Alabama Infantry*
Lieutenant Louis McFarland..................................*Ninth Tennessee Infantry*
Colonel James Fannin..*Georgia Reserves*
Belle Boyd...*Confederate spy from Virginia*
Seth Coogler......................................*Private, Thirtieth Georgia Infantry*
Dash...*Confederate volunteer from Gascony, France*

The North

Colonel Oscar Hugh LaGrange.........*Wisconsin Abolitionist and cavalry officer*
Captain Wallace LaGrange......................*Hugh's brother and cavalry officer*
Colonel Edward Daniels........................*Wisconsin geologist and Abolitionist*
Jennie Stowell...*Wisconsin student and Abolitionist*
Sherman Booth..*Abolitionist newspaper editor*
Colonel Daniel Ray..*Second Tennessee Cavalry*
Al Walton...............................*Drummer, Seventy-Fifth Indiana Infantry*
Sergeant Steven "Nick" Nichols.....................*Choctaw, First Wisconsin Cavalry*
Captain Roswell "Ross" Hill..*Second Indiana Cavalry*
General James Wilson.........................*Cavalry Corps, Army of the Cumberland*
Major General Alexander McCook...........*XX Corps, Army of the Cumberland*
Colonel Edward McCook.................*Cavalry Corps, Army of the Cumberland*
Major General George Thomas................*XIV Corps, Army of the Cumberland*

1

LAGRANGE, GEORGIA
MARCH 1856

"**M**iss Hill! Another demerit for you!"

Sixteen-year-old Nancy Colquitt Hill stopped halfway up the portico steps of LaGrange Female College. Turning, she searched the gabled windows and manicured grounds for the source of that unfair indictment. Was Mrs. Smith spying on her again? That old bat crowned with the severe bun of gray hair was always stalking her with the marks journal. What absurd transgression had she committed now? She examined her feet to make sure the skirt of her gray starched uniform covered her ankles. Finding no violation with her attire, she ticked off the endless list of regulations the dean had forced her to memorize: *Pupils must not leave books or other articles out of place; sit in windows, make undue noise, borrow jewelry, leave pianos open, or—*

"Communicate with young gentlemen."

She spun again but couldn't find the culprit. Had she heard correctly, or was an oracular voice intruding on her innermost thoughts? A shade from Delphi or Cumae, perhaps. Yes, one must have attached itself to her soul during her many hours of reading the Roman classics. Just last week, she had playacted a blind priestess at the grotto in the garden terraces, evoking the spirits by breathing in the applewood tea vapors to substitute for the mind-altering gases that rose through those ancient Greek crevices and—

"Naughty on you, Nannie!" Ten-year-old Leila Pullen leapt out from behind a fluted column, wagging her finger.

Nancy turned red as a Troup County peach. "You little boll weevil! Have you been following me?"

"President George Washington made it a free country," said the pig-tailed sprite, who was not much taller than the portico's wrought-iron railing. "I can walk wherever I please."

Nancy grabbed her tormentor's arm before she scampered away. The clever urchin had somehow learned to mimic Dean Smith's screechy voice and throw it like a ventriloquist. "Who taught you to do *that?*"

"I ain't telling."

"You *aren't* telling. If you were in primary school right now instead of playing hooky, maybe you'd learn correct grammar."

Leila shook off her hold. "Mama says your face is gonna turn way too common if you keep strolling downtown the way you do every morning."

Nancy was aghast to discover she was being discussed on Gossip Row. "I swear I will haul you off and sell you to the next circus—"

"Lawyers don't make suitable husbands. They're too stodgy."

Nancy spun to confront another voice whispering behind her. One of her two best friends, Mary Cade Heard, stood grinning at the prank she and Leila had pulled. She accused Mary, "*You* put her up to this?"

Mary patted Leila's head. "She's a fast learner. She may hogtie a man before you do."

Nancy fussed with the pleats in her skirt, trying to deflect the implication sheathed in that observation. "Hogtying a man, if you must use such a crude expression, is the furthest thing from my mind."

Mary locked arms with Nancy and hurried her toward the doors of the classroom building. "We will be late for Natural Sciences."

"If you hadn't tailed me like a lurking thief—"

"Did you see him?"

Nancy played dumb. "See whom?"

"Don't act innocent. Brown Morgan."

Nancy glanced over her shoulder and saw Leila trailing them. She stopped and brought her fists to her waist. "Where do you think *you're* going?"

Leila stuck out her tongue. "Mary arranged for me to sit in today. My teacher says I'm precocious. So there, Nannie with the Face-Too-Common!"

Nancy harrumphed as she launched herself onto the second flight of stairs. "Has this school dispensed with all age and moral requirements?"

Mary, as usual, didn't take the bait.

Nancy meant the complaint for Leila but aimed it at Mary, whose wealthy Heard family had long been a college benefactor. Twenty-two and married for five years, Mary was blessed with lush crimson hair, soft green eyes, and the delicate features of a proper Yorkshire manor lass. For every reprimand Nancy received from the instructors for impudence and unladylike behavior, Mary won a plaudit for her selflessness, reticence, and refined Southern demeanor. As one of the oldest students, Mary insisted on playing mentor to the younger girls. Nancy suspected she was so protective of them because she married so young, a decision that required her to take on the added responsibility of helping run her minister husband's Methodist church affairs while also studying for her degree. Nancy appreciated Mary's maternal concern, but though she would never admit it, she envied her wonderful fortune in marrying well and living in one of the stateliest mansions in town.

"You didn't answer me," Mary said.

"Yes, I saw him."

"And?"

Nancy abandoned her affectation of indifference. "He spoke it."

Mary stopped her rushed walking. "He proposed to you?"

Nancy shushed her. "No, you goose! He turned to me, doffed his hat, and—"

"Asked you to save him a dance at Saturday's ball?" Leila said.

Nancy was about to blow a cork. "Will you two let me finish a sentence?"

"Well, get on with it," Mary said.

"I'm not telling you now."

"Nan, I'm sorry," said Mary. "Please, I want to know."

Nancy studied her with suspicion. Finally, she relented. "Mr. Morgan looked directly at me and said, 'Good day, Miss Hill.'"

Behind them, Leila chortled. "That's all?"

"It was the *way* he said it!" Nancy insisted. "And his eyes. He spoke volumes with those misty eyes."

Leila looked to Mary for an assessment of the disappointing report. "That would never cut the Yorkshire cheese in a Brontë story."

Nancy rounded on the urchin. "They're letting you read risque romance novels now? What's next? The Shelleys?"

Mary brought a finger to her lips for Leila to stay silent. "Brown Morgan is a man of few words and—"

"He's a lawyer," Leila chimed, not taking the hint. "I thought lawyers trained to talk fast because they get paid by the minute."

Nancy sized up an open second-story window, calculating the effort to send Leila flying through it like a winged piglet. Before she acted on the impulse, Mary hurried them both down the hall and toward the classroom. She opened the door and herded Mary and Leila inside.

Nancy stood frozen at the threshold. Every student in the room turned to gawk at her for being late. The morning had been full of unwanted surprises, but she could not accept what now met her eyes. At the lectern stood Dr. Augustus Ware, her cousin and the elder brother of Caroline Poythress, her second-best friend. Baffled why *he* was in the teacher's spot, Nancy looked to Caroline in the front row for an explanation, but she just shrugged.

Dr. Ware narrowed his bespectacled glare on the late arrivals. "Are we interrupting your promenade this morning, ladies?"

"What are you doing here, Gus?" Nancy demanded.

Gus huffed at the informality. "For the rest of the semester, Miss Hill, I would prefer you address me as Professor Ware."

Nancy cackled. "Are you going to treat us to sodas at your apothecary after class, *Professor* Ware?"

The other girls laughed.

The instructor flushed. "That will be quite enough."

"Come on, Gus," Nancy said. "You're not *really* going to teach this class."

"Had you arrived on time, you would have heard me explain that Professor Morris has taken ill. He will recuperate at Warm Springs until the end of the semester. President Woolford didn't find a replacement on such late notice, so he asked me to fill in."

What more could go awry today? Nancy slid grumbling into her desk chair, distressed the grand mysteries of the natural world were to be taught by her family physician. Her mother had paid an exorbitant tuition for *this*? Gus Ware was a grumpy eccentric who harbored strange ideas, including a deep skepticism about the traditional curriculum in medical schools. Most of the locals attributed his dour temperament to his barely surviving the Yellow Jack fever as a boy during the Mobile Bay epidemic of 1843. She remembered her mother's stories of that scare, and only three years ago, another low-country chill rage hit New Orleans. The harrowing newspaper reports of that ordeal said the delirium victims bled black ooze from their noses and vomited until their insides were dry as chalk downs.

She stared at Gus and tried again to comprehend how two siblings could be so different in personality and features. His sister, Caroline, was short, attractively buxom, and cherubic in her round face; she allowed her straight black hair to fall bouncing onto her shoulders, and the only aspects at war with her congenial disposition were her deep-set, unblinking jet eyes, which, in tandem with her thin mouth that naturally turned down at the corners, evoked an aura of pouting sadness.

Six years older, Gus, in contrast, remained thin as a rail and bald, except for a few tufts around the ears, and his skin had yellowed from the jaundice. He had always been sickly, which did not help his medical practice flourish, and if the ravages of the yellow fever weren't affliction enough, his constitution was so weakened by early rheumatism that he walked with a cane. Folks around town whispered why anyone would go to a doctor who couldn't heal himself, but Caroline confided he attended medical school in Philadelphia to learn to help others avoid what he had endured. When not at work in his drugstore and examination office, Gus indulged his lone avocation, tending to a small grove on the edge of town, where he grew a species of tree from Peru that supplied the bark to produce quinine, the only known antidote to a variety of fever diseases. Despite his mixed reputation with white customers, the plantation slaves flocked to him for magical remedies, believing the touching hand of God had rendered him immune from the swamp scourges after passing through his own hour of testing.

"We'll start with a lesson on herbs," Gus announced.

"Herbs?" Caroline protested. "Shouldn't you first teach us the stars and constellations? This is Natural Sciences, not Botany."

Gus leaned against his silver-tipped walking stick as he limped down the row with his narrow head hung so low that his chin thrummed against his sunken chest. "Has anyone in this class been mended by a heavenly orb?"

The girls shrugged.

Gus pulled a small packet from his breast pocket and poured its brownish contents into the palm of his right hand. He held the slight mound of granules under Leila's nose. "What's its aroma?"

Leila's face twisted. "Yuck. Spoiled apricots."

"*Agrimonia eupatoria*," Gus said. "The mountain folk call it 'church steeples' and the Cherokee called it the 'plant of gratitude.' Does anyone wish to hazard a guess why?"

The girls shook their heads.

"*Bald's Leechbook* recommended it as far back as the ninth century as a cure for impotence."

"Gus!" Caroline admonished. "Remember your place."

Not one to tolerate the courtesies of *haute* society, Gus ignored his sister's warning and persisted in recounting, in the most graphic terms, the herb's properties. "It is also effective for healing diarrhea, urinary infections, and as a balm for musket wounds. Every garden in Georgia should have a patch of this."

Bored, Nancy looked out the window toward Broad Street. The liveries were transporting their passengers and freight from the Atlanta train and loading it onto the cars bound for Montgomery. She smiled with pride at the foresight of their city's founders, who had changed the rail gauges to prevent the locomotives from the North to pass through town without stopping to shop. Plantation owners from a hundred miles in every direction brought their cotton here to send to the distant corners of the world; the tariffs and exchange fees alone had made LaGrange, with a population of only fifteen hundred and nearly twice that many slaves, one of the most prosperous towns in the South.

An idea struck her. Maybe it wasn't too late to change schools and enroll in the Southern Female College across the quad. Besides the two women's colleges, her beloved town was home to four academic institutions for men, one a military academy. Sitting so near to the Alabama state line, LaGrange drew its fair share of wealthy sons from Montgomery, Atlanta, and New Orleans. Visiting scholars called it the Cambridge of the South.

If she failed to find an eligible husband here, it wouldn't be for want of resources or favorable odds. Yet she had set her sights on the one gentleman whose name she couldn't whisper without causing her heart to flutter. Why waste time on college men when she could marry a local lawyer, one already well on his way to becoming established and wealthy? Problem was, several young ladies—some in this classroom—had devised the same plan.

She didn't need to be told she wasn't the comeliest belle in Troup County. Her face was too long, her limbs gangly, and her gaze too unchecked for her to be considered the top prize. Mary, the genuine beauty of the class, had been plucked at seventeen by a wealthy planter. She, on the other hand, was fast approaching that age when a girl risked being relegated to grubbing around in the dregs barrel. She was not about to let *that* happen, so she would have to rely on her one asset the others lacked: a talent for calculation and strategy. She read at a voracious pace and kept a secret journal of guideposts and rules by which to live. One maxim she had never forgotten: When choosing generals for his army, Napoleon searched for one trait above all—not if the officer was talented, or fearsome, or calm under battle, but if he was lucky. So, she applied the same test in choosing a husband. And from her observations during the past ten years, the luckiest man this side of Atlanta was Jeremiah Brown Morgan. Oh, Lord, if only—

"Are you still with us, Miss Hill?" asked Gus. "Or have you cast yourself into a trance?"

Nancy looked around to find herself surrounded by smirks. She had learned the best defense was to go on the assault, so she raised her hand.

Gus nodded for her to answer. "Perhaps, like Persephone, you've returned from your interminable journey through the netherworld to offer us a soupçon of wisdom?"

Nancy straightened to the challenge. "We needn't know about herbs. The darkies harvest the medicinals for us. So, may we get on to something useful?"

"For example?"

"I was born under the sign of Aries the ram. What I'd like to know, what would be very useful to me, is ... am I compatible with a Capricorn?"

Gus sighed. "For the love of all that is holy."

Andelia Bull, in the front row, turned and piped at Nancy: "We know who *your* Capricorn is."

"You haven't the foggiest. You can't even tie your shoes properly."

To her horror, Andelia saw one of her strings had become loose. She glared at Nancy, silently accusing her of the sabotage.

"Mr. Morgan possesses the personality of a goat," Ella Kay said. "All horns and bleating."

"He does *not* have the personality of a goat!" Nancy insisted. "And he certainly doesn't rut around like some field hare—"

"Enough!" Gus shouted. The girls fell silent and he circled the classroom, ominously tapping each desk with his cane as he passed. He came to Nancy's seat and hovered over her. "So, you don't feel the need to know herbs?"

"Of course not."

"Do you wish one day to marry, Miss Hill?"

"What does that have to do—"

"Answer the question, please."

"Of course."

"And have children?"

"Yes."

"Say your husband travels to Macon on business. You're left alone with your children. One night, the door to your cabin—"

Nancy scoffed. "Cabin? I think not."

Gus rolled his eyes. "The door to your *mansion* slams open. A gang of armed foreigners bursts inside and demands to know the whereabouts of your husband. What do you do?"

Nancy glanced at her classmates, wondering if Gus was suffering one of his odd spells. "That is preposterous! I'd simply tell them to leave."

"And if they refused?"

"Could never happen to a Southern lady," Nancy insisted. "The gentlemen here wouldn't allow it. Duels and repercussions would ensue."

Gus shook his head at her naiveté. "Anyone heard of Wilkes County?"

"East of Athens," said Caroline.

Gus nodded. "A freezing February there in 1779. A man by the name of Ben Hart owned a cabin off by itself. He was no hermetic mountain man, mind you. He came from a distinguished family. Thomas Hart Benton and Henry Clay called him kinsman."

The girls shifted in their seats, impatient to get on to their next class.

Caroline asked, "What on Earth does this have to do—"

Gus tapped his cane against the floor to warn against being interrupted. "One night, while Ben Hart was away fighting with General Dan Morgan, six Tories broke into his humble log abode. Ben's wife, Nancy, stood at the fireplace in front of her terrified children. The Tories demanded she reveal where an escaped prisoner was hiding. Nancy Hart insisted she didn't know, but the Tories didn't believe her. To show they meant business, they shot her only turkey and ordered her to cook it for them."

"We *have* a History class, Gus," Nancy said.

Gus refused to be denied his tale. "Nancy Hart stood a good six-feet tall and cross-eyed, and she had wild red hair and a face pitted from smallpox. She invited the Tories to sit down at the table and stack their muskets in the corner while she got the stove hot. The intruders did as she suggested and passed around a jug of wine that Nancy provided for their enjoyment."

"What a coward," Nancy muttered.

Gus ignored her remark. "While the Tories drank and told ribald jokes, Mrs. Hart smoked up the turkey and added several herbs and spices according to her favorite new recipe."

"Now we're in Cookery?" cried Nancy.

Gus mimicked placing a platter on the desk in front of her. "When, at last, the turkey had been roasted to a juicy perfection, Mrs. Hart served it to her uninvited guests. Several minutes later, the Tories slouched in their chairs, feeling the effects of the meal. While they slumbered, the wily lass of the Revolution slid their muskets, one by one, through a chink in the cabin wall."

The girls, suddenly interested, leaned closer.

Gus lowered his voice for effect. "Mrs. Hart kept the last two guns by her side. When one of the Tories woke and saw what she was doing, the traitorous knave lunged at her." He paused and stared out the window for several moments.

"Gus!" Nancy shouted. "What happened?"

He spun and aimed his cane at her. "Mrs. Hart pulled the trigger and dropped that damnable Tory dead. Then she picked up the second gun and held the five remaining Tories at bay until her neighbors, hearing the shot, came running. The men wanted to shoot the trespassers on the spot, but Nancy Hart, heroine of our independence, preferred to see them hang. And hang they did."

Nancy studied him. "You contrived that story."

"You think so?"

Mary agreed. "Gus, those Redcoats didn't fall asleep from eating a leg of turkey."

"Wasn't just any old turkey. Nancy Hart cooked it with her special recipe."

"What was in this recipe?" Leila asked.

Gus put a finger to his chin in mock thought. "Oh, let's see. Thyme, if I recall. And pepper, plenty of that. And a healthy dash of salt."

Nancy snorted. "Oh, well, *that* makes it believable now."

The tower bells rang the time for the next class. The girls gathered up their books and started for the door.

"Oh, and I forgot one more ingredient," Gus said.

The girls turned, impatient to get away.

Gus pulled another small apothecary packet from his inside breast pocket and opened it. He held his palm at head's height as he walked among the girls and displayed several shiny black berries, dried. "Beautiful lady."

Nancy blushed. "Why, Gus—"

"Not *you*, frivolous girl. That's the name of the herb made from these berries. *Belladonna.*

Nancy picked a berry from his palm and sniffed it.

"In ancient Rome," Gus explained, "drops from these were used to make women's pupils dilate and appear seductive."

Nancy considered pocketing a couple to use for the ball on Saturday night. She brought one to her lips to taste. "How long would it take you to make such a potion?"

Gus grasped her wrist to prevent her from eating the berry. "Not advisable."

"Why?"

"Five berries can be lethal to a man. Who knows what one might do to a vapid girl."

Horrified, Nancy dropped the berry and shivered with disgust. "You just walk around carrying poison, do you?"

Gus winked at the other girls. "Did I mention the cranberry sauce that Nancy Hart made to serve with the turkey that night?" When they shook their heads, he revealed, "Nancy Hart was a master herbalist. But you nymphs have no interest in the natural science of how to charm men."

Before the girls, now even more intrigued, could ask for their next assignment, Gus limped out of the classroom and headed back to his apothecary on the town square.

2

FOND DU LAC COUNTY, WISCONSIN
MAY 1856

"Not as a slave, Hugh!" Wallace LaGrange shouted as he scattered wheat seeds from his knapsack. "But as a brother above a slave! St. Paul sent Onesimus back to Philemon as a brother!"

Seventeen-year-old Oscar H. LaGrange—"Hugh" to his family and friends—calmed the draught horse pulling the single-blade plow. He could always tell when another fire-breathing circuit rider had set up a revival tent in Ripon. His younger brother would return from these nightly sermons filled with that same holy fervor. Although only fourteen, Wallace took in the preaching of the Holy Spirit like an arrow through the heart. Hugh, on the other hand, was a critical thinker who demanded scriptural references for any question and weighed them as a lawyer poring over case precedents. He had seen hundreds of staunch believers flounder here on the frontier, their faith shaken when God abandoned them to starvation and penury.

His brother was too young to remember when their father loaded up the wagon at their sapped homestead in western New York and followed the trace across what the old-timers called the Burnt-Over District. The land there was scorched not from grass wildfires, but the flaming tongues of whatever spiritual enthusiasm ignited that season: Millerites, Mormons, Adventists, Shakers, Table-Rappers, Mesmerists, Swedenborgians, Fourierists, and sundry other societies of mystics and seers, most of whom didn't have a clue what they advocated. Hugh learned to be wary of all sects and fevers of the soul, having listened to his mother, rest her soul, tell how the papists tied their Huguenot ancestors on barges and drowned them in the rivers of France.

"The Old Testament forbade the Israelites from enslaving one another!" Wallace insisted. "It's right there in the Book!"

Hugh kept a tight rein to prevent the horse from spooking at Wallace's preaching. He picked up a rock before it could nick the plow blade and, in the steel's rubbed sheen, glimpsed his own reflection. His high cheekbones and broad forehead, which a stranger once said gave the impression of Cossack fierceness, were so burnt from the unrelenting sun that he barely recognized himself. He tossed the rock over his shoulder at Wallace a few steps behind him. "The Book also says that adulteresses should be stoned. Are you going to brain every lass who's had a frolic around here?"

Wallace fired the rock at Hugh's back. "What do you know about frolics? I haven't seen you even wink at a gal."

"Keep your nose to the ground. You're supposed to be clearing shards, not evangelizing the crows."

"I'm bored. Let's have us a theological dispute."

Hugh ran a hand through his thick shocks of black hair to sop up the sweat. "I don't fire on the mentally unarmed."

"You ain't got any more of an education than me."

"Yeah, but unlike you, the Good Lord blessed me with inborn intelligence."

Wallace persisted. "Resolved. A Christian nation cannot abide slavery."

"Where was that last tent preacher from?"

"Boston."

"Figures. You're giving me the evil side of the argument."

Wallace grinned at having drawn Hugh into the debate. "With all that natural inborn intelligence, you should be able to hold your own."

Hugh shrugged and nodded wearily, if only to keep Wallace moving. "Come out blazing, then. I'm sure you've memorized those Scripture quotes that Bible thumper churned out last night."

"For starts, you can answer my conundrum about St. Paul and Philemon."

"That one is easy enough. If St. Paul had wanted to abolish slavery, he would have said so. Instead, he sent Onesimus back asking Philemon to take him as a *favor*."

Wallace protested, "What twisted thinking is that?"

"Verses Twelve through Seventeen." Hugh quoted from memory. "'I am sending him—who is my very heart—back to you. I would have liked to keep him with me so he could take your place in helping me while I am in chains for the Gospel. But I did not want to do anything without consent, so that *any favor you do will be spontaneous and not forced.*'"

Wallace reddened. "You're cuttin' the apple too thin!"

"You worded the resolution, not me."

"Slavery ain't Christian! Love thy brother!"

"Morals and the law are two different kettles of fish. St. Paul may have looked sideways at slavery, but he never called for outlawing it."

"That's a lawyer's trick!"

Hugh kept his sputtering brother on his heels. "The patriarchs of the Old Testament owned slaves. Even Abraham."

"Wait now, the Book ordered the Israelites not to enslave one another! That preacher last night said so!"

"Did you think to ask your pulpit Abolitionist if the Israelites enslaved Canaanites?" Before his brother could manage a retort, Hugh let loose with another fusillade of quotations. "Ephesians Six-Five. Slaves must obey their masters. Colossians Three-Twenty-Two. Slaves must obey their masters. Titus Two-Nine. Slaves must obey their masters. Peter Two-Eighteen—"

"Jesus changed all that!"

Hugh hid a smile; he had his brother trapped, as usual. "I don't read anywhere in the New Testament that says Jesus outlawed slavery. And if He did, how come St. Paul allowed slaveholders into the Church?"

"Maybe not everything written in the Bible has equal authority?" a third voice bellowed.

The two boys turned to find a short, long-bearded man in a black suit kneeling under a limestone bluff. His unkempt auburn hair was speckled with ground dust and gray gravel chips, and his eyes had become swollen and red from the assault of upshooting chisel shards. Hugh thought the man looked like a hairy leprechaun burrowing around in search of a pot of gold.

Armed with a hand pick, the odd fellow with no neck to speak of hammered furiously at the layers of multicolored rock until a smooth, bulbous fragment covered by a pattern of snowflake-shaped rosettes fell into his grasp. Excited, he donned a pair of spectacles, inspected his precious find, and held it aloft to display the fruit of his digging. "It's a bryozoan. A moss animal. Very common here. How old do you figure it is?" When the boys shrugged, he insisted. "Come now, lads. Hazard a guess."

"Can't be over six thousand years," Wallace said. "The Bible says so."

The man grinned as he shook his head. "Ah, Genesis. Would it rattle the foundations of your faith if I told you this insignificant creature wriggled around here over three hundred million years ago?"

"That's impossible," Wallace said.

The man tapped away at the limestone cleft. "What I'd give to find a mastodon. Just a femur, even. Wouldn't have to be a full skeleton. I have a theory why I've never unearthed one here. There was vast erosion in this region over the many centuries. Mesozoic remains washed away long, long ago."

"Not to be inhospitable," Hugh said. "But you're prospecting on our patch."

The man leapt from his perch and vigorously shook their hands. "Professor Edward Daniels of Ripon College. I'm the state's geologist. I hope you will forgive my trespass, but when I inquired in town, no one knew the owner."

"What's a state geologist do, exactly?" Hugh asked.

"Those oligarchs in Madison would tell you they pay me to apply my noble subterranean science to find the minerals and oil to fuel their empires," Daniels said. "Just between the three of us, I'm out here on a secret mission."

"You're a spy?" Wallace asked.

Daniels winked. "A spy for the Lord. ... I overheard you trading theological salvos on the question of Abolition."

Hugh didn't know if he could trust this interloper. Even this far north, there were reports of Missouri bounty hunters posing as preachers to ferret out Negro sympathizers. "We're just passing the time."

Daniels put his arm around Hugh's shoulders to reassure him. "No need for alarm. We're soldiers in the same army."

"Army?" Alarmed, Hugh looked toward his water gourd across the field and realized he had left the muzzle-loader at the cabin.

The professor gesticulated wildly as if addressing an auditorium. "The army of the righteous battalions serving the Almighty. As we speak, many of our brethren muster to rid this nation of its natal pestilence."

Hugh sniffed the intruder's breath, wondering if he was drunk on the local corn mash.

The professor grasped the boys by the napes of their necks and walked them to the face of the rock cleft. "Geology holds the secret to how we must prevail in our noble struggle against the Southern malefactors. Look at those sediment lines. What do you see?"

"Layers?" suggested Hugh.

"Eons of time," the professor said. "Each band represents lands, once dry, inundated by deluges that killed off the species. Now, lads, what you must understand is that the ebb and flow of these periods was cataclysmic. Societies are akin to geological eons. Catastrophe brings on glorious changes in the evil ways of humans, too."

Hugh didn't have a clue what the professor was talking about, but it sounded like a prophecy. "My brother and I have to turn this field before sundown, or our pa will inflict a catastrophe on our backsides."

The professor removed his hat and jacket, hung them on the branch of a nearby tree, and rolled up his white sleeves. He walked around the plow to inspect it. "That blade is nicked and dulled. Won't last you through the spring."

Hugh couldn't argue that point. "Not with Wally here hitting every third rock in his path."

"There's an inventor in Indiana, a Scot chap named Oliver. He's perfecting a novel method for forging plow steel. Calls it 'chilling.'"

"Chilling?" Wallace chortled. "Does he keep it in the icehouse?"

Daniels laughed. "No, no. He drops the molten cast into vats of boiling water. That allows the gases to escape and keeps them from weakening the bonds. He plans to patent the procedure. Those blades will last several seasons."

"They'll probably cost a pretty penny, too," Hugh said.

Daniels stared at Hugh intently, as if sizing him up. "You impress me as a bright young fellow."

"He ain't that bright," Wallace insisted. "He's still out here cutting sod with me, ain't he?"

Daniels examined each boy from toe to scalp. "You lads could pass for giants. How tall are you?"

"I'm six-foot-two," Hugh said. "Wally here's a shade under that."

Daniels formed a 'V' with two fingers and mimicked shooting a slingshot at their chins. "David and *two* Goliaths."

Not one for aimless talk, Hugh glanced at the lowering sun, hoping the chatty professor would let them get back to work.

Detecting their doubt about his *bona fides,* the professor walked along the limestone cleft until he found the object of his quest. He hammered out a piece of the quartz rock with his pick and tossed the fragment to Hugh. "Next to a diamond, this is the hardest substance you'll find." He scuffled over to the plow and turned it onto its handles. Feeling the blade's ragged edge, he began stroking the jags with the quartz stone, smoothing out the bevel. After five minutes of this honing, he yanked the plow upright again. "Try it now."

Hugh snapped the reins to get the horse moving again. The plow cut through the sod like a knife through cider cake. Amazed, he asked the professor, "Are you some kind of magician?"

Daniels laughed. "Along with my geological passion, I've long harbored an interest in progressive farming techniques."

"What's that mean?" Wallace asked. "Progressive techniques?"

"Where does your father sell his wheat and corn?"

"We take it into Martin's granary in town," Hugh said. "Providing there's enough left over from feeding us through the winter."

"You get a fair price?"

Hugh shrugged. "We take what he offers. Martin's the only buyer with the wagons to send the grain east."

"The man takes advantage of you," Daniels said. "We will change that, and soon. First, we'll get a railroad out here. Then good folks such as you and your pa need to set up communal cooperatives to pool your resources."

Hugh was skeptical. "Communes? Sounds like those crazy ideas we got away from in New York. I heard one of those Utopian farms went belly up in Indiana."

Daniels dropped his chin in regret. "Robert Owen's place. He didn't know what he was doing. I've got a different notion on how to go about it." He grabbed the handles of the plow and, motioning the boys to lead the horse, threw the reins around his shoulders and began slicing the sod.

"Mister, how come you're helping us?" Hugh asked.

"I believe in cooperation," Daniels said. "The Good Lord admonished us to teach others to fish so they might feed themselves, did He not? The disciples went out on the boat in the Galilee together. Each contributed to the handling of the nets and the sharing of the catch. You don't hear of Jesus going forth alone. No, he joined with others."

Hugh detected an Eastern accent, and that usually meant only one thing these days. "Are you an Abolitionist?"

Daniels met Hugh with a sideways glare, impressed with his perspicacity. "I am a Christian and a progressive. That should tell you all you need to know."

"What about the ants," Hugh said.

Daniels blinked hard and looked down at his feet, as if fearing he had just stepped on a hill full of the fire-eaters. "What ants?"

"I've been told slave-holding ants exist."

"Define your terms, young man. What do you mean by 'slave-holding?'"

"Some ants force other ants to do their work."

Daniels purpled. "Where did you hear such a claim?"

"A fella came through town a month ago with the circus," Hugh said. "He was regaling everyone about these slave ants, saying he was going down below the Equator to bring back a colony and take them on a tour through Mississippi and Georgia. He figured he could make a fortune showing the plantation owners how to raise slave ants with their cotton."

Daniels looked as if he might pop a vein in his temple. "And what nugget of wisdom do you claim to extract from this preposterous carny tale?"

"Well, if there *are* slave ants as that circus fella said, then it seems to me an argument could be made that God designed the world to include slavery as natural."

"You see what I gotta put up with?" Wallace cried. "Don't humor him, Professor. He'll paint white streaks on a beaver and convince you it's a skunk!"

Daniels wasn't listening to Wallace's rant; instead, he kept boring in on Hugh as if a teacher chastising an impudent pupil. "First, even assuming the existence of such an unnatural abomination, those ants were likely enslaving *another* species of ants."

Wallace egged him on. "You tell him, Professor!"

"The Israelites had slaves," Hugh countered.

"They did *not* enslave their own kind," Daniels insisted. "The black man in America is of the same species as the white man."

"The Negro came from Africa," Hugh said. "That's farther away than the Canaanites were from the Israelites."

"Still—"

"And if those black pagans hadn't been rounded up and brought over to this land," Hugh added, "they'd never met Christ as their Savior, now would they? If being saved is all that matters, as Wally here always insists, then shouldn't the darkies be thankful for working their way to Heaven?"

"You, son, possess the Devil's tongue!"

"You got *that* right, Professor!' Wallace piped. "Watch out for him. He has a dastardly talent for twisting your words around Beelzebub's pitchfork."

Exasperated, Daniels snapped the reins to send the plowhorse forward, eager to abandon the disputation he was losing. "Do you two have names? Or do you just lurk around the wilderness, living off the wolves as Romulus and Remus did?"

"I'm Hugh LaGrange. This here's Wallace."

"Ah, LaGrange, an old French surname," mused Daniels. "I'd wager from your impressive stature and dark Gallic bearing that you gents hail from Capetian royal stock. Perhaps you had ancestors among the fallen heroes at Agincourt. Two Wisconsin knights in King Charlie's court!" The professor enjoyed a merry laugh at his own wit, but the boys stood mute, mystified. "I'll tell you what, Sir Hugh LaGrange of the Range, I'll throw in and help you plow your field if you'll do something for me in return."

Hugh suspected a swindle. "Such as?"

"Enroll in my class next week at Ripon College."

Hugh figured the professor wanted to belittle him in front of his students as revenge for having just put him in a rhetorical corner. "I ain't had but a little schooling."

"I've got a keen eye for scholarly talent. You show promise. You needn't worry about the tuition. I'll find you employment."

Hugh wrapped the reins of the plow around his shoulders and motioned for Wallace and the professor to resume removing stones from the path of the advancing furrow. They walked up and down the field in silence until, an hour later, when the sun was nearly spent, Hugh halted the horse and unharnessed it from the plow. He threw the livery over his shoulder and began walking toward the path that led to their cabin a half-mile away.

"Well?" the professor asked, waiting for his answer. "Are you going to cut sod for the rest of your life?"

Hugh stopped and turned. "My pa would never allow it. He needs me for the planting."

Daniels wiped his forehead with a kerchief. "Let me talk to your father. There might be a new plow in his future if he sees things my way."

"What about me?" Wallace asked. "You want me in your class, too?"

Daniels winked at Hugh and patted his brother on the back. "Wally, my good lad, *you've* got the makings of a fine farmer." Seeing his disappointment, the professor tried to soothe the boy's hurt feelings. "Some of my friends from the college have been meeting each week in Ripon to debate politics and ideas. Come to our next gathering on Tuesday night. You love to argue. You and your brother here would fit right in."

Wallace brightened. "How will we find you?"

"Stand in front of the schoolhouse on the square and shout 'free labor, free land, and free men!' We'll send an escort into our *sanctum sanctorum*." The professor gathered up his pick and rock-filled haversack and hoisted them onto the saddle of his waiting horse. He mounted and tipped his hat as he rode north toward Ripon.

"Hey, Professor!" Wallace shouted. "You debating fellas got a name?"

Daniels answered over his shoulder. "The Republican Party!"

As the professor disappeared on a trot over the horizon, Wallace ran to catch up with Hugh, who was making fast tracks home to avoid being late for supper. "You hear that, Hugh? Sounds as if them boys in town are fixing to shake things up in Washington city. Might be fun to join them."

Hugh snorted his disgust at the suggestion. "Just what this country needs, another herd of politicians trampling through our crops. I wouldn't give it a plug nickel's chance of amounting to much with a sorry name like the Republican Party."

"It don't sound that bad to me."

"You think people don't know the United States of America is a republic already? Why would anyone vote for a party that claims to stand for what we already got? Why not just call it the Free Air Party? Tell people they can breathe all the free air they want."

Wallace scratched his head. "That don't make a lick of sense!"

"Now the Whig Party, there's a perfectly reasonable name!"

"Why do you say that?"

"Not everybody has wigs. Gives people a prize to strive to attain."

Wallace, now even more befuddled, looked to trees, as if expecting the crows to offer an explanation.

Hugh hid a smile as he kept walking, leaving his gullible brother to grapple with the profound mystery of political nomenclature.

3

LAGRANGE, GEORGIA
MAY 1856

Nancy gathered the crinoline folds of her hooped white gown and slipped unnoticed through the rear door to the bedroom's third-story veranda. She kicked off her slippers and climbed the narrow stairs that led to the banistered promenade crowning the Bellevue mansion, a white Greek Revival temple overlooking the plantations of LaGrange. As she hid behind the corner, she watched the guests arriving through the iron-cast gates on Broad Street. Her gasp of delight nearly gave her away.

Under the cloudless night sky, flickering oil lamps lit the way for the caravan of carriages rolling in on the tree-lined lane from town and the neighboring plantations. Every movement from miles around appeared choreographed as if in a dream; the conveyances pulled up to the entrance, and the doorman bowed and placed a footstool to assist the ladies. She squinted to catch her first glimpse of the latest fashions from New Orleans and Atlanta. The necklines were lower this year. She reached for the underwire girding her petticoats and pulled the apparatus down an inch to show more décolletage. On the portico, the young men gathered in their cravats and tails and vied to escort the ladies into the grand hall, now cleared of furniture to serve as the ballroom.

And they were all coming to see *her*.

Well, almost all. Her ecstatic smile gave way to a grumpy frown. Why did Sallie Fannie Reid have to be announced to society on the same night? It wasn't fair. The petite blonde tart didn't even live in LaGrange. Yet because she was the daughter of the wealthiest plantation owner in West Point—the next town down the rail line—*that* nouveau pedigree gave her the right to make her debut in the most elegant mansion in Troup County. Heavens, Sallie's backwater burgh couldn't even decide in which state it resided; half the town sat on the Alabama side, the other half in Georgia. Worse, Sallie had graduated a year early from the Female College, allowing her to flaunt her degree while Nancy still waited to earn hers.

Wasn't it enough that every man in the county could talk of nothing else but Sallie's beauty and grace and selflessness? *Sallie Fannie Reid is holding a charity bazaar for the church. Sallie Fannie Reid sat in the pew next to me. Sallie Fannie Reid intends to travel to Europe. Sallie Fannie Reid smiled at me. Sallie Fannie Reid accepted my—*

"Nannie!" Mary Heard glared at her from the bottom of the promenade steps. "What are you doing out *there?*"

"I need air. I can barely breathe in this corset."

"The announcements will start soon! We haven't gotten your hair braided. Sallie Fannie Reid—"

"I have heard my fill of Sallie Fannie Reid!"

Mary straightened from the force of that complaint.

Nancy glanced across the roof at the far window. "She's over there plotting how she will trip me—"

Mary corralled Nancy by the arm and hurried her back into the bedroom assigned for their preparations. While the mulatto house servant, Marie, knelt on the floor adjusting the hem, Mary raised the border of Nancy's neckline to a proper height and fluffed out the folds in her gown. "This is the night you become a woman. You might wish to act it."

Nancy refused to stand still. "Just because you're married doesn't make you the queen of society."

Mary applied the finishing touches on Nancy's hair, teasing the soft loops and ringlets on each side to give her long face as much an illusion of roundness as possible. She glanced at the door, as if expecting a summons at any moment, and told the domestic, "Marie, you are dismissed."

"Yessum." Marie gathered her sewing basket and hurried out.

Alone with Nancy, Mary lowered her voice. "There are things I need to say to you." When Nancy escaped to the mirror and adjusted the brooch to sink lower into the valley of her breasts, Mary pulled a worn booklet from under the frills of her sleeve. She smoothed out the bent corners of its cover and opened it to a marked page. "My mother read this to me on the night of my debut."

"Didn't we cover that era in Ancient History class?" Nancy was about to drive her gibe to the hilt when she saw tears well up in Mary's eyes. She softened and nodded, affecting an eagerness to hear what was so important to her best friend, who was always so serious.

Mary cleared the emotion from her throat. "These are the maxims young ladies must memorize before attending their first ball."

Nancy saw the name of the booklet's author. "Written by a *man?*"

"Please, for once, pay attention."

Nancy cracked the door and stole a glance across the hall at the bedroom where Sallie Fannie Reid was dressing. "Are you going to read it to *her,* too?"

Mary ignored the taunt and pressed on, reciting: "'Dancing is the only rational amusement wherein the man of business can forget the manifold cares of an active business life. The social pastime, when joined with delightful music, is a panacea for the innumerable ills resulting from the continuous strain on the heated and overtaxed brain.'"

Nancy rolled her eyes. "There are plenty of overtaxed brains in *this* town."

"You'd best harness that sharp tongue. Or you will find yourself ostracized by every gentleman present tonight."

"Go on, then. Let's get this done."

Mary circled the room while reading the dictums in a matronly voice. "'Avoid slang phrases. Do not contradict. Give your opinions, but do not argue them.'"

"So, I must endure college to hang as an ornament from a man's elbow?"

Mary pointed at the page to show the next rule was timely. "'While dancing, endeavor to wear a pleasant face.'" Her voice trailed off, and she muttered something else under her breath.

"I heard that!"

Mary read faster, as if concerned the cotillion elders would judge her poorly for failing to prepare her initiate. "'Do not speak in a loud tone, indulge in boisterous laughter or actions, nor tell long stories. Never seem to be conscious of an affront, unless it be of a very gross nature.'"

"Sallie Fannie Reid tells stories so long, the ice cream melts."

Mary raised the page in question to Nancy's eyes. "'Never repeat in one company any scandal or personal history you have heard in another.'"

"What in heaven's name are we to talk about, then?"

"'Contending for a position in quadrilles indicates an irritable and quarrelsome disposition. Do not form an engagement during a dance—'"

"What? No engagement?"

"'Or while a lady is engaged in any manner. A provocation to anger should never be answered in the presence of ladies.'"

Nancy hovered near the door, desperate to steal a glimpse of the entrance hall below the stairwell. "Hurry, will you? Caroline has brought everyone inside."

"Let me see you practice your promenade one more time."

Nancy sashayed across the room, exaggerating the ladylike steps.

Mary threw her head back, exasperated. "Allow your arms to hang. When you enter the quadrille, you must avoid the appearance of agility or familiarity with the calls."

"I spent the last month learning the steps! And now you want me to act as if I forgot them?"

"The trick is to perform the dance with ease, as if it comes naturally."

Nancy had reached her limit. She plugged her ears with her fingers.

Resigned to what was clearly a losing battle, Mary hurried through the last few rules. "'While conversing with one person in a crowded room, let it be in an undertone. Avoid affectation, frowning, quizzing, or the slightest sign of ill temper. Loud conversation, profanity, stamping the feet, writing on the wall, using tobacco, spitting or throwing anything on the floor, are glaring vulgarities.'"

Nancy peeked past the door again. "Why aren't the oil tapers along the walls lit? They will barely be able to see me."

Mary hesitated, as if attempting to dredge up the courage to broach a subject too long delayed. "The house servants have lowered them for one of the guests."

Nancy spun back on her. "*Which* guest?"

Mary fussed with Nancy's gown. "I didn't tell you earlier for fear you might become too excited. Your cousin, Ben Hill, has a good friend in attendance. An *important* friend."

Nancy waited for the revelation. "Well, who is it?"

Mary eased the door closed. "Mr. Jefferson Davis."

"The planter from Mississippi?"

"He's more than a farmer now. He's the government's Secretary of War. A very influential man in Washington."

Nancy reddened with pique. "Why doesn't he *stay* in Washington?"

"What has gotten into you? It's an honor to have such an esteemed dignitary at your coming-out. I thought you'd be pleased. He has taken the train from his home south of Vicksburg to Montgomery and is en route to Atlanta. Rep. Hill invited him to stop for the occasion and spend the evening."

"Everyone will look at *him*! Talk to *him*!" Nancy fought back tears. "And in the shadows! What is he, a vampire?"

Mary glared at her. "The stars do not orbit around *you*! Mr. Davis suffers from a painful eye condition that nearly renders him blind under harsh light. I'm questioning if you are truly ready to be a lady. Maybe you should just put your jumpers back on and run around the room sitting on everyone's laps!"

"This is to be *my* night. And now, not only do I have to share it with Cleopatra of West Point, I have this Mexican War hero and his martyr's wounds with which to contend. Brown will barely have the time to notice me."

"Oh, Brown will certainly notice you. How could he not? With the way you have thrown yourself at him these past months?"

Nancy's sneer, aimed through the wall at the adjacent bedroom, sharpened. "Sallie Reid has her fluttering blue eyes on him. I've seen the way she flirts with him. You just watch. She will pull every trick in her—"

The bell rang below, the signal that the announcements were to begin.

Mary wiped the tears from Nancy's eyes. "You must compose yourself."

"At least I'll have the first shot at Brown. I'm sure Mother chose him for my escort. I made my preference quite clear."

Mary led Nancy to the door. "I'm sure you did."

"Are you feeling puny?" Nancy asked. "You look pale. I'm the one who's supposed to be on the edge of fainting."

Deflecting Nancy's questioning stare, Mary fumbled for her booklet again and found the one maxim she had saved for last. "If you can remember only one rule to live by, Nannie, let it be this: 'True politeness costs nothing, but yields the largest interest and profit to the possessor of any known securities.'"

Nancy blessed her friend with an endearing kiss on the cheek. "You've always worried for me. Now, if you are out of admonishments and bromides, may I go forth to become a lady?" She opened the door and looked back over her shoulder. "Oh, I forgot to tell you. I've arranged a surprise for the dancing."

Mary's eyes rounded. "Nannie, what have you—"

The bell rang a second time. Nancy pushed open the door and walked onto the balcony that overlooked the entrance hall. Mary had advised her to keep a distant gaze so as not to appear too familiar or eager, but she couldn't help sneak a glance at the guests gathered around the bottom step. The tapers were aimed to illuminate the two debs of the hour; as a result, she could not make out the upturned faces. She scanned the favors table next to the ballroom entry arch, guarded like fairies by Leila Pullen and the other buds. Ribboned with flowers, the *escritoire* sat stocked with sealing wafers and the stack of stationery for the men to pen poems or notes requesting the honor of a call. She smiled with anticipation. Under the desk's legs rested the small canister she had secreted into the house earlier that morning; its contents were destined to make this night one to remember.

The door to the bedroom across the hall creaked back, and Sallie Fannie Reid slithered out, accompanied by her father.

Nancy blushed with hot anger. Her nemesis wore not the traditional white for purity, but a brilliant gown of *golden satin* fluffed with tulle. And Sallie had studded her strawberry-blonde hair with hyacinths and crowned it with a lavender plume, as if intent on convincing the stupid coxcombs that she was a Greek goddess rising from the foamy sea. How *dare* she. Hearing a gasp of delight from the guests, Nancy colored another shade darker. She resembled a peasant waif next to *that* indulgence. Sallie Fannie Reid turned on her with a smile that would launch a thousand daggers. Nancy waited for Sallie to make the first move to the head of the stairs, but the Little Princess of Half Georgia and Half Alabama refused to budge.

They stood facing in a standoff, neither willing to relinquish the honor of descending last. Nancy felt a shove in the small of her back. Mary was trying to nudge her forward, but she dug in the heels of her slippers, taking a wide stance, hidden under her hoops, to resist her urging. The guests began murmuring, wondering what was happening. Nancy returned Sallie's sugary smile with a glare of determination, making it evident she was prepared to wait there the entire evening.

Finally, releasing a smothered huff, Sallie declared victory in defeat. Pasting on another smile—this one tinged in a promise of revenge—she swished across the balcony to the top step with her ostentatious gown glittering in the flickering shadows.

"Miss Sallie Fannie Reid of Sunny Villa!" State Rep. Benjamin Harvey Hill, host and master of ceremonies, announced the Grand March. "Miss Reid is escorted by her father, our esteemed friend, Colonel Reid."

While the West Point interlopers took their time descending the stairs, Nancy seized the opportunity to search the floor for Brown Morgan. *There* her darling stood, awaiting his turn to come up and sweep her into their shared destiny. Lord, he looked so gallant with his slender form and coiffed goatee. Such a portrait of the perfect gentleman. Her heart fluttered. She congratulated herself for having carefully arranged this moment. Her father, rest his soul, had passed to his reward three years ago. By tradition, her older brother, Miles, should stand in her father's place, but she had secretly arranged, through an admirer in the courts, for a law case in Savannah to require his presence that week. Left no alternative for her escort, the cotillion society held the responsibility for appointing a substitute gentleman. Yet that was a mere formality; she had pestered her mother for weeks to convey her choice to the ladies on the planning committee. Yes, Sallie might wrap herself in gold, but she, Nancy Colquitt Hill of the renowned Hills of Georgia, would enter society arm-in-arm with the most eligible lawyer in Troup County.

At last, Colonel Reid and his daughter made it to the main floor. Rep. Hill cleared his throat to announce the next candidate, and Gus Ware began climbing the staircase, rattling the boards with each thump of his cane and gnawing on his ratty cravat.

What in God's name is he doing?

Nancy set her teeth. The rickety old fart was so hard of hearing that he didn't know the announcements were in progress. She tried to wave him off with her eyes, but he kept climbing, determined to ruin her moment by hanging his coat or using the wash basin or whatever numskull task he was contemplating. When he was halfway up the stairs, she muttered under her breath, "Gus, go back."

Gus looked over his shoulder at the mountain of stairs he had just scaled. "I am not making that trip twice."

She performed her best imitation of a smiling ventriloquist. "Get ... away ... now."

"Miss Nancy Colquitt Hill!" announced Rep. Hill. "I take great pride this evening in noting that Miss Hill hails from two families of which I share a bloodline."

The guests applauded, but Nancy seethed at the new change in protocol, which now required the assigned gentleman to escort the debutante down the stairs after an unfortunate fall by one young lady two years ago. Resisting the urge to kick Gus back down the precipice, she muttered, "You're blocking the way for Brown!"

Gus cupped a hand over his ear. "Who?"

"Stop rattling that cane," she whispered.

Rep. Hill elevated his booming voice another octave. "This evening, remembering fondly as we do the late Dr. Hampton Wooten Hill, our city's solons have chosen in his stead the man who assumed Dr. Hill's practice. Escorting Miss Hill this evening in her public *entrée au monde* is Dr. Augustus Ware."

On the balcony, Nancy stood frozen, praying she had not heard correctly. Amid a smattering of applause, her cheeks flushed, and she reached for the banister to steady herself. Mary's hand braced her back, but Nancy held a forced smile and snarled a warning over her shoulder, "I will never forgive you."

"I had nothing to do with the choice," Mary whispered. "Although he is precisely what you need."

Nancy, mortified, could only wait and watch as Gus attacked the final few stairs, stopping to rub his knees with each new elevation. She whispered to Mary, "Need? What did I ever do to—"

"Humility, Nannie," Mary confided. "Your mother thought you needed to learn humility on your first night as a lady."

At last, Gus, breathing hard, reached the balcony. He turned to stand aside Nancy and offered the elbow of his free arm. She reluctantly took it while fighting back tears. To her added horror, her cousin insisted on the side next to the staircase wall, forcing her to risk a fall over the railing. Each step was excruciating and tenuous. She feared Gus might stab her toes with the cane and send them both plummeting in a heap.

Gus, struggling to maintain his balance, whispered into her ear, "Time to feed the virgin to the lions."

She clenched her grasp on his elbow, drawing a wince. "What a vulgar clod you are."

"I don't wish to be here any more than you do. And if you're still upset about that 'C' I gave you in Natural Sciences, you can take it up with—"

"I couldn't care less about your travesty of a class." Nancy felt every uplifted eye boring in on her. "Just get me to the parlor in one piece."

After what seemed an eternity, she reached *terra firma* and curtsied to Rep. Hill. "I wish to thank you, dear cousin, for allowing me the privilege of debuting in your magnificent home."

Rep. Hill beamed. "Never has it been so radiant as tonight with your presence. I think we owe Dr. Ware here a hand of gratitude for delivering yet another blessed child into our world."

Nancy cut off a stiff bow to her enforced escort.

Rep. Hill took Nancy by her gloved hand and, parting a path, waved forward a man who was besieged with heated conversation by several gentlemen rudely oblivious to the proceedings. "Nannie, may I introduce you to one of my oldest friends, Mr. Jefferson Davis."

A corpse-like figure shuffled toward her to extend his palsied hand. His frail condition appalled her. Given the Secretary of War's legendary exploits on the frontier, she had expected a vibrant giant in the cut of a Davy Crockett or Sam Houston. Instead, despite maintaining an erect military bearing with much effort, Davis seemed a haggard soul who suffered from the slings and slashes of a hundred chronic ailments. His high, sharp facial bones hung with hollowed cheeks, pale and puckered, and his goatee and thinning hair had grayed prematurely for a man of only forty-seven years. An aura of penetrating sadness followed him, and she could not break off her attention from his most alarming feature: a painful neuralgia contorted his face, and his left eye, sunken and filmed, gave him the mien of an ancient Druid.

"You remind me of someone, Miss Hill," Davis said.

"Your lovely wife, Varina?" Rep. Hill suggested. "Such a pity she could not join you on the journey. We miss her."

Davis kept his filmy gaze fixed on Nancy. "No, not Varina."

The guests waited for an explanation for the odd observation, but when Davis offered none, Rep. Hill broke up the uncomfortable silence. "Perhaps we should return to the gaieties?"

The men, eager to dance with the debutantes, applauded that suggestion.

"What say the majority?" Rep. Hill asked. "An opening contredanse to give every gentleman a chance?"

"That sounds lovely," Sallie Fannie Reid pipped. She turned toward Nancy, her hooded eyes shooting a reminder she held the reputation as the most graceful dancer in the county. "Don't you agree, Miss Hill?" Not waiting for an answer, Sallie swiveled in her hoops and nudged her father in a signal to lead her into the ballroom.

"In fact," Nancy said. "I have planned a new dance. That is, if it meets with the approval of the cavaliers."

Sallie stopped in mid-swish. "*You* devised a dance?"

Mary, forgotten on the balcony, bristled with apprehension. Before she could intervene, Nancy nodded for Leila Pullen to retrieve the canister she had hidden under the entry table earlier. She opened the container, pulled out small flags on sticks, and distributed the favors she had bribed Leila and her fellow grade-school tadpoles to make in secret. A murmur grew into a buzz of excitement as the guests realized what the flags represented.

"The Flag Dance," Nancy explained. "It's all the rage in France."

Sallie narrowed her eyes. "Do tell."

With Leila trailing behind with the canister, Nancy handed out flags to the participants. "There are two identical flags for each state. Ladies and gentlemen must take their positions on the floor without looking at the flags of the other dancers." She turned to Rep. Hill. "Will you call the dance?"

"Delighted."

"When a state is called," Nancy explained, "the lady and gentleman with that state's flag pair off."

"Marvelous!" Rep. Hill exclaimed.

Mary did not share in the enthusiasm. "Nannie, may I have a word—"

Nancy ignored her friend. "Into the parlor! Everyone! At once!"

The guests, waving their flags, bustled into the grand room and formed a circle along the walls. Nancy would have patted herself on the back for her brilliance if only she could reach around her hoops. She had neglected to reveal the one wrinkle to the game that promised to solve her problems with Sallie Fannie Reid and Gus Ware and the rest of the boobs determined to thwart her: She kept one flag pinned to her petticoat under her skirt—and it was the twin to the flag that her conspirator, Leila Pullen the brat, gave to Brown Morgan. That West Point china doll won the first battle with her gaudy gown, but Sallie Fannie Reid was no match in strategy for a sophisticated LaGrange belle trained at the Female College.

With Secretary Davis retiring to the corner to watch, Rep. Hill took to the center of the floor and motioned for the town's five-man orchestra to strike up a rousing rendition of "Hell Among The Yearlings." As the LaGrange patriarch read off the names of the states, adding flair by keeping with the order of their admission into the Union, the dancers paired off and strutted hand-in-hand across the waxed ash floor. Rev. Heard led Mary into the fray, followed by Frank and Caroline Poythress. Many of Nancy's older college classmates joined in when their state flags were trumpeted until the entire room was awhirl.

Nancy's heart beat faster as the states announced by Rep. Hill edged closer to the Mississippi River. The unpaired dancers thinned along the periphery, and Sallie's frown grew darker; it was becoming clear what was happening. Two men still holding flags—Brown Morgan and Sam Eakin, a rotund, homely elf who owned the town's lone haberdashery—remained unattached.

"California!" cried Rep. Hill.

Sam Eakin looked at the gigantic bear painted on his flag. He grinned, unable to believe his stunning fortune. Sam dashed over to Sallie and waved the little strip of linen in front of her paling face to confirm that it matched the flag now shaking in her hand from her fury. He bowed and offered his hand. Sallie snapped the folds of her gown and took his hand, unable to refuse without incurring the displeasure of the onlooking guests. Yanked off onto the floor to join the other dancers, she shot a vengeful sneer over shoulder at Nancy.

Brown Morgan stood alone now, a confused look on his face. Rep. Hill, thinking his task completed, backed away, hoping to join Secretary Davis in the observing gallery.

"One more!" Nancy shouted to the legislator, waving her flag.

Brown Morgan stared at the flag in his hand, noticing its details for the first time. The blood drained from his face. He tried to warn Nancy with his pinning eyes, but to no avail.

Rep. Hill turned. "Darling, I'm afraid we've run out of states."

Nancy, giggling with anticipation of soon being held in Brown's arms, held her flag up for everyone to see. "No, Kansas has yet to be called."

The music came to an abrupt halt. The dancers stopped in fractured steps, and the room fell silent.

Gus Ware limped up from his position in the shadows near the wall and whispered into Nancy's ear. "Kansas is a territory."

"But is it not the same as—"

"Say nothing more of this," Gus insisted under his breath.

Sallie Reid, seeing an opening for a punishing sortie, abandoned her escort and came swishing up to Nancy. Affecting an air of courtesy, she took Nancy's hands into hers and announced, "I'd have made the same mistake." She led Nancy toward Brown Morgan in a *faux* gesture of magnanimity when she stopped to examine the Kansas flag that Nancy held. "I've never seen this symbol. Why, you must forgive my blush. Is it not a painting of a bare-breasted woman?"

The guests, murmuring with astonishment, crowded around the two debutantes to gawk at the Kansas flag that Nancy had crafted.

"Kansas and Lady Liberty," explained Nancy. "It represents the Fair Maid of Kansas. I found its depiction in a book in the college library."

"There, then," Brown Morgan said testily, trying to brush everyone away. "With that geography lesson finished, shall we return to the dance?"

"That's a Free-Soil flag." Frank Poythress said. "I saw one in Missouri. Those meddling Abolitionists from New England devised the abomination. It depicts Kansas as a virgin lying on her back being seduced by armed Southern men."

"Black-souled miscreants!" Rev. Heard said. "Those slave-stealing hooligans won't stop until they have us digging our own graves!"

To Nancy's horror, the guests abandoned her dance and clamored for Secretary Davis to come forward to expound upon the political situation in Congress and the prospects for the presidential election in November. Such conduct was unheard of during a cotillion. For the next thirty minutes, the men argued over Kansas and Free-Soilers and the new Republican Party and the tariff and the conniving manufacturers up north and Know-Nothings and popular sovereignty and who should be the Democratic candidate and where will we ship our cotton and whom Oh Lord will save us from the Northern aggressors?

She found a hiding spot in the far corner of the dining room across the hall, too ashamed to say goodbye to the guests when they ran out of debating steam and made their way to the carriages. She hadn't even danced with Brown Morgan; he left with several of the men, still in heated conversation, without saying goodnight. Secretary Davis prepared to ascend the stairs to retire for the evening when he spotted her alone in her covey. He walked in, his face looking even wearier from the strain of the night's tense discussion. Seeing him blinking and rubbing his glazed eye, she extinguished the nearest lamp, remembering his sensitivity to light.

Davis regained his sight. "Miss Hill. Why are you not out on the portico accepting cards from the departing young gentlemen?"

"I shouldn't think they would wish to be seen with me now."

"The most radiant lady in the house? Come, I assure you, I heard several whisper hopes you might grant a beneficial eye to their approach."

She smiled through tears. "I am sorry to have put you through that boorish blustering and crowing."

Davis took her hands. For the first time, he smiled. "You forget I am a politician. I've become accustomed to such blustering."

"I was told you attended the Military Academy in New York."

He nodded. "And barely graduated. I was not the most diligent of students. But during the Mexican War, I learned to assess the lay of a battlefield. I couldn't help but notice that you had your gun sights set upon one gentleman in particular this evening."

She blushed. "Was it that obvious?"

"Well, the fireworks sparking between you and Miss Reid brought to mind the cannonade at Monterrey. Is Mr. Morgan your first love?"

His keen perception astonished her. "I fear he does not share the same feelings about me."

Davis turned to the window to watch the carriages rumble over the macadam lane toward downtown LaGrange.

"You miss Mrs. Davis," Nancy said. "You must love her dearly."

Davis kept his gaze askance to hide a surge of grief. "I startled you during our introductions. I apologize."

"You said I reminded you of someone."

He nodded as a pall of sorrow fell over his features. "Sallie Knox Taylor was her name. She had your deep obsidian eyes and fierce spirit. She was the daughter of my commanding officer at Fort Crawford in Wisconsin. He didn't think much of me. Forbade me to court her."

"Did you obey him?"

"I wish I had. Perhaps then ..." His voice trailed off. He coughed back the emotion, collected himself, and bowed to take his leave.

She risked placing a hand on his arm to delay him a moment more. "Secretary Davis ... I've been told a lady on the evening of her debut should always ask the wisest man in attendance for advice as to the conduct of her life."

Smiling sadly, Davis pressed her hands in his. "In my experience, Miss Hill, the Almighty rewards those who throw abandon to the wind to attain what their heart desires. But as the Good Book tells us, He is a jealous God, and He will not hesitate to take from us that to which we so desperately cling."

Before Nancy could ask for an explanation of that dark prophecy, Davis bowed and escaped to the stairs to end his social night.

4

FOND DU LAC COUNTY, WISCONSIN
MAY 1856

Hugh knocked on the door to the professor's office, screwing up the courage to beg a release from his matriculation agreement. After a week of attending lectures, he now regretted the deal he had struck to attend Ripon College. Besides enrolling him in Grammar and Rhetoric, Professor Daniels insisted he take his Natural Science class. That curriculum, as far as Hugh could figure, consisted mainly of debates on biblical support for progressive communal farming and hidden codes of wisdom the Almighty wrote into Creation's sedimentary layers. None of this study was practical for a farmer. Besides, he had missed the first half of the semester, and the walk into town was four miles uphill.

The door glided open, but before Hugh got a word out, the geologist announced they were going on a spelunking field trip that morning to catch up on the missed science classes.

Hugh had never been inside a cave, didn't know such holes existed around Ripon. He wasn't eager to worm into tight spaces led by a man who functioned with his head in the clouds. To make matters worse, the eccentric instructor insisted they wear underwater diving outfits jerry-rigged from canvas overalls, leather helmets fitted with goggles, and oxygen rebreathers devised from peach cans stuffed with sponges soaked in lime juice. The bantam professor's garb was so baggy that he resembled a deflated balloon. Asked why they didn't carry the paraphernalia until needed, the professor explained their lungs had to acclimate to the breathing regulators before they descended into the earth's bowels.

Despite his misgivings, Hugh climbed into the diving suit handed to him and slid on its itchy headpiece. Strapped in, he slung his rock-hounding knapsack over his shoulder and, squinting through the scratched goggle lenses, followed the professor across the one-acre campus toward the commercial heart of Ripon. The only thing queerer than their appearance in the diving suits was the reaction they received from those they passed on the sidewalk boards lining the storefronts. The residents, accustomed to the professor's quixotic ways, smiled and offered him salutations. The professor garbled greetings through his breathing canister and made it a point to let everyone he passed know he was escorting another initiate to the abode of Persephone and Demeter.

Whatever that meant.

Trudging five steps behind, Hugh noticed a stranger with a shabby beard sitting astride a roan horse in front of the jail. A coiled whip hung on the rider's pommel next to a holstered musket, and several pistols dangled like fruit from his oilskin overcoat. He had seen rough characters pass through Ripon, but none as sinister as this hinterlander with the oily hair stringing to his shoulders. Perhaps his immediate dislike had something to do with the fellow's drawling speech, stretched and foreign, or with the way he spit tobacco near the boots of the sheriff, who sat inspecting his domain in a rocking chair on a platform above the muck.

Before Hugh could ask why they were extending the embarrassment and misery of the heat by taking the long way through town, Daniels veered off from the duckboards and slogged across the muddy street to converse with the sheriff and the mounted stranger.

"Morning, constable." The helmeted professor scraped the stinking glops of muck off his boots. "I can dehydrate this boulevard of morassed carbons for you. All it requires is a thin film of ignited petrol."

The mounted stranger glared at them as if confronting the town lunatics.

The sheriff picked up a pebble from his platform and tossed it off the professor's goggles. "Why should I want to do that, Docent?"

The professor's reply reverberated through the peach can riveted to his helmet. "When the street dries, we cut its caked effluvium into peat bricks and sell it as fuel. For a healthy profit, I might add. Close off traffic for a day, and people will soon call you Midas. The compressed horse dung here is congealed gold. Bestow upon me a mercantile conferment for the operation, and together we can flourish, fifty-fifty partners."

The sheriff snorted. "And I suppose *my* fifty is the pecuniary half of the contribution?"

"Neither yet bread to the wise, nor yet riches to men of understanding." When the sheriff and the stranger reacted with blank stares, the professor cited the source for his claim to poverty. "Ecclesiastes."

The rider shifted in his saddle and farted in the professor's direction. "Do the fools up here always travel in pairs?"

"From time to time, we encounter them solitary," the sheriff said. "And the more weaponry they carry, the softer in the head they usually prove."

That insult took several moments to hit its thick mark. Hugh saw the rider twitch a hand toward his nearest pistol. The roughneck, seeing the sheriff respond in kind, didn't follow through on the impulse.

"Allow me to introduce my latest matriculant, Hugh LaGrange," the professor said. "His father farms a patch up west of the Longhouse."

The sheriff gave a half-hearted nod, and the rider shot a stream of black tobacco juice at the professor's feet to register his lack of interest.

Daniels tipped his imaginary hat. "We'd best be on our way. I find noon to be the most auspicious hour for the practice of physiography. The stones come alive with the rising sun and surrender their innermost secrets."

"When you talk to your rocks today," the sheriff said, "let me know if they tell you the whereabouts of Ferdy Hanson's lost cow."

Hugh watched, confused, as the professor held a forced smile, willingly playing the butt of their jokes. Daniels backed away and turned to leave when the rider's firearm, holstered in the leather sheath embroidered with rosettes and studs, caught his eye again. "That is an impressive scabbard, sir. A Kentucky long rifle within its swaddle?"

The stranger glowered menace. "You scribbling my memoirs, are you?"

"I hold to the dream of one day visiting the Bluegrass state. I've heard tell of a cave there called the Mammoth, the largest east of the Mississippi."

"It do exist. Nearly big as your mouth."

Nodding to concede he had overstayed his welcome, the professor bowed and made a fast retreat.

"Good hole hunting!" the sheriff yelled, cackling.

Hugh stumbled along behind and risked a look over his shoulder at the whip tethered to the Kentuckian's saddle. Were those bloodstains on the rawhide? The professor was now navigating the five remaining blocks up Broadway on a near run, so Hugh huffed and heaved to keep pace. They passed the Arcade Flouring Mill on the outskirts of town and scampered across the railroad tracks into an expanse of woods that bordered the marshes near Rush Lake. When they reached the shade of the grove, Hugh stopped and dropped his hands to his knees, gasping for air through the regulator.

The professor meandered around in the brush as if hunting mushrooms. He fell to his knees, discovering his marker. After making sure no one else was observing him, he grubbed and clawed away the loam near a boulder.

Hugh turned his torso like a turret and tried to piece together a panoramic view of the environs through his gauzy goggles. He wasn't versed on the propensities of geologic formations, but he thought grottoes were found around limestone and dolomites, where water burrowed through the soft core. This flat mud ground more resembled the biblical descriptions of the Nile marshes where Jochebed hid the baby Moses. "There's a cave around *here*?"

Muffled by the homemade regulator, his question went unheard. The professor hammered at the earth with a pickaxe. After a few minutes of this furious excavation, he pulled out a sieve brush from his knapsack and began whisking away leaves and twigs, exposing what appeared to be a circular wooden lid for a well.

Had someone nailed those leaves to the lid?

The professor slid off the covering and exposed a vertical shaft. He plunged into the darkness feet first and motioned for his student to follow, but Hugh held back. This was not what he expected for a cave. Wary, he sat aside the hole and dangled his boots. He felt the professor's hand pulling on his heel, urging him to hurry. How far was the jump? He'd have to trust that the professor knew what he was doing. He launched himself into the void and landed with a jarring thud. Surrounded by darkness, he became disoriented, unable to see or hear because of his helmet.

A match sizzled against the rock wall. Hugh turned and found Daniels holding a torch. The professor's diving suit and canvas helmet lay in a heap at his feet. As the flame took life, the light revealed they were standing in a tight niche that led into a tunnel. Why did the professor remove his spelunking gear? Daniels handed him the torch, climbed back up along the jagged edge of the hole, and repositioned the wooden lid over the mouth of the shaft. The professor clambered back down and yanked off the regulator mask from Hugh's sweating head.

Hugh gulped for air. "Why wear these animal skins on the walk here if—"

"Shed those overalls."

The professor no longer spoke like a scatterbrained scholar, but a man consumed with determination and purpose. Hugh scanned the walls again, trying to gain his bearings. He saw pick notches. "This is a man-made tunnel."

Daniels scooped up his diving gear. "We haven't much time."

Before Hugh shook his foot out of the body-suit dungarees, the professor disappeared into a narrow niche. He carried his diving suit above his head in one hand and the torch in the other, wiggling sideways for clearance.

Hugh tucked his overalls and helmet under his arm and hurried to keep up with the professor. He feared, with the suffocating air here, the light would go out. He chased after the fading shadow, squeezing and grunting through the zagging canal. If the torch died, how would they find their way out? The smoke from the torch thickened, fouling the air. After another fifty paces, the embankments of the tight maze eased and flared. He finally managed a full breath.

The flickering light ahead became weaker. The professor had hurried on without him. Hugh forced his cramping legs to keep churning. Minutes later, he came to another small chamber. The tunnel split into branches. Which one had the professor taken? He cursed every swear word he could remember. There was no response to his shout. Exhausted and dazed, he slid to his haunches and dropped the bulky gear to his side. He called for the professor again. The echo of his own voice repeated one thought.

This is Hell.

He laughed grimly. If Wallace could see him now. How many hours had he listened to his brother repeat the descriptions those tent preachers painted of the route that sinners walk on their underground sojourns to the demonic fires? Hot enough here to be Hell, too. Would he die from thirst, or from starvation? What awaited him on the other side—were those footsteps?

"Professor?" He heard the approach of bare feet loping against stone. He retreated into a corner and searched the floor for a stone to use as a weapon.

A bear?

Heavy breathing. The beast was inching closer. He pressed his lips, making sure it wasn't his own inhalations. The snorting and breathing became louder. A looming presence hovered over him. It smelled sulfuric—was a demon attacking him? He balled his fist and reared back to strike the malignant spirit—

A light flickered. An enormous black face, streaked with sweat and stippled with the wide yellow eyes of a panther, hovered inches from his nose. His heart jumped into his throat. The fiend clamped his hands and pinned him to the floor. "Off me! Christ Jesus help me!"

"You ain't takin' me!" the demon shouted.

"And you ain't taking *me!*" Entangled in the hellion's tentacles, Hugh struggled and kicked, but he threatened to succumb to its monstrous force. He squirmed a hand loose and recoiled his balled knuckles to land right into— something grasped his wrist.

The torch came flaming over him.

"Calm yourself, lad."

Hugh blinked hard, blinded by the blast of light. Recovering his sight, he crawled to his hands and knees. The black demon who had attacked him cowered in the corner. "Don't you see him, Professor?"

"See what?"

Hugh pointed at the beast. "Satan's minions inhabit these subterranean worm lairs."

The professor brought his torch around the bend and discovered what had so frightened his student. "Praise God. Mister Jeffries, I've been looking for you." He extended a hand in greeting.

The black intruder curled his knees to his chest, reluctant to accept the professor's handshake.

"You needn't be frightened, Mr. Jeffries. I'm your conductor."

Conductor?

Hugh was still gulping for breath. That word eased the stranger's alarm, and he lurched to his knees to press the professor's hands in gratitude.

"This is my coal boy," the professor said. "I see you two have met."

Hugh protested. "I'm nobody's coal boy!"

"Come, Hugh, say hello to Mister Alfred Jeffries from Louisiana. The Lord's angels have brought him to us."

What pagan necromancy was the professor plying?

"Have you never seen a man of African descent?" When Hugh shook his head, the professor said, "Consider yourself blessed this day." Daniels reached into his breast pocket, pulled out a sliver of rabbit jerky, and gave it to Jeffries. "This should keep you sustained until we can get you to the next station."

"Thank you, massah."

"None of that plantation jarble here. Call me Edward. You're a free man now."

Jeffries, by habit, lowered his eyes. "Much o-o-obliged, Mister Edward."

"We haven't much time. Hugh here will take you—"

"Me?" Hugh knifed to his feet.

"This man's life depends on you." The professor handed his diving suit and helmet to Jeffries. "You take mine."

Hugh now understood why the diminutive professor had chosen spelunking gear so oversized that he resembled a circus clown.

"Quarter mile ahead," Daniels said. "When you reach the shaft to the basement storeroom of Grumald's butcher shop, put on the diving suits."

"How are we going to get *there*?"

The professor handed Hugh the torch. "Follow that branch. Black smudge dots mark the way. If you become lost, just backtrack and look for the signs."

"Why aren't you going with us?"

The professor tilted his chin to his chest, disappointed his student hadn't figured out his ploy. "Two went into a cave. They'll expect two to come out."

Hugh's mouth gaped. The professor had schemed this diversion. Daniels was no airy-headed scholar; his teaching was just an act, a cover to allay suspicion of his true purpose in Ripon. That's why he insisted they wear the diving suits in town. When he and this Negro reappeared on the streets, no one would be the wiser. "And that rider at the jail?"

"A bounty hunter," Daniels said. "The fugitive slave law pays evil men like him a year's worth of what Mister Jeffries here goes for at auction. That is if the scoundrel brings him back to those Southern sinners who claim to own him."

Stunned, Hugh watched the man trembling before them. He examined the dirt and found evidence of past campfires. "You've taken others through here."

The professor nodded. "It is my calling. And if you *are* a man of God, Hugh, it will become your calling, too. The first day I encountered you in that field, the Lord told me you were one of His soldiers in the cause."

"What cause?"

"All will be understood in good time. Take Mister Jeffries's hand and go. Do not lose him."

Hugh extended his hand, but the Negro balked, as if not accustomed to touching a white man. The fugitive's gnarled knuckles were scratched and swollen. Had his hands become enlarged and arthritic from years of picking cotton? He asked Daniels, "What am I to do with him if we reach town?"

"Josiah Strong at the butcher's shop will have your instructions. I'll stay here until nightfall and make my way back to the campus. If anyone asks, we were rock-hunting all day." The professor braced Hugh with hands to his shoulders. "God be with you both."

Before Hugh could ask about the criminal penalties for assisting refugee slaves, the professor disappeared into the darkness. Resigned to his plight, he tied the boots and canvas helmets to his belt and wrapped the sleeves of the jumpsuits around his neck. Gripping the torch, he found the Negro's grasp with his free hand and entered the tunnel that led to another shaft for the storeroom in town. He prayed they didn't hit a pocket of stale air and lose the flame. What if explosive gases lurked in this sap? With each step, he braced for the possibility of being blown to smithereens. When he calmed enough to feel his heart settle back into his chest, he risked speaking. "Mister Jeffries?"

"Yes, sir?"

"Could you ease your grip?"

"Sorry."

"Thank you."

"The professor called me a coal boy. What did he mean by that?"

The Negro hesitated. "I'm not right sure I'm supposed to say."

"You think you can't trust me?"

"To be honest, I'm ain't sure who I can trust up here."

"Up here?"

"North of the River Jordan."

Hugh decided not to press the slave on his peculiar manner of talking.

Moments later, Jeffries said, "Fueling the engine."

"Engine?"

"You asked what a coal boy does. He shovels the fuel for the conductor. So the train can keep a-movin'."

Hugh had no clue what the man was trying to explain. Did the professor and this escaped slave share a secret language full of codes and mysteries? "You a Christian, Mister Jeffries?"

"Yes, sir."

"What's the Bible say about breaking the law?"

"I ain't never read it, to be honest."

"How can you be a Christian if—"

"I ain't never read nothing."

Hugh felt the prickle of embarrassment rise in his face. "I'm sorry. I didn't mean …"

"Most of what I know of the Good Book I hear from the preacher."

"Your people have preachers?"

"No, sir. Our owners allow us to come Sundays to listen to their holy men."

"So, everything you've learned has come from a white man telling you what Christ taught?"

"I reckon that's the way it be."

Hugh pondered that disturbing discovery. "I'm no student of divinity, but I've listened to a fair number of traveling baptizers coming through here. No two preach the same interpretation."

"I can't rightly say I follow?"

"What I'm getting at is, I'd question if those plantation oligarchs are giving you the straight story about Christ."

"My folk may not be learned, but we ain't born feeble. I'd be lying if I said that possibility hasn't crossed my thoughts."

Hugh lifted the torch near the walls to look for the black smoke dots. "Some say what I'm doing here is a sin, breaking the law." When the man did not respond, Hugh debated aloud with himself. "Romans Thirteen. 'Obey the rulers who have authority over you. Only God can give authority to anyone, and he puts these rulers in their places of power. People who oppose the authorities are opposing what God has done, and they will be punished.'"

"Yes, sir."

"So, am I sinning by doing this?"

As they plodded deeper into the tunnel, a silence fell between them. After several moments passed, Jeffries spoke again. "You sound like an educated man."

"I'm just a student."

"Didn't Moses break the law when he stole the Israelites from Pharaoh?"

"That wasn't God's law. It was the law of Egypt and the heathens."

"Yes, sir, but for those heathens, it was *their* God's law, wasn't it?"

"I suppose."

"So, does God's law depend on whose side you're on?"

"I don't think it works that way."

"Maybe I'm not seeing things as they are, but didn't the Christians break the God law of *my* people when they chained us and brought us over on the ships? And didn't President Washington break the God law of England when he took up arms agin' the redcoats?"

Hugh conceded the point. "Where are you headed, Mister Jeffries?"

"They tell me a place called Milwaukee."

"What are you going to do when you get there?"

"I don't know."

"Well, you have the skills of a barrister."

"You poking fun at me, sir."

"No, I'm serious. I doubt the Supreme Court of these United States could refute the argument you've just made—" Hugh stopped and motioned for the fugitive to be quiet. He cocked his ear toward a thumping sound in the darkness just ahead. He whispered over his shoulder, "Stay here."

Jeffries didn't want to release his hand.

"I can't take the chance of anyone seeing you."

Jeffries finally let go, and Hugh gave him the torch and groped his way along the chiseled surface. After twenty paces, he stumbled over a stone step. He inched his foot up and, finding the landing, climbed a shaft to a wooden door. He placed his face against a crack, just enough to see a man in a bloodied apron hacking away at a hanging side of beef. Was this his contact? With a deep breath, he pounded on the boards. The door to the cellar creaked open.

The butcher held a dripping cleaver. "What took you so long?" He glanced at the window. Assured that no one was around, he motioned for Hugh and Jeffries to climb into the slaughter room. He nodded for them to put on the spelunking gear they had brought with them.

"You know where the funeral home is?" the butcher whispered.

Hugh untied the gear from his belt and handed the professor's jumpsuit to Jeffries. He fixed his goggled helmet against his shoulders and nodded to confirm his readiness. "Four blocks west on Seward Street."

"Walk toward campus. There's a side alley just beyond the fountain. Make sure no one sees you, then go into the funeral home from the delivery door."

"And if people speak to us on the street?"

"You answer for the professor," the butcher said. "Say that Mr. Daniels developed a debilitating case of laryngitis and lost his voice from the dampness in the cave. Do you understand?" When Hugh nodded, the butcher pushed the disguised Jeffries toward the door. "Mr. Daniels walks with a slight hitch in his right knee, sir. Godspeed to you."

Jeffries brought his hands together in a gesture of gratitude. Encased in their spelunking gear, Hugh and his charge sneaked out the butcher's rear entrance and turned right onto the sidewalk. Hugh hoped most people were back home from their shopping. With the Almighty's help, they navigated the four dangerous blocks without being accosted. They slipped into the alley.

The embalmer motioned them into a back room where he drained the blood from the corpses. Jeffries took off his helmet and stood terrified, surrounded by bodies. The embalmer handed him a white silk shroud. "Step into this, sir, and I will tie it above your head."

"Oh Lord," Jeffries muttered as the embalmer prepared him like a corpse.

Hugh tried to reassure the shaken man, even though he had no idea of the chances for his survival. "I'm sure the professor has taken many of your folks to safety this way."

Before pulling the shroud over Jeffries's head, the embalmer handed him a square of cloth and piglet's bladder filled with water. "You've been instructed what to do?"

Jeffries nodded, his hands shaking.

"The next station is the Hartford cemetery. A full day's ride."

"Hartford?" Hugh said. "That's going back south."

The embalmer nodded. "We bring the refugees up here and into north Milwaukee before we transfer them to Canada. The law agents hunting fugitives expect them to enter the city from the south, so they keep a watch on those streets." He turned to Jeffries and clasped his hand. "Ready?"

Jeffries muttered a prayer and clung fast to the water bladder. He turned to Hugh and thanked him. "You have God in your heart, Mister LaGrange."

The lump in Hugh's throat cost him his voice.

The embalmer tied the shroud over Jeffries's head and lowered him into a pine coffin. He lifted the lid into place and nailed it shut, leaving a few slender cracks for air. He rang a bell on the wall, and two assistants appeared from the next room and carried it to a waiting flatbed carriage in the alley.

"Your work's done," the embalmer told Hugh. "Go home. Speak to no one about this."

Hugh knew he should return to the college and wait for the professor, but he couldn't abandon the trundle hearse that rolled up Broadway. He moseyed along a block behind it so as not to draw suspicion and watched as the coffin bounced from the ruts in the road. He feared poor Jeffries might suffer a concussion before he cleared town. He dawdled along the boardwalk, silently urging the carriage to reach the safety of the outskirts.

"Friend of yours?"

Hugh turned and saw the mounted Kentuckian walk out of the tavern behind him. "No, sir."

"You seem awful interested in that box. Who's the poor sap on his way to meet his Maker?"

"I'm not sure."

The Kentucky bounty hunter, two sheets to the wind, rolled a cigarette while watching the carriage. "You ain't seen any darkies in town, have you, boy?"

Hugh wasn't practiced at lying. "No."

The bounty hunter narrowed his glare. "Have we met?"

"No, sir."

The man lit his cigarette. "You ever witnessed a man buried alive?"

"Can't say I have."

"It's not a pleasant experience, particularly for the one under sod."

Hugh held his breath. Did the fugitive hunter suspect him? He tried to act nonchalant. "I'd best be getting back home."

The slaver yanked his whip from the pommel of his saddle and, with a flick of his wrist, wrapped its tail around Hugh's waist. "Come with me, boy. I'm gonna teach you a lesson you won't learn in that schoolhouse of yours."

The Kentuckian mounted and cantered up the street, dragging Hugh behind him. He pulled his pistol and fired into the air, signaling for the two men driving the hearse flatbed to stop. He caught up with them and circled the carriage to inspect the coffin. "How long?"

"How long what?" the driver asked.

"Since the deceased has been presumed departed."

"He died night 'fore last."

The Kentuckian sniffed the air. "A body gets a little ripe."

"Our boss is the best blood-drainer in the business. I've seen a few linger a week before the flies gather."

"Cause of demise?"

"Consumption."

The bounty hunter rode up close enough to touch the coffin lid.

"You got a fondness for dead flesh?" the driver asked.

"I do if it's negrah flesh." The Kentuckian snorted as he caressed the pine box. "Got a plot picked out for yourself yet, undertaker?"

The driver, hearing the threat in that question, turned mute.

"Back in Casey County, we devised a surefire way of winnowing the living from the dead and helping the Lord before the Judgment Day. You fancy a demonstration?"

The driver kept looking straight ahead. "Suit yourself."

While Hugh struggled to extract himself from the whip's coil, the bounty hunter leaned over the flatbed and traced the burning end of his cigarette along the crease of the coffin lid. Then he took a deep inhalation and blew so much smoke into the coffin that Hugh saw some curl out from the other side. After a minute passed, the bounty hunter flicked away the cigarette, satisfied. "You can plant the lilacs in the bosom of this tender soul."

The driver tipped his slouch hat. "Yes, sir, just as I said."

The Kentuckian snapped his whip and spun Hugh to the ground, releasing him. He rode back toward town.

When his tormentor was out of sight, Hugh jumped onto the wagon and put his ear to the pine box. He heard a gasp from under the coffin lid, followed by coughing through the water-soaked cloth. Before he could ask Jeffries if he was suffocating, the driver pushed Hugh off, snapped the reins, and sent the flatbed careening down the rutted road toward the next station on the Underground Railroad.

5

LAGRANGE, GEORGIA
JUNE 1856

Nancy spied Gus Ware limping along Broad Street toward his apothecary and surgical office across from the square. The curmudgeon's morning itinerary on his class days never varied. Breakfast at ten, followed by a stroll through the garden terraces owned by Sarah Farrell. Then, he circled back to harangue the codgers on the courthouse benches about the evils of the new Republican Party, all before attending to his medical duties, which ranged from pulling human teeth to putting down foundered horses.

Flitting in the shadows, she tailed him from column to column of the Presbyterian church. Although her cousin often annoyed her, she felt sorry for Gimpy Gus, the nickname folks used behind his back. People here could be unkind, and many refused to seek treatment from a physician so marred by disease. Living as a bachelor with his sister didn't help his sour disposition. That and the fact that his brother, Eugenius, younger by three years, was as dashing and jaunty as Gus was dour and forlorn.

At last, Gus arrived at his door, fumbling as always for his key.

She clutched the folds of her skirts and dashed across the street to catch him before he entered. An avid observer of politics, Gus was the only person in town who might know the answer to the mystery that had tormented her since the night of her disastrous debut. Certain no passersby saw her, she tiptoed to his turned back and whispered to his ear, "Sallie Knox Taylor."

Startled, Gus staggered and dropped his cane. "Stalking imp!"

She picked up the silver-capped cane and saw a crease, barely detectable, near its handle. She slid her fingernail into the groove, flipped open a lid, and found a flask built into its shaft. "Does Caroline know of this?"

He plucked the cane from her grasp. "I designed it for the transport of pharmaceuticals." When she slanted her head to remind him she was no fool, he warned, "If you tell my sister—"

"You'll be in the doghouse. Oh, wait, that's a term used for cuckolded husbands." She angled a finger to her lips in affected thought. "What *is* the word for a celibate monk who must ask permission from his sister before slathering a second dollop of jam on his toast?"

Exasperated, Gus took out his pocket watch. "You should be in class."

She felt the roll line of his starched white collar. "You look different today." When he slapped away her hand, she said, "Someone is pressing your shirts."

"You think me a sloven?"

"Caroline hasn't the time to coddle you. You've commissioned a laundress."

His eyes darted, betraying his guilt. "What is it you want?"

"Two matters of inquiry."

Gus's jaw sank. "I am *not* the justice of the peace!"

She stood between him and the door. "You flinched when I spoke her name."

"Whose name?

"Sallie Knox Taylor."

He glared suspicion at her. "What did Secretary Davis tell you?"

"Very little."

"You must have pried until he could no longer suffer your impertinence. He never talks of her."

"He said I reminded him of Miss Taylor."

Gus leaned in, raising his spectacles, and squinted at her features. "That is passing strange. You haven't the slightest resemblance."

"How do *you* know her?"

"*Did* know her. Everyone in the South knew her, until ..." He turned aside.

"Until what? Are you going to tell me, or must I spread a rumor that you stuff your healing herbs with grass?"

Gus gritted his chaw-stained teeth. Unable to stand in one place for long, he ushered her by the elbow to a nearby bench. "Speak to no one of this. If it gets around that I peddle in idle gossip, I'll lose business." When she nodded her agreement, he sighed and explained, "Sallie Knox Taylor was President Zachary Taylor's daughter. Secretary Davis fell in love with her while serving under Taylor's command in the West. He married Sallie and took her to Mississippi in the summer, against her father's wishes."

"And?"

"She caught malaria and died three months later."

Nancy now understood the pain she observed in Secretary Davis's eyes that night. "But he married again."

Gus nodded. "On his honeymoon, the Secretary insisted his new wife, Varina Howell, visit Sallie's grave with him. Is that not morose and cruel? Sallie was his first love. Some say the Secretary has never gotten over her."

Nancy lowered her chin, confused. What did Secretary Davis see in *her* that brought to his mind such memories of sorrow? Had he divined in her future a similar black fate? "Gus, I shamed myself at the ball."

"Yes, you did."

"Do you think Brown despises me now?"

Gus traced her glances across the square toward the row of law offices. "Is that why you ambushed me?"

She refused to meet his glare, deflecting the charge. "I need an excuse to make amends with him."

"What does that have to do with *me*?"

"You stood in his way during my debut. It was Brown who was to walk me down that staircase."

Gus bristled. "I had no choice. Ben Hill commissioned me with the task. Ever since your father passed, he looks after you as a daughter. And you repaid him with that flags-dance fiasco."

"Why did he choose you?"

"Did it occur to you that no other gent offered his service?"

Nancy bounced to her feet. "Are you implying—"

Gus tapped his cane around her shoes, driving her back to sitting. He waited a moment, allowing her to gather her composure. His strident tone turned paternal. "Nannie, gentlemen prefer young ladies who wait to be courted. The flower does not chase the bee. I fear the advanced schooling at the College has subverted you, as it has so many of our fairer sex."

"Subverted?"

"Dangerous ideas infiltrate your minds. *Scientia potentia est.*"

"What does *that* mean?"

"Knowledge is power. The maxim is often attributed to Sir Francis Bacon, but its origins run much older to the Bible. Proverbs Twenty Four, Verse Five. 'A wise man is strong, a man of knowledge increaseth strength.'"

"So, knowledge is beneficial."

"For a man."

The blood drained from her face.

Before she could explode, Gus raised a finger to warn her. "Remember St. Paul's rule. 'I do not permit a woman to teach or to assume authority over a man; she must be quiet.'"

Nancy scooted away and stewed, wondering if her boldness *had* chased Brown Morgan away. She had intended to ask Gus to suggest a physical malady grim enough to consult Brown for a last will and testament, but that strategy was now dashed. Gus would snitch on her and leave her in an even deeper hole of her own digging. No, she must resort to her reserve plan.

Gus, impatient, thrummed his cane against her ankle. "You wished to discuss a second matter?"

Nancy rose and smoothed the folds in her dress. "Never mind."

Gus frowned, confounded by her abrupt reticence. "You are a mercurial creature."

She hiked her chin in a taunt. "I shall find someone else in town to ask. A real man who possesses proper authority."

"What?"

"You said it yourself. Knowledge is power. So, if I wish answers, I will henceforth make inquiries to the mayor and the town council, *not* to veterinarians."

Gus lurched to his feet, tottering against his cane. "Veterinarian? Now, look here, young lady, explain yourself!"

Nancy strode off. At the corner, she pivoted and made a buttoning motion across her pressed lips, mocking a subservience to St. Paul's admonition for female silence.

Gus risked stumbling to a heap by aiming the point of his cane at her. "Do not miss my class this afternoon!"

Walking on, she raised her parasol and snapped it open, the nearest gesture a Southern lady could make to giving one the middle finger. She crossed the street and stopped at the far corner, counting off the seconds, enough time for Gus to tire of staring at her. When he disappeared into his office, she hurried west on Broad Street, passing the many law offices, until she arrived at a two-story brick building with the same engraved bronze plate that she had conjured so many nights: *Jeremiah Brown Morgan, Esquire.* She stared at those recessed gold letters, imagining them next to her own name on a card of introduction. *Nancy Colquitt Hill Morgan.* Three of the most renowned families of Georgia merged into one appellation. How grand it sounded. Brown gained admittance to the bar only last year, at age twenty, after reading the law with Rep. Hill. Yet already he was being spoken of as a rising Demosthenes, arguing cases for the Atlanta & LaGrange Railroad Company and serving as local counsel for New Orleans cotton traders. Some considered him a future judge for the circuit court.

She slapped color into her cheeks and arranged the strands of curls, hoping to camouflage her large ears. She drew a deep breath for courage and reached for the polished handle—

The panels opened of their own accord. Out walked Sallie Fannie Reid on the arm of her father, Colonel William Reid. Sallie stood sheathed in a stunning hooped skirt of layered turquoise crinoline that featured a high bodice and a plunging neckline. She resembled a confection of white chocolate dimpled atop a round brandy cake.

How dare she!

The petite tart with her signature blonde ringlets was exposing her pale bosom and flaxen arms, a scandalous impertinence. The two girls stared at each other, Nancy towering over her diminutive rival, both spinning their parasols while trying to comprehend the other's presence.

Sallie finally spoke. "Miss Hill. My father. You met at the cotillion."

Nancy curtsied. "Colonel Reid."

The colonel studied her blankly. His eyes widened, now reminded. "The battle of the flags."

Nancy flushed. "I assure you, sir, it was not my intent—"

"We just left Mr. Morgan, who treated us to lunch at the Chattahoochee Hotel," said Sallie. "He has a most robust appetite for a man of such refined proportions." She turned to her father. "What was the entrée he ordered, Papa?"

"The Brunswick stew."

Sallie twirled her parasol faster. "And he followed it with the largest helping of cherry cobbler I have ever seen. He shared it with me. He prefers the crust, I fancy the filling."

Nancy gripped her parasol so hard that her knuckles turned white. What purpose did the Reids have to endure the ten-mile carriage ride up from West Point to consult with Brown? Did Sallie connive the meeting as a pretext to fling her ringlets at him? Colonel Reid held many business interests, including his vast plantation and mansion, Sunny Villa, which he built overlooking the new rail line that ran from LaGrange to that scratch on the map out in the sticks. She remembered hearing about some recent courthouse wrangling over the variance in rail gauges. LaGrange, with the larger population, risked losing its lucrative livery trade to its upstart neighbor. Passengers traveling from Atlanta to Montgomery changed trains here, requiring them to lodge overnight and spend their money in town. West Point was scheming to steal that transit business. Perhaps the Reids hoped to poach Brown on retainer to rid the LaGrange merchants of their most effective defender.

Colonel Reid glanced toward the sun. "We have a long journey back."

Sallie curtsied to take her leave. "I shall see you tomorrow."

Baffled by that threat, Nancy said nothing as Sallie and her father strode off toward a waiting carriage. She shrugged off the mystery and entered Brown's office. A miasma of dust assaulted her, accompanied by the horrid stench of moldy paper. The alcove was so dark that she required a moment to adjust her eyes. She expected a grand chamber crowned with an elevated desk, lit by elegant lamps, and lined with ceiling-high oak shelves filled with the monumental volumes of civilization. Instead, she confronted a mayhem of files and bound volumes scattered across the floor, their only apparent connection being the cobwebs. She pulled a kerchief from her sleeve and, stepping across the detritus, dusted the leather bands and raised ribs of those tomes still on the shelves.

"May I help you?"

She found Brown on his knees in the shadows, riffling through correspondence and court filings. If an earthquake hit, he would be buried alive. "Good Lord in Heaven, have you been ransacked by ruffians?"

Brown took off his reading spectacles. "Miss Hill?"

Nancy kicked a path through the small pyramids of volumes to reach the window. She drew back the curtains and lifted the pane to allow in fresh air. "How can you work amid this mess?"

Brown laughed. "You've never seen a law office, have you?"

"You will ruin your eyes. Fire a lamp, at least."

Brown found a chair and swept several files from its seat. He situated it in front of his desk and offered it to her. "First rule of practicing law. An overturned candle can consume an entire library in three minutes."

Nancy lifted the hem of her skirts an inch as she tiptoed to the chair. "You need a secretary."

Brown conceded that point with a nod as he leaned back in his swivel chair behind his desk. He glanced at the slanting light through the window. "It's the middle of the afternoon. Shouldn't you be in class?"

"Does everyone in town know my matriculation schedule?"

Brown grinned at her feigned outrage. "So, to what do I owe the pleasure?"

"No pleasantries first? Are barristers so consumed with billing hours that they cannot find time to ask as to a client's contentment and happiness?"

"Client?" Brown interrogated her with a twinkling eye. "And *barristers*? You've been reading that insufferable Dickens again."

"What if I have?"

"Novels are trifling distractions. Toxic to the female disposition."

"You mean they expose the shenanigans of shysters, villains, and pettifoggers who prey upon widows and orphans. Jarndyce and Jarndyce drones on."

Brown could not hide his amusement. "If you plan to gain knowledge of the law from *Bleak House*, I fear you will come away with a cynical view of me."

Nancy deflected his mirthful inspection by acting as if she were examining her gloves. "You will never guess who I chanced upon this morning."

Brown brought a finger to his lips, as if trying to solve a mystery. "Let's see, I will guess … Sallie Fannie Reid."

Nancy affected amazement. "How did you know?"

Brown swiveled, his habit when thinking. "This is how lawyers are trained to analyze a conundrum. Miss Reid left my office two minutes before you entered. In jurisprudence, that's called circumstantial evidence. If I am prosecuting a murderer, I don't need my witness to testify that he saw the scoundrel fire the pistol. It is enough if he hears the shot and finds the body of the victim next to the smoking gun while the defendant runs away."

Nancy sensed a playful patronizing tone. She could do what her best friend, Mary, always counseled, act stupid and allow the gentleman to feel superior, but that wasn't in her constitution. She observed dryly, "You are a savant."

He grinned. "I hold my own—"

"Let me see if I understand this concept of circumstantial evidence. You took the Reids to lunch. That means *you* are courting Colonel Reid for *his* business. Yet Colonel Reid has lawyers who handle his cotton exports. That's not your specialty, anyway. And Sallie Fannie accompanied her father. … Ergo, I'm thinking their visit had something to do with Sallie's inheritance."

Brown appeared astonished by her understanding of his business and that of the Reid family, not to mention her deductive powers. "You know I cannot discuss client matters. Confidentiality."

She skimmed his chaotic desk until her attention landed upon a circular at the top of the pile. The corner of the document appeared to have a red thumb-print stain on the corner. *Cherry cobbler.* She played nonchalant as she read the title line upside down and rearranged the bold letters. *Dred Scott vs. Sandford.* Before he could thwart her reach, she snatched the paper and saw that it was a court opinion with a recent post date. "This looks interesting."

"Not in the least."

She narrowed her glare, always capable of telling when he was lying. "I will sit here and read it, word for word. You might as well summarize it for me and save yourself the time."

Brown sighed. "It's a Missouri case."

"Missouri? What relevance could it have for Troup County?"

"The case is being appealed to the United States Supreme Court. A slave named Scott was taken up North to a state that grants freedom to Negroes. When Scott's owner returned with him to Missouri, the slave claimed he was a freeman."

Nancy thought for a bit, tying the evidence together. "So, Colonel Reid *also* has slaves lost to that same network of Northern thieves. Sallie is the Colonel's only child. The man she marries will inherit the plantation." She looked up at him in triumph. "They hired *you* to sue for the return of their escaped darkies."

Brown's jaw dropped. "Not a word of this to anyone, you understand?"

Nancy thrilled at knowing they shared a secret. "My lips are sealed." She batted her lashes. "For now."

Brown waited as if expecting her to explain her presence. "Was there another reason, other than spying on Sallie Fannie Reid, that you came to see me?"

She straightened in her chair, returning to business. "Now that you've agreed to represent me in return for my preserving your confidence—"

"Represent you?"

"I wish to sue for extreme pain and suffering."

Brown examined her. "Are you injured?"

She curled her lower lip into a pout. "My heart is shattered."

"I wasn't aware you had become betrothed. Alienation of affections is a hard case to prove and—"

"I am *not* engaged." She removed the glove on her left hand and waved her bare ring finger at him.

"Well, what happened?"

Nancy wiped a forced tear. "My future was utterly ruined at the Cotillion."

"The soirée at Ben Hill's home?"

"I can barely speak of it, so devastating was the tort perpetrated on my soul."

Brown edged closer to his desk, concerned. "Did a gentleman take liberties with you that night?"

Nancy waved off that line of inquiry with her kerchief. "No, no. It was my bumbling cousin."

"Dr. Ware?"

She nodded through her fake sobbing. "He botched my entrance. A lady comes out once in her life. I must suffer that harrowing memory for the rest of my life." She glanced up at him, hoping for empathy. "How can I go on?"

Brown stood, rolled his chair around his desk, and set it next to hers. He sat again and took her hands in his to comfort her. "Miss Hill—"

She risked resting her head on his shoulder. "Please." She looked up at him with her swimming eyes. "Call me Nannie."

He smiled at her overture. "Nannie, then. There is a doctrine in the law called contributory negligence. If a plaintiff holds any blame, in whole or in part, with the injury inflicted, no damages can be awarded."

She abandoned her woe-is-me act. "What are you suggesting?"

"As I recall, that evening was splendid until someone brandished a state flag representing the territory of Kansas."

Nancy catapulted up. "How was I to know Kansas hasn't been admitted into the Union? The education I am receiving, for good money, I might add, is useless on such matters of common discourse."

Brown eased her back into her chair and slid his seat closer. "Thing is, Nannie, I cannot take your case because I might be called as a witness. And I'd have to testify, truthfully under oath, that Miss Nancy Colquitt Hill came into society during the most successful cotillion ever held in the history of Troup County."

She glowed, grateful for his praise, as he stood and walked her to the door. "Off to class you go." She was halfway out when he added, "I enjoyed our discussion on the law. You have a talent for rhetoric."

She curtsied, suppressing a grin, and took one last lingering, judgmental look around the office, imagining how she would soon redesign it.

An hour later, Nancy hurried into the college's lecture room. She was the last to arrive. Burned by the suspicious glares of her classmates, she lowered into her seat while Gus, with his back to her, leaned against his cane and scribbled with chalk on the blackboard the hierarchy of Georgia fauna species. She sneered at the brat Leila Pullen, who had talked her way into the class full-time now, and Leila stuck her tongue in and out like a gecko. Nancy was about to congratulate herself on the success of her subterfuge sneaking in—

"Miss Hill. Please stand."

She suppressed a curse. Her annoying cousin seemed to have compensated for his buckled leg by growing eyes on the back of his head. She inched up, screwing her pinched lips at the smirking Leila. Mary shook her head in a warning, trying to defuse another confrontation with the substitute instructor.

Gus continued his writing on the board. "Miss Hill, do you know the singular attribute of the red-throated loon?"

Nancy rolled her eyes. "I've studied only the one-legged bobtail."

The girls giggled, and Gus turned, peering over his spectacles. He tossed the chalk to the tray. "The red-throated loon devotes its entire life span to finding a mate. One can detect the success or failure by the loon's distinctive calls. A goosey cackle"—he barked a loud *kak-kak-kak,* startling the girls—"warns a target is in the female's sights. A short wail—*aarOOao! AarOOao!*—confirms another generation of loons has been conceived. And a long, soft coo, called the 'long call,' announces that the female loon's usefulness has ended."

Nancy glowered a promise of revenge, horrified by the implication and his veiled threat to reveal her whereabouts that morning. She went on the offensive. "And what is the call made by a male loon who *never* mates?"

As the giggles erupted into laughter, Gus reddened. "Sit."

Nancy, triumphant, plopped into her seat, accepting the smirking accolades of her friends.

Gus strode across the front of the room, banging chair legs with his cane. "Mosses, ferns, conifers, and fungi. Members of the plant kingdom. Each has its uses for mankind, set upon the Earth by the Almighty—"

"Tell us about Missouri," said Nancy.

Gus waddled to a ragged halt. "Missouri?"

"Why is Missouri a slave state?" Nancy asked. "The Kansas territory sits next to it, and it's not slave."

Martha Beall, whose nickname was 'Pack' because she always stuffed her canvas tote with enough Monte Cristo sandwiches and pralines to feed half the cadets at the Fannin Military Institute, raised her hand. "Iowa is a state and borders Missouri, too. Yet Iowa is a free state."

"That makes no sense," said Nancy. "You mean one of our darkies could swim across the Mississippi River to freedom?"

"I don't think anyone can swim the Mississippi," said Mary.

Gus watched in rising dismay as his class disintegrated.

"That's not the point!" Nancy insisted. "If they rowed a canoe—"

"A canoe?" exclaimed Sally Bull. "You cannot row across the Mississippi in a canoe. The currents would drift you to New Orleans. My brother once rode a barge from Vicksburg, and he barely made it past—"

"Silence!"

The girls hushed, stunned by Gus's outburst.

"Again, may I remind you, this is a class on Natural Sciences."

Nancy crossed her arms. "All the men talk of now is politics and the election in November. How are we to converse with them if we know nothing of what goes on around us?"

"Politics is no proper concern for young ladies," Gus insisted.

"Nannie just wants to impress Brown Morgan," said Leila.

Nancy scowled at the troublesome sprite who possessed a maddening gift for reading her mind. Truth was, she *had* come to an epiphany that morning in Brown's office. She would never match Sallie Fannie Reid in beauty and charm, but she might win Brown with her wit and conversational skill. *I enjoyed our discussion on the law.* Yes, she would learn the affairs of government and statecraft, and thus gain an edge over Sallie. But first, a more immediate matter demanded resolution. She pointed at Leila in a protest. "Is *she* now a permanent member of this class? She's too young and foolish!"

Gus harrumphed. "If foolishness were the standard for non-admittance, I would send half of you back to Sunday school." He aimed his cane at Nancy. "And *you* would lead the parade."

Mary, the mature one in the class, tried to help the physician restore order. "Dr. Ware, she will persist until you agree to her request."

Head thrown back in disgust, Gus waved his cane like a maestro conducting an orchestra. "Chairs to the perimeter!"

The girls erupted from their seats and scooted their desks against the walls.

"Form a line." Gus walked across their ranks, counting off almost half the girls with his cane. "You gather to the North."

The girls chosen first retreated to the north end of the room. Gus counted off another set of students and motioned for them to stand at the south end.

He left Nancy, Leila, Mary, and four girls to await their assigned station. Taking center stage, he pointed to the first group and asked Nancy, "Free states. How many?"

Nancy counted them. "Sixteen."

Gus spun toward the southern group of girls. "And slave states?"

"Fifteen," said Nancy.

"Fifteen!" Gus circled Nancy and the six other girls near the window who were not assigned a group. "What do we have *here*?" Met with shrugs, he shouted, "Territories!" He walked around them, tapping each on the head. "Minnesota. New Mexico. Nebraska. Utah. Oregon. Washington." He came to Nancy. "And the most troublesome! Kansas!"

Nancy chafed at being tapped to represent the black sheep of the territories. She was also having second thoughts about getting Gus agitated. He seemed even more animated than usual. Had he stolen a few drinks from his hidden flask in the cane before class? "I want to be Nebraska."

"You are *Kansas!*" Gus ruled. "Fractious! A thorn in the side of every state in the Union! A godforsaken land that knows *not* what it wishes to be. If ever there was born a termagant to represent Kansas, it is you."

Nancy threatened to explode until Mary firmly gripped her arm.

Gus toddled across the room, full of steam. "Since 1830, the free states and the slave states have stood in balance, each holding the other in check in Congress." He paced around Nancy and the girls bunched in the center. "But *these* upstarts from the virgin frontier come along wanting inclusion as states. Yet more territories exist in the North than in the South. What will happen if Congress admits them by geographic location?"

"They will outvote our slave states," said Mary.

Nancy studied the two clusters of her fellow students, trying to imagine them as states on a map of the country. "Why not just allow each territory to vote on whether they wish to be free or slave?"

Gus, stumbling, thrust his cane toward the heavens like Zeus sending forth a thunderbolt. "Kansas speaks! Bloody Kansas! Kansas wants popular sovereignty! And the result? Free-Soilers from the fire-and-brimstone abolitionist states pour in across the borders like the locusts of Egypt." He closed in on Nancy. "I ask *you*, Kansas, do we Southerners have enough immigrants to send there to win the day at the ballot box?"

Nancy hazarded a guess. "No?"

"Look through those windows at the wilderness surrounding us," said Gus. "We have vast Creek and Cherokee forests yet to civilize. Why should anyone in Troup County pull up stakes and walk a thousand miles to that flat hellscape of savage plains in Kansas when they can make a homestead here?"

Nancy pondered the conundrum. "So, we are doomed."

Gus paused to gather his breath. He lowered his voice, as if to underscore the danger of the current political quagmire. "The Negro-loving Pathfinder, John C. Fremont, and those Constitution-torching Republicans wish to eradicate our way of life. Fremont and his Jezebel of a wife are in league with Millard Fillmore and the Know-Nothing Party. If the Republicans whip James Buchanan in November ..." He could not bring himself to utter the words.

"There will be war," whispered Mary.

The girls glanced at each other, worried, but Nancy refused to accept such a frightful future. "Surely men of good will can come to an accommodation?"

A vein in Gus's temple throbbed. "Accommodation? Allow me to enlighten *you*, Miss Kansas, on the sin of accommodation!"

Nancy retreated a step. All could see the craze in his bloodshot eyes.

"Last month, an Abolitionist scoundrel from Massachusetts, Charles Sumner, took to the Senate floor. Do you know what he said to Preston Brooks? One of our most esteemed brethren from South Carolina?" When Nancy shook her head, he said, "The vile Abolitionist called the gallant Brooks an unchivalrous knight who had taken the harlot slavery as his mistress."

Leila Pullen had enough gumption to ask Gus what the others wished to know. "Did Senator Brooks demand a duel to avenge his honor?"

"A duel? No, my darling. Only gentlemen of equal stature in dignity accept duels. Senator Brooks did what any righteous Southern man would do to a Northern knave. He walked into the Senate chamber, strode to the well, came to the slanderer Sumner seated at his station, and—" Gus slammed his cane into an empty school desk. With trembling hands, he raised the cane again and pummeled the lid on the desk until its sides splintered.

"Dr. Ware!" Mary risked a beaning as she rushed to restrain his arm.

Gus reclaimed his composure, brushing back the loose strands across his balding head and straightening his lapels. He looked at the shocked girls and explained his conduct with an alarming calmness. "*That* is how Senator Brooks avenged *our* honor." He glared at Nancy to assess if she was now satisfied with the lesson she had demanded on politics. Finding her at a loss for words, he limped to the teacher's lectern. "Next week, we shall explore our local native flora. Red cedar, scaly-bark, sweet gum, and my favorite, flowering quince." He placed his straw hat on his beading head and walked out.

Nancy released a held breath.

The next afternoon, Nancy walked with Mary to the Ferrell Garden terraces and the small meadow where they often enjoyed picnics. "Why are you being so mysterious?" Nancy demanded. "Are we taking calisthenics outside today?"

"Not exactly."

"Why, then, did you tell me to change into my riding dress?"

"It suits you so."

Nancy could always discern when Mary was not being forthcoming; she veiled her prevarications with compliments. "If you baked another of your cranberry cakes, I told you, I can barely fit into my corset as it is."

"I want you to promise me something, Nannie."

"Anything. You are my dearest friend."

"Be on your best behavior today."

Nancy stopped. "When have I ever not been? Why are you so coy?"

Mary threaded arms with Nancy and led her around the corner to the meadow. Nancy froze. Waiting for them on the shorn grass not twenty yards away stood Sallie Fannie Reid and another girl from West Point. Instead of parasols, the two intruders held long-staffed mallets and wooden balls the size of giant oranges. Sallie, attired in a fashionable blouse, waved to her unidentified friend to rush around the green expanse and plant U-shaped wooden wickets in a double-diamond pattern.

Nancy backed away a step. "What is *she* doing here?"

"Smile and wave," Mary insisted under her breath. "The West Point alumni offered to play us in a match."

Nancy watched, baffled, as Sallie imitated an unmounted polo player and sent her wooden ball flying across the park. "A match of *what?*"

"A new game called croquet," said Mary. "One of Colonel Reid's visitors from New Orleans introduced it to Sallie. It is all the rage in France."

"You didn't tell me *she'd* be here."

Mary grasped Nancy's hand to prevent her from huffing off. "The college master insisted we take part. You are our best athlete. Just play along. What harm can come from it?"

Too late to back off, Nancy put on the best face she could manage and walked over to her nemesis. "Miss Reid, what a surprise."

"Surprise? Why, I told you yesterday that I would see you today."

Nancy shot a vexed glance at Mary. She mustered a forced poise and told Sallie, "I understand you have chanced upon a new entertainment."

Sallie swung the mallet around her skirts, showing off a deft stroke. "This is a most addicting game. You will fall madly for it. There is very little natural skill required. It rewards pluck."

Nancy reddened.

Sallie picked out two mallets from her collection. She handed the one with the shortest handle to Nancy. "With your long arms, I should think this will fit you." She handed the other mallet to Mary.

"Are we confined to hitting balls only?" asked Nancy.

Mary kicked Nancy's ankle under her skirts.

Sallie stared at Nancy and giggled. "Oh, Miss Hill, you have such a blessed sense of humor." She beckoned her playing partner. "This is Celestia. Her father is a doctor."

"How nice to meet you," said Mary.

Celestia curtsied. "Sallie speaks so well of you."

Not falling for that lie, Nancy was impatient to finish with this nonsense. "We just bang balls?"

"Oh, no," said Sallie. "There are intricate rules."

During the next five minutes, Sallie held forth on how points were scored, which balls had to go through which wickets first, how a stroke was to be made, on and on, until Nancy felt her head swelling from the maddening terminology: jaws, pushes, pegs, hoops, spooning, pushing, swinging, hindered, double banking, bisques, half bisques. She couldn't take it any longer. "Let's play. We call our own penalties?"

Sallie burst out again with laughter. "Oh, heavens, no. This game requires an umpire."

Nancy turned to Mary. "An umpire?"

Mary deflected Nancy's demanding glare.

"Someone with experience in interpreting and applying laws," said Sallie. "I have arranged the perfect arbiter."

Nancy spun and saw Brown Morgan walking into the meadow. He removed his hat and bowed. "Ladies, apologies for my tardiness."

"Not at all, Mr. Morgan," said Sallie. "I was just instructing our friends here on the objectives of the contest. Did you familiarize yourself with the rules book I gave you?"

Brown pulled a pamphlet from his coat pocket. "I have seen state budgetary bills with less codification, but I think I understand the gist of it."

Nancy glared at Brown, who shrugged as if to plead he was helpless to decline the request. Had Sallie set her up for this challenge? She must have recruited him yesterday to serve as referee.

"Mr. Morgan," said Sallie. "I believe you have a preamble to recite."

"Ah, yes." Brown opened the rules booklet to its first page and read aloud: "'Croquet is a genteel game, suited to genial conversation rather than strident competition. It promotes etiquette, sportsmanship, and happiness. Amiability and unselfishness are the first requisites of an adept player.'"

"We can agree on that." Mary turned to Nancy. "Don't you think, Nannie?"

Nancy beat the mallet against her hand, feeling the weight of its head. "Who goes first?"

"That's the spirit." Brown consulted the booklet. "Players toss their mallets in the air. The handle pointing closest the line gains the first stroke."

The four girls let fly, and Sallie's mallet fell just inches from Nancy's feet. Nancy glared at her, suspecting *that* was not an accident.

Brown examined the distances between mallets. "It appears Miss Reid has won the honors."

Sallie shrugged. "The rules are the rules."

Brown lined up the balls of different colors on one end of the field, facing the first wicket. Sallie addressed her ball. With a sharp smack, she sent the ball through the wicket with a perfect spin. She proceeded to smack and pop her way across the meadow with the precision of a surgeon until, at last, she bounced her ball off one of the far wickets.

Nancy caught Sallie waving at Brown while casually lifting the front of her skirts over the ball to hide it. When Sallie backed away, the ball sat a foot from its original position, now facing the wicket for her next turn. Nancy complained to Mary, "Did you see that?"

Mary whispered, "Say nothing."

"Say nothing?"

"Do not be small of spirit in Brown's presence," Mary cautioned. "Sallie will only benefit, and you cannot prove the infraction."

Denied her challenge, Nancy stood stewing.

"Well-played!" Brown said to Sallie. He turned to Nancy and offered the way to the starting line. "Nannie, it's your turn."

In the short time she had observed this infuriating game, Nancy had come to two conclusions. First, she could get more power on the strike if she stood sideways to the ball, avoiding the hindrance of her skirts on the backstroke. Second, her ears perked when Sallie mentioned a rule allowing one opponent to knock another's ball away from the wicket as far as possible. Sallie, she realized, had been practicing this game for weeks. She knew she could not defeat her nemesis by points, but there was another way to skin a West Point polecat. She stood next to her ball and gave it a whack. The ball split the wicket clean.

Brown applauded. "Fast learner, you!"

Nancy threaded the remaining wickets, one by one, until she came to the shot to put her even with Sallie's ball on the far end of the court. Rather than play through the jaws, she zeroed in with one eye and calculated the precise amount of power required to perform her desired outcome. She took aim and sent her ball spinning. It came to rest against Sallie's ball. When Sallie glared at her, Nancy played dumb and asked Brown in her best distressed damsel voice: "Whatever do I do now?"

Brown scanned the rules pamphlet with Mary and Celestia looking over his shoulder. He marked a subsection. "'Should an opponent's ball come to rest against another player's ball, and the first player has a stroke left, that player may strike his own ball and send his opponent's ball by force of transferred inertia in any direction.'"

Sallie's confident smirk vanished. "That seems unkind."

Nancy shrugged. "The rules are the rules." She looked around the flowery terraces, having memorized every inch of the grounds since she crawled there as a child. The gardens cascaded into a series of grassy steps until leveling off onto an incline. The major artery into town was a road of packed dirt, but because of the heavy carriage traffic past the gardens, the city fathers macadamized a quarter mile of smooth pavement. When it rained, the water tended to run toward the rail tracks, which sat on the far side of the courthouse square. She searched the confines of the garden and saw a drainage ditch cut into the terrace. *There* was the slope.

"The rules require a player to take a stroke within one minute or forfeit the turn," said Sallie, impatient.

Nancy twirled her mallet in a taunt. "Well, we *must* follow the rules."

Sallie counted the seconds with her fingers.

Nancy turned to Brown. "How much time left?"

Brown checked his pocket watch. "Five seconds."

Nancy circled her ball, squatting over it and waving the air as if to chase away a flea. *Four ... three ... two ...* She straightened, round-housed her mallet over her head, and smacked her ball as hard as she could.

Sallie's ball flew toward the drainage ditch.

Brown and the girls hurried to the edge of the terrace and watched the ball hover and drop to the next terrace.

Sallie traced its progress with rising consternation as the ball rolled and rolled, descending each terrace and gaining speed. At the bottom, it caromed off a lamppost and bounded down Broad Street, disappearing from sight. She protested, "That's out of bounds!"

Nancy turned to Brown with a wry smile. "I don't recall the rules mentioning an out-of-bounds."

Brown, flustered, thumbed through the pamphlet. He stopped at a page and his face paled.

"Well?" Sallie insisted.

Brown read his discovery aloud: "'A ball is out of bounds when its vertical axis crosses the boundary line. If no boundary is designated before the game begins, the ball shall be played where it comes to rest.'"

Sallie's pert mouth dropped. "That will take me a hundred strokes to return! I have no choice but to concede."

Brown gave Nancy the stink eye, blaming her for putting him in the middle of their feud.

Nancy shrugged and returned her mallet to Sallie. "The rules *are* the rules." She tossed the back of her hand to her forehead as if spent from the exertion. "That was a most invigorating frolic. You know what I have a sudden craving for?"

The girls waited to hear her suggestion for a post-game treat.

She shot a lording smirk at Sallie. "Cherry cobbler."

6

SOUTHWESTERN IOWA
SEPTEMBER 1856

Hugh's soaked socks were rubbing his blisters raw, but he pushed on through the endless waves of waist-high prairie grass. Clutching his hat to prevent it from blowing to Mexico, he searched the undulating horizon for the next Lane Chimney, the nickname his fellow Free-Soilers gave to the rock cairns piled at intervals to mark the way into Kansas. Rain clouds blotted out the sun, costing him his sense of direction, and he couldn't be certain if he was walking toward or away from the Missouri River. His plan was to retrace his steps back to Professor Daniels's encampment at Tabor, but no one warned him this lush range grass devoured footprints. The afternoon light was fading fast, and if he didn't find the Lane Trail soon, he would be stuck out here all night, easy prey for the wolves and renegades.

We are upon the Lord's work, Hugh. His angels will guide and protect you.

Arming him with that blessing and nothing more, Professor Daniels had sent him ahead on foot that morning to scout the next leg of their exodus from Wisconsin to help Kansas remain a free territory. The professor's wagon train with two hundred State Aid Society recruits left Ripon three weeks ago, but it still hadn't reached the Nebraska line. Threadbare and destitute, Hugh and his fellow Abolitionists had consumed the last of their grain, and their draft horses were lame for lack of decent shodding. Worse, an unruly gaggle of teachers, politicians, hotel managers, and gold-dusting crackpots had joined them along the way. No one seemed in charge, and rather than plan how they intended to turn back the Missouri slavers without rifles or artillery, most of the men spent the lonely hours at night around the campfires arguing theology and rehearsing political speeches.

His father had begged him not to go with the eccentric geologist and his Republican clubhouse cronies, warning he would end up as roadkill for those clay-for-brains Southern butchers running roughshod around Lecompton. But saving fugitive slaves was more exciting than farming, and after outfoxing that Kentucky bounty hunter, Hugh had helped the Fond du Lac conductors deliver five more escaped Negroes up the Underground Railroad to Canada. He wasn't a fervent faith believer like his brother, Wallace, but the gratification of seeing those poor black folk shed their chains was as close to a calling as he had ever experienced. Besides, when the professor got one of his Utopian ideas stuck in his head, there was no saying no to him. So, Kansas it would be.

If only they could find it.

To keep his mind off the hole burning in his stomach, Hugh parsed the many rumors he had overheard at the stagecoach stations. Best as he understood the political situation, Franklin Pierce kicked the slavery can down the road by signing the Kansas-Nebraska Act, which allowed the residents of those territories to decide whether to allow the vile institution within their borders. Nebraska was certain to vote against slavery, and if Kansas followed, it'd be just a matter of time before the Free-Staters outnumbered the Southerners in Congress. Desperate to hold on to their wealth earned on the backs of Negroes, plantation owners east of the Mississippi recruited mercenaries to frighten Kansans into setting up a pro-slavery government. When the Abolitionists retaliated by sending freedom homesteaders, the slavers burned the Free State Hotel in Lawrence, setting off another round of attacks and counterattacks.

Most folks hoped the slavery question would be resolved with the presidential election in two months. Frustrated by President Pierce's waffling, the Democrats had cast aside the irresolute New Englander for the feckless James Buchanan of Pennsylvania. Professor Daniels expressed confidence in their own Republican nominee, John Fremont, the great military hero of California who vowed to abolish slavery, but the national vote promised to be close. Seemed the only thing all Americans could agree on was the road to the White House started along this winding Iowa wagon trail out here somewhere—

A gunshot echoed across the grasslands.

Hugh ducked below a scruff of thistles. Were the Meswakies using rifles now? He held his breath, one cough away from being listed in the obituaries as just another dead Free-Stater. If the Indians *did* have guns, they'd likely save their bullets and finish him off with tomahawks. A braining would be quicker than starving, at least. He finally bucked up his courage and, resolving to go down swinging, sprang through the grass with his fists balled.

Three white men on frothing horses circled him.

He swallowed hard. An arsenal of swords, axes, and meat cleavers dangled from their livery straps. Were they Missouri reivers on the hunt across the border for hostages? He backed away, picking thistle needles from his shirt while thinking Meswaki scalpers might have been preferable. The overworked mounts suggested these men weren't out on a pleasure ride. How had they gotten the jump on him? There wasn't a tree around in miles to hide behind.

The leader of the gang—a fearsome-looking patriarch with glassy gray eyes focused on some distant epiphany—rested the butt plate of his smoking musket on his thigh. He lifted the brim of his headgear to better see what species of prairie dog he chanced upon. He spat at the ground, not impressed with his discovery. "The Lord saith in Genesis it is not good for a man to be alone."

Hugh kept a close watch on the shorter rider to the frowning geezer's right; that one acted nervous, with his hand trembling over his holstered pistol.

"You got a working tongue?" the old man asked.

Hugh tipped his hat and tried to act nonchalant, as much as one could while cornered on the plains without the comfort of weaponry. "Yes, sir. You fellas preachers?"

The mounted elder pulled a powder round from the pocket of his riding cloak. He bit off the end of the paper cartridge and drove the ball into the barrel of his musket with a ramrod. "That depends on how sound you are on the goose."

Hugh looked around. "No geese in these parts that I've seen."

The twitchy younger rider on his left climbed down from his saddle. "I'd best inspect him, Pa."

"Leave off that," the old man ordered his son.

"Lemme give him the once over."

When the old man didn't enforce his command to desist, the son approached Hugh cautiously, with his right hand never leaving the reach of the firearm at his belt. Hugh saw that the son's long fingernails were caked with dried blood. He braced to be searched, but the frisker began caressing his skull. Hugh tried to fight him off. The man retaliated by tightening his grip and running his thumbs across Hugh's temples.

Satisfied with his phrenological examination, the pawing intruder released Hugh's head and nodded to his father. "He's a truth-teller. And I assay him to be right with the Almighty."

The patriarch kept a suspicious eye fixed on his catch. "Lost in Satan's desert, are you?"

Hugh scratched at his scalp to shake out any lice planted by the son's grubby hands. "I'm searching for the Lane Trail."

"You a follower of Colonel Lane?"

Hugh was getting damn fed up with the inquisition. "I'm a follower of his steps."

The old man's lips pinched pale. "That is a slippery answer, and I have heard my share to know. I will not suffer false testifying. The Lord saith I will destroy the wisdom of the wise and the cleverness of the clever."

"I'm telling you the truth. I don't know the man, just *of* him."

"If it is as you say, your ignorance will soon be disabused."

"I never said I was ignorant."

For the first time, the old man betrayed what for him passed as a smile. "You mistake my meaning. We broke bread with Jim Lane in Nebraska City two nights back. Those Missouri scoundrels indicted him for treason. He's making his way east under an alias to meet up with a battalion of the Lord's avengers from Wisconsin."

Hugh brightened, hoping the Kansas colonel was bringing food for their starving wagon train. "That's likely my party. They're still a ways off ..." He turned to point, but then remembered the futility of trying to identify a direction. "Somewhere around here."

The hoary patriarch spat another wad of phlegm. "Well, Johnny, it appears your skull augury has hit its mark again."

"Never fails, Pa."

The old man scowled at his son's boast. "To never fail is the sole provenance of the Lord. Proverbs saith let another praise you, and not your own mouth. A stranger, and not your own lips." Before his son could protest that chastisement, the patriarch turned to Hugh and inquired, "What news from the East of Senator Sumner's condition?"

"I don't know anyone named Sumner."

"Senator Sumner of Massachusetts."

Hugh shrugged. "Like I said, don't know the fella."

The old man's scoured forehead flamed. "The martyr's countenance should crown every Christian hearth in this nation! Do men of the cloth not accompany your army?"

"Army? We're just—"

"How could they not preach of Sumner's passion under the rod?"

That burst of unprovoked fury drove Hugh to his heels. The old man was now testifying so vehemently that spittle was flying from his mouth.

Mistaking Hugh's vexed silence for insolence, the old man fanned more fire steam into his bellows. "The whoreson Brooks from South Carolina thrashed him to a bloody pulp on the floor of Congress! Caved his brain with a cane! Are we now to speak with bated breath in the presence of our Southern masters? Are we to be whipped as they whip their slaves? Are we to cower when we do not comport ourselves to please them? Never! Never, I tell you!"

Hugh feared the armed evangelist might burst the veins raised in his neck. He patted the firebrand's horse to soothe its skittishness. Yet no sooner had the old man's temper erupted than he calmed and pointed to a ridge several hundred yards to their rear. In a voice as pleasant as that of a store proprietor identifying a can of peaches, he said, "Yonder is the trace that will lead you to Megiddo."

Hugh hadn't seen *that* stop on the Lane trail maps. "Is Megiddo a town in Iowa or Nebraska?"

The old man sneered down his long nose. "Do you study your Scripture?"

"Yes, sir, but—"

"Judges Five: Nineteen. The kings came and fought the kings of Canaan in Taanach by the waters of Megiddo. They took no gain of money." He swept a hand across the flat environs. "You must learn to see this country in the geography of the Holy Land."

Unless Kansas's flapjack topography was a lot different from Iowa, Hugh couldn't fathom how there could be much similarity with the Judean wilds.

The third mounted man, the one who until that moment had remained silent, kept looking over his shoulder. "We'd best get moving, Pa."

The patriarch raised his palm for patience. "Nothing must interfere with the instruction of a new generation in the strictures of the Almighty."

"They'll be on our heels soon," the second son said.

"Enough of your faithless cowardice, the both of you!" the old man shouted at his sons. "Had you heeded my orders, Frederick would still be with us!" The two brothers retreated into a grudging silence, and when their father patted the breast pocket of his overcoat, they traded worried glances behind his back. The patriarch leaned across his saddle and hovered a hand over Hugh's head in what seemed a blessing. "Go forth and tell your people to come by way of Lawrence. Favor the sinistral side of the town's thoroughfare. Wagon axles have been known to snap in the gun pits."

Gun pits? In the middle of a city street?

"Avoid the den of iniquity known as Pottawatomie Creek," the old man said. "There, the tables of the moneychangers have been upturned and the sword of the Apostle Peter unsheathed."

All of this cryptic religious talk made no sense, but Hugh nodded with a grim smile just to humor the old man; he'd seen enough of those professors back at college who delighted only in the sound of their own pontifications.

"Should anyone ask again if you are sound on the goose," the old man instructed, "you look them straight in the eye and tell them the Lord created every manner of fowl for His purpose alone."

The damn goose, again. Hugh waited for an explanation of that repeated reference, but none was offered. The strange manner in which this prairie prophet communicated sounded like a code. Was the man telling him to lie to the slavers about his purpose for coming to Kansas? He asked in a tone as humble as he could manage, "Does the Lord permit deception?"

The old man reached into the inner pocket of his cloak. Hugh flinched, expecting to meet the business end of a pistol. Instead, the old man pulled out the item that had been the object of his distracting concern throughout their conversation, a small Bible bound in ragged leather. He fingered a verse from Exodus and held the Bible aloft as if calling upon the divine hierarchies for witness. "Did Moses not lie to Pharaoh for the Almighty?"

This prickly crank might be deranged, Hugh conceded, but he knew his Scripture. "I reckon he did."

The patriarch snapped his Bible shut and returned it to safekeeping under his cloak. He looked up to the heavens, muttered something, and reined off into a gallop east with his sons following him.

"Wait!" Hugh shouted. "Professor Daniels will want to know your names!"

After several hours of blind walking into the night, Hugh heard a distant voice yammering what sounded like funeral poetry.

> "Bear him, comrades, to his grave;
> Never over one more brave
> Shall the prairie grasses weep,
> In the ages yet to come,
> When the millions in our room,
> What we sow in tears, shall reap."

He staggered up the Lane Trail in the moonless darkness, rubbing his eyes to stay awake and taking care to keep the wagon ruts at his heels to avoid becoming lost again. He figured he must have wandered another five miles, and his legs, scraped from ankle to knee, were cramping. He cupped a hand over his ear to pick up the twanging accent that seemed to mock his suffering. He had encountered all manner of strange noises out here—the maddening barks of the prairie dogs, the shuddering cries of a small deer ravaged by a pack of coyotes—but this piercing dirge shivered his blood.

> "Bear him up the icy hill,
> With the Kansas, frozen still
> As his noble heart, below,

And the land he came to till
With a freeman's thews and will,
And his poor hut roofed with snow!"

He stumbled across a dry creek ford and inched his bleary eyes over the mash of bramble. His heart leapt. A crowd of men stood around a raging bonfire, listening to a rangy fellow with an expansive liverish forehead and strident green eyes hold forth while waving a stovepipe hat tall enough to shelter a litter of rabbits. Was this his destination, or was he hallucinating from the hunger pangs? He dropped to his knees, exhausted. Unable to rise, he crawled closer to get a better look. Tears flooded his eyes. He was saved—there stood Professor Daniels in the crowd. And those were the Ripon wagons parked in a half circle behind the men to protect themselves from predators.

Perched atop a makeshift podium on the bed of a wagon, the orator kept blasting away and flailing his arms as if fighting off demons:

"Frozen earth to frozen breast,
Lay our slain one down to rest;
Lay him down in hope and faith,
And above the broken sod,
Once again, to Freedom's God,
Pledge ourselves for life or death."

Was this versifying gesticulator a traveling actor? Hugh gritted his teeth, angry that his comrades had left him for dead just to enjoy a carny performance. He struggled to his feet and stumbled toward the assembly, determined to give them a hot piece of his mind and—

"The Lecompton blackguards are on us, boys!"

The orator atop the wagon pulled a Colt revolver and fired a bullet that whizzed inches above Hugh's scalp. Dazed by the near miss, Hugh knifed to his knees and felt his matted hair for blood.

"Get me the rope!" The orator dropped his stovepipe hat and planted his right foot atop its crown to steady his aim for the next shot.

"There ain't a tree in miles around here, Colonel," one man said. "Anyways, don't croak him until he tells us where his slaver conspirators are hiding."

Colonel?

Hugh squinted through the shadows. The orator had stringy, unshellacked hair that stood out from his triangular head as if frizzed by lightning. His crazy eyes darted and his nervous mouth looked as if it might snap at anything that came within flying range. The so-called officer wasn't wearing a uniform, but sported a ragged evening jacket with long tails and shoulders fitted with homespun golden epaulets made from weaved corn husks. If this was what passed for colonels out here, Hugh didn't want to see the generals. He stood up slowly with hands raised, trying to swerve from the barrel's aim.

With their vision occulted by the flickering campfires, the men angled around Hugh in threat. One drew a knife and was preparing to begin a bloody interrogation when Professor Daniels broke through the ranks. "Wait! Hold off, lads! That's LaGrange!"

Only then did the men recognize Hugh in his bedraggled condition. They lifted him to his feet and clapped him on the back, thrilled to see him alive.

The professor embraced him. "We'd thought the natives got you."

Hugh was in no mood for celebration. "I've been out there trying to find that poor excuse of a trail that some jackass named Lane—"

The orator jumped from the wagon and cocked the hammer on his revolver. "And what are you planning to do if you ever meet that jackass?"

The professor pushed between them. "Now, Colonel Lane, the boy just suffered an ordeal."

Hugh's eyes bulged. He realized he had insulted the Grim Chieftain, the self-proclaimed military leader of the Free-Staters in Kansas.

Lane spun the cylinder of his revolver. "We've all suffered ordeals in the service of the Cause. I'd like to hear Mister LaGrange here finish his thought."

Despite the colonel's violent reputation, Hugh refused to back down. "I meant no insult. But I'd damn well like to know why everyone is standing here listening to rhymes instead of sending out a search party for me."

Lane stopped the spin of his cylinder. "You know what model this is?"

Hugh couldn't fathom what *that* question had to do with his abandonment to the wolves. "No, sir."

"Navy 1851 piece. General Scott gave it to me in appreciation for my valor at the Battle of Palo Alto. That engraving on the cylinder commemorates the Second Texas Navy's glorious victory at Campeche. This darling has seen—"

"Hell, Jim, my pa was in Mexico with Scott, too," said one of the men. "He told me those old Navy Colts were sold to civilians."

Lane wheeled on the doubter. "Then your old man is a damn liar!"

The offending man raised his palms. "Just making small talk, Jim."

"I don't countenance *small* talk! Not when my soldiers are being gutted like Sunday spit meat in Lawrence." With a snort, Lane turned and blew the powder residue from his revolver into Hugh's face. "That rhyming nonsense, as you called it, was written by the patriot John Greenleaf Whittier to memorialize a brave soldier of mine, young Tom Barber. The slaver bushwhackers shot him last year."

"I'm sorry for him," Hugh said. "But that still—

"How do I know you aren't a spy planted by that bastard Sam Jones and his Douglas County ruffians?" Lane circled his suspect. "Awful convenient for you to return to camp when I happen to be here."

Daniels tried again to intervene. "Colonel, I can vouch for him. He was one of my college students."

Lane veered a venomous glare toward the geologist. "You know your Roman history, sir?"

The geologist blinked hard. "I do, but—"

"Marcus Junius Brutus."

"Colonel, we need to get back to planning—"

Lane kept waving the revolver in the air, causing the men to duck and weave. "Educated by the great Cato himself. But that didn't stop Brutus from thrusting a knife into the back of Julius Caesar, now did it?"

One of the volunteers tried to get Lane to refocus on their current predicament. "Our supplies are damn low, Colonel."

Lane paced in front of the ranks of the alarmed Abolitionists, causing them to back away. "You wanna know how I know who taught Brutus? Now that you asked, I'll tell you. I taught myself from the books I scrounged up in the wilds of Indiana. I learned the law that way! And by God, I don't need some fancy college choirboy coming out here and telling me how to run my state!"

"Kansas ain't a state yet," another volunteer muttered to his comrade next to him. "Not until we get there. And if we don't get rolling soon—"

Lane got into the face of the whispering recruit. "What did you say?"

"I said Kansas—"

"Kansas is the Italy of America!" Lane lifted his watering eyes to the stars and fired a shot into the heavens. "The corn and the vine grow so lush there, they thank the farmers for planting them. It is a climate akin to that of Illinois, but milder. Invalids, instead of going to Italy, will go to Kansas to gather new life beneath its fair sky and from its balmy airs. The wild grapes of Kansas are as large and luscious as those that grow in the vineyards of Southern France."

Hugh was starting to wonder if Kansas was just one giant, grass-padded insane asylum. This Jim Lane fellow was the first politician of any note he'd ever met. Were they all this hair-triggered and moonstruck?

Another Abolitionist dredged up the courage to interrupt Lane's soliloquy. "Colonel, we ain't doubting the enticements offered by your fine territory. We just want to survive to see it."

Lane folded his arms, keeping the revolver pressed to his chest. "Please, gentlemen! Do not inquire further about my sacrifices in Mexico! We veterans of the glorious battles do not talk of the horrors we have endured for the nation."

The men looked at each other, confused. Several shrugged.

Lane climbed atop the wagon again and swiveled on his heels as if address-ing the House of Representatives. "Yes, I stood side by side with the gallant Bissell at Buena Vista, and again in Congress. I wish I could recreate the scene on the morning preceding that glorious conflagration. On a ridge we formed ranks, prepared to die. Twenty-thousand armed enemies arrayed their ranks before us. It was a stunning morning, and the sun shone bright upon the polished lances and muskets of the enemy, and their proud banners waved in the breeze. In our rear, the lofty mountains reached skyward, and their bases swarmed with enemies ready to rob the dead and murder the wounded when the battle was over. Around us hovered five ragged regiments of volunteers, two from Illinois, two from Indiana, and one from Kentucky."

Hugh stumbled, feeling faint. The professor rifled through his coat pocket and slipped him a stale crust of a month-old biscuit. Hugh nodded his grati-tude and cracked down on a corner of the morsel as Lane shifted his harangue an octave higher.

"Then, my friends, followed a most vivid and awful narrative of the outrages perpetrated upon the Free-State men by the Missouri ruffians! So vivid that the Osawatomie murders seemed but unmerited retaliation, and most sweet revenge to his excited hearers! The Missourians poured across the border in thousands with Bowie knives in their boots, their belts bristling with revolvers, their guns upon their shoulders, and three gallons of whiskey per vote in their wagons."

Hugh opened his mouth to finish his last bite when the colonel aimed the revolver at him.

"And I ask *you*, intruder!" Lane shouted. "How did you, with such facile timing, find your way back after claiming to be lost for a day and a night?"

Hugh choked on the mouthful of dry crumbs. Between coughs, he said, "Three travelers came by and showed me the way to your trail."

Lane turned a skeptical smirk to the men gathered around the wagon. "Did you hear that, my fellow warriors? The boy conveniently claims to have been visited by angels of mercy." He rounded on Hugh again, this time in mocking accusation. "And how were these three Good Samaritans attired? With white wings and flowing robes?"

"Didn't see much to remark on about their garb," Hugh said. "But they had enough cleavers and blades to butcher a herd of heifers."

Lane's smirk gave way to a stare of astonishment. "Did one of them look to be kin to the biblical Moses?"

"He had a preacher's way of talking, if that's what you're getting at."

Lane raised his hands to the heavens and fired off another round to celebrate. "You, sir, had the high honor of trading words with John Brown of Osawatomie. Finer defenders of freedom you will not find than Mr. Brown and his sons."

After the few bites, the blood flowed again in Hugh's brain. "Yes, sir. He mentioned he'd shared dinner with you in Nebraska City."

"Brown and I together have carried on the burdens and struggles in Kansas."

"I remember him now saying something else."

"Did he give you an accounting of my victories in the Wakarusa war?"

"No, but he said you'd been indicted for treason."

Lane's pocked cheeks paled.

The men moved closer to Lane to demand an explanation.

"That right, Colonel?" the professor asked. "Are you running from the law?"

Lane grabbed his lapels as if preparing a jury defense. "An illegal document!"

"Issued by whom?" Daniels demanded.

Lane acted shifty, refusing to meet their glares. "Well, now, there's some dispute about that. I blame those scoundrels in Douglas County—"

"Was the indictment rendered by a federal judge, sir?" the professor asked.

Lane launched into a rambling encomium on the many luminaries he had befriended during his brief tenure as the lieutenant governor of the Hoosier state. While the congressman filibustered on, Daniels and his Abolitionists gathered a few feet away to confer in whispers. After a few minutes of this private debate, the professor interrupted Lane's summation of his career with an exaggerated cough. "Colonel, on behalf of the State Aid Society of Wisconsin, I cannot express enough our appreciation for your service."

"If you wish to draft me for the presidential nomination—"

"Sir, we regretfully report that we can no longer be of further association."

"Of further association with whom?"

"You."

Lane leapt from the wagon's bed and, fingering his revolver, landed directly in front of the professor. "You're scheming to decommission me?"

"With respect, sir, you were never commissioned," Daniels said. "You took on the mantle of military commander yourself without—"

"This is *my* army!"

The professor lowered his head to deflect Lane's ire. "Named for you, true. But this is not an army, and even if it were, it's not yours."

"Perhaps you have not been told of the last man who besmirched my honor. Stephen Douglas of Illinois refused to meet my demands for a duel—"

"Because you were not a senator," the professor said. "Mr. Douglas, you will recall, deemed you of inadequate social status to merit a meeting of pistols."

Purpling with rage, Lane cocked his revolver and drew a defiant arabesque in the air with its barrel. "Anyone else here agree with that sentiment?"

After a hesitation, all two hundred of the skittish volunteers inched their hands up, bracing to hit the ground if the irascible congressman started firing.

The revolver in Lane's hand shook from the force of his own fury. He spun the pistol's barrel to his temple.

"Hold on now, Jim," a voice called out from the rear.

"I'll do it, Sam!" Lane shouted. "You know I'd do it!"

"Captain Walker," the professor pleaded. "Tell him. He'll listen to you."

Samuel Walker, one of Lane's loyal captains, stepped forward from the shadows to confront the colonel. "Jim, if you lead these men into Kansas with that federal indictment on your head, they'll be arrested for aiding a traitor."

"There's no law *in* Kansas!" Lane shouted.

"I will take them there to change that," Walker said. "It's not fair, Jim, but if headlines across the country say we Free-Staters are flouting the government, we'll lose the vote on outlawing slavery. It's what the Missouri boys are trying to trick us into doing."

Lane pressed the barrel deeper into his temple. "Walker, if you say the people of Kansas don't want me, I'll just blow my brains out! I can't go back to the states and look my people in the face and tell them that as soon as I got these Kansas friends of mine into danger, I had to abandon them! I can't do it! No matter what I say in my defense, no one will believe it! I'll end the thing right here!"

The colonists backed away, convinced the volatile Lane would follow through on his threat. Lane's finger pressed the trigger—

"We need you in Washington!" Hugh shouted.

Lane eased his finger off the trigger. "Speak up, boy!"

Hugh cleared his throat to throttle the nervousness in his voice. "The way I see it, Colonel, we're gonna require a superb military man to champion our rights when Mr. Fremont gets into the White House. You served with him, from what I've been told. You could convince him to send us troops and make sure we become a state as soon as possible."

The men nodded at Hugh's play on the congressman's vanity.

Lane stared at Hugh for a dangerous moment, and he holstered his revolver. "Finally, a fella talking some sense around here!"

The professor released a breath in relief. "Three hurrahs for Colonel Lane to Washington! Huzzah! Huzzah! Huzzah!"

The men cheered as they escorted the Grim Chieftain to his horse. Behind his back, they shook Hugh's hand in gratitude for his quick thinking.

* * *

A week later, a rendition of "Amazing Grace" roused Hugh from his tent slumber. He dismissed the hymn as a dream and turned over in his bedroll to catch more shut-eye before he had to walk the trail again. Lord, he was more tired than he'd ever been in his life. After crossing the Missouri River and cutting the corner through Nebraska, their soggy wagon train had entered Kansas earlier that night, six miles back. Muddy Kansas, is what he called it, not Bloody Kansas. Given the trouble this territory was causing, he expected to find something more monumental than a lick-stone to mark its border. The only difference he could see between this stretch and Iowa was the violent intensity of the rain. He couldn't blame the climate for taking on the temperament of the inhabitants. Heck, from what he'd been told, Kansans had a hard time telling the artillery booms from afternoon thunder.

Still, despite their fatigue and the severe case of the foot rot spreading around, the volunteers were in high spirits. They had been joined at the Missouri River ford by Colonel Shaler Eldridge, the most famous resident of Lawrence and owner of the Free State Hotel. Seemed anyone who purchased a weapon out here received the rank of colonel as a side dish, but Hugh was willing to concede Eldridge was the first man he had met since leaving Wisconsin who deserved the promotion. Many of Eldridge's fellow Free-Staters had fled the butchery, but the colonel, a stubborn Massachusetts native, stayed to fight and rebuild his burned establishment, which rivaled in style the best lodgings in St. Louis even. They now sat camped just a few miles from Lawrence, and Eldridge had promised Hugh a thick beefsteak at his restaurant. Another two days of walking, and he'd be enjoying the first decent meal in—

There was that singing again. He rubbed his eyes, convinced now the booming hymn was no dream. He kicked out of his roll and slipped on his boots to find its source. Emerging from his tent, he found Professor Daniels and Eldridge standing with fifty volunteers around a fresh grave. He inched closer to read the name of the board stabbed into the muddy mound: *Charles T. James. Buried Oct. 1856 by the State Kansas Aid Society of Wisconsin. May he one day rise again to do the work of the Lord.*

As the men sang another stanza, several glanced south with worried looks. When the hymn was finished, Eldridge closed his Bible and walked back to his tent, followed by Daniels and the mourners, all chatting cheerfully and patting themselves on the backs as if leaving the first Sunday service in springtime.

"Somebody die last night?" Hugh asked.

Professor Daniels turned and, finding Hugh up and moving, braced him at the shoulders. "We didn't want to disturb you. One of the men succumbed in his sleep. Be happy for him, Hugh. He rests in the arms of his Maker."

Hugh studied the grave's head plank. "Charles James ... I don't remember meeting anyone here by that name."

"He kept to himself."

"What'd he die from?"

"We're not sure. The Lord taketh when the hour—"

"They're coming!" shouted a picket on the outskirts of the camp.

Alerted by the guard's warning, the Abolitionists sprang from their tents like ants sprayed with a wash of vinegar. On the horizon, a column of U.S. Army dragoons galloped toward them. Within the minute, the onrushing troopers were on them, circling the camp and forming an unbreachable cordon.

The officer leading the cavalry company rode up and confronted Daniels "Are you the leader of this little invasion army?"

The professor straightened and pulled at his cuffs, as if trying to affect a pose of dignified authority. "This is neither an army nor an invasion. We are lawful settlers, come to stake our farm claims in this land which, by last account, is free to travelers."

The officer swept a keen eye across the Abolitionists herded together. Not finding what he was looking for, he cantered through the park of wagons and beat his saber against the canvases as if rousting rats. "Eldridge! I know you're here, you old polecat! Come out, or I'll have my men set fire to your tentage."

Moments later, Colonel Eldridge stuck his head through a crease in a tarp. He yawned and stretched as if rising from a sleep. "Colonel Cooke, what brings you to the border? Inclement weather to be out on practice maneuvers."

"Orders from the governor," Cooke said. "All weapons brought into Kansas must be surrendered."

"An illegal confiscation!" Daniels protested. "We have every right as American citizens to carry arms to protect ourselves and hunt game. If you do not believe me, you may search our tents."

Cooke spotted the new grave a few yards from the trail. "You lose a man?"

The professor removed his hat in reverence. "Yes sir, we did, God bless his soul. Perhaps if we had been given an Army escort across the state line, Mr. James might have made it to Lawrence in time for the medical care he so desperately required."

"You certain he was dead when you laid the sod over him?"

"I am a learned man of science, Colonel," said Daniels. "I know when the life force has left the body."

"You ever hear of Maggie Dickson?"

"There is no woman by that name in our—"

"She was a housemaid in the auld country. My grandfather saw her hanged in Edinburgh for having the poor luck of delivering a stillborn babe. The way he told the story, she kicked and swung on that gibbet for a half an hour before the executioner declared she had given up the ghost. Fortunately for her, the teamsters charged with delivering her coffin to the charnel field stopped on the way for a couple of pints. When they emerged from the pub, they found ol' Maggie sitting up in the coffin and wondering why Hell looked so similar to Scotland."

A few of the men chortled until Eldridge glared at them for silence.

"Lord save us," Daniels said. "Did they hang her again?"

"No, the authorities pardoned her for coffin time served." Cooke rode to a wagon, picked out a shovel, and threw it at Hugh's feet. "But ever since my grandpa told me that story, I've always been a firm believer in making sure the duly departed have departed duly."

"Sir, you cannot mean to violate the corpse of a good Christian!" Daniels said. "It goes against every law of human decency!"

Cooke signaled for Hugh to get started. "Dig him up and check for a breath."

Hugh looked to the professor for what he should do. Daniels glanced at Eldridge and the other men for their support. Powerless to challenge a company of dragoons, he reluctantly nodded Hugh to the distasteful task.

Hugh cursed under his breath as he attacked the soft ground with stabs fueled by anger. He was damned put-out at being chosen to undertake this miserable excavation just because he was the youngest of the volunteers. Hell, he hadn't even known the deceased. He felt like a plow mule on this journey, always being tossed the dirty work that nobody else wanted to do. He threw two spadefuls of mud at the hooves of the horses out of spite, forcing the dragoons to move back.

After fifteen minutes of noxious digging, he hit something hard.

Cooke rode nearer the hole and peered into it. He asked the professor, "Casket handle, you reckon?"

Daniels refused to look at the officer. "Likely."

"We're not accustomed to such fancy burials out here on the frontier," Cooke said. "Must be quite an exquisite coffin to make such a rich ringing sound." He motioned one of his troopers forward and commandeered a loop of rope. He threw one end of the rope at Hugh and tied the other end to his trooper's saddle pommel. "Give it a double knot," he ordered Hugh. "We wouldn't want to disturb the dead on the way up."

Hugh tethered the rope to the coffin handle. After double-checking to make sure the knot held, he climbed out of the muddy grave to stand clear of the resurrection. Cooke signaled for his trooper to backtrack his horse. The rope snapped taut, and the barrel of a cannon emerged from the mire. Stunned, Hugh turned toward the professor for an explanation, but Daniels merely shrugged and pulled his hat over his brow. Hugh studied the foundry marks above the barrel's breech and compared them to the name on the grave marker.

"Charles Tillinghast James," Cooke said with a smirk, reading the barrel engraving aloud for Hugh's benefit. "May he rest in peace, or should I say, rest in war? I served with Senator James in the Rhode Island militia. He patented the six-pound smoothbore. I'm sorry I wasn't here to say goodbye to old Charlie on his premature deathbed."

"I know nothing about this," Eldridge insisted.

Cooke didn't buy the innocent act. "Eldridge, you and your new shavetails here will have to become more imaginative with your lies if you expect to out-wit that Douglas County crowd." He waved up the rest of his troopers. "Arrest them all. We're taking them to Lecompton."

Daniels blanched. "That's bushwhacker country! Those slavers will kill us."

Cooke shrugged. "You should have thought of that before you smuggled contraband into Kansas."

"We are influential supporters of Governor Fremont!" the professor shouted. "When he wins in November, your military career will be finished!"

Cooke appeared unfazed. "It will be an incalculable loss to be denied the en-joyment of riding these godforsaken grasslands and rounding up lunatics such as yourself." He signaled for his dragoons to proceed with his orders. "Inspect every inch of their grain wagons. I'll wager a month's pay we'll find a stash of new Sharps rifles germinating under their corn."

Led away with a rough shove, Hugh glared an accusation of betrayal at his mentor Daniels, who had now twice conned him into playing his dupe.

7

LAGRANGE, GEORGIA
MARCH 1857

Two months earlier, Nancy and her classmates rang in New Year's Eve with a toast of gratitude. The Democrat James Buchanan defeated John Fremont and the Abolitionist Republicans for the presidency, and the newspapers were rife with eyewitness claims that Buchanan, during his inaugural ceremony, held whispered consultations with the chief justice of the Supreme Court on sanctioning the extension of slavery into the Western territories. With Buchanan's victory easing the feverish talk of war, the men of Troup County were now free to turn their attention to more important and pressing matters: the spring balls and eligible ladies.

Yet no sooner had the gaiety of the season started than another pall fell over the town. Reverend Joseph Montgomery and his brother, who founded the LaGrange Female College in 1846, announced they could no longer afford to support the institution. Confronted with bankruptcy, the beloved family of educators sold the building and confines for forty thousand dollars to the Georgia Conference of the Methodist Church. Even if the college remained open, the conference would install a new administration and faculty.

Distressing as this news was, Nancy counted herself fortunate compared to her younger friends. She had graduated with the Class of 1856, yet poor Leila Pullen and her own sister, Augusta, completed only their freshman year, and Pack Beall her sophomore year. More than a hundred other girls in the underclasses, many of whom she and Mary took under their wings, faced the possibility of never attaining a degree or learning from the wisdom and generosity of Professor Chase in music, Miss Hort in art, and Miss Loyd in speech. She spent the first week of the new year depressed and walking the Ferrell terraces while lost in the memories of performing her vocal solo in the conservatory and arriving on the fresh-clipped grounds for her first day in her uniform of gray dress flannel with matching hat. For that fleeting moment, arrayed as they were in ranks and classes, she understood what men must feel when they muster on the field of battle.

Oh, to do it all again.

Now, time oppressed her. Half the girls in her graduating class were engaged, and many had scattered to the far corners of the South. Mary and Caroline would start families soon. Nancy felt a premonition that something foreboding was hurtling toward her. Did all women feel such a dread when they approached eighteen? Perhaps it was a deepening of the apprehension she had suffered since her father died six years ago, leaving her mother to put food on the table by lodging a dozen college girls during the terms. Ben Hill looked after them, but he was often away on political business. If the school closed, her family might become destitute, and any chance she had to win Brown Morgan would vanish.

She refused to wallow in self-pity and came up with an idea to save the coming school year: a benefit theatrical put on by the graduates and students. Mrs. Hannah Judge, a silver-haired impresario who had tutored many of the South's most successful thespians, agreed to direct the production on one condition: no somber tragedies or ancient melodramas. What the citizens of LaGrange needed, the grand dame insisted, was a romping comedy to leave them rollicking in their chairs and the donations flying into the college coffers.

And so, on this afternoon, Nancy found herself in the auditorium rehearsing the British farce, *She Stoops To Conquer* by Oliver Goldsmith. Mrs. Judge had assigned the roles: Mary would play Mrs. Hardcastle, the vain and greedy biddy who spoils her son. For the male parts, Mrs. Judge recruited Dr. Ware to inhabit Mr. Hardcastle, the patriarch of the bumbling clan, and his brother, Eugenius, for the street-smart but uneducated Tony. To no one's surprise, the male lead of Marlow went to the dashing Brown Morgan, who had to be bribed onto the boards with a promise that the ladies in the cast would drop pastries off at his office every day for the next two weeks.

That left the two female leads.

To Nancy's dismay, Mrs. Judge cast her as Constance, the niece of Tony, the clichéd "nice" girl with little allure. Adding insult, Constance, having lost her father at a young age, was a ward of Mr. Hardcastle. Nancy was furious at being typecast, but she bit her tongue and accepted her fate with a veneer of equanimity, as was expected of a LaGrange Female College graduate. All of this would have been tolerable had the star character in the play, the beautiful Kate, love interest of Marlow, not gone to the belle who won at everything.

Sallie Fannie Reid.

Nancy suffered the entire week watching Sallie cast alluring glances at Brown, sidling up to him with her sashays and pirouettes.

"Ladies and gentlemen, we are behind schedule!" Mrs. Judge clapped her hands for the cast members to climb the steps to the stage. Seated in the front row with Leila, her line reader, the elegant director motioned everyone to their marks. "I needn't remind you we have less than a week to prepare."

Gus tapped his cane, irked. "And I needn't remind everyone that *I* have a medical practice to attend."

"You can neuter the dogs tomorrow," said Nancy.

"Dogs! Why, you venomous sprout—"

"Oh, speak to me no more!" cried Mrs. Judge, quoting Shakespeare, as she was wont to do. "These words like daggers enter my ears!" She stood and glared Nancy and Gus to silence. "If you two want to perform King Lear, take the train to Atlanta."

From the corner of her eye, Nancy caught Brown chuckling at her come-uppance. She waited until Mrs. Judge descended again into her chair before sticking her tongue out at him. He recoiled at her bratty act and brought his fists to his chest, staggering as if pierced by a lance.

"Leila," said Mrs. Judge. "Please instruct our strutting troupe, whose conceit lies in their hamstrings, and doth think it rich to hear the wooden dialogue and sound 'twixt their stretch'd footing and the scaffoldage." When Leila stared blankly at her, the director pointed to the pamphlet in Leila's hand. "Remind them what the play is about. Without looking at the summation."

Leila closed her eyes to squeeze her memory. "Marlow arrives at the home of the Hardcastles to engage Kate. But Tony has misled Marlow into believing he is staying at a common inn. Everybody thinks the others are somebody else. Marlow is too shy to court refined ladies because he is a bumbling idiot around them. So, Kate must trick him into believing she is a barmaid. Only then can she make him reveal his genuine nature."

"Well done. I may put you up there in the stead of these scrapping cats."

"She can have my role," said Nancy, pouting.

Mrs. Judge wagged a finger at Nancy. "Now, let us rehearse again the crucial scene in Act Four. The play and its conceits hinge on this crucial moment when Kate must prolong her guise while yearning to share her growing affections for Marlow." She waved everyone but Brown and Sallie to the wings and signaled to Leila for the cue.

Leila announced, "Enter Miss Hardcastle!"

Sallie floated across the boards, fluttering her fan. She projected her lines to the imaginary audience in the upper reaches of the auditorium. "'I believe he begins to find out his mistake. But it's too soon to undeceive him.'"

"Splendid enunciation, Sallie," said Mrs. Judge. "But dispense with the fan. Remember, you are a tavern maid. You cannot afford a fan."

"But, Mrs. Judge, it's such a habit."

Mrs. Judge motioned for Mary to confiscate the fan and nodded for Brown to continue with the scene.

Brown plopped into a chaise, extending his feet and wrapping his arms around the backing as if in a New Orleans boudoir. He leered at Sallie, trying to make sense of her. "'Pray, child, answer me one question. What *are* you, and what may your business in this house be?'"

Sallie glided around the stage, her blonde head as steady and immovable as a jewel set upon the axis of a spinning wheel. "'A relation of the family, sir.'"

"'What?'" asked Brown. "'A poor relation?'"

Sallie waltzed across the boards. "'Yes, sir, a poor relation, appointed to keep the keys, and to see that the guests want nothing in my power to give them.'"

Brown narrowed his glare. "'That is, you act as the barmaid of this inn.'"

Sallie angled over him in her hoop skirt, her lashes doing the work of her confiscated fan. In a delicate voice that dripped smooth as sorghum, she replied with a restraint at odds with the lines. "'Inn? Oh, dear, what brought that in your head? I nevah. One of the best families in the country keeps an inn? Why bless your heart, sir. Mr. Hardcastle's house an inn!'"

"Stop, please." Mrs. Judge studied Sallie with vexation. "My dear, you are playing a woman of low means, not the wife of Commodore Vanderbilt." The director stood and paced in front of the proscenium. "Have you ever known a tavern hussie to speak with the elevated inflection and cadence expected in a Montgomery society salon?"

"I've never been in a tavern."

Mrs. Judge closed her eyes in exasperation. "We call it *acting*. Has the great Edwin Booth ever ruled Denmark?"

Sallie hazarded a guess. "No?"

"And yet he conjures Hamlet night after night to standing ovations. How? He reaches into his soul and pulls Hamlet forth from the afterlife."

Sallie, exasperated, threw up her hands and landed them into the pillowing folds of her hoops skirt. "I have devoted years to elocution classes! And now you wish me to abandon that custom in which I have become so ingrained?"

"It was my delivery," said Brown. "I threw Miss Reid off her lines."

Mrs. Judge, seeing through his self-interested chivalry, climbed the steps to the stage and motioned the cast members and stagehands to gather. "In 1849, I attended a production of *Macbeth* at the Astor Opera House in Manhattan. That night, Edwin Forrest and the esteemed British actor William Macready squared off on the boards in front of a standing-room-only audience. Do you know what happened?"

The cast members shook their heads.

"Riots broke out in the theatre and spread across the city. By morning, twenty-five people lay dead and more than a hundred wounded."

"My heavens," said Sallie. "All over a little play?"

Mrs. Judge's powdered face flushed. "When the lights rise, you accept a sacred duty." She pointed to the empty seats in the auditorium. "Come Saturday, you will own the power to reach into the hearts of our fellow citizens seated out there. It is a divine commission with which no one should trifle."

The cast members hung their heads, all but Sallie, who winked at Brown to catch his attention. Nancy wiped a tear, moved by Mrs. Judge's story.

Mrs. Judge noticed her reaction. "What upsets you, Nannie?"

"This could be the last performance here. My father brought me to this hall as a child to see a play about the Revolutionary War hero, Israel Putnam."

Mrs. Judge studied her. "I knew your father, Hampton. A man of most commendable character. He went to his reward when you were only eleven, if I remember correctly. That must have been difficult for you."

Nancy nodded. "Mama has worked hard to see me earn my degree."

"You have risen to the challenge, despite your circumstances." Mrs. Judge waved the cast back to their marks and descended to the well, taking her position again. She studied Nancy. "Let's begin where we left off."

Sallie, flirting with Brown, glided to her spot and waited for her cue.

"Oh, and Nannie. Try reading this scene with Brown ... as Kate."

Nancy's eyes popped, and Sallie straightened with a frisson of affront.

Mrs. Judge motioned for Leila to take her copy to Nancy.

"I don't need it," said Nancy. "I have Kate's lines memorized."

Mrs. Judge applauded. "Dedication!"

Nancy snickered at Brown. "The star must always have an understudy ready, isn't that right, Mr. Morgan?"

Brown slanted his eyes at her.

Nancy stepped toward him and waited for Sallie, still recovering from the shock, to give way. At last, Sallie retreated, her alabaster face red as a turnip.

Brown, relieved the potential for a clawing match was defused, cleared his throat and restarted the scene. "'Mr. Hardcastle's house? Is *this* Mr. Hardcastle's house, child?'"

Nancy pulled a kerchief from her sleeve and dusted the chaise, slapping its pillows with her palm and raising puffs of lint. She moved with hurried steps around Brown, as if fearful the master of the manse might discover her lagging at any moment. "'Aye, suh! Whose else should it be, sugah?'"

She delivered those lines with such force that Brown rocked to his heels. Recovering, he matched Nancy's overblown manner, pacing like a criminal just discovered in his robbery. "'So, then, all's out! And I have been damnably imposed on. Confound my stupid head, I shall be laughed at by the entire town. I shall be stuck in caricatura! To mistake this house of all others for an inn, and my father's old friend for an innkeeper! What a swaggering puppy must he take me for! What a silly puppy do I find myself! There again, may I be hanged, my dear, but I mistook you for the barmaid.'"

Nancy flung the kerchief at Brown and moved to him, nose to nose, her balled fists digging into the sides of her hips with her elbows flared like pitcher handles. "'Barmaid!? *Barmaid?* I'm sure there's nothing in mah behavior to put me on a tankard rack with one of *that* ilk.'"

Brown stared agog at her sudden transformation into a common wench.

She kicked his ankle to bring him back to his lines.

Playing mortified was not a stretch for Brown now. He dropped his head into his hands. "'Nothing, my dear, nothing. But I was in for a list of blunders and could not help making you a subscriber. My stupidity saw everything the wrong way. I mistook your assiduity for assurance, and your simplicity for allurement. But it's over. This house I no more show my face in.'"

Nancy glanced at the wings toward Sallie, whose eyes were wide with astonishment. Just as swiftly, Nancy retreated into a creature of reticence, her voice quivering with affected shame. "'I hope, sir, I have done nothing to disoblige you. I'm sure I should be sorry to affront any gentleman who has been so polite and said so many civil things to me. I'm sure I should be sorry'"—she broke out in tears, blubbering so profusely that Brown searched his pockets for a kerchief. Before he could produce it, she calmed—"'if he left the family upon my account. I'm sure I should be sorry if people said anything amiss, since I have no fortune but my character.'"

Brown was undone, at a loss how to explain her chimeric talents.

"By Heaven!" shouted Leila, giving him the line.

Alerted back to the scene, Brown nodded, grateful for the cue. "Ah, yes." Remembering he was to turn to the audience and speak an aside, he caught Sallie's icy glower, and that distraction nearly unfettered him again. At last, recovering, he fixed his gaze upon the empty seats in the back row. "'By Heaven! She weeps. This is the first mark of tenderness I ever had from a modest woman, and it touches me.'"

Nancy, sobbing in character, turned her back to him.

He confided to her over her shoulder. "'Excuse me, my lovely girl. You are the only part of the family I leave with reluctance. But to be plain with you, the difference of our birth, fortune, and education, makes an honorable connection impossible.'"

Nancy frowned. Was it her imagination, or did he speak *that* line with more than required emphasis? Was this his veiled way of telling her she held no chance with him? She stole another glance at Sallie and found her rival taking comfort from her nettled reaction.

As if sensing her retreat to reality, Brown moved an inch closer, until she could feel his warm breath against her neck. He whispered, "'I can never harbor a thought of seducing simplicity that trusted in my honor, of bringing ruin upon one whose only fault was being too lovely.'"

Mrs. Judge and the other cast members leaned in to understand him.

Nancy trembled from the effect of his intimacy. She imagined being taken into his arms, pressed against his chest and kissed. *Is he playing the part? Or are those his true intentions?*

"Nannie, no pause there," said Mrs. Judge. "You should answer him immediately to maintain the momentum of the deception."

Nancy gathered her wits and motioned for Leila to repeat the last line.

Leila rolled her eyes. "'Only fault was being too lovely.'"

Nancy risked another glance at Brown, confirming the impact of that line. Casting off her weepy affect, she turned to the absent audience to deliver a heartfelt aside. "'Generous man! I now begin to admire him.'"

Sallie risked a step closer, as if suspicious there was a third level of beguilement being played out between Nancy and Brown.

Nancy turned to meet Brown's gaze. "'But I am sure my family is as good as Miss Reid's. And though I'm poor, that's no great misfortune to a contented mind. And, until this moment, I never thought it was bad to want fortune.'"

Brown was so nonplussed by her *faux pas* that he lost his next line. Sallie's pert mouth fell agape. Unsure if she had heard correctly, Mrs. Judge looked at Leila, who nodded and shrugged. Nancy, clueless, waited for Brown to proceed, but he had fallen mute. She looked around the stage and found the cast members whispering and smirking. What on earth had she done?

Mrs. Judge, the last person in the auditorium to perceive the rivalry being played out onstage, gently corrected Nancy. "Hardcastle, dear. 'My family is as good as Miss Hardcastle's.'"

Nancy blushed with embarrassment. Had her lips betrayed her heart? She was ruined. She could never look at Brown again. What if she repeated the mistake on—

"'And why now, my pretty simplicity?'" Brown came to her rescue by smiling and offering his hand.

She swallowed hard, desperate to regain her voice. She allowed him to take her trembling hand between his reassuring palms. Reverting to her role of the common lass again, she pulled away and recited with more earnestness than that called for in the play's instructions. "'Because it puts me at a distance from one that, if I had a thousand pounds, I would give it all to.'"

Brown's next line was written to be an aside to the audience, but he spoke it to himself. "'This simplicity bewitches me.'" He turned his gaze inward.

Leila, thinking him lost again, read his line aloud. "'I must make one bold effort and leave her.'"

Brown put a finger to his lips and nodded as he walked in a tight circle, deep in thought. He glanced nervously at Sallie, avoided her silent inquisition, and then asked Mrs. Judge: "That last line seems disingenuous."

Sallie burned him with another glare, twice heated.

"Disingenuous?" exclaimed Mrs. Judge. "Good sir, you question the intent of Oliver Goldsmith?" She took the play pamphlet from Leila and reread the line. She looked up, suddenly understanding Brown's wish to avoid humiliating Nancy by publicly associating her with penury and humble family circumstance. Yet he had already run offstage, in the opposite direction from Sallie's entrenchment. Mrs. Judge waited, expecting his return after such a dramatic and improvised exit, but Brown was gone for the day.

Leila muttered to Mary, "Coward."

Now needing a replacement, Mrs. Judge surveyed the astonished cast members. "Dr. Ware, would you stand in as Marlow? Just for this instance."

Aggravated by the entire fiasco, Gus limped forward to Brown's marks, his cane scraping across the boards. "May I remind everyone that I have patients waiting in my office?"

Leila made a snorting noise. "Mahoney's pig is gonna croak on the operating table lest Doctor Ware comes carving!"

Gus staggered to the edge of the stage and targeted his cane at the smart-mouthed girl. "Whippersnapper! Wait until you need a tooth pulled! See if I waste my ether on you!"

"Leila! Gus!" Mary admonished. "Behave!"

With order restored, Mrs. Judge nodded for Nancy to carry on.

Still flustered by Brown's inexplicable retreat, Nancy pulled herself together for the grand finale. She walked to the edge of the stage and addressed the world. "'I never knew half his merit till now. He shall not go, if I have power or art to detain him.'" She dropped to her knees and raised her eyes to the heavens. "'For I shall stoop to conquer!'"

An ominous silence filled the auditorium.

Mrs. Judge bounded to her feet and applauded.

The other cast members joined in the ovation—except Sallie Fannie Reid, who stood frozen at the curtains.

8

RIPON, WISCONSIN
OCTOBER 1858

Late for his first day of teaching, Hugh hurried across Liberty Street tugging at the short sleeves of his new sack coat while cursing the haberdasher who sharped him an inch on the wool. Professor Daniels persuaded him to purchase the outfit on credit, insisting an educator was also an entertainer who must dress the part. Passersby edged away and nodded sternly. Perhaps they saw him, festooned in his beaver hat, choking cravat, and flaming red vest, more as a circus ringleader than a scholar.

It was just a grammar school, but he was more nervous than when those Army troopers dragged him into the Lecompton jail. He had lost more than a year of his life to that godless Kansas territory. And to show for it? Calloused feet, empty pockets, and an appreciation for the depths to which humankind could sink. By the time the State Aid Society petitioned his release, the territorial governor had reduced the border war to a simmering burn. With their guns confiscated, he and his fellow Free-State emigrants hadn't fired a shot in the defense of liberty, weren't even allowed to vote in Kansas or stake a land claim. Worse, that fence-straddler, John Buchanan, edged Fremont for the White House, and now the old hot potato of slavery was being tossed around Congress again. The election didn't change a damn thing, and he and the other Wisconsin Abolitionists became so tired of being shunned like ministers in a Lawrence saloon that they packed up and walked home.

Good riddance to Bloody Kansas and the lunatics who rule it.

Problem was, Professor Daniels wasn't a man to abandon a dream without a fight, and he was already scheming another invasion by the Lane Trail, this time at the head of a proper army.

Hugh balled his fists in riled determination. No more ferrying escaped slaves up to Canada for the geologist for him. The Negro-conveying business had become too dangerous. Daniels took his desertion better than he expected. Instead of throwing a tantrum, the geologist cajoled him into papering the lampposts in town with broadsides offering to prepare students of any age for the rigors of college. For a cut of the tutoring fees, Daniels also rented for Hugh's use the old Ceresco commune schoolhouse, where their Republican comrades gathered for weekly meetings.

Hugh turned the corner and gazed up at the cupola crowning the runty octagonal building. The place wasn't much larger than a corn bin. He shrugged. Why worry over lecturing to an empty room? No upstanding family would pay to have its children indoctrinated by a failed Free-State filibusterer. He would humor the professor, confess his teaching career started and finished on the same day, and then find a plot to furrow to be left alone in peace. He rattled the door open and shouted into the darkened room to chase the rats. "Shake your tails, you Democrat devil rodents! Line up and recite for me the three unities of Aristotle!"

"Time, place, and action," a female voice answered.

He peered into a thick haze of smoke to find its source. Was the roof on fire? He rushed gagging to a window and lifted the pane for air and light.

"The time, eight sharp," the female voice groused. "The place, a presentable classroom, not a coal hamper. And the action, well, is tardiness."

He waved away the soot puffs and, in the glint of sunlight, found his brother, Wallace, heaving anthracite chunks into a pot stove. "What the hell are *you* doing here?"

Wallace started to explain—

"Such foul language in a classroom?" the female voice chided.

The smoke dissipated. On the front bench sat a young lady, tall for her age and tressed with long strawberry blonde hair, with her back arched in a pose of disgust. She pressed a kerchief to her mouth to avoid being suffocated. Perched on either side of her, shrouded in the shadows and thinning smog, were ten children of various ages, all holding prayer books borrowed from the church across the street.

"She's a firecracker," Wallace warned Hugh. "We've been getting to know one other."

The girl rolled her eyes. "By which he means I have been trying my best to ignore him."

Hugh pried open the stuck flue on the stove's pipe.

"Are you the chimney sweep?" the girl demanded, studying his outfit from head to toe. "Dickens said they wore grotesque attire."

Hugh's mouth dropped. "Now, there's no cause for—"

"This evangelist"—the girl pointed an accusing finger at Wallace—"has been forcing us to sing hymns and speak in tongues."

Hugh glared at his brother, who raised his eyes toward Heaven as a reminder of his first allegiance.

The girl dusted the smoke residue from her bench. "I was led to understand this is a school, not a revival."

"You were late," Wallace explained to Hugh. "I thought I'd help you out and get the sprouts started down the right cornrow."

Hugh collected the hymnals from the confused students and shoved them into Wallace's arms. "My brother is leaving."

Wallace grinned. "I think I'll stay."

"You can't afford my services."

"I'll bet a day's wages I can."

Hugh found an empty cigar box on the bookshelf and placed it with the lid open on his desk. "Ten cents a day. Students must deposit the tuition before class starts." He waited for the students to line up and drop their coins in, but no one moved.

Wallace yanked a crumpled flyer from his coat pocket and smoothed it out. "Says right here that Mr. Oscar Hugh LaGrange will offer his instruction *gratis.*" He looked around the room. "Can anyone tell Mr. Hugh what *that* word means?"

"A gift," the girl piped.

Wallace nodded as he read the rest of the broadside. "'*Gratis* during the first week, and that all are welcome to attend and become enlightened.'"

"It derives from the Latin *gratia*," the girl continued. "As in gracious, gratuity, grateful—"

"I understand the word," Hugh snapped.

The girl persisted. "Also means complementary."

Hugh's eyes bugged. "Let me see that!"

"Also means without charge," she said, waving her copy at him.

Hugh snatched Wallace's broadside and saw that someone had replaced his terms with a new offer.

"'Freely given,'" the girl continued. "'On the house, without recompense, from love alone.'"

"From love alone," Wallace repeated while elbowing his brother and making smooching sounds. "Professor Rock Brains must have figured you needed a kick in the recruiting pants."

Red-faced, Hugh required a moment to recover his composure. "I'll fulfill this commitment, though it was not me who—"

"'I'," the girl said, interrupting him.

Hugh blinked hard. "Excuse me?"

"It was not 'I,'" she corrected. "You intended to use the pronoun as a subject in your sentence."

"I *intended?* You know what I intended? Are you a gypsy fortune teller?"

Impatient, she tapped her toe. "'Who.'"

"Who *what?*"

"You said 'it was not me *who.*' Signaling to the listener you were preparing to take action, which, by the way, would have been the first time this morning."

"Do you have a name? Or do you just pester people anonymously?"

"Jennie Stowell."

Hugh ignored Wallace's snickering. "You sound educated, Miss Stowell. Much more so—"

"Than you?"

"Can I finish a thought, please?"

"That remains for you to demonstrate. But you *may* try."

Hugh's brain felt like a dartboard. He now hesitated with each sentence, gun-shy he would commit another breach of grammar. "I was going to, uh, ask why you'd waste your time with my instruction?"

"Don't be absurd. I didn't come for your instruction. I attend the Lyceum down the street."

Even more vexed now, Hugh glanced at his brother before turning back to the impudent girl. "I'll probably regret asking this, but—"

"I want to know more about Kansas."

Hugh bristled. "I am not a traveling carny poet spinning tales of the Great Frontier. Now if you will kindly—" He fell mute, stunned to see Jennie open her draw purse, pull out a silver dollar, and drop it into the cigar box. He paced in front of her. "You think you can indenture me?"

Wallace edged closer to the cigar box. "That *is* a dollar, Hugh."

Jennie aimed her chin at Hugh. "I understand you took out a loan at the First National to pay for your botched invasion of Indian country."

"Am I the target of gossip at every quilting bee in town?"

"My father is one of the bank's directors."

Hugh, apoplectic, stood motionless until Wallace slapped him on the back to rouse him. "Showtime."

Hugh fixed an eye on the girl as he circled to his desk. "How old are you?"

"That's not a proper question to ask a lady."

"When you behave like a lady, you'll earn that prerogative."

"Ooh, big word. Prerogative. Are you going to enlighten us as to its meaning, Dr. LaGrange?"

"I'm not a doctor."

"You're not a teacher, either. But that doesn't stop you from advertising your-self as one."

"Your age, Miss Stowell? For my records."

Jennie flicked a curl across her forehead. "Eighteen."

"I don't teach fiction."

"Seventeen."

"I see we need work on your subtraction skills, too."

She huffed. "Sixteen and eight months."

"If you aren't here to learn from my curriculum, what *is* it you want?"

She inched toward the edge of her bench. "Tell us about John Brown."

Hugh couldn't believe her audacity. "That's not a proper topic for children."

Jennie patted the head of the barefoot boy sitting next to her and asked him, "You want the story of the Pottawatomie Creek avenger? How he gutted those evil slavers like a scad of catfish on a string?"

"Yes!" the boy and the other students shouted. "Yes!"

"Aye, may we have a story, suh?" Wallace crooned, conspiring with Jennie in a mocking plea.

Jennie arched her brow, taunting Hugh to get on with it.

Hugh saw she was hellbent on disrupting the class until he relented. He took a seat atop his desk while pondering how best to answer her. "To be honest, I don't know what to make of John Brown."

"That's it?" Jennie reached to retrieve the dollar from the cigar box.

Hugh grabbed her wrist and forced her to drop the coin. When she sat back and nodded her agreement to behave, he continued. "I met Brown briefly. I saw no soldier-fighting in Kansas. Sorry to disappoint you."

Jennie lobbed a barb. "Rumor is you got yourself arrested."

"Illegally," he insisted.

"The United States Army with a federal warrant seems pretty legal."

"You believe everything you hear on the street?"

"Did you give that cannon the proper reburial it deserved?"

"You've got a smart-alecky mouth. I'm your elder, don't forget that."

"Not by much. And if we went by semester years, *you'd* be a lot younger."

Wallace chortled. "Harsh talk ain't conducive to catching a husband."

Jennie wheeled on Wallace. "I'm not planning to marry! No man in these parts is worth the trouble. I'll sail to the Continent. Europeans understand how to treat a *jeune femme* of noble birth."

"Yeah, just ask Marie Antoinette," Hugh said.

A runny-nosed boy in the second row raised his hand. "Will we be cipher-ing today?"

"How far can you count?" Hugh asked.

"Ten."

Hugh dug around his pocket and found a chalk nub. "Go write your figures backwards a hundred times on the wall. If you can do it without asking for help, Miss Stowell here will buy you some sugar taffy at the drugstore." When the boy leapt to the task, Hugh shooed the other kids off with Wallace. "Make sure he scribbles it right."

Abandoned by the other students, Jennie pinned Hugh with a look suggesting she hadn't gotten her dollar's worth yet.

Hugh lowered his voice. "Why do you care so much about John Brown?"

"The judge here in town says Brown has written a new national constitution," Jennie said. "A constitution that requires equality for all races."

"Anybody can put words on a piece of paper."

"I also hear Brown's been using your Lane Trail for something besides guiding emigrants into Kansas."

Hugh fiddled with the buttons on his coat. "I wouldn't know."

She lost her smirk and turned serious. "I would think you do."

Hugh shot a worried glance at Wallace, who was straining to overhear. He edged closer to his fetching interrogator and whispered to her ear. "I don't know what you've been told, Miss Stowell, but if I were you, I wouldn't put any stock in the local calumny."

Jennie pulled a folded newspaper from her purse and opened it to the front page. "I haven't had the chance to peruse this morning's *Free Democrat*." She rustled the paper to smooth out a column below the fold. "Now here's an item that mystifies me. Politically astute as you claim to be, perhaps you can enlighten me as to its meaning. The correspondent says the editor of this gazette, Sherman Booth, has been in and out of prison five times. Why did the government shackle such an upstanding member of Milwaukee society?"

Hugh felt the hair on his neck rise. Was she a spy planted by the Democrats? Or worse, a government informant? Four years ago, the Racine sheriff arrested his Abolitionist friend, Sherman Booth, for violating the Fugitive Slave Act after organizing the rescue of a hunted Negro. Professor Daniels introduced him to the controversial newspaper editor during a Republican Party meeting, and he and Booth hit it off. Everyone involved with the Underground Railroad remained on edge these days, worried the federal marshals might blow open their doors at any hour. There were rumors that Booth's enemies intended to frame the Republican Abolitionist with phony morals charges.

Jennie angled her head in a taunt. "Prairie dog got your tongue?"

"Booth is not a felon."

"Why was he thrown into prison?"

"His situation is complicated."

"I see. A woman could not possibly understand statecraft."

"That's not what I meant."

"What *did* you mean?"

Hugh glanced at the fidgeting younger students, who stood at the board looking over their shoulders, expecting his instruction. He motioned for them to continue practicing their figures, and told Wallace, "Keep them occupied."

Wallace tarried. "I'd rather listen to you answer Miss Stowell's question."

"Get over there!"

Wallace did as ordered, but he kept his ear cocked.

Huddled with Jennie, Hugh turned his back to the other students. He leaned toward her, close enough to detect the vanilla fragrance of her perfume. "What game are you playing?"

"Game? Why, I'm simply interested in learning about the law."

"I'm running a school, not a legislature."

The corners of her delicate mouth curled with amusement. "Let's say you give me a civics lesson for that dollar. Isn't the United States Supreme Court the highest legal authority in our nation?"

Hugh glanced toward the window to make sure they weren't being spied on. "You know very well there are human laws so repulsive to God that no man, however haughty his robe, should be required to abide or enforce them. The Supreme Court of *our* state has ruled the Fugitive Slave Act unconstitutional."

Jennie didn't flinch from his accusing glare. "Yes, but from what I've read, the federal justices in Washington, D.C., have *not* so ruled. And they ordered our state court to deliver Mr. Booth's case for their decision. That was four years ago, and his trial files remain locked in Milwaukee. Some might call disobeying a federal court an act of treason, Mr. LaGrange."

"What would you call it?"

She lifted her chin to allow her lips to hover near his breath. "Oh, no, I'm just a frivolous girl who has no proper opinions on such matters."

"I should start class."

She opened her purse again, pulled out a small pouch full of coins, and slipped it into his coat jacket. Locking her blue eyes with his perplexed gaze, she ran her hand along the lining of his coat. "My father wishes to pay my full tuition in advance."

"I thought you attended the Lyceum."

Her sultry inspection rose again to his eyes. "I've had a change of heart."

"But this is much more than—"

She stood so abruptly that her curls bounced and brushed his face. Spinning toward the door, she winked at Wallace and gathered the folds of her skirt. "If you gentlemen will excuse me, I'm expecting a shipment of precious goods from New Orleans. I've been waiting weeks for the delivery. I hope the *package* arrives safely." She pronounced "package" as if to underscore its veiled importance. "Otherwise, I must go to Canada to locate such rarities."

Wallace jumped in front of Hugh and offered his elbow to escort her to the door. "May I treat you a soda some afternoon, Miss Stowell?" He winked, showing off his correct use of grammar.

Jennie reached into Wallace's pants pocket and pulled out the lining, revealing it to be empty. "You *may*," she said. "But, alas, it appears you *can't.*" She sashayed out of the schoolhouse, leaving the brothers speechless.

Hugh opened the pouch and stared at the coins. He dug his hand into the cache and found the local embalmer's card with words and numbers scribbled on the back referencing a date: *Baggage Claim 11:7.*

He had seen such code words with numbers before.

The nervy girl, he realized, was a conductor for the Underground Railroad.

9

TROUP COUNTY, GEORGIA
OCTOBER 1859

Nancy spread her quilt across a grassy knoll overlooking the confluence of the Chattahoochee River and Yellowjacket Creek, a few miles west of LaGrange. From this vantage, the marshlands stretched toward the vast expanse of cotton fields where the Negroes, singing their hymns, brought in their burlap sacks to waiting wagons. She sat at the crest and closed her eyes to savor the cooling breeze.

She vowed no matter how old she grew, she would never miss Orpheus Day.

The men thought her daft, but she didn't care. To protest her exclusion from their annual wild boar hunt, she had devised a companion event five years ago, recruiting Mary, Pack, Caroline, and Leila—all students or graduates of Professor Judge's Classics seminar—to join her on this makeshift acropolis for a sacred duty: Drink Madeira, pilfered from Gus's cellar, and recite their favorite poems from the past year while watching the hoplites of LaGrange ride through the cane breaks like Spartan cavalry and—

A dog yapped behind her ear.

She recoiled from the drooling mutt licking her.

Leila, cradling her new greyhound pup, dropped a picnic basket onto the quilt, nearly crushing Nancy's feet. "What did *you* bring this year?"

"The Romans buried Vestal Virgins alive inside the city walls for not respecting their elders."

"Virgin? Look who's talking. At least I'm not an old maid."

Nancy bolted up and surveyed the knoll, calculating how long it would take for Leila with one push to reach the bottom.

Leila stuck out her tongue. "You'll go tumbling down with me."

Nancy wrestled the little she-wolf into a headlock and was about to send her rolling when a carriage pulled up. The Negro driver climbed off the seat and opened the doors for Mary and Caroline.

"Must you two reenact the Wrath of the Furies every year?" Mary stepped out and displayed her precious jug of elixir. While the driver took the horses to shade in a nearby copse of red maples, she led Caroline, arm-in-arm, to the quarreling twosome on the quilt.

Nancy pointed to Leila as the cause of their spat. "I vote we ostracize her for the day. Like the Athenians did to Aspasia."

"Overruled." Caroline hovered her hand over the picnic basket and closed her eyes, as if divining its contents.

Mary relished this traditional soothsaying ritual. "Speak, Oracle of Delphi!"

Caroline rolled her eyes up into her head and trembled as if possessed. "Rice pie ... sweet-potato biscuits ... I'm getting a powerful sensation of ... candied yams ... no, the gods say it's ... apple fritters."

Leila stared dumbfounded at Caroline. "How do you do it, Linnie? Every year? You truly are a priestess of the ancient ways."

Nancy lifted the basket lid to reveal Caroline's secret. "She cooked them, you hobby horse! We've pulled this trick every year on you since you were nine."

Leila reddened from being duped. Before the headstrong girl could pounce on Nancy, Caroline brought four copper cups from the basket, and Mary filled them with the Madeira. Leila pulled out a fifth cup, requesting a libation for her puppy. Mary debated the request, then mixed in a few drops with water.

Nancy lifted her cup for their time-honored toast to open the ceremony. "To Gus. May the goddess Mnemosyne cast her spell again and make him forget he ordered five bottles instead of four."

The women raised their cups. "To Gus."

Nancy sipped the wine as she watched the men in the meadow trot their horses in circles to loosen their joints while the hunt overseer, an elderly darkie owned by Mary's husband, stoked the hounds by rubbing their noses with rags dipped in boar grease. Brown rode with them. He arrived home yesterday from St. Louis, where he had been litigating the case of Colonel Reid's escaped slave for months. He was on the dappled Arabian, his favorite, a frisky purebred purchased in Macon that could run all day without a break. She prayed Brown would look up just once at her before the bugler sent him off toward the river, but he remained absorbed in an animated conversation with the other hunters. She thought of Sallie again, and whether her bitter rival had traveled with Brown and her father to St. Louis. After their performance together in the play, Brown failed to follow up with a card. Had he lost interest in her? Or did he simply find her too common for—

"Nannie! Are you listening?"

Mary's demand yanked Nancy from her spiraling thoughts. "A very poignant reading."

"We haven't started yet," Caroline scolded.

Nancy feigned interest and, without taking her eyes off Brown, elbowed Leila to the task. "The youngest always goes first."

Leila scooted to the poet's corner of the quilt and brought her puppy to her lap. "'An Ode to Flush, My Dog.'" From memory, she recited:

> "'Loving friend, the gift of one,
> Who, her own true faith, hath run,
> Through thy lower nature.
> Be my benediction said
> With my hand upon thy head,
> Gentle fellow-creature!'"

Nancy clapped. "Lovely reading. Who's next?"

"I'm not done," Leila insisted.

Nancy rolled her eyes. "You're not performing *The Iliad.*"

Leila ignored the jab at the poem's length and finished with a flair:

> "'Yet be blessed to the height
> Of all good and all delight
> Pervious to thy nature,
> Only loved beyond that line,
> With a love that answers thine,
> Loving fellow-creature!'"

"I do so adore Elizabeth Barrett Browning," said Mary.

"What do you think the poem was about?" Caroline asked Leila.

"Her dog, of course. It's right there in the title."

"Yes," said Mary, "but is there a deeper meaning?"

Leila thought hard on that conundrum.

"I read once that Browning was a lifelong invalid," said Mary. "Her pooch, Flush, always waited at her bedside until she woke."

In the field below, the bugler sounded the chase, and the dogs leapt to the hunt, barking and howling as they stalked the river canes. Nancy watched Brown hang back and tail the pack of riders. He rode with a slouch. Was he not enjoying the thrill of the kill? She whispered to herself, "Loyalty."

Caroline asked, "What did you say, Nannie?"

"Loyalty." Nancy kept her eyes pinned on Brown. "The poem is about loyalty." The women waited for an explanation, but Nancy persisted in monitoring the distant hunt.

Caroline shrugged off Nancy's inattentiveness. "What will you share with us, Mary?"

Mary sighed. "I have lately been meditating on nature and its gifts."

Nancy torqued with her mouth agape. "No, you're not going to read from that frog-pondian Yankee again, are you?"

"Emerson has touched my heart, more than any poet this year."

"The man is an Abolitionist!"

"Even so," said Mary. "One can be mistaken about politics and still touch the divine."

Incensed by that suggestion, Nancy gulped the rest of the Madeira in her cup and angled her head toward the driver watering the carriage horses. "You cannot allow *them* to know you harbor such thoughts."

"Such thoughts?" Mary suddenly took her implication. "I am not reading Harriet Beecher Stowe! It is a poem praising a flower."

Nancy grabbed the wine jug and filled her cup again. "You just said a poem always has a deeper meaning."

"We agreed not to comment until after each reading," Caroline admonished. "And slow down with the Madeira."

Nancy swilled her second pour and folded her arms in protest.

Caroline nodded for Mary to continue with her recitation.

Mary cleared her voice. "'On Being Asked, Whence is the Flower?' by Ralph Waldo Emerson." She began reciting from memory:

"'In May, when sea-winds pierced our solitudes,
I found the fresh Rhodora in the woods,
Spreading its leafless blooms in a damp nook,
To please the desert and the sluggish brook.'"

Nancy sat glaring a harsh judgment at Mary. Feeling tipsy, she lifted the jug for a third round of wine as her friend finished the last stanza.

"'Then Beauty is its own excuse for being:
Why thou wert there, O rival of the rose!
I never thought to ask, I never knew:
But in my simple ignorance, suppose
The self-same Power that brought me there brought you.'"

Caroline and Leila applauded, but Nancy repeated the last line of Mary's poem to protest its biblical heresy suggesting the equality of all races and species. "'The self-same Power that brought me there brought you?'"

Her reaction baffled Mary. "The Almighty makes both us and the flowers."

"And what else does the Almighty make *just like us*?" Nancy glanced pointedly again at Mary's carriage driver again.

Mary shook her head in dismay. "So, I may not admire a dandelion?"

Caroline moved to defuse the argument. "Let's listen to the Bardess of Broad Street. Perhaps she can set us on the straight and narrow."

Nancy, oblivious to Caroline's sarcasm, folded the wrinkles in her skirt and straightened her sitting posture.

"'Once upon a midnight dreary, while I pondered, weak and weary,
Over many a quaint and curious volume of forgotten lore—
While I nodded, nearly napping, suddenly there came a tapping,
As of someone gently rapping, rapping at my chamber door.
"'Tis some visitor," I muttered, "tapping at my chamber door—
Only this and nothing more.'"

Mary's eyes narrowed. "That is quite enough."

"I'm not even a third finished."

"You *are* finished," Mary insisted. "Those lines were written by that opium-riddled addict from Richmond."

"Edgar Poe?" Caroline covered Leila's ears. "The ravings of that dead man are not proper."

Nancy huffed and threw her cup to the grass. "Just because Poe didn't gawk at his own reflection through pond scum?"

Mary edged closer to console her. "My love, *this* spoke to your heart this year? Such darkness and melancholy?"

"Poe wrote of monsters," said Caroline, agreeing with Mary. "The man was so disturbed in the head, he dropped out of the military academy. Morose ideas are not proper for ladies of the Chivalry."

"Monsters *can* be real," said Leila.

Aghast, Caroline turned on Nancy again. "You see what you've put into her young mind?"

"The poem speaks of a raven," insisted Nancy.

Mary reached for her hand. "Dear Nan, from what hurt does this darkness in your spirit spring? You were always so joyful and optimistic." She caught Nancy still being distracted by the baying of the hounds near the river. "You are brooding over *him* again."

"And if I am?"

Mary tried to console her. "You must not take offense if Brown has been preoccupied these past months. This Kansas business—"

"Kansas!" Nancy huffed. "Again? That godforsaken wasteland?"

"There is much at stake with the territory's impending decision to go slave or free," said Mary. "Peter will not speak of it with me. I know my own husband's moods, and he is deeply worried."

Caroline agreed there was a growing apprehension in the town. "Just last week, ten men from the county rode off to defend the slave constitution there."

"You see?" said Nancy. "Soon there won't be *any* men left here to marry."

Mary pulled Nancy to her embrace. "Darling, there are still plenty of eligible men."

"Where?" demanded Nancy.

Exasperated, Mary abandoned her soothing manner. "Cease thinking only of yourself. There are much worse fates than to be unattached at nineteen."

That suggestion astonished Nancy. "Such as?"

Mary's eyes angled toward Caroline, who appeared lost in her own sadness, as if seeking solace in the panels of the quilt. A moment passed before Nancy understood that Mary was referring to Caroline being widowed at twenty-four. That tragedy forced Mary to take care of Gus, a circumstance that did not bode well for attracting a second husband, even if she *had* inherited one of the most beautiful homes in LaGrange.

Leila broke the uncomfortable silence. "Gus says monsters live underground out here. Thousands of them."

"Gus was pulling your leg," Mary insisted.

"I don't think so," Leila said. "He called them Maroons. Slaves that ran off years ago. He said they live in caves and tunnels."

Alarmed, Mary looked around the knoll. "Caves? Here?" She turned to Caroline for support. "Tell the child this notion is absurd." When Caroline remained silent, Mary persisted. "*You* believe the tale, too?"

Caroline angled her head toward the driver waiting in the copse with the horses, and she lowered her voice. "Our overseer found an escaped slave last month living in the wilds of Long Cane."

"What was he doing there?" Nancy asked.

Caroline's breathing quickened. "They pulled him from a hole he dug years ago. The slave devised a trap door covered with brush to pull over him. He had constructed a living compartment and lived off scraps and—"

Nancy leapt to her feet. "I've had enough of this dread mongering! You won't even allow me to finish my poem before diverting off into this hobgoblin nonsense. I will join the men. At least they won't bore me."

"Absolutely not!" Mary stood.

Nancy marched toward the carriage. "I'll take one of the horses."

"They are shooting down there," Mary warned. "It's dangerous!"

"Yes, they might mistake you for a ferret!" Leila shouted, egging her on.

Nancy called the driver. "Did you bring a spare saddle?"

The driver came hurrying up. "Yes'm, but Massah Heard told me to keep this horse here should one pull up lame."

"Saddle it."

The driver looked to Caroline for direction.

Caroline sighed and nodded him to the task, whispering to Mary, "Let her ride the anger out of her craw."

When the driver got the horse strapped up, he set the stepping box in position and gripped the pommel. "Ain't a saddle made for--"

"I'll manage."

"This one's got a wild streak."

As if she were a practiced equestrian, Nancy slid her foot into the stirrup, threw her right leg over the saddle, and snapped the mount into a trot down the knoll toward the barking dogs.

Twenty minutes later, she reached the low river plain, out of sight of the other women. The only landmark she recognized this far from town was the covered bridge over the Chattahoochee. The hounds had stopped baying, so she figured Brown and the other hunters had either cornered a boar or struck out.

Broiling under the sun, she headed for the shade of the bridge to wait until the men returned to water their horses. She adjusted herself to the pommel, trying in vain to prevent the buckles on the saddle straps from irritating her ankles. With a huff, she gave up the effort, slid off the sweating horse, and led it on foot toward the river. She immediately regretted that decision when the knee-high switchgrass cut at the hem of her skirt.

Compounding her misery was the guilt she now felt from abandoning the others after her angry eruption. Why couldn't they all be carefree schoolgirls again? More and more, the world and its burdens intruded on their friendships. Mary and Caroline seemed much older now, and Leila was still immature. She herself had helped keep the college alive for another year, but the new faculty members were distant to her. Earlier that year, her widowed mother remarried and moved to Atlanta, accepting the proposal of an older man named Winship, who owned a cotton gin factory, and leaving her to take care of Augusta—

The horse spooked and reared. The reins slid from her grasp—the animal galloped off toward the bridge.

Alone in the canes, she heard a hissing behind her.

A coiled viper.

She turned and backed away a step. Dark brown bands? No. Terrified, she struggled to remember Gus's class lecture on identifying snakes. Wasn't a copperhead. No striping or triangular head. That ruled out a timber rattler. Its slithering black body had pale, chain-like stripes down its slithering length. She released a held breath. Only a chain kingsnake. Harmless. She congratulated herself on her frontier survival skills—

"Don't move!"

She spun and saw Brown a hundred yards off, cantering closer with his rifle aimed at her. She tried to reassure him. "Not to worry! It's only—"

"Quiet!" he shouted.

She froze, baffled by his demanding tone.

He rode fifty yards closer and dismounted, keeping the rifle leveled in his sight line. "Don't turn."

She ignored his order. "Whatever are you—" She stifled a scream.

The cane rushes rustled—and split open.

A boar snorted and bobbed its tusks.

"It's wounded and riled!" he shouted. "Don't run."

He had one shot, she knew. If he missed, it would take him several seconds to reload a ball and ram it into the barrel, enough time for the enraged boar to gore her. If she gave into her fears and ran, the beast would chase her, presenting an even more elusive target for Brown. She closed her eyes. All she could think of was her obituary in the *LaGrange Herald:* Miss Nancy Colquitt Hill, lead actress in the college production of *She Stoops To Conquer,* gnawed to death by a feral hog in the Chattahoochee wilds. She left no husband or children.

His gun fired—the ball whizzed past her ear. The boar dropped.

Her heart nearly catapulted into her throat. She screamed and ran for the bridge, but Brown caught her and held her trembling in his embrace until she calmed. Her tears streamed across his shirt.

He sniffed her breath. "Are you cork high and bottle deep?"

She pulled away. "It's Orpheus Day."

Brown nodded. "Ah, yes. The Feast of Gus's Madeira."

"You mock me."

He wiped the tears from her cheeks. "Did you walk here?"

"My horse ran off." She circled in a huff. "I'm sorry I ruined your hunt."

"You didn't ruin it. I left early."

"But why?"

He whistled for his waiting horse. "My grandfather hunted these marshlands with a spear." He looked north into the distance. "A boar doesn't stand much of a chance these days. Still, when cornered, it fights to the death. Not much of a sport when technology gives one combatant such an advantage."

She sensed something deeper than hunting was troubling him. "Does the hunt also lose its allure when the prey remains too elusive?"

Brown didn't take her bait. Instead, he handed her the reins, loosened the saddle straps to allow for two riders, and hoisted her onto the saddle sideways. He stepped into the stirrup and climbed on behind her.

"Are you not taking your prize?" she asked.

He sent the horse into a trot. "The dogs will find it. Gene Ware will claim he shot it and have its head stuffed to lord over Gus."

Her pulse raced as his arm wrapped around her waist. She tightened her throat, hoping to prevent her voice from breaking. "Mary and the others will be waiting for me at the carriage."

"They can wait. There's something I want to show you first."

They rode south several miles, until they reached a ridge overlooking Long Cane Creek, a meandering tributary that split off from the Chattahoochee below West Point. They climbed to a clearing that crowned a thick woodland. Brown reined up, dismounted, and tied the horse to a tree. He lifted her from the saddle and, taking her elbow into his arm, walked her across the chin of the ridge until they came to the best view.

"The Creeks believed you can see into the future from here," he said.

"It's a lovely spot."

"I'm thinking of buying a hundred acres of it and building a home. Ben Cameron has agreed to the commission. It will take two seasons to clear. But the breeze is cooling and the soil will support cotton."

"Leave town? What about your law practice?"

"Not that far a ride."

"You have only a few slaves to work it."

"The Nashville litigation has been lucrative. I will manage."

Why was he telling *her* this? Did he see her as a friend only, to offer counsel? A homestead here would not be far from LaGrange, true, but it would also be closer to Colonel Reid's plantation and Sallie Fannie. She studied him. The man was inscrutable. It took all the restraint she could muster to avoid requesting an answer to these questions, but Mary's admonishing voice whispered in her ear: *Do not press the matter. Allow him to decide in his own time.* She picked a few yellow leaves from a nearby pecan tree, crushed them, and breathed in their bracing aroma. "So, can you see *your* future from here?"

A sad smile crossed his face, and he shook his head. "I have no Creek blood." He opened her hands and gazed into the pulverized leaves. "The more I look into the cup of the prophesying goddess, the more obscure everything becomes." His voice trailed off as he turned toward the river in the distance.

"What troubles you, Brown?"

He shrugged off her concern. "I am melancholy by nature. Surely you've observed that in me."

"Not in the least. I consider you a paragon of gaiety and cheer compared to my mercurial disposition."

"You? Why, Nannie, I've never known you to be sad. You have too much willpower and determination."

"I admit I don't understand politics, but—"

"We live on borrowed time."

That strange warning stopped her short. "Then we must make the most of it." She felt him staring into her eyes and feared she might dissolve from the intensity of his inspection. Searching for a way to brighten his mood, she ran to the horse and pulled his weapon from its holster loop. "Show me how to shoot your musket."

His jaw dropped, and he laughed. "Why?"

"Should I ever again find myself charged by a raging beast and you're not with me, do you want my goring to be on your conscience?"

"First of all, it's not a musket. It's a Pennsylvania Long Rifle, and it cost more than a closet full of your gowns."

She shrugged. "A rose by any other name.... Please?"

"You should have been born an Amazon in ancient Greece." Melted by her pouting face, he shrugged and took the rifle from her. He measured out a thimble of powder from his horn, dropped it into the barrel, centered a small cloth patch over the hole, and set a ball atop it. He pulled the wooden ramrod, drove the ball and patch into the barrel, and primed the flash pan.

"Heavens, Brown. I could bake a pie in less time."

"Have you ever baked a pie?"

"No, but that's beside the point."

He drew back the flint hammer and eased the butt of the stock against the crease of her right shoulder. Wrapping his arms around her, he supported her arms to hold the barrel steady. "Aim at that hive on the tree."

"Are you trying to get us stung?"

"If you hit it, I promise to draw the bees away."

She bent her knees to firm her stance.

"The secret to marksmanship is *not* concentrating on the importance of the shot. You must relax." His cheek rested against hers as he adjusted the aim. "Just above the barrel."

His minted breath tingled against her neck. Her hands trembled.

"Slow your inhalations," he whispered to her ear. "Give up all determination to hit the target. Allow the shot to find it."

He placed her finger on the trigger.

She closed her eyes and pulled. A cloud of smoke erupted in her face, and the flash and force of the gunpowder explosion drove her backwards. She dropped the rifle and fell atop Brown on the ground, still in his embrace. She risked opening her eyes. "Am I dead?"

He laughed so hard she could feel his abdomen shake.

She pretended to wrestle from his arms, determined to scold him for not warning her about the kickback. "I should sue you for whatever it's called!"

He held her tight until she surrendered. "You should thank me."

"Thank you?"

"You're safe from the bees. Your shot didn't come within ten feet of the hive."

She huffed and levered herself to sitting.

He sat astride her, still holding her in his arms. "Nan, there's something I have been meaning to ask you."

She braced for it. "Yes?"

"War may soon come, and—"

A pounding of hooves interrupted him.

Drawn by the shot, Gene Ware and the other hunters galloped up the hill, leading Nancy's horse on a rope. Ware pulled up his snorting horse, lathered from the forced ride. "We've been searching half the damn county for you!"

Brown and Nancy stood and brushed off the leaves.

"You can have the boar," said Brown. "My compliments."

Ware, perplexed, saw Brown's rifle on the ground. "What boar?"

Nancy realized from their alarmed looks that these men were in no mood for banter. "What's wrong, Gene?"

"The militia is mustering," said Ware. "Telegram came from Atlanta. That Kansas cutthroat John Brown captured the armory at Harpers Ferry. He's got armed Negroes in his gang. They're scheming slave uprisings in Virginia. If word gets out to the slave cabins here, there may be Hell to pay."

Brown hurried Nancy to her horse and lifted her to the saddle. He ordered Ware, "Take her with you to find Mary Heard and Caroline Poythress near Yellowjacket Creek. I'll warn Colonel Reid and his family at Sunny Villa."

She wanted to beg Brown to let her go with him, but he was already racing south toward West Point.

10

Hugh always felt wistful on the last day of a semester. As dusk fell, he inspected the schoolroom, making sure the stove ash was cold and the windows were latched. He gathered the gifts his students had brought him—marbles, carved root knobs, a rusty penknife, fruits and candies—and stuffed them into his pockets. Back to the wheatfields for the summer with Wallace and the plow.

On his way out, he glanced at the profile of George Washington that one of his freed Negro pupils, Gabriel, had sketched on the ciphering wall. A clever likeness, he reckoned, although he had never seen a painted portrait of the great man. Professor Daniels once told him that Washington was the only founding father who emancipated his slaves in his will. Yet during the Revolution, several of Washington's house servants chose not to wait for their master's death and instead escaped to the British Army. If the first president thought bondage was wrong, why did he sign the first fugitive slave law in 1793 and supply guns to the French colony of Saint-Domingue to crush a plantation rebellion and—

"A girl could grow old waiting for you."

He saw Jennie Stowell at the door. "Did you forget something?"

"You gave me a 'B' in geography."

"Well done. You've graduated knowing your alphabet."

"Why did you dock me a grade?"

"You misidentified the Duchy of Tuscany. The territory became part of the Kingdom of Sardinia."

"Since when?"

"Last month."

"That's not fair! We covered Italy during the first week!"

"You're behind on your newspaper reading."

"That was the only 'B' I received! I could have had a perfect record!"

A perfect record. He shook his head at the mortal conceit in that quest. Her complaint recalled for him that miserable day four years ago when he lost his way on the Lane Trail. *John Brown lies a-mouldering in his grave.* Army regulars gibbeted that Old Testament prophet after he attacked the Federal arsenal at Harpers Ferry. The slavers now cited Brown's botched raid as evidence for their charge that Northerners were conspiring to incite slave uprisings.

"Did you hear me? A *perfect* record!"

He plopped on his hat and headed for the door. "A dreamer nearly as round the bend as you once told me perfection is the sole provenance of the Lord. I live by that advice. I suggest you do the same. Now, I'll say good evening and wish you success in whatever mischief you choose to apply your pestering talents."

Jennie blocked his path. Her frown mutated into a scheming grin. "You think I give a hare's care what some hayseed marks as my grade?"

He sighed and tipped his head back to look for deliverance from the rafters. This girl had been a burr under his saddle for two years. To be finally rid of her was a relief. He searched for a way to pass her, but her expansive skirts would require an ambitious leap, and he didn't need to start the farming summer with a broken ankle. "I gave up long ago trying to fathom what runs through that overheated head of yours. You've remained an enigma."

"Enigma. Ooh, that is right high and mighty. Gargantuan words don't impress me. You can make amends for your abecedarian shortcomings as a pedagogue by escorting me to the lake tonight to listen to the frogs croak. You could use a good dousing of Thoreau's transcendentalism to wash off that phony urbane pretense you're always putting on."

His jaw dropped. "I will not be escorting *you* to the lake, or anywhere else, for that matter."

"Afraid of me?"

"Why would I be—"

"You've never had a sweetheart, have you?"

"I'm your teacher. It's not proper."

"You can't hide behind that excuse now. School's over. You're just another Ripon rooster crowing to get my attention."

Hugh strained to control his exasperation, posing with his hands behind his back. "I do not crow, and as for your attention—"

"Let's compromise." She thrust out her elbow for him to take. "You walk me to the lake, and I'll grade your courting manner and decide if you're worthy to call on me again."

"How is that a compromise?"

She casually examined her cuticles. "Let's see, how many months are you behind on your bank loan payments?"

His ears turned red. "Have you been riffling through the confidential files at your father's office?"

"I help him with the paperwork."

"You are Jezebel's evil daughter!"

"You should work on your nasty swearing habit." She snapped her fingers for him to hitch up. "Let's take the path around the mill. More romantic. Unless you'd prefer to buy me a pastry on State Street?"

Denied an escape, Hugh grumbled and marched her out of the school-house, slamming the door behind him. He walked with her in silence toward the Old Gothic Pond on the shadowy outskirts of town. She glanced at him periodically, as if to check the pressure level of the steam building against his eardrums. She may have extorted him into squiring her around, but he wasn't about to partake in sweet musings. So, together they forged ahead, he forcing the pace and she applying the brakes. After twenty minutes of lurching along like two mismatched carriage horses, they reached the pond and he released her elbow. "There, have it at. Listen to the croaking to your heart's delight."

Jennie stared across the water at a distant grove.

Her sudden pensiveness confounded him. "What are you looking for?"

She didn't answer but kept a keen watch on the far bank.

"Did you not hear me?"

She brought a finger to her lips for silence. After a minute passed, she whispered, "Do you see those fireflies over there?"

He looked around. "What fireflies?"

Lights flickered in the woods ahead. His shoulders tightened with alarm. He pulled her behind him and yelled at the skulkers. "Who goes there?"

The lights inched closer—a voice called out. "Are you awake?"

His belly knotted. Had those slaver bushwhackers tracked him this far north? He balled his fists. He shot no border ruffians in Kansas, but he damn well knew how to scuffle. "Come out and show your faces!"

"Are you awake, my son?" the voice asked again.

"What the devil are you jawing about?" he demanded.

Fifty men with six-foot-high torches burning whale oil emerged from the brush and surrounded him. They wore blue robes with capes and black glazed hats. One waved an enormous flag blazoned with an eyeball.

Professor Daniels split their ranks and stepped into the flickering aura. "Hugh, it's a simple question."

Hugh's brow pinched as he spun Jennie around. Did she conjure these mantled knights by employing some pagan craft of female sorcery? He fingered the professor's cape to make sure it was real. "What are you doing out here dressed like a Musketeer?"

"Allow me to introduce my comrades, the Wide Awakes."

Hugh suspected Jennie arranged this prank for his last school day. "I'm not falling for it."

Yet the professor sounded solemn. "We prepare for what is coming."

Daniels was knee-deep in more skulduggery, Hugh realized, and the geologist had used Jennie to lure him here to test his resolve in abandoning the Abolitionist cause. When she shrugged to confess her complicity, he felt betrayed. "That's the only thing you've been honest with me about."

Jennie placed a hand on his arm to beg his forgiveness.

He brushed it away. "All this time, I thought the slavers were the enemy." Livid, he confronted the professor. "You planted her in my class."

"She's one of us."

Hugh walked off. "I told you. I'm done with that work."

"Good men cannot stand aside, Hugh. We need you."

He stopped and wheeled. "Need me for what?"

"The Democrats are recruiting gangs to intimidate our citizens to vote against Lincoln in November. We can't let them steal the election."

"This isn't Kansas," Hugh reminded him.

"War is coming," the professor warned. "The Federals will arrest us if we drill in the open. So, we've formed a secret militia under the guise of a social club."

"You're sanctioning vigilantism."

"The Fugitive Slave Act is immoral."

"It's still the law."

Jennie went on the attack. "You taught me the righteousness of the Boston Tea Party."

"That was different," Hugh said.

"The British law imposing a tax was technically legal," she said. "But it was also an affront to God's higher law."

Hugh saw these Abolitionists that Daniels recruited were armed with clubs "You plan to fight the government with baseball bats?"

"When the South breaks from the Union," the geologist promised, "we know where to requisition weapons."

"Looks as if you've got plenty of help. You don't need me."

The Wide Awakes tightened their circle to muffle the professor's next whispered revelation. "Sherman Booth has done God's work. And now, our friend, *your* old friend and fellow conductor, languishes in the Federal Custom House in Milwaukee for freeing one of the Lord's souls from his chains."

It all made sense now. That's why Daniels mustered this nocturnal band of minutemen to accost him. Earlier that year, Booth, the traveling speaker, newspaper editor, and temperance advocate, proclaimed he would hang every Federal agent in Wisconsin before he allowed fugitive slaves rounded up and returned to their masters below the Mason-Dixon Line. Hugh admired Booth's convictions, but the firebrand was hellbent on sparking a civil war in the state. Booth had sat incarcerated for months for helping a Missouri slave refugee named Joshua Glover escape from bounty hunters. Hugh surveyed the determined faces of the Wide Awakes and understood the drastic measure the professor had in mind. "The newspapers say that jail is a fortress."

Daniels held that same peaceful and confident gloat of divine sanction that Hugh witnessed four years ago in John Brown's glassy gray eyes. "The Israelites faced such odds against the Canaanites," the geologist said. "But the Almighty rode in His chariot with them on Mount Tabor, and not one Canaanite was left alive." He pulled a Colt revolver from his belt and handed it to Hugh. "There's a train ticket inside the barrel. Ten of us leave for Milwaukee in the morning. I pray you will join us."

Hugh felt Jennie take his hand and pulse it, begging him to trust them.

* * *

Hugh had never visited a city so vast and populous as Milwaukee, but Daniels allowed him no time to stop and admire the wide streets bordered by gabled Greek revival homes or sample the bratwursts peddled by the barkers in front of their saloons. From the train station, the geologist led him briskly across the bridge and past bustling shipyards along the river. Ten Wide Awakes, disguised as dockworkers and armed with pistols under their rain ponchos, followed them. The city residents, in a festive mood, celebrated the Fourth of July by ringing bells and shooting off fireworks. The frenzied crowds and rocket bursts made Hugh even jumpier. He and the Ripon men moved against the tide of roisterers who surged in the thousands along the banks for picnics and rowing contests. They turned onto Wisconsin Street, and before them stood their target, looming over their heads like a Venetian palace.

The Federal Custom House.

He counted three floors, each with seven arched windows that offered riflemen a sweeping view. The thick granite edifice took up an entire block, and even on this holiday, the trade emporium was a hive of activity. Lawyers, bankers, merchants, and cops hurried in and out of an entrance winged by towering cast-iron doors. On the portico steps sat the customs collector sunning himself next to the local United States marshal. Local Wide Awakes had warned the Ripon men that the portly German lawman was a former boxing champ. Each day, like clockwork, the marshal and the customs agent lunched at an outdoor table set near the door. Getting past those two would be like squeezing between champion veal calves at the county fair.

The professor nudged him forward. "Go walk a scouting circuit."

While the other Wide Awakes hid behind a delivery tram, Hugh crossed the street, dodging carriages, and ambled over to the Custom House steps. He whistled a tune and tipped his hat to the marshal, who replied with a loud fart while shoveling another spoonful of beans into his mouth.

"You got something to declare?" the customs agent asked.

Hugh pressed his folded palms across his heart. "I wish to declare the love of the Almighty for all humanity."

The customs agent unbuckled his belt, loosened it a notch, and shooed Hugh aside. "You're blocking the rays, rube."

Hugh tipped his hat again in a request for forgiveness and shuffled a step to the left, allowing the porker to broil unimpeded. He played the bumpkin. "This here place a church?"

The marshal nearly choked on his mouthful of spiced sausage. "You ain't too bright, are you, *dummkopf?*"

"No, sir, I reckon not. Whadya keep inside here?"

The marshal aimed his fork at the sky. "You see that window above you?"

Hugh lifted his gaze to the second floor, trying not to act overly interested. His heart sank. A Federal marine armed with a rifle stood guard behind the pane. He scanned the other windows and saw marines posted in those rooms, too. An entire company looked to be camped up there.

The marshal belched. "That's where we lock up the loiterers and riffraff. You stick around much longer, I'll give you a week's tour."

Hugh tipped his hat and withdrew. "The Lord be with you, gentlemen."

The marshal spat a shred of gristle. "Amen and *wiedersehen.*"

Hugh hoofed it back across the street, taking a different route so as not to alert the marshal to the Ripon men watching in the shadows. He hurried into an alley and circled around behind another building to rejoin the professor and the Wide Awakes. The Abolitionist conspirators crowded around him.

"They're holding Booth on the second floor," Hugh whispered.

"Just one flight up," Daniels said. "We will have no trouble—"

"Marines guard him. A lot of them."

Distraught, the professor braced a hand against the wall. "Someone betrayed us." The Wide Awakes argued among themselves and vowed to ferret out the traitor, until the professor signaled for their silence. "Our plan is impossible now. We must return to Ripon before the federals discover we're here."

The men slumped and prepared to backtrack to the train station.

Hugh had done his damnedest to avoid this preposterous mission, but once the professor and Jennie dragged him into its web, he wasn't prepared to waste an entire week of preparation. Daniels, as usual, was a short fuse, quick to take a flame but just as hasty to give up if the string fizzled. Hugh pondered their predicament and saw a longer-term victory seeded in this temporary setback. "Wait!" He called the professor and his men back. "Where's Booth's wife?"

Daniels tilted his head to the side and pursed his lips, impatient to get out of the city. "She lodges at the Newhall House hotel. Why do you ask?"

Hugh ordered one of the Wide Awakes, "Go fetch her. The rest of you round up a crowd. Tell them Booth plans to make a speech today."

Daniels's eyes widened. "He can't give an oration from jail."

"We'll see about that." Hugh was determined to show the professor that he was not the callow boy who had been the butt of the Free-Soilers' jokes in Iowa. He instructed the courier, "When you've delivered Mrs. Booth to the Custom House entrance, make yourself scarce. I'll take it from there."

An hour later, Hugh, accompanied by Mrs. Booth and a rowdy crowd of Abolition agitators, marched up the Custom House steps and shouted at the second-floor window. "Sherman Booth, the citizens of Wisconsin wish to be inspired by your speech on this Day of Independence!" His hollering and the applause drew scores of holiday carousers and onlookers, until the street in front of the Custom House teemed with Republican partisans, dockhands, and general malcontents clamoring for an appearance by the jailed editor.

The marshal burst through the doors to track down the rabble-rouser causing the commotion. He saw Hugh on the soapbox and turned redder than a skinned sausage. "You're the pissant who ruined my lunch."

Hugh played along as if Booth had secreted to him a copy of the speech announced in the newspapers. He pulled a handwritten letter from his breast pocket and waved it at the window. "Sherman, I can't read your handwriting! Throw down the manuscript of your speech and Mrs. Booth will translate it!"

The Abolitionists stoked the agitation of the motley assembly by chanting their hero's name. "We want Booth! We want Booth!"

To his horror, the marshal saw he'd soon have an angry mob on his hands if he didn't comply with their demands. He clambered down the steps and rammed a finger into Hugh's chest. "What are you trying to stir up?"

"The newspapers promised us a sternwinder." Hugh monitored the windows where the marines stood loading their muskets. "We're entitled to hear Booth on Independence Day!"

The jeering protesters, simmering into a boil and fueled by jugs of beer passed around by the unrecognized Wide Awakes, surged onto the steps and demanded to see Booth, who had been denied the opportunity to give an oration for fear he would incite violence. Pressed against the doors, the marshal looked up and reluctantly nodded for the marine to bring Booth to the window.

Moments later, Booth appeared and waved to his wife, drawing a cheer that rattled the panes. No doubt fearing he'd be torn apart if he delayed, the marshal ordered the marine to unlock the iron-bars grille and hinge it open.

Booth bathed in the adulation as he stuck his pale, high-crowned head out the window and waved to his admirers. During his many months of incarceration, his once stocky torso had thinned beyond recognition and his thick beard and bushy eyebrows had turned so feral that his nose resembled a doorknob on a gate overgrown with vines. "My fellow Americans!" he shouted. "Liberty this day for all Negroes!"

The street shook from the approving clamor, and Hugh seized the moment to heave a ball of twine into the upper window. He shouted at Booth, "Your manuscript! Send it down!"

Booth caught the orb of cord, tethered the pages of his written speech, and lowered them. Hugh displayed the transcript to the chanting crowd. "Who here wishes to read aloud the words of the great Sherman Booth?"

Several of Booth's admirers begged for the honor until one Abolitionist spotted a dignitary trying to thread a path to the courthouse. "Justice Paine!"

Hugh rushed the pages into the hands of the bewildered Chief Justice of the State Supreme Court. Paine scowled and bristled at the attempt to draw him into the political fray. He pushed Hugh aside. "Read it yourself!"

Hugh made an exaggerated bow and pranced through the crowd, hamming it up like a carny barker to make the marshal think he was a harmless buffoon. "I hereby declare this meeting of the Sherman Booth Appreciation Society open for business! As its first order of agenda, I nominate Justice Byron Paine as president of the club! All in favor say 'aye'!"

The delirious throngs, more tipsy by the minute from the free holiday beer, boomed their approval despite Paine's disapproving glare. Hugh seconded his own nomination. Assisted by Mrs. Booth's translation of her husband's script, and in Paine's trapped presence, Hugh bellowed Booth's speech while the jailed paladin stood at the window preening and grasping his lapels to pose for the sketch artists. When finished, Hugh began babbling incoherently, citing passages from Cato the Elder and interspersing them with lines he remembered from his reading of Shakespeare's *A Midsummers Night's Dream*.

The confused crowd, insistent on hearing more from Booth, threw rotten vegetables at Hugh. Caught in the epicenter of this mayhem, Hugh shielded his head with his coat and dashed for the Custom House wall. He shouted loud enough for the marshal to hear: "Who brought the ladder?"

The crowd hushed and retreated several paces.

Hugh stood abandoned, slouched in an affection of humiliation while praying his ploy to convince the marshal to ease his vigilance worked.

The merrymakers dissipated, cursing the lunatic who thought he could break Booth out of jail with a ladder in full view of the marshal and the marines. Newspapermen had rushed from their offices to cover the long-expected rescue of the Abolitionist editor, but they shook their heads in disgust at having wasted the holiday afternoon. Several boys pelted Hugh with bottles. Above the fray, Booth waved off the fracas and returned to his cell, infuriated and convinced his drunken friend had ruined his panegyric.

The marshal lingered on the steps, laughing at Hugh's sorry predicament. He motioned Paine over to enjoy the spectacle of Hugh splattered with tomatoes and offered the justice a cigar. "Rarely do I get to share a stogie with an Abolitionist president, Your Honor."

Paine enjoyed a long puff and snickered at Hugh being abused like a dunking target at a county fair. "Who is that clodhopping harlequin?"

"Apparently," the marshal quipped, "the brains behind the treacherous conspiracy to rescue Booth."

Converged upon by newspaper correspondents, Paine billowed like a topsail and held them off with the lit end of his cigar, as if fearing the Democrats had set a trap for him. "My god, *The Sentinel* will roast me on its editorial spit tomorrow. At great expense to the taxpayers, I've turned this building into an arsenal to fend off hayseeds? President Buchanan will tear a hole in my hide for requesting a company of marines for this nonsense."

"I told you we didn't need them," the marshal said. "My boys can handle the security here just fine."

Paine slammed his top hat onto his head. "I'm sending the marines back to their barracks tonight."

As Hugh skulked off along Wisconsin Street, pummeled by jeers and debris, he suppressed a smile of triumph.

* * *

A month later, Hugh stood eating a bratwurst at the end of the Schneitzal Saloon bar, a position he chose for its direct view of the Custom House across the street. After he rushed those walls on the Fourth of July begging for a ladder, the newspapers lampooned him as a hapless crackpot copycatting John Brown's raid. One caricaturist even depicted him as a bumpkin Don Quixote tilting at a windmill fashioned in the likeness of Booth. He had waited these weeks until the hubbub blew over, then returned to Milwaukee this morning as planned, relieved to find his notoriety in the city short-lived.

City folk had short memories, but he was going to make certain they would not soon forget him for *this* day.

He ordered another beer, nursing it to prevent the barkeep from becoming suspicious and kicking him out for loitering. He checked his watch. When the second hand struck noon, he peered through the window and traced the crush of men pouring out the Custom House doors on their way to the many establishments along Wisconsin Street for lunch. In the bustle, he spotted Irving Bean, one of his Abolitionist comrades from Ripon. Bean pulled out a handkerchief and wiped his lower lip.

One swipe ... one guard.

Bean swabbed his left cheek—the lone guard was a deputy marshal.

Hugh felt a surge of elation. His playing the dolt with Justice Paine had worked. The marines were gone, and the entrance had been left unguarded. He threw a quarter on the bar, tipped his hat to those around him, and hurried out of the saloon. From his periphery, he saw Professor Daniels on the opposite side of the street, marching toward the doors with grim determination. He avoided eye contact with the geologist and timed his ascent of the Custom House steps so they would both enter together. Inside the lobby, they saw muskets stacked against the far wall, set at the ready should the marshal need to deputize citizens. Bean and another Wide Awake named Morton, carrying a large documents satchel to hide his cargo, joined Hugh and Daniels. Provided cover by the clamor of commercial negotiations on the main floor, the four men climbed the stairs unnoticed.

On the second floor, the deputy marshal, armed with a musket, sat in front of the cell. Hugh walked up and reached into his own breast pocket. The deputy leapt to his feet, expecting Hugh to pull a pistol. Instead, Hugh drew a calling card. "Easy there, constable. You're a might skittish today."

The deputy squinted at the name on the card, unable to make out the small type. "No one said anything about visitors."

"Oh, we're not visitors," Hugh said. "Read the back."

Confused, the deputy rested the butt of his musket between his feet as he fumbled with the card, turning it over several times while searching for a script that might explain why these strangers stood before him.

"Poor eyes?" Hugh asked.

"They ain't what they used to be," the deputy admitted.

"Maybe we can help," Hugh said.

Bean grabbed the deputy's arms from behind. The musket fell to the floor.

Hugh kicked the weapon to the corner and pulled a revolver from his coat. "*This* is my calling card."

When Hugh lifted the brim of his slouch hat, the deputy recognized him. "You're that Ripon hick! Fool! You've walked right into your own prison! The marshal has the only key. And he's three blocks away."

Smiling, Morton reached into his breast pocket, flashed a key, and unlocked the cell door.

The deputy's eyes bulged. "Where did you get that?"

"We made it by stuffing a wad of wet bread crumbs into the lock," Hugh said. "Do we need to render you senseless?"

The deputy reluctantly shook his head as Bean tied his hands.

Hugh kicked open the cell door and imitated the marshal's heavy German accent. "Booth! Time for your beans and sauerkraut!"

Booth lay on his cot with his eyes closed. "You know I don't eat that dreck!"

"Ah, but I give you no choice! You eat beans or you face a firing squad!"

Outraged, Booth bolted from his cot to launch a fiery editorial protest when he found Hugh and the professor laughing at him through the bars. A grin of recognition creased the editor's hairy face. He looked down the hall, saw the tethered deputy marshal in a state of agitation, and shook hands with his old friends. "You loved my speech."

"I thought it benefited from my elocution," said Hugh.

Booth slapped Daniels on the back as Hugh gagged the deputy marshal, shoved him to the cell, and locked the door. Hugh retrieved a coat and hat from Morton's satchel and gave the garb to Booth for a disguise. He whispered to the editor, out of earshot of the deputy, "You have another speech scheduled in Ripon the day after tomorrow. You don't want to miss your train."

*　*　*

Two days later, Jennie rushed through the waves of wheat on the LaGrange farm near Ripon and found Hugh scything staves into piles. "You've gone and done it now, Hugh LaGrange!"

He took a break and wiped his brow with a kerchief. "I hope you brought some lemonade."

She kicked at him but missed. "I'm not a milkmaid tending to the hired hands. Especially when they're hunted felons."

"You've been reading too many Dumas novels again."

"Federal marshals are in town. They're banging on doors and asking questions."

"I guess that's what marshals do."

"They're calling it the Booth War."

"I haven't the foggiest notion what you're talking about."

"Don't play dumb with me. It's in the papers." She unbuttoned the top latch on her blouse and pulled out a page of newsprint. She smoothed it out and read the first story above the fold. "Mr. Hugh LaGrange of Ripon is believed to be one of the conspirators who broke into the Milwaukee Custom House and released the editor Sherman Booth into the wilds of Wisconsin."

"Wilds of Wisconsin? Why those highbrows!"

"Did you do it?"

"I don't see how that's any of your concern. And *you're* the one who got me back into this business."

She stood on her toes to get into his sweating face. "I didn't suffer two years of your warbling in that schoolhouse to see you carted off to jail. You should have been smarter about it. I didn't think you would start a riot and then bring Booth back *here.* "

"That was the professor's idea. And nobody's taking me to jail. That's just your imagination running off from the bridle bit again."

"Oh, really? I guess I wasted my time coming out here to warn you that two badged gunmen are making themselves at home in your stepma's kitchen."

"What? Where's Wallace?"

"They're putting him in chains! They think he's *you*!"

Hugh threw aside the scythe. "I have to help him."

"No!" She caught his wrist to stop him. "They'll arrest you."

"I can't let Wallace take the blame."

Jennie scanned the farmland. "You stay put in those woods. When it's dark, make your way into town and sneak into City Hall by the back door."

"What are you planning?"

She ran for the LaGrange farmhouse without answering him.

Jennie sauntered into the LaGrange cabin without knocking. She found Hugh's stepmother sitting terrified at the table and Wallace cornered at the window with his hands chained behind his back. "Didn't know you had company, Mrs. LaGrange. I just stopped by to pick up a book that Mister Hugh left for me."

The two marshals, armed with shotguns, emerged from the shadows. One studied Jennie while the other circled behind her to block the door. "Mister Hugh, you say. You know Hugh LaGrange?"

"Oh, everyone knows Mister Hugh. He's my teacher."

"Teacher?"

"At the grammar school."

The interrogating marshal looked her up and down. "You're a little old for grammar school, aren't you, darling?"

She contrived a blush and lowered her eyes. "I'm not too bright, so I have to repeat classes."

"Well, you make up for it in looks."

She curtsied. "I don't believe we've met. I'm Jennie."

He pressed a lascivious kiss to the back of her hand. "I'm Marshal Saxe. My partner over there is Lewis."

"Saxe and Lewis," she said, fluttering her lashes. "Or is it Lewis and Saxe?"

Saxe sidled up to her and lifted her chin to his admiring inspection. "Lewis there is married. I perform solo."

"Solo ... does that mean you shoot so low you always miss your target?"

Saxe grinned, enjoying her flirtatious attention.

"Hey!" Wallace shouted. "I need some air over here!"

"Lift the window," Saxe said.

Jennie laughed. "Now, Marshal! You're funny! You know he can't lift that window with his hands all chained up."

Saxe grinned. "I guess I didn't think of that."

Jennie flitted to the window and lifted the pane. Before fixing the latch open, angled her head slightly at Wallace to warn him that Hugh was hiding in the woods. "There, Wally. Now you won't get the vapors."

Saxe ceased his flirting. "What d'you call him?"

"Wally," she said. "My mama says I should be proper and call him by his Christian name, Wallace, but everyone knows him as Wally."

"So, this isn't Hugh LaGrange?"

Jennie giggled. "Hugh? Oh, heavens no."

Wallace, alerted to her act, started whistling "She'll Be Coming Round the Mountain" as if to annoy the two lawmen.

"You see that?" Jennie asked. "Mister Hugh never whistles idly. He's very stern. Wally here is much more fun."

Wallace raised his whistling an octave, hoping Hugh heard his signal.

Lewis, not amused, barked at Wallace. "Stop calling for your dog!"

Wallace snorted. "If I had a dog, I wouldn't let him bite a marshal for fear the putrid flesh might kill him."

Lewis raised a fist until his partner told him to hold off.

Jennie broke the tense silence. "I can see you folks are busy, so I'll be heading back into town."

"Wait," Saxe ordered. "When was the last time you saw your teacher?"

"Why, just an hour ago."

"Where?"

"On the county road. He was hauling a load of hay to Fond du Lac." She turned to Wallace. "Shame on you, Wally, for staying in the shade here while your brother does all the farm work."

Saxe snapped his fingers to reclaim Jennie's wandering attention. "Does Hugh LaGrange take many trips to Milwaukee?"

Jennie acted puzzled. "Why would he go there?"

"Two days ago? You happen to notice he wasn't around?"

She raised another fake blush. "I'd rather not answer that question."

Saxe traded a grin with his partner. "So, he conveniently took a day off from classes."

"No, school's over for the year."

"Why did you hesitate just now?"

"I'd rather not say."

Saxe pointed at his badge. "You see this, missy? It means that I can call you before a grand jury. I don't think you want that, do you?"

"I guess not, but—"

"Don't waste my time. Just confirm your teacher was not in Ripon on the Fourth."

"But he *was* here," Jennie said.

Both marshals hovered over her. Saxe whispered to her ear, "You'd better have proof."

"He was courting me at the pond. Please don't tell my father!"

"Courting you?" Saxe asked. "You mean—"

"Bussing me. My Hugh hasn't said it in so many words, but I think he means to marry me. A girl can tell, you know."

Foiled in his investigation, Saxe kicked a chamberpot over, pulled out his keys ring, and released Wallace from the manacle chains.

That night, Hugh slipped through the rear entrance of City Hall and found the assembly room packed with Ripon residents listening raptly to Sherman Booth's impassioned speech against the Fugitive Slave Act. Hugh lurked in the shadows until someone in the crowd recognized him.

"LaGrange is here! LaGrange to the podium!"

The crowd cheered and pushed the hero of the Milwaukee jailbreak onto the stage. Grinning, Booth stepped aside and offered the center mark to his rescuer. Hugh coughed and hawed, not knowing what to say, until an unidentified woman shouted from the audience below the podium.

"They say Booth seduced a child!"

The blood in Hugh's temples spiked. "That's a damn lie spread by the Democrats to sully the reputation of this great man! You see what lengths the slavers will go to see their evils maintained? Failing to win the argument on the merits, they resort to the oldest lawyer's trick! Attacking a good man's morals? Do you really believe that Sherman Booth climbed into bed naked with his fourteen-year-old babysitter?"

"No!" a hundred voices shouted. "It ain't true!"

Hugh kept riling the crowd. "The well-paid Democrat street thugs think so little of your intelligence they expect you to swallow their lies!"

"Lincoln or war!" the crowd shouted.

Hugh was on a roll. "He was exonerated of all charges!"

"You're forgetting Booth's wife!" a man shouted. "She didn't believe him! She left him!"

Hugh peered into the fractious crowd to find the source of that scurrilous claim. "Show your face!"

"McCarty's my name, if you can't read my badge."

Hugh was stunned. Jennie hadn't told him there was a third Federal lawman prowling around the town. Now *this* marshal had heard him confess his participation in the jailbreak. He tried to put up a carefree front. "You're a brave man, Marshal, walking into the lion's den! I'll concede you that!"

"He's not brave enough to take *me!*" Booth shouted from stage left.

Unable to corral the wiry Hugh, McCarty elbowed through the crowd and leaped onto the stage to catch the larger fish. "Mr. Booth, you are my prisoner!" He slammed a hand hard onto the fugitive editor's shoulder and tried to hustle him off. Booth pulled back his coat lapel and reached for a revolver at his side. Before the Abolitionist editor could draw the weapon, McCarty pinned Booth's hand against his side and reached for his own holstered pistol.

All hell broke loose, and the hall erupted with the zing of knives and shouts to kill the intruder.

Hugh charged and floored McCarthy with a bear hug.

In the melee, several Wide Awakes dragged Booth away and hurried him out. After rolling across the stage boards in the clench, McCarty shoved Hugh aside and elbowed his way through the jeering crowd.

He was too late.

Booth had escaped with hundreds of his supporters.

Crawling away, Hugh peered into the roistering hall and saw Jennie seated on the rear balcony, watching with an amused smirk as he scrambled to avoid jail. He suddenly realized *she* had shouted that question challenging Booth's morals to goad him into publicly praising the Abolitionist editor. Now, thanks to her, he could never turn back from the Booth War. He was a fugitive, just like those slaves he had helped transport to Canada.

Jennie blew him a taunting kiss and waved goodbye.

As Hugh scrambled out the rear door before the marshal could circle back and arrest him, he turned, pointed at Jennie, and mouthed a promise above the brawl that the cunning girl had not seen the last of him.

11

TROUP COUNTY, GEORGIA
DECEMBER 1860

"Nannie, come sit with me," said Senator Ben Hill.

Thrilled to be offered the chair next to the most admired man in western Georgia, Nancy accepted the assistance out of the carriage from her elder cousin, who had been elected to the state senate earlier that year. She held onto his arm as he walked her to the grandstands built for the occasion. Shaded by a canvas panoply, the podium for dignitaries overlooked the finish line at the county's horse racing track in Mountville, a few miles east of LaGrange. Hundreds of conveyances arrived carrying ladies and gentlemen from as far away as Savannah and Selma for the faddish spectacle sweeping the South: The Tournament of the Rings.

"I'm told last month's joust at Charleston drew five thousand," said the senator. "The winning Hussars team may compete today."

Nancy patted his mottled hand. "You were born twelve centuries too late. You should have been a knight at King Arthur's Round Table."

The senator met that observation with a wistful sigh. "I wish the breaking of lances between two knights could resolve our problems."

"The election of that Illinois agitator worries you."

The senator found their reserved box and seated her. "The Northern states refuse to enforce the fugitive slave laws."

"Did Lincoln not promise to avoid meddling with our property?"

While acknowledging with a forced smile his constituents' greetings, the senator explained the political impasse to her under his breath. "The slippery fellow plays both sides. Lincoln says he personally abhors the institution, but he will not allow opposition to it to rend the Union. He swings with the wind. It will be only a matter of time before the New England Abolitionists gain control of his marionette strings and make him dance to their tune."

"So, you *are* for secession?"

"Between us ... no." The senator no longer could sustain the pretense of confidence. When the fawning spectators filed back to their seats, he slumped, dispirited. Propping his chin on his fist, he turned inward as if debating anew a question that had plagued him for years. After several moments, he lifted his shoulders by sheer force of will. "It's the Christmas season. Let's put aside our woes for the day and enjoy the festivities."

"Agreed." Nancy turned and waved at Caroline and Mary, whose husband, Peter, was taking part in the matches. Below the stands, Leila, dressed up as the Greek goddess Nike, pranced across the grass carrying around her neck the victory wreath she would award to the champion. All present put on a show of gaiety and good cheer, but Nancy felt a tension beneath this façade of merriment. Earlier that week, South Carolina seceded from the Union, and Governor Joseph Brown set a vote for the day after New Year's to choose the Troup County delegates for the state convention at Milledgeville. The town's patriarchs sponsored this joust, they said, as a diversion from the war talk.

She knew better. The tournament rules committee changed the format from the traditional runs with wooden lances and medieval helmets to a competition more practical for honing modern military prowess. The scaffolding along the track resembled the ribs of a long, unfinished barn. Bronze rings dangled from the rafters and poles, and at the finish line, effigies of Abraham Lincoln and the Abolitionist firebrand, William Lloyd Garrison, sported rings around their necks. The cavalier who sweeps off the most rings with his saber at a gallop would be the Knight of the Black Plume. That honor brought with it the privilege to present the Lincoln Ring—a less grisly proxy for the vanquished's severed head of yore—to any lady in attendance, crowning her the Queen of Love. She whispered to the senator, "You don't fool me." When he feigned innocence, she fluttered her fan over her mouth to prevent anyone from overhearing. "This is training for the home guards."

Senator Hill studied her afresh, astonished by her perceptiveness. "I mistook you for a romantic. You are as hardened as Toledo steel."

"The college taught me sewing *and* reading. The newspapers are filled with warnings that Lincoln plans to seize the armory in New Orleans if our men drill in public. And don't think I haven't noticed the Negro drivers and servants being allowed to watch at the railing. You're sending them a veiled warning."

"What warning?"

"Should another John Brown incite an uprising *here*, we have the cavalry to suppress it with bloody consequences."

He pulled out a kerchief and wiped his forehead. "Such brazen talk for a young lady. Is it any wonder you remain unmarried?"

"I hear John C. Fremont's wife informs his military decisions."

"You've been listening to the prattle of those courthouse buzzards again. And speaking of reading habits—"

"Don't tell me. Mary and Caroline snitched to you my preference for the dark Gothics. They are sniveling spies!"

"Why not enjoy proper literature, such as *Ivanhoe?*"

She straightened with affront. *"Ivanhoe?* Or, I could just confine myself to a *McGuffey's Reader!"*

The senator tipped his hat to the guests distracted by Nancy's conniption. When their attentions returned to the band marching down the track playing *Camptown Races,* the senator chided her. "There is much you can learn of our Southern cause from Sir Walter Scott."

Nancy borrowed the senator's field glasses and scanned the competitors gathered at the starting line, a furlong away. She searched the muster of riders sporting floppy musketeer hats with ostrich plumes and outlandish tunics embroidered with gold fleur-de-lis and red sunburst crosses. The men clasped gloved hands and toasted their matches with tankards of rum. Gus's brother, Gene, threw his lot into the hat, as did her cousins, Alfred and Peyton Colquitt, and John Gay, an accomplished horseman.

Brown Morgan led his Arabian from the hitching post and onto the track. *He is back from Nashville.* Her heart leapt, but a numbing sadness overwhelmed her impulse. She hadn't spoken ten words to him since the hunt four months ago. He had been away from LaGrange for weeks at a time, consumed with his litigation and accompanying Senator Hill to political meetings across the state. Her chance to win him had passed, she knew. Love withers on the vine if not picked at the hour of ripeness.

"The Scot bard understood the vital importance of Chivalry," Senator Hill said. "Society cannot hold together without it."

She half-listened to the senator's blather while dialing in the focus on the field glasses. Brown was conversing with a man she didn't recognize. Tall and broad-shouldered, the newcomer appeared to be younger than Brown, but there was the elegance of fine breeding in the manner he carried himself. Brown and the stranger looked toward her, as if divining her thoughts. She lowered the glasses and fiddled with the pleats in her gown, hoping the two men did not detect her inspection.

They are looking to my left.

She turned and saw Colonel Reid arriving in his box. Sallie was with him. The West Point princess smiled thinly and nodded to her. Then she waved at Brown and his mysterious friend. Nancy's face flushed. *So,* that *is why Brown has not called on me.*

"Our conflict with the North is as old as England itself," said the senator, still lecturing her. "The Puritans with their brutish religion of intolerance descended from Cromwell and the Roundheads. Those pike-wielding thugs swarmed King Charles and his Cavaliers—"

"Who is that man speaking with Brown Morgan?"

The senator took the glasses. "Ah, William Grant from Walton County. The son of Colonel Grant in the railroad business. Superb pedigree."

The bugler sounded the signal for the first run, and Gene Ware sped down the track, thrusting at the rings but not finding even one. The crowd met his dismal performance with a tepid spattering of applause.

Nancy rolled her eyes. "We're off to a bleak start. Gene has Gus's surgical stabbing skill."

The senator could not suppress a chuckle. "You are terrible, Nannie."

While watching where Sallie was fixing her attention, Nancy tried to will Brown to move away from the Grant fellow, but they stood talking, arm in arm, as if the best of friends.

"You'd do well to model yourself after Rowena," said the senator.

Nancy did a double-take. "Rowena?"

"She is the very paragon of Southern womanhood."

He is still babbling about Ivanhoe? She drew a deep breath to calm herself. "That placid blonde parvenu? Rowena had the comportment and personality of a damp dish rag!"

"Rowena came from Celtic-Saxon stock. Her bloodline was impeccable. Whom do *you* prefer to emulate?"

"If I must choose ... Rebecca."

"The Jewess?"

"I liked her better."

"The woman was an outcast, despised by both Saxons and Normans. Child, never forget that you are of Hill and Colquitt lineage. Our families traces back to William the Conqueror. Feared warriors, all. The Jews are an itinerant people, living off usury and unskilled in the defense of Chivalry."

"Rebecca was also a healer. At least she did something useful with her life, instead of lounging on chaises and pining for rescue. And didn't you just say Rowena was a Saxon? I thought the Saxons were mortal enemies of the Normans."

"Yes, but—"

"Well, then, which ancient tribe of savages do you wish me to worship, the Saxons or the Normans?"

Senator Hill yanked his pipe from his pocket and lit it, puffing on it furiously. "You are impossible!" He turned back to the competition and discovered to his dismay that he had missed three runs. "What is the score?"

Nancy squinted at the tally board being marked by Leila. "Al Colquitt leads with five rings taken, five fumbled."

"No Lancelots in *this* group."

"At least you have your Rowena in attendance." Nancy angled her eyes toward Sallie, who sat fanning herself several chairs away.

The senator connected her reference. *"She* has soured your mood?"

Nancy locked her gaze straight ahead. "I should relocate to the North. I cannot escape her."

Senator Hill smiled and pulsed her palm in a paternal gesture. "I will turn you into a romantic yet. Before the day is over, even."

She extended her hand in a dare. "Wager?"

He shook her hand to seal the bet. "Loser walks down Broad Street singing 'Old Gus Ware, He Ain't What He Used To Be.'"

She giggled. "I have the advantage on you. I can outrun Gus."

The senator surveyed the stands. "Where *is* that bellyaching sawbones?"

"Probably back in his dungeon boiling sheep livers for his Druidic incantations. He abhors pageantry."

The spectators rippled with anticipation as the next rider took the line.

"Down to two," the senator said. "Brown Morgan is up."

The crowd rose to cheer on the county's champion.

Nancy could hardly bear to watch. She sneaked another peek at Sallie and caught her smiling daggers back. She huffed and slumped in surrender. *He is yours. You have won. Take him, Rowena.*

The horn blew—Brown lashed his Arabian into the chute. He held his saber over his head like a Moslem ghāzī, thrusting at each dangling ring with a dexterity that stole her breath. The secret, Nancy saw, was to avoid dropping the rings collected while maneuvering the saber to pierce the next target. Brown had perfected the tactic of lifting his arm to the sky with each conquest to gather the rings on his shoulder. He swept past her without so much as a glance, snagged the Garrison ring, and took dead aim at Old Abe. The crowd exploded. Brown stabbed at the ring around the mannequin president-elect's neck, but the oval slid off his saber. The LaGrange faithful groaned.

"Eight rings," said Senator Hill. "Well done. That should win it."

Nancy studied Brown's every move as he reined his horse into a turn and cantered past the stands, tipping his hat to acknowledge the applause.

Did his eyes meet Sallie's?

When Brown rode off the track, the crowd hushed, waiting for the bugle signal for the last run. Nancy covered her ears to avoid the blare. William Grant, astride a sleek black stallion, attacked the chute. He reversed his right hand, turning the saber guard up, so that the curved edge aimed to the sky.

"Lord help us," muttered Senator Hill. "Grant appears trained in the army dragoon style of the charge. They hold their sabers like hussars."

The rings slid onto Grant's saber like doughnuts on a pastry pin. He swept up the Garrison ring and made quick work of Lincoln's ring. The crowd had barely time to comprehend what just transpired when Grant trotted over to Leila and dropped his booty of ovals onto the blanket.

Leila counted them twice and looked up, astonished. "Nine rings! A record!"

Disappointed, Nancy saw Brown smile and nod to concede the match. As Brown saluted Grant in commendation, she glanced over at Sallie, who also seemed deflated by the result.

All eyes turned on Senator Hill as he stood to call for silence. He summoned Grant to trot his mount in front of the stands to accept his honor. "Mister William Grant of Walton County, superb riding. Fairly earned, indeed." He motioned for Leila to present the Wreath of Victory.

Leila lifted to her toes to hand Grant the prize, and the handsome champion placed it around his neck. He shouted to the guests: "I humbly welcome this accolade from the citizens of Troup County! And may God save the South!"

The crowd cheered.

"As Knight of the Black Plume," the senator said, "should you so choose, you may present a ring to a lady and crown her the Queen of Love."

Grant bowed and scanned the stands. Nancy felt his gaze meet hers. He nodded and doffed his hat. *Such directness.* A mix of emotions churned inside her as he circled his horse and rode toward her. She gathered her skirt to stand and accept the ring—

He rode past her and turned his stallion to face Sallie. "Miss Reid, will you accept this ring as the Queen of Love?"

Nancy's mouth fell agape.

Sallie appeared just as surprised, flustered even. The West Point belle looked toward Brown, still mounted several yards away. Pinned by the crowd's expectations, Sallie stood and extracted the ring from Grant's sword. She curtsied and placed the makeshift crown on her head. The spectators applauded and prepared to leave the stands to retrieve picnics from their carriages.

"A moment more of your time," said Senator Hill to the crowd. "If I may?"

The guests turned, wondering what remained in the closing ceremony.

"We have another presentation," the senator said.

Brown Morgan, balancing his saber grip on his thigh in the ready position, cantered his Arabian onto the track and halted in front of the senator. Brown dismounted and, with the saber resting against his shoulder, walked to the railing. He knelt and lowered the blade until its point hovered within the senator's reach. He moved it a foot to the senator's right.

Nancy stared with incomprehension at the weapon pointed at her—the tip held a gold engagement ring.

"Miss Nannie Colquitt Hill, will you take my hand in marriage?"

The citizens of LaGrange erupted with the loudest cheer ever remembered in the history of Troup County.

Nancy's eyes flooded. Her mind went blank. She turned to the senator and saw from his beaming smile that he had given Brown his blessing on the bonding in her deceased father's stead. Nearly a minute passed before the applause eased enough to allow her to answer. "Yes, Mr. Jeremiah Brown Morgan, I will marry you." She took the ring from the saber's tip, careful not to slice her gloved palm, removed her glove, and placed the ring on her finger. She held it aloft for all to see. Mary, Caroline, and Leila threaded through the throngs to hug her. As the citizens of LaGrange crowded around to give their congratulations, she glimpsed to her left.

Sallie Reid and her father had departed.

Senator Hill offered his arm to escort Nancy on a celebratory parade to the carriages. Brown gave the reins of his horse to his steward and hurried to Nancy's other side. Together, they walked her through the gantlet of well-wishers.

The senator muttered an aside to Brown. "A ditty just came to my mind, but I can't quite recall the words."

"Which song is that, Senator?" Brown asked.

Senator Hill whistled to find his starting note. "It goes something like 'Old Gus Ware, he ain't what he used to be, ain't what he used to be, ain't what he used to be.'"

With a tearful nod, Nancy accepted his hint that she had lost their bet. In the flash of a life's turn, the romantic idealism that lay beneath her shield of cynicism was exposed, just as the senator predicted. She kissed his jowled cheek and whispered, "Thank you, my King Arthur."

He savored a deep, satisfying sigh. "You owe me a ballad, Rowena."

"I still prefer Rebecca."

"Of course, you do."

She brushed her damp eyes and joined the senator and Brown in singing the "Gus Song" as they led her to the picnic prepared in her honor.

* * *

"Nannie, come away from that door," Mary whispered to the freshly consecrated bride.

Nancy kept her ear pressed to the crack, determined to hear what Senator Hill and Brown were discussing with the election council in the study of Bellevue mansion.

"You have wedding reception guests waiting," Mary insisted.

Nancy pawed away Mary's attempt to pull her back into the grand room, where dozens of the town's society had gathered to feast on ham and jellies and offer their congratulations.

Caroline tried her luck. "People will talk."

"Let them talk," Nannie said. "I won't be shunted aside from the discussion of consequential matters on my wedding day."

Mary shot a fleeting look over her shoulder, nodding and fabricating smiles at the other women who kept looking in Nancy's direction. "You are no longer the carefree belle whose eccentricities will be overlooked. You married a gentleman of great consequence, and you must now play the part."

"You mean I must sacrifice my desires and convictions."

Mary huffed. "I thought this was what you wanted? What you had dreamed of for years?"

"I did *not* dream of becoming engaged and then a week later walking into a parlor instead of down a church aisle dressed in a plain gown of linsey-woolsey while political hacks with mud on their boots tramp in from the polling station shouting updates."

"We didn't have time to sew you a proper dress," said Caroline. "The lace store was closed for the holiday. And *you* wanted to hold the wedding before Brown left for the state capitol."

Nancy fought back tears. This day was nothing as she imagined it would be. Not just the weather, cold and rainy, had betrayed her. After South Carolina seceded from the Union, the governor called an immediate election for three delegates from each county to decide if Georgia would follow. Mississippi and Alabama were threatening to leave soon, and all anyone could talk about was war. Tomorrow, Brown planned to go with Senator Hill to Milledgeville for the convention, and they might be away for weeks. Should hostilities be declared, Brown would likely postpone their honeymoon. Such grievances she could bear if only Brown and the men kept her informed regarding affairs of state; they confided in her more when she was unattached.

She ordered Mary, "Bring that tray of cookies."

Suspicious of her intentions, Mary reluctantly retrieved the platter from the table laden with delicacies. "What are you scheming now?"

"You and Caroline follow me."

Nancy opened the door to the study and found the men—including Brown; Senator Hill; Mary's husband, Peter; and Pack Beall's husband, James—hovered over a map of the Troup County precincts. She whimsically announced, "I will not allow the Roman Senate to go hungry while they debate how to dispose of Julius Caesar."

The men laughed and eagerly accepted her offerings. Brown kissed her cheek and caressed the ring he had placed on her finger aside the engagement ring an hour ago, after the senator presided over their vows. "You must forgive me, my love, for ignoring you."

Nancy leaned her head against his shoulder, playing the dutiful wife. "So, have the wise solons of LaGrange picked Gus Ware for mayor yet?"

The men laughed at her charming innocence, while Mary, seeing through her friend's acting, rolled her eyes at Caroline.

"Not that kind of election, Nannie," said Senator Hill.

Nancy placed the cookie tray into Caroline's hands and pulled out her fan, fluttering it to hold the attention of the men. "It is beyond my ability to comprehend. But I do hope you gentlemen afford us ladies enough notice to stitch and tailor your uniforms."

"Uniforms?" exclaimed Senator Hill. "No, no, it is much too premature to talk of uniforms."

Nancy circled the table that held the election map marked with updated tallies for each precinct. "I must have been misinformed."

"Misinformed?" asked Brown. "Of what?"

"Oh, no doubt just idle gossip. One of the ladies from Newnan—who was it, Caroline?" Nancy answered her own question before Caroline could inquire what she was blathering on about—"Mrs. George Hanvey, if I recall, mentioned that the Coweta County Guards have decided upon a dark calico blue for their infantry blouses. I thought that choice might clash with the butternut pantaloons, but she assured me—"

"Coweta County is commissioning uniforms?" asked Brown.

Nancy played dumb. "Well, I can only assume—"

Brown fixed on Senator Hill with a look of apprehension. "George Hanvey is captain of the Newnan militia."

The men became agitated. Senator Hill paced the length of the study in deep thought, as if trying to decipher the meaning of this intelligence. He turned to Nancy and, with a newfound air of gravity, asked, "Did Mrs. Hanvey mention muskets by any chance?"

Nancy put a finger to her lips, now adopting a pose of befuddlement. "Muskets? Heavens, muskets?"

Brown led her to a chair, and he and the other men surrounded her as if preparing an interrogation. "Nannie," said Brown. "Tell us word-for-word what the woman said to you. This is important."

Nancy feigned a strained effort to recall. When the men, impatient, began spinning conspiracy theories and arguing among themselves, as if the women were no longer present, she winked at Mary and Caroline.

"Coweta County will vote to secede," said James Beall. "That could tip the balance."

Brown stared out the window and watched the town's citizens, bundled against the downpour, trudge along Broad Street to the polling station at the courthouse. "If Coweta goes secession, Heard County will follow."

Mary's husband, Reverend Heard, finished Brown's thought. "They will confiscate every cloth bolt from the mills on the upper Chattahoochee. And they'll have first crack at trains heading south from Atlanta with armaments."

Senator Hill raised a hand to beg a pause. "Gentlemen, we are getting ahead of ourselves." He turned to Nancy. "My dear, you must learn more of this development from Mrs. Hanvey and report back to us."

"Any way I can help the cause, but ..."

"But what?" Brown asked.

"I fear my obtuseness about this secession business might betray my real motive to Mrs. Hanvey."

Brown nodded at Senator Hill. "She's right."

Determined to educate her, Senator Hill pulled another map from his cabinet, this one of the entire state, and spread it across the table. "Each county will send three delegates to Milledgeville to vote the sentiments of their citizens. I will accompany Dr. Beall here, and William Beasley."

"So, you have already won the election?" asked Nancy. "Why are men still voting?"

"Ah, a perceptive question, my dear," said the senator. "We run together as a slate, unopposed. Yet the size of the vote is of paramount importance. A robust attendance at the polls will arm us with leverage in the capital." He cringed at the driving rain pounding against the windowpane. "This weather, I fear, will not help us in that regard."

Now genuinely perplexed, Nancy looked to Mary and Caroline for help in understanding these revelations, but they shrugged.

Brown brought his hands to his bride's shoulders to soothe her. "Electioneering is complicated. Delegates sent to the convention will declare themselves 'immediate secessionist' or 'cooperationist.'"

Nancy ignored his patronizing tone and turned to the senator. "You three will be cooperationists?"

Senator Hill nodded. "We wish to keep exploring options for compromise with the Northern states."

She pivoted to her husband. "And you agree with remaining in the Union?"

Brown hesitated. "We must attend the convention with a united voice."

Nancy tried to make sense of it all. "What is Secretary Davis's opinion on secession?" She caught the men trading worried glances.

Brown confessed, "He gave a speech in Boston opposing it."

Nancy traced her finger across the map, counting the number of counties and recalling the character of those she had visited. "The northern counties have fewer slaves. They will vote to stay."

"Most likely," the senator conceded.

"And our governor?" she asked.

Brown sighed. "Strong for leaving the Union."

"Will the secession vote by each county be made public?" she asked.

The senator diverted his glance, a sign her question hit the essence of the secession issue. "I suspect not."

Nancy pondered their conundrum. "Our music teacher in college, Professor Chase, always asked us to write on pieces of paper which sonata we wished to perform for our spring concerts."

"Nannie," said Brown. "Now is not the time—"

"After each vote, we girls compared our choices." She stood and walked around the study. "Professor Chase never selected our preference. He merely wanted us to *think* he had, believing we'd take responsibility for the sonata and practice with more diligence." She looked hard at Mary and Caroline. "We must plan a cloth drive at once."

Caroline and Mary waited with the men for an explanation.

Nancy slowly rolled up the map and returned it to the senator's cabinet. "If the governor wants secession, he will ensure the secret delegate vote supports that outcome. We are going to war."

*   *   *

Three months later, Nancy's prediction came true.

On April 26, a cloudless spring day better suited to frolicking and ice cream socials, she hurried Brown from their residence toward the Ferrell Garden terraces, where the LaGrange Light Guards were mustering in preparation to parade through town amid the cheers of their fellow citizens. At the depot, a train waited to take the volunteers to Augusta to join the Fourth Georgia infantry regiment in camp. She walked so fast she nearly had to drag him. "Bless me, Brown, I can move faster in this skirt than you can in that fighting garb. They will leave without you."

Brown slowed his steps to taunt her. "I have the requisition order for the conductor. Without it, the lads will have to pay their own fares, and they are much too cheap."

She fussed with the collar of his dark frock coat, cut to her specifications by his Negro seamstress. "Second Lieutenant Morgan, reporting for duty. Why they didn't elect you captain instead of Bobby Smith is beyond my comprehension."

"Now, Nannie, don't start up with that again."

She rested her cheek against the golden epaulet on his shoulder. "You look as dashing as a French *chasseur.*"

He clicked the heels of his new brogans and imitated a Prussian accent. "I prefer to be an Austrian *jäger.*"

She poked his ribs with the end of her parasol. "Whatever am I going to do without your worldly instruction?"

"Harass Gus, I suspect." He angled his red-plumed shako hat. "Does this cover my balding scalp?"

"Stop it." She unbuttoned the knapsack he carried over his shoulder and checked again that the cook had packed enough roast turkey sandwiches, pickles, and johnnycakes to last him three days. "You'll write as soon as you arrive in Augusta."

He turned serious. "Nannie, the darkies—"

"No more talk of this."

"Should they cause you women any trouble, summon Gus."

She puffed a jet of disgust. "We'd be kidnapped and hauled off to Jamaica before Gus got out of bed."

She felt him draw closer, as he always did when she became anxious. With his many journeys to Montgomery to help Senator Hill form a new government, she had spent no more than a week at a time with him since the wedding. He promised to be home within a month. Yet when she cornered the senator on the prediction, her sagacious cousin sounded less optimistic about the timing of the company's return. Although many counties voted against secession, Governor Joseph Brown declared Georgia's unanimous entrance into the Confederacy, joining eight other Southern states. After Charleston's capture of Fort Sumter, Jefferson Davis, the new provisional president of the Confederacy, called for 100,000 volunteers. Every train south of the Mason-Dixon Line was converging on Richmond with men spoiling for a fight.

They turned onto Broad Street, and Nancy came to an abrupt stop, horrified. Before her stood a gaggle of the city's finest, attired in every variety of uniforms imaginable and fresh from having their daguerreotypes taken as framed mementos for their wives and sweethearts. Some volunteers wore kepis with countersunk crowns, others foppish slouch hats, yet others in top hats and straw-farm monstrosities and Corsican bandannas trimmed with lace. Their jackets ranged from kersey coarse wool to fine tweed, dyed in dizzying shades of cadet gray, robin egg blue, butternut, and copper. Worse, they were armed with Kentucky flintlocks, bushwhacker shotguns, pocket Deringers, dueling pistols, Bowie knives, and a few conversion muskets that looked over ten years old. She spied Mary and Caroline, who stood speaking with one of the Guard's elected officers, John Gay. She cried, "This is *not* what we agreed!"

The soldiers and their beaus turned, drawn by her outburst.

She abandoned Brown and marched into the gathering of soldiers, fingering the sleeves of their tunics and frocks, her dismay growing with each inspection. She spun on Mary and Caroline. "We cannot send them off to battle looking like a caravan of gypsies!"

Mary tried to calm her. "Not everyone has the resources—"

"I've seen more martial discipline at a clambake," said Nancy. "We agreed to precise measurements and color." She came to Gene Ware and ran her finger along the crease of his coat, counting twelve large buttons instead of the standard fourteen. She ordered the men, "Fall in."

Brown nodded for his fellow volunteers to humor her, and they shuffled into a line. Nancy walked along their ranks. This was unacceptable. Senator Hill had confided to her that an immigrant artist named Nicola Marschall was designing a standard uniform for the Confederate armies, but her letters with suggestions for fashion to the haughty German in Alabama went unanswered. She set the stem of her parasol at the hem of each soldier's frock coat, using it as a measuring stick to demonstrate the inconsistency. She stopped in front of her brothers and shook her head at how Joe's coat came below his knees while Miles's hem was a foot shorter. "Even *you* two can't get it right? My own kin?"

"I didn't stitch it, Nannie," said Joe. "Don't blame me."

"You're marching in a sleeping gown."

Miles pointed at Brown. "Get your own house in order. He's not even wearing his peacock tail straight."

Nancy turned a disapproving eye on her husband. "Set an example, Brown."

Brown shrugged and straightened his shako.

John Gay dredged the courage to step forward. "Nannie, Governor Brown won't disburse funds for regimental uniforms. He says it's a waste of money for just a few weeks of fighting."

"That's not the point," said Nanny. "We're sending you North to represent us. I've never met a Yankee, and most of you haven't, either. Those people think lowly of us. We must not give them a reason to confirm their prejudice. LaGrange is the Cambridge of the South. You will remind them of that when you come to blows."

The men nodded, moved by her pride in their town.

Mary took Nancy's hand and motioned Caroline, Pack Beall, Leila Pullen, and the other women to her side. Mary promised the men, "When President Davis chooses a design, we will sew you new uniforms." She smiled and hugged

Nancy to mollify her nerves. "And we will have Inspector General Nannie count the threads on every coat before we send them."

The men cheered their approval, causing Nancy to blush. When at last they quieted, she took Brown by the arm and told the ladies, "Let's give our heroes a send-off they shall never forget!" She nodded to Leila.

Leila opened a haversack and pulled out a flag the ladies had quilted. Leila held one corner as Nancy unfurled its blue background to reveal "LaGrange Light Guards" above a Greek temple with three columns. Below this symbol of wisdom read the embroidered Latin warning, *In hoc signo vinces.*

"In this sign thou shall conquer!" announced Leila, translating.

The band struck up "Dixie," and the appreciative volunteers fell in, four abreast. With the women waving kerchiefs and twirling parasols on each side of the street, the Guards marched past the courthouse driven by the cheers and tearful embraces from families and friends. At the depot, they boarded the waiting train while shooting their guns into the sky for a salute.

The locomotive fired up and the departure whistle blared.

Nancy kissed Brown one last time before he stepped onto the rolling car. Pressing his scabbard against his thigh, he waved to her and shouted, "Do *not* rearrange my law books!"

She cupped a hand to her ear and shook her head, acting as if she could not hear his order. The train receded from view, and the cheering throngs dissipated and walked back toward the town square. She remained a few minutes more on the platform, lost in her thoughts, until Mary, Caroline, and Leila came up to comfort her.

"Darling," said Mary. "Join us for lunch, won't you?"

"I'll be along shortly."

Mary and Caroline hugged her and departed with Leila.

Nancy saw Gus standing alone, several yards away. He had kept his distance from the festivities. She walked toward him and caught him wiping his eyes. He turned away.

"Gus?"

He limped to a bench under the shade of a tree and sat with his head dipped to his chest.

She understood the disappointment he felt, watching his brother, Gene, and his cousin, Joe, and the other men go off to war while he, an invalid, remained behind, never to share in their glory. She sat beside him, saying nothing for several minutes. Finally, she tried to raise his spirits. "Mary's got red cake. I could be bribed to bring you a piece at the office."

He pulled out his watch and opened its lid.

"Gus, are you okay?"

He kept staring at the ticking hands. "I'm a sight better than you will be in two minutes."

She looked around, baffled by his prophecy. She stole his cane and checked the volume of whiskey in its hidden compartment. "Have you been hitting the medicine before noon again?"

As the seconds ticked off, he began singing in a breezy tempo. "'We are a band of brothers, natives of the soil. Fighting for our property we gained by honest toil.'"

She laughed, relieved to see his spirits revived, and she joined him in the new patriotic ditty that was sweeping the South. "'But when our rights were threatened, the cry rose near and far. Hurrah for the Bonnie Blue Flag that bears a single star.'"

Gus clicked his pocket watch shut and grinned the devil at her.

Before she could insist on an explanation for his odd behavior, she heard another locomotive coming from the south. She looked to the right and saw coal smoke billowing from its stack. As the train drew closer, she detected the faint thrum of voices. The locomotive chugged past the depot pulling a dozen cars filled with soldiers smartly attired in cadet gray coats and white trousers festooned with blue stripes, all armed with shiny new Springfield rifles adorned with bayonets. They waved their kepis and sang the song Gus had been humming: "Hurrah! Hurrah! For Southern Rights, hurrah. Hurrah for the Bonnie Blue Flag that bears a single star."

She leapt to her feet. "Who are *those* soldiers?"

Gus widened his smirk. "Right on time."

"Are they Regular Army?"

Gus tapped his cane on the platform boards with a suppressed glee of anticipation. "Wait for your answer."

The caboose hurtled past, crowned with a mast carrying a giant battle flag snapping in the wind. A banner strapped across the length of the caboose read: *Huzzah for the Sallie Fannie Reid Guards!*

Nancy's mouth dropped. She squinted to identify the two passengers who stood at the railing of the rocking caboose. They fluttered kerchiefs to the LaGrange residents walking back into town. "Is that—"

Gus slapped his knee and returned the waves as their wealthy neighbors chugged north. "Yes, indeed. Colonel Reid and the Princess of West Point."

Nancy recoiled—did Sallie just pucker an impudent kiss at her?

Gus levered to his feet and leaned to her ear. "Bless her kind little heart. Miss Sarah Frances Reid financed the entire West Point company with a draw on her inheritance. In gratitude, the volunteers named their unit for her. Colonel Reid and his daughter are accompanying the troops to Atlanta. The education one gains when one reads the newspapers. I suppose Miss Reid will become famous on the great battlefields in the North." He angled his cane as if shooting at a charging brigade. 'There come those hard-fightin' Sallie Fannie Reids!' the Yankees will cry as they retreat. 'Who is this gallant belle these Southerners fight so fiercely to defend?'"

Nancy, incredulous, suffered Gus's jibes as she watched the festive train disappear into the distant haze.

Gus tipped his hat and offered an exaggerated bow to rub salt in her wounded pride. He limped toward his office, tapping his cane to the tune. After a few steps, he stopped and swiveled back. "Oh, I certainly admired the cut of their uniforms, didn't you?" He blew a puff of insolent air at Nancy's cheek, imitating Sallie's distant kiss, and ambled away, singing to himself:

> "Hurrah! Hurrah! For Southern Rights, hurrah.
> Hurrah for the Sallie Reid Flag that bears a single star."

12

RACINE, WISCONSIN
JUNE 1861

Hugh projected his hunting call toward a far grove to distract the provost guards. His ruse accomplished, he slid unseen into the canoe borrowed from the Racine College dock, pulled his kepi low over his eyes to avoid being recognized, and paddled out into the unusually calm waters of Lake Michigan. Leaving the confines of Camp Utley without permission was technically desertion, but he was desperate for a few hours alone. Two months ago, the Wide Awakes from Fond du Lac County answered President Lincoln's request for troops by forming the Ripon Rifles. The armies in Virginia were sparring and feinting for a big showdown a few miles south of Washington, but here in the West, he and his Abolitionist comrades sat idle in their spiffy gray jackets and blue blouses, compliments of the legislators in Madison. The politicians ordered the new campaigning coats studded with bronze buttons engraved with the state seal and burnished to a reflective shine, evidently to give the Johnnys a clear target for lining up their musket sights.

Private Oscar Hugh LaGrange of Company B, Fourth Wisconsin Infantry, reporting again, sir, for no duty whatsoever.

He slapped the water with the oar to vent his frustration. Soldiering was already getting old and he hadn't even left the state. The extent of the regiment's action could best be summed up as one long, never-ending parade to nowhere. An hour of general drill before breakfast. Company drill from eight to ten. Battalion drill from ten to twelve. Dinner of boiled potatoes and whatever roadkill the commissary officer stumbled upon that morning. Company drill again from one to three. Battalion drill again from three to five.

Repeat the next day.

Four thousand men crammed together, four to a tent, brewed an odor that drove even the rats to the hills. At least on his Kansas invasion, the wagons kept moving. Still, he reckoned they had it better than most Union volunteers.

The lake here cooled the summer humidity and provided laundering water. Yet nerves were fraying. If the regiment didn't get the call to pack up and head East soon, the boys were liable to start the war without waiting for the Secessionists. Two days ago, the Black Hawks from Fort Atkinson refused to muster in with Company G because the sergeant of that unit was a drunken kraut who laced the beer rations with his own piss.

As the waves lapped against the canoe, he stretched out in its hollow, able to relax at last. These early evening escapes provided his only moments of peace. He discovered soon after mustering in that he was a loner by nature. Jennie should count herself fortunate to be rid of him. Sure, he felt guilty leaving without saying goodbye, but it was for the best. During their courting—*her* courting and his running, to be more exact—she tried everything short of slipping a bridle on him and tethering him to the marriage post.

He pulled a rolled newspaper from under his pant leg and shook its pages open. He cursed at seeing the masthead. That peddler's boy in town sent him the *Sentinel-Gazette*, a Democrat rag that lampooned him as a dimwit after his Booth hoax. He had just enough daylight left to get in twenty minutes of fast reading, so he scanned the headlines.

The New York Yacht Club offered Lincoln its boats for the cause. How will those rich boys survive without their sailing toys? Edmund Ruffin and Jeff Davis must be quaking in their sashes at the prospect of gimcrack schooners manned by cricket players tacking into Charleston harbor armed with their regatta trophies. He moved down the page to the report of military actions. Not much fighting yet. In Alexandria, a Southern sympathizer shotgun-blasted a Zouave named Elmer Ellsworth for ripping a Confederate flag from a hotel window. In Missouri, one of his old bushwhacking enemies from the Kansas wars, Jo Shelby, routed a small force led by Franz Sigel. And at a place called Big Bethel, near the Revolutionary War earthworks of Yorktown, a Southern unit commanded by the grandson of Thomas Jefferson roughed up a detachment of four thousand New Englanders. To add insult to that defeat, many of the eighteen Northerners were shot in confusion by their own comrades. Not an auspicious start—

A projectile caromed off his chest and splashed into the water.

He ducked under the brim. Damn! Had the Rebs made it this far north?

Another whizzing ball nearly clipped his ear. The sides of the canoe pinged from a furious fusillade. He rolled over in the hollow and kept his scalp below the gunwale. Those six-pound smoothbores in Kansas coughed out solid balls, but these grapeshot rounds peppered him like hail. Had the slavers invented a rapid-fire howitzer? Tired of being used for target practice, he screwed up the courage to launch head-over-feet into the water. He'd swim for the bank to alert the—wait, why wasn't he hearing explosions? He risked breaking the surface. On the far side of the lake, his company stood in two lines. As if on drill, they took turns loading their fists with rocks and firing them at his canoe.

"Ripon Rifles!" an unidentified officer shouted. "By the Left Oblique!"

The front rank, moving shoulder to shoulder, turned ninety degrees.

"Fire!"

The Ripon soldiers launched their loads skyward.

Hugh dived under just in time to avoid being brained. He bobbed up spewing curses. The bastards were *laughing* at him. He kicked and paddled toward the shore, determined to make the pranksters pay for the lost newspaper.

"Ripon Rifles!" the officer shouted. "Prepare for enemy charge!"

Hugh detected a familiar cadence in the voice barking those commands. He blinked to clear his burning eyes. Was that Wallace marching across the line brandishing a stick for a saber? What was his brother doing in Racine? And why was he sporting a black beaver hat and an oversized sack coat? Not only did Wallace disobey his order to stay on the farm, he had, in just minutes, disrupted what little discipline remained in the company. He doubled the pace of his breaststrokes, determined to deliver Wallace a severe beating.

Wallace didn't flinch. "Bayonets!"

With practiced precision, the Ripon men stepped onto walking staffs positioned inches from the toes of their boots and flipped them upright. They grabbed the spear props and held them at the ready.

Drenched, Hugh staggered to the muddy water line and hunted for an opening to reach his smirking brother, but Wallace's buddies kept him at bay with their poles. "Wallace, I'm gonna skin you!"

Wallace performed his best imitation of a Southern dandy. "Why, I do declare, gents, I believe yonder Yankee has his hackles raised."

Hugh spewed backwash. "Who's helping Pa with the crops?"

Wallace shrugged. "He got along fine before we arrived."

Hugh wrung the water from his sleeves. "You can just hightail it back to Ripon. Civilians aren't allowed in camp until Sunday."

Wallace shared smirks with the other soldiers. "That won't be a problem."

"Why not?"

"I just joined up."

Hugh froze. "Enough of the tomfoolery."

"I'm as serious as Jeff Davis on auction day."

Hugh surveyed the sniggering men around him and realized his brother had indeed enlisted. Enraged, he lunged at Wallace, but the soldiers held him back. Hugh clawed and shouted, "You're too young! I told you!"

Wallace shadowboxed him. "Not according to President Lincoln."

Hugh fought to escape the soldiers' restraining arms. "Who's the sonofabitch recruiting scum who took your signature for his cut of a dollar?"

"That would be me."

Hugh turned to find Halbert Paine, a former congressman and the organizer of the Fourth Wisconsin, watching the encounter from under a shade tree.

"Halbert, I don't—"

"It's Colonel Paine now."

"Colonel or not, you have no right to take Wallace without my permission."

"I've read the President's proclamation. Any able-bodied man qualified for the militia may volunteer. Wallace here assures me he is seventeen and—"

"One brother from a family's enough," Hugh insisted.

Colonel Paine removed his campaigning hat to suspend the formality of his rank. "Hugh, it's only for a few months. Think how you'd feel if you were in Wallace's shoes. You can't run off and take all the glory. There won't be another chance in his lifetime."

Hugh studied his mischievous brother, who pleaded to stay with a fake pout. Against his better judgment, Hugh nodded his grudging agreement. "Looks like I don't have a say in the matter. But I won't allow him to run me roughshod with his roguery. He nearly swamped me with this shenanigan—"

"That rock barrage on your boat—stolen, I might add—was on *my* orders," said Paine.

Hugh's jaw dropped. "I'll not be played a fool and drowned on the same day!" He marched toward headquarters. "I'm taking this up with the governor."

Paine called him back. "It was their last chance."

Hugh turned. "Last chance for what?"

"To have a little fun with you."

Wallace draped an arm over Hugh's shoulder. "In my opinion, they chose the wrong LaGrange. The men voted you captain of the Rifles this morning."

Paine reached to shake Hugh's hand. "From now on, you'll receive salutes instead of peltings."

"Huzzah!" the Ripon men shouted as they crowded around Hugh. "Huzzah for Captain LaGrange!"

Hugh sheepishly accepted their slaps on his back. "I don't know whether to thank you boys or kick your asses for the misery you'll inflict on me."

Paine waved off the aw-shucks act. "If you lead these men with the same verve you just demonstrated in your marine assault, they'll be well-served." He pulled from his pocket two shoulder straps, gold-trimmed with a light blue field. "Before we stitch these on you, there's one more item of business."

"Yes, sir. I can have the paperwork finished before—"

"I'm told you possess an admirable grasp of Shakespeare."

Hugh glowered at Wallace for spreading blether about his reading habits. "I've taught his plays in school, sir. I'm no expert."

"How do you rank *Much Ado About Nothing* in the Bard's pantheon?"

"A clever comedy, but I prefer the tragedies."

The colonel paced with his hands clasped behind him. "I've never attended a performance of *Much Ado*. The thought of taking a bullet before filling out my education weighs on me."

"Sir, I'm sure the college library has a copy. If you'd care to read—"

"Not the same as seeing it performed on stage, you'd agree?"

Hugh was puzzled where this was heading. "I suppose."

Paine fidgeted, distracted, glancing at the tents on the flats above the bluff. "Some of the men have offered to entertain me with an excerpt." He turned to a private. "Remind me again which scene you fellows chose?"

"Act Five, Scene Four," the soldier said.

Paine seemed to enjoy Hugh's confusion. "Familiar with that passage?"

"A frivolous riff, to be honest. I'd suggest the band-of-brothers scene in *Henry the Fifth*. More inspiring for soldiers off to war."

"Too late," the colonel said. "Our troupe has been learning its lines."

Our troupe? Confounded by that absurdity, Hugh glanced at the stone-faced men, wondering when they'd found time to practice.

The colonel asked his sergeant, "Where's Jenkins?"

"Infirmary, sir. The runs."

"Curse the misfortune! He was our Claudio, was he not?"

"Aye, sir, and he had the role down pat," the sergeant said. "He would have made Edwin Booth green with jealousy."

"Damn shame," the colonel muttered as he scanned the ranks. "Anyone here know Claudio's lines?"

The soldiers shook their heads.

The colonel turned back to Hugh. "The Lord taketh, and He giveth. Captain LaGrange, why don't you fill in for Jenkins."

Hugh retreated a step. "Sir, it's been over a year since I read the play."

The colonel motioned up an orderly who delivered to Hugh a page with handwritten scribbles. "You can crib off my script."

Before Hugh could renew his protest, the men circled him.

"Sergeant Billings!" the colonel barked. "Set up the scene."

The sergeant strutted forward with his shoulders pinched back. He bellowed out the context notes as if announcing drill commands. "Sir, we are in Sicily! Enemy soldiers have surged into the city of Messina, sir!"

The colonel clapped his hands for action.

"Aye, sir!" The sergeant addressed an imaginary audience. "And the ladies in Messina scheme to find husbands! Days of nonsense have ensued, sir! Claudio and the beautiful Hero have fallen in love and plan to get married! But the villain, Don John, has slandered Hero with false charges! Hero has fainted! The wedding has been called off! The family of the bride is pretending that Hero died from shock. As we enter Act Five, Scene Four, sir, Claudio mourns Hero's death, believing he was the cause of it! To make amends to Hero's family, he has agreed to marry her cousin! They now enter the church for the wedding!"

The colonel traipsed around the inner perimeter of the circle as if a stage director. "Who plays the bride?" When the men pushed forward a blond boy, the regiment's drummer, the colonel patted the boy's head. "You forgot his veil!"

The men tucked a kerchief under the boy's cap to cover his forehead and eyes. Satisfied with the prop, the colonel signaled for the play to continue.

A squat private draped a sack coat over his head and, entering from ranks left, slouched to mimic a hunchback friar. He pulled one of his comrades to his side and whispered, "'Did I not tell you she was innocent?'"

The colonel joined in the theatrical playing Leonato, the Duke of Messina. He swaggered among the actors and skipped ahead several lines in the script. "'When I send for you, come hither masked. The Prince and Claudio promised by this hour to visit me. You know your office, brother. You must be father to your brother's daughter. And give her to young Claudio.'"

The sergeant, assigned the role of Antonio, Leonato's brother, replied, "'Well, I am glad that all things sort so well.'"

Another player came forward to speak the lines of Benedick, but the colonel cut in. He flipped up the makeshift veil covering the drummer boy's face and winked at him. "'Well, daughter, and you gentlewomen all, withdraw into a chamber by yourselves.'"

The sergeant bowed. "'Which I will do with confirmed countenance.'"

The colonel waved away the boy to go hide. When an embarrassing silence extended in wait for the next line, the colonel *tsked* the crouching private playing the humpback to rouse.

Alerted, the tardy friar squeaked, "Here comes the prince and Claudio!"

The colonel motioned Hugh forward. "On the double-quick, Claudio."

Hugh risked two uncertain steps forward, skimming the page for his lines.

The colonel crossed his arms and puffed out his chest to caricature royalty. "'Good morrow, Claudio. We here attend you. Are you yet determined today to marry my brother's daughter?'"

The soldiers opened a path to allow Hugh a glimpse of his bride. He rolled his eyes, unimpressed by the drummer boy's getup, and read his next line with little enthusiasm. "'I'll hold my mind, were she an Ethiope.'"

"'Call her forth, brother!'" the colonel ordered. "'Here's the friar ready.'"

Two privates escorted the boy bride back to their imaginary church in the round as other soldiers made bugle noises to imitate a renaissance fanfare.

"Hold off!" the colonel ordered, departing from the written scene again. "You call this stagecraft?"

"Sir?" The sergeant seemed unsure if that line was part of the play.

"The bride should be masked. Claudio must not see her face."

Hugh tapped his toe, bored. *What in hell's name is Paine up to now? The boy is veiled. Get on with it.*

"I have it!" the colonel announced. "We will blindfold Claudio! The effect will be the same."

Hugh resisted that ad-libbed tomfoolery. "Wait—"

"Excellent suggestion, sir!" The sergeant tied a bandanna over Hugh's face.

"Can you see her comely features, Claudio?" the colonel asked.

Hugh nearly gagged from the stench of tobacco stains on the kerchief. "No, sir, but might I remind the Colonel we have battalion drill in ten minutes?"

"Art takes precedent. Now, on with the show!"

Wallace bounced a pebble off Hugh's chest to alert him to his cue. "We're waiting for your line, Claudio!"

Still blinded, Hugh groused, "And how am I supposed to read it?"

The colonel sent Wallace to help his brother and signaled for the sergeant to recite Antonio's next line.

"'The bride has arrived!'" the sergeant announced.

Wallace muttered Claudio's lines into his staggering brother's ear, and Hugh repeated them in a half-hearted monotone. "'For this I owe you. Here come other reckonings. Which is the lady I must seize upon?'"

"'This same is she,'" the sergeant said. "'And I do give you her.'"

Feeling more foolish with each passing minute, Hugh hurried his next lines to get the scene finished. "'Why, then she's mine. Sweet, let me see your face.'"

"'No, *that* you shall not, 'til you take her hand,'" the colonel bellowed. "'Before this friar and swear to marry her.'"

Hugh felt the drummer boy's hand placed between his palms. The lad had skin soft as a woman's. How did the youngster avoid calluses after beating that sheepskin from dawn to dusk? He sputtered his next line from memory: "'Before this holy friar, I am your husband ... if you like of me.'"

"I hope you make a better husband than a teacher."

That verse is not in the play.

Hugh released the boy's hand and ripped off his blindfold.

Jennie stood before him in a wedding dress.

His mind went blank.

Wallace revived him with a whack on the shoulder blades. "Can any soldier here offer a reason my brother shouldn't marry this fetching lass? Other than she's twice as smart and much too superior for his lowly rank?"

Recovering from the shock, Hugh fixed on Jennie's taunting eyes, trying to divine her feelings. "Was this your idea?"

"No, but I went along with it."

"Who put you up to it?"

The circle parted and Professor Daniels appeared. "Your best man. I won't let you go to war without putting a ring on Jennie's finger. She's been with you during the worst of times, and she's the best thing that's ever happened to you. After meeting me, of course. You're fortunate I'm married, or you'd not stand a chance with her. Now, do what you know is right. We don't want you getting tangled up with those Southern jezebels."

Hugh studied Jennie's reaction. "Why would you wish to marry a man who may never come back?"

"Don't be melodramatic," she said. "Three months, at most. You'll be home before I can get decent dressings on the house's windows."

"House?" He turned to Wallace, demanding an explanation.

Wallace shrugged. "That signing bonus you asked me to put in the bank?"

"You didn't."

Wallace nodded. "A down payment on old lady Bensham's place." He plucked a small Bible from a knapsack to use for their vows. "I'm no certified preacher, but I reckon I've attended enough tent revivals to qualify in the eyes of the Lord. So, do you want to become married as a private or a captain?"

Hugh surveyed his many longtime friends around him. They removed their kepis for the matrimonial sacrament while biting back grins. He examined the shoulder boards for his new rank and returned them to his pocket. "I'm still taking orders instead of giving them, so I guess I'd better go into this conscription as a private answering to a female commander."

Jennie intertwined her fingers with his and whispered Hero's lines from the play. "'If it proves so, then loving goes by haps.'" She kissed him and stood with him in front of Wallace.

Wallace placed their hands together in the knot of binding. Winking at Jennie, he prefaced the blessing of their union with the only line he ever cared enough to remember from *Much Ado About Nothing.* "'Some Cupid kills with arrows, some with traps.'"

13

LAGRANGE, GEORGIA
JULY 1861

Gus hobbled up the porch steps of his sister Caroline's house carrying several newspapers. He limped inside and dropped the pile on the parlor table used by the LaGrange women to sew uniforms. Unrolling the most recent edition of the *Atlanta Intelligencer*, he displayed its gaudy headlines:

BATTLE OPENED AT MANASSAS
The Lincolnites Attempt To Cross At Bull Run!
They Are Three Times Repulsed With Heavy Loss!
THEY RETREAT IN GREAT CONFUSION!
Fighting Lasts Four Hours!

Nancy bounded to her feet and sent the needles and thimbles scattering. "The rumors are true! Read us the details."

Gus stored his cane on the umbrella rack and plopped into his favorite high-backed chair, set near the porch window to take advantage of the river breeze. The women gathered around, some scooting their chairs closer, others sitting on the floor. He cleared his voice as if an actor preparing a scene.

"Get on with it," said Nancy.

Gus retaliated by taking his time removing his reading spectacles from his pocket, opening and closing the case, and polishing the lenses with his kerchief. "I pay for the subscriptions to these publications. You'd think *that* might entitle me to a lemonade."

Caroline threw up her hands. "Leila, would you please be a dear and bring the pitcher from the cellarette to pour my helpless ward here a libation?"

Gus waved Leila to the task. "Oh, and whippersnapper, if a dash of spirits were by accident to fall into the glass to smooth the elocution ..."

Leila huffed. "Why am I always the one sent on errands?"

"You're the youngest," said Nancy. "It's the price you pay to sit at our feet and imbibe our wisdom. Do you think the students of Socrates and the solons of Athens complained of having to wash their tunics?"

Leila stormed off, grumbling something about harpies.

Gus rustled open the *Intelligencer* and creased the front page to frame the most important stories above the fold. He read aloud: "'General P.T. Beauregard of the Confederate forces met the Northern aggressors today and won a glorious victory.'"

"Praise God," said Pack Beall.

Mary clasped Pack's hand. "And praise President Davis for his wise choice of our gallant commanders."

Leila returned with the lemonade and threatened to drop the glass into Gus's lap before he stole it from her. He smelled its aroma and sighed, disappointed. Shrugging, he sipped to lubricate his tongue and read on. "'At dawn, the enemy approached in large force at Bull Run and attempted to cross. The scene of the battle was three miles northwest of Manassas Junction.'"

"Where is Manassas Junction?" Nancy asked.

"A few miles south of Washington capital," said Gus. "In Virginia."

"I hope Lincoln suffers nightmares from it," said Leila. "Maybe now he'll sulk back to the frontier and leave us alone."

Gus became so entranced while silently reading the written account of the battle that he forgot the women.

"Gus!" Nancy admonished. "This is not your nap time."

Roused, Gus jerked and adjusted his spectacles. "Most remarkable. Says here the battle was going against us when one of our generals, Thomas Jackson, held his position. They've given him a nickname. Stonewall. Washington residents rode out in their carriages to watch the action as if attending a carnival. Our forces sent the Northern frolickers retreating in mayhem with the Federal army across a lone stone bridge."

"How many casualties?" asked Mary.

The women shared worried glances and clasped hands.

Gus scanned the newsprint to find the tally. "Estimates for the enemy are three thousand killed and wounded. Our losses were half that number."

Impatient, Nancy leapt up to hover over Gus's shoulder. "Was the Fourth Georgia engaged?"

"There is no mention of the regiment. The wags at the tavern say our boys left Augusta too late. The War Department assigned them to an encampment near Norfolk."

The women slumped with relief and pressed their palms together in prayerful gratitude for their brave men being spared the carnage—except Nancy, who felt a mix of emotions. She was grateful Brown was unharmed, but she feared he would stew for the rest of his days over missing the field of glory.

Mary dared to speak what all were hoping. "The war is over, then."

Gus seemed less confident of that prediction. "A defeat so close to Lincoln's office. I'm sure he can smell the gunpowder, but who knows what that conniving Illinois demagogue will do next?"

Caroline glanced at the bolts of wool purchased for the new Fourth Georgia uniforms. "I shouldn't think we'll need these now."

While the other women discussed plans for a celebration to greet the returning victors, Nancy plucked another newspaper, *Harper's Weekly*, from Gus's pile. Its front page featured a crosshatched caricature of a giant snake whose tail sat on Richmond and its slithering body wrapped across the Confederate states, down the Atlantic coast and turning past the tip of Florida before heading west along the Gulf. She tried to make sense of the disturbing graphic. The snake's head climbed inland through Texas and Arkansas, and its fangs took aim at the confluence of the Mississippi and Ohio rivers. The headline read: *General Winfield Scott's Anaconda Plan.*

"Nannie," said Mary. "Should we return the fabric?"

Nancy was paying her no attention. She glared at Gus, suspecting he was withholding pertinent information. "What is the Anaconda Plan?"

Gus snatched away the periodical. "You needn't worry over that. Way beyond your comprehension."

Nancy grabbed back the paper. "Where is this published?"

Gus hesitated. "In New York City."

"And just why are you taking a Yankee newspaper?"

"The Bible says if we are to defeat the darkness, we must know our enemies."

Nancy walked around the parlor displaying the snake illustration.

Intrigued, Caroline asked her brother, "What does this depict?"

Gus reached for his cane, opened its secret compartment, and refreshed the lemonade with a jigger of whiskey. "General Winfield Scott commands the Northern forces. He has proposed a strategy to Lincoln to blockade our ports and gain control of our rivers."

Nancy pondered the implications. "Such a campaign would strangle us. We'd be prevented from selling our cotton to England and importing furniture and clothing."

Gus nodded. "Hence, the name. The anaconda slowly envelops its victims until they die of asphyxiation."

Alarmed, Nancy studied the drawing again. Her attention fell upon the mid-section of the snake. "The Yankees plan to capture Mobile and Pensacola." When Gus averted his eyes, she shook the sketching a few inches from his nose.

"Theoretically, but—"

"The rail line runs from Mobile to Montgomery, and then east ..."

"Toward us," said Mary, finishing Nancy's thought.

Nancy quickened her pacing as she ran the calculations aloud. "If the train travels thirty miles an hour ... two hundred and fifty miles from Mobile. Say the transfer in Montgomery takes an hour." She turned back on Gus. "Union troops could be here in eight hours, ten at most. Sooner if they sent cavalry straight north from Pensacola."

The other women studied her with concern, fearful the strain of the recent months had sent her over the edge.

Gus pounded his cane against the floor to put a stop to such nonsensical talk. "Lincoln is *not* sending an army into the middle of Georgia. He has no way to supply and feed such a pack of locusts."

Mary studied Nancy. "What are you suggesting we do?"

Nancy picked up one of the cadet-gray shell jackets they had stitched to-gether. She placed the jacket against her bosom, comparing the fit and calculat-ing the alterations required if—

"Absolutely not!" Gus shouted.

"But we have no militia to protect us now. The nearest force of any size is in Augusta. That's a march of ten days to reach us should we be attacked."

"Attacked?" exclaimed Caroline.

Nancy dumped a cigar box full of thimbles onto the table and positioned them in an arc to represent the eastern and southern coasts of the Confederacy. "If I were Lincoln, this is what I'd be thinking. Capture one of the obscure ports on the coast of Florida, near the Chattahoochee." With a flick of her thumb, she sent that thimble flying off the table. "Send a raiding party north. A few hundred armed men could incite a Negro insurrection here in the thousands."

Gus rapped his cane like an irate woodpecker. "I will hear no more of this!" He gathered up his newspapers and marched out.

When the door slammed, Nancy turned to assess the opinions of the others. "Well?"

"We don't even know how to load and fire a musket," said Mary.

Nancy had kept secret her shooting tryst with Brown on Orpheus Day. "*I* know how."

"You?" exclaimed Leila. "I don't believe you."

"I'll prove it."

"Where will you find a musket?" Leila asked.

Exhorted on by Nancy's demanding glare, Mary sighed and nodded to Caroline. "We might as well humor her. She will pester us with this notion until we prove the absurdity of it."

Caroline smiled and winked at Mary, hinting she had just devised an impossible proposition to put a quick end to their impulsive friend's fantasy. She offered a deal to Nancy. "Providing you can even find a gun, if you manage by some miracle to load it and hit anything of value, we'll put this militia nonsense of yours to a vote. If you miss, no more talk of it. Agreed?"

Nancy came to attention and saluted. "Meet me at the creek in the field behind Morgan Street in two hours."

Word spread fast of Nancy's planned marksmanship demonstration, and by mid-afternoon, forty LaGrange women had gathered in Harris Grove, a shaded feeding pasture just a hundred yards from the rear entrance to Gus's office. At the appointed time, Nancy walked up from Broad Street carrying a slender musket, a powder horn, and a ball pouch.

Caroline examined the markings on the gun. "That's Gus's fowling musket. How did you convince him to lend it to you?"

Nancy slid her a sly look. Before Caroline could interrogate her about the theft, she searched the field for potential targets. Her attention alighted on a jug hanging from a tree thirty yards away. "How about that one?"

Caroline squinted, then turned a nervous glance over her shoulder toward the back of the offices on Morgan Street. "That jug holds Gus's emergency stash of peach brandy. If he finds out—"

"You said I won't hit anything. So, why worry?"

Caroline looked for support in her protest, but Mary just shrugged.

Nancy set the butt plate of the stock on the ground between her feet and pulled the ramrod. "Gather around, ladies, and watch how it's done."

The women backed away, worried she was about to blow herself to smithereens. For the past hour, Nancy had rehearsed from memory the drill that Brown taught her on the Long Cane knoll. She pulled a ball from her pouch, dropped it into the barrel, and poured black powder to chase it.

"How much powder are you supposed to add?" asked Mary.

Nancy shrugged. "It's like a recipe. I measure from feel."

Leila rolled her eyes and made a gesture suggesting Nancy's head was about to go "poof."

"Here's the most important step." Nancy shoved the ramrod into the barrel to make sure the ball and powder were sufficiently compacted, like flour into dough. When she deemed the concoction perfected, she reached into her pouch again, pulled out a flint, and attached it to the hammer cock.

Mary shielded her face with her elbow. "Nannie, are you sure—"

Nancy firmed her stance and raised the musket, struggling to steady it. She didn't remember Brown's gun being this heavy. She drew a bead at the jug, imagining in her mind's eye the delicious moment when Gus's peach brandy would spray across the azure sky. As the women around her stuck their fingers into their ears, she remembered Brown's instructions. *Relax, breathe, and give no care to success. Allow the ball to find the target.* She closed her eyes and—

Boom! The shot echoed across town and the recoil drove her to her rump. When her focus returned, she found the smoking musket on the grass, ten feet away. Several distressed faces hovered over her.

"Am I bleeding?"

Mary wiped Nancy's eyes with her sleeve. "My lord."

Caroline pulled a small folding mirror from her handbag and opened its lid. If Nancy blushed from embarrassment, no one could tell. The powder explosion had blackened her cheeks and forehead. Mary and Leila lifted her. She blinked at the target. Her heart dropped.

The jug still dangled from the tree.

Several men, alerted by the shot, came running from the town square. Gus fought a path through the gawking onlookers. His striated roseate cheeks flushed. "Is that *my* musket?"

Nancy feigned outrage. "I may very well sue you for negligence in its maintenance. The gunk in this barrel nearly killed me."

Gus lurched to his heels, his cane thrumming in a paroxysm of anger. He scanned the pasture and released a held breath on finding his peach brandy unscathed. Suddenly, a painful baying erupted from beyond the creek. He walked closer to locate the source of the eerie sound and stopped, staggered by his discovery. He turned toward Nancy and aimed his shaking cane at her. "You clooted miscreant! Clotpoled dewberry! You shot my bull!"

Miffed at her inaccuracy, Nancy stayed on the offensive. "Allowing farm beasts to run wild within the town limits is a misdemeanor. But in the interest of conciliation, if you promise to restrain your feral animals, I won't file a complaint."

Gus tremored with such fury that he looked to be on the verge of spontaneous combustion. "*You* won't file a complaint? *You?*"

Nancy called over a local butcher who was watching their argument. "Mr. Willen, would you be so kind as to assist Mrs. Poythress here by delivering the meat to her home? We will be serving ribs donated by Dr. Ware for the vote tomorrow, and you are welcome to join us."

Before Gus could protest, the butcher waded across the creek and put the dying bull out of its misery with a pistol shot to its forehead.

Mary, baffled by Nancy's celebratory barbecue announcement, confronted her. "What vote?"

"For our militia."

Mary exchanged a suspicious glance with the other women. She reminded Nancy, "We agreed to take a vote *if* you hit your target."

Nancy brought a finger to her mouth and looked to the sky as if trying to recall their conversation. "I remember our agreement differently." She smiled devilishly while elevating her voice for the men to hear. "The precise terms were that we vote if I hit *anything of value*."

Mary pursed her lips at Nancy's legal cunning.

Without a hint of remorse, Nancy airily asked Gus in the presence of dozens of witnesses, "Dr. Ware, was your donated bull of any value?" Seeing Gus's jowls fading from red to purple, she picked up his musket and began walking back to Caroline's house. "I'll take that as a 'yes.'"

"My fowler!"

Nancy turned and inspected the musket in her hands. "You mean this slipshod antique? I'm confiscating it as evidence. It will be retooled and stored in our armory."

* * *

A week later, forty volunteers of the LaGrange Female Militia, smartly attired in gray cadet shell jackets, snood hair nets, and loose skirts, emerged from their new headquarters, the old one-room schoolhouse on Senator Hill's property. Some carried family muskets on their shoulders, but most were armed with broom handles painted black to mimic gun barrels.

Nancy blew Morgan's hunting horn to stir the townspeople for a parade down Broad Street to admire her company's debut. Shutters flew open and residents stepped out onto their verandas, drawn by her shouted commands and the beat of a drum. Rumors of her shooting mishap had swept across the county, but Nancy managed to turn the referendum for a militia into a vote for officers, skipping whether such an unprecedented and unladylike unit should exist. Mary and Caroline capitulated to her stubborn insistence, knowing there was no stopping her. There was also the inconvenient truth that they were enjoying their newfound notoriety.

With Nancy at her side, Leila led the column in ranks of four while carrying a banner stitched with their roster of officers:

Mrs. Jeremiah Brown Morgan, Captain
Mrs. Peter A. Heard, First Lieutenant
Miss Aley Smith, Second Lieutenant

Miss Andelia Bull, First Sergeant
Miss Augusta Hill, Second Sergeant
Miss M.E. Colquitt, Third Sergeant
Mrs. James "Pack" Beall, First Corporal
Miss Lelia Pullen, Second Corporal
Miss Sallie Bull, Third Corporal
Mrs. Caroline Ware Poythress, Third Corporal
Miss Ella Kay, Treasurer

Smirks and a smattering of tepid applause greeted the women until they reached the benches on the courthouse square called the Buzzard's Roost. One of the perching old-timers hooted and yelled to his buddies, "Lock up your bovine, gents! Here comes Nannie the Sharpshooter! Andy Jackson could have used her at New Orleans."

"Yeah," cracked another crank. "As a beef forager."

Nancy halted her column and executed a smart left-face to confront the hecklers. She zeroed in on the toothless wiseacre who tried to pin her with the nickname. "Tuskegon Gray, why haven't you joined up with the Fourth?"

"Nannie, you know darn well why. I'm too old to fight."

"You're not too old to flap your gums."

"Now, there's no cause for—"

"Given your decrepitude, you have no use for that flintlock piece you used to help paddle General Washington across the Delaware."

The men cackled and elbowed Gray for getting the worst of the exchange. Gray lifted his straw hat and scratched his bald head. "Hell's hornets, Nannie, I ain't a hundred and ten!"

Nancy reached into Gray's breast pocket and found three nickels. She confiscated the money as a contribution to the militia. "Leila will stop by your place this afternoon to pick up that weapon." She glared at the other coots, who had fallen silent, averting their eyes. "Anyone else patriotic enough to step forward and donate to the defense of the town?" The windbags shared sheepish glances. A few surrendered timid nods and reached into their pockets.

Lazarus Cofield, the proprietor of the local general store and tobacconist, ran across the street waving a newspaper. "We're famous!" As the women broke ranks and gathered around him, he caught his breath. "Copy of the *Southern Confederacy* just arrived from Atlanta. It quotes our local paper."

"Read it to us, Lazarus," said Mary.

Nancy decamped the old galoots from their roosts so that Cofield could stand on the bench for everyone to hear.

"Front page," said Cofield. "Headline: 'Gallant Belles of LaGrange Defend the Glorious Cause.'"

The women whooped and hugged themselves.

"Quiet!" ordered Nancy. "Go on, Lazarus."

Cofield pressed his reading blinkers up the bridge of his nose. "'We have learned from the *LaGrange Reporter* this week that Mrs. Jeremiah Brown Morgan, wife of Lt. Morgan of the Fourth Georgia regiment, has organized the brave ladies of LaGrange into a militia to protect their homes against the dastardly Lincolnites and their secret agents who lurk in the darkest dens of our venerable Confederacy. Such feminine gallantry recalls the grand exploits of another Georgia heroine of glory past, Nancy Hart, the patriotic spy for General Washington's colonial army, who outwitted a pack of armed Tories to defend her frontier cabin. We salute these modern Nancies of LaGrange and hereby bestow upon their company the agnomen: The Nancy Hart Rifles.'"

As deafening cheers erupted around her, Nancy stood lost in her thoughts, confused. Their vote took place four days ago. How did an Atlanta newspaper learn of their plan so quickly? And who in town knew of ... Wait, the college lesson years ago about the heroine, Nancy Hart. She glanced across the square toward Gus's office. He stood outside his door, watching the parade. He caught her glaring with suspicion at him and hurried inside, locking the door behind him. *That rapscallion. He telegraphed the* LaGrange Reporter's *item about them to Atlanta. If he did it to humiliate me, I'll make certain his ploy backfires.*

"Nannie!" said Mary. "Are you not thrilled?"

Nannie swiped the newspaper from Cofield and scanned the article. She threw it back at him. "Brigade," she insisted. "We are not a mere company. We will call ourselves the Nancy Harts Brigade."

"We don't have enough members for a regiment, let alone a brigade," Mary reminded her. "Let's just call ourselves the Nancy Harts."

Nancy lifted her chin in a gesture of defiance. "I'm commander of this militia, and I've made my decision. 'Brigade' sounds more poetic. Besides, the town's fire brigade has only a dozen—"

"How wonderful! Is there a costume ball this evening?"

Nancy and the LaGrange women turned to find Sallie Fannie Reid and her father stepping out of the general store.

"A militia," said Nancy, icily. "Not a costume ball."

Sallie led her father across the street to examine the women's uniforms. "What a grand idea for a social club. You should start a gazebo band."

Nancy moved in to correct Sallie again, this time without mincing words, but Mary clamped a firm hand on her irascible friend's arm.

"What brings you to LaGrange, Miss Reid?" Mary asked.

While her father talked politics with the men, Sallie broke away to converse with the women. "My stock of stationery required replenishment. You will remember Captain William Grant, who honored me with the crown at the Tournament of Rings."

"We do, indeed," said Mary, tightening her grip on Nancy.

"Captain Grant has adopted such a prolific correspondence. It is all I can do to keep up with him. He leads a regiment of cavalry under the command of Colonel Nathan Bedford Forrest in Tennessee. I pray every waking hour for his safety." Sallie turned to Nancy. "And you, Mrs. Morgan, I trust your husband is at the front?"

Nancy brushed off Mary's restraint and set a musket between her skirts and Sallie. "The fighting in Virginia is more intense than in Tennessee. He has less time to take pen to paper."

Sallie held her pleasant expression, but the corners of her lips twitched. "This is the first opportunity I've had to congratulate you on your wedding."

Using her musket as an anchor, Nancy offered a stiff curtsy.

Sallie, barely suppressing a smirk, returned the gesture and turned to inspect Pack Beall's broomstick. Presently, she stiffened and sniffed. "I shouldn't keep Papa waiting. Maintaining a real company of soldiers is so costly and time-consuming, but the sacrifice is its own reward."

Nancy watched with set teeth as Sallie led her father to their waiting carriage. She looked toward Gus's office. His window shades slammed closed. Gus had still been watching her, no doubt gloating over her comeuppance. She monitored the window and, after a few seconds, saw Caroline's Negro laundress, Marie Harrison, carrying a basket of pressed shirts and pants toward the rear entrance of Gus's office. What was *she* doing making afternoon deliveries? Nancy smiled while hatching a plan for revenge. *Gus Ware, you have picked the wrong combatant.*

14

BALTIMORE, MARYLAND
JULY 1861

Hugh hurried with Wallace past the hundreds of sullen residents who crowded the walking boards on Pratt Street. The Secesh men they passed tucked their right hands into their vest creases, as if itching to pull pistols, and the women spat at their boots and kicked at their ankles with their heels. Irked by the abuse, Hugh glanced over his shoulder at the earthworks on Federal Hill, where General Butler installed a battery of Union artillery to enforce martial law and the suspension of *habeas corpus* writs. Dozens of local Confederate sympathizers—including the mayor, city council, and police commissioner—sat incarcerated in Fort McHenry on the point of the peninsula.

Wallace kept a keen watch for the next civilian attack. "You chose an exemplary time to stroll us into this slaver cesspool."

Hugh glowered at his brother to lower his voice. He had been on edge since they arrived, and those glistening cannon barrels in the distance did little to ease his apprehension. That week, a grand jury indicted seven Secessionists for inciting a riot that left forty men of the Sixth Massachusetts dead and wounded on this very street. Mixed in with this powder keg were thousands of German and Irish immigrants just off the ships, who sulked with their own grievances in the slums that lay on the perimeters of the rail yards. Baltimore might be north of the Mason-Dixon line, but this city was just as treacherous as Richmond and Montgomery.

Wallace licked his lips. "That tavern over there looks—"

"For once, keep your mouth shut," Hugh snapped. "And your eyes pinned on those railings above us?"

"You think these Rebs are gonna just stroll out on their stoops and shoot us like turkeys? More likely they'll stab us in the back with their frog giggers or let us die of boredom in this stink-hole."

Hugh angrily kicked a rock into the street. "This wasn't my idea. Colonel Paine ordered a requisition of shoes. Let's be done with it and get back to camp before all Hades breaks loose again."

"One drink."

"No."

"I haven't grappled the rails since we left Racine. My tongue's pickled from that salted pork they feed us."

"Hasn't kept it from flapping."

"You've been all vinegar and green lemons since we voted you those stripes. Some of the boys have been discussing a recount."

Hugh stopped. "I'll save them the trouble!" He shoved his shoulder insignia into Wallace's face. "Go ahead! Rip them off and put them on! You think you can do better?"

Several locals, drawn by the outburst, turned.

Wallace waited until the gawkers returned to their strolls. "Simmer down, or you *will* draw fire on us. You need that shot of poteen worse than I do."

Hugh huffed. In the few weeks since joining up, his brother had quickly graduated from his religious fervor to become the regimental jester and forager for liquor. He resumed his vexed march on the boardwalk, not waiting for Wallace. He felt utterly exposed to sharpshooters, festooned as he was in his Prussian blue coat and chasseur cap. *Damn this saber!* The infernal scabbard banging against his thigh left a bruise the size of a baseball. Little good the blade did him. He hadn't used it for anything except roasting apples. He wasted his first month's pay on it and a Colt revolver to replace the government-issued cap pistol that couldn't hit the Wisconsin state capitol from the front steps. A small fortune squandered to be sent halfway across the country to guard the lone railroad into Washington at Relay House station, a miserable bend of B&O track twenty miles west of Baltimore.

Wallace was right about one thing, he conceded. He hadn't been himself during these past three months. Although he wouldn't admit it to the men in his command, he was homesick beyond cure and missed Jennie terribly, hadn't even given her a proper honeymoon. Worse, he feared the war would be over before he fired a shot. All this hullabaloo and lost time for nothing.

Wallace caught up. "The politicians treat us Westerners like yesterday's slop, sure, but maybe they did us a favor keeping us north of the Potomac. Those Madison scions in the Second got their noses bloodied good at Bull Run."

"They rode first-class carriage all the way to Manassas Junction. Sons of legislators. Money and family pull."

"That money and pull didn't help them run any faster from Beauregard. The papers said two hundred paid the coffin rate back to Washington."

"I'll still take my chances in Virginia rather than be stuck here on latrine duty," Hugh grumbled. "At least we'd be able to see the enemy and—" A furled parasol slammed against his chest. He heard a swish from above—a foul-smelling wave of offal came crashing onto the walking boards, just steps ahead.

Wallace pressed a kerchief to his nose to avoid gagging. From a second-story window, a woman swung a bucket and began singing "The Bonnie Blue Flag."

Hugh reached for his pistol, but the parasol at his chest slapped his hand away from the holster.

"Sir, I fear you Yankees will not survive long enough for our boys to shoot you properly on the field of battle."

Hugh's eyes traced up the staff of the parasol that had saved him from the dousing. The gloved hand holding it belonged to a tall lass with a long nose and gray-blue eyes that fixed on him with an unsettling intensity. He reckoned she could be no older than a schoolgirl, but she wore the gaudiest outfit he'd ever seen: a gold palmetto tree leaf hung from a chain beneath her chin, and a velvet band with seven gold stars creased her forehead, giving her the appearance of an Amazonian. She sported a Rebel cavalry hat, with one side brim turned up, and a CSA belt buckle cinched her slender waist.

"Are you as deficient in manners as you are in reconnaissance?" the young woman asked. "In civilized nations, speaking to a lady not of your acquaintance while in cessation of motion is unseemly."

"I did not—"

"Walk with me, and I shall do my best to deliver you across the Valley of the Shadow of Death." She glanced behind her and saw Wallace arguing with the woman on the balcony who had tossed the refuse. "Your orderly?"

"My brother, but—"

Their female rescuer hooked her arm around Hugh's elbow and pushed him onward. As they walked and dodged stares, she smiled with condescension at the insignia boards on his shoulder and sighed. "A mere captain. Why not a colonel?"

"Where I come from, we choose our officers by democratic vote, not by the number of humans we own."

She stabbed the sharp end of her parasol into the top of his boot. "Now *that* remark was uncharitable. We must find a way for you to make amends. What brings you into our fair city?"

He looked over his shoulder again, wondering why Wallace was malingering. "I'm on official military business."

An expression of astonishment creased her face. "Your superiors could spare you from flagging trains at the Relay Station?"

"Who told you of our encampment there?"

She ignored his question and held out her hand. "I am Isabella Maria. Lately of Martinsburg, Virginia."

He awkwardly accepted her hand and kissed it, not sure if that was proper etiquette.

"I see why you ascended the ranks, Captain LaGrange. You are a ready learner."

"How do you know my name?"

She smiled thinly and averted her eyes. "Will you keep a lady's secret?" When he gave a hesitant nod, she drew closer and said, "I must confess our encounter is not a coincidence."

He bristled. "You conspired with that harridan on the balcony?"

"Shame on me for saying so, but you have been the talk of the debutantes here in Baltimore since your regiment arrived. I hesitate to tell you for fear your campaign cap may no longer fit your head. You have even gained a sobriquet from your many admirers."

"A sobriquet?"

She lightly ran a finger across the decorative flourishes of his saber scabbard. "The Wisconsin Adonis."

Hugh colored crimson from embarrassment. Before he could manage a response, Wallace came rushing to catch him.

"You abandoned me!"

"I don't see any wounds," said Hugh.

"I should box your ears for—"

"It was entirely my fault." Isabella Maria examined Wallace's left hand and saw he wore no ring. "Sir, I see, unlike your brother, you are not married. How fortunate!"

Wallace stared at her, and then at Hugh, as if trying to comprehend what the two of them had been discussing.

"I was explaining to Captain LaGrange here that I am on a mission of mercy." She turned and pointed to an impressive three-story octagonal building that sat on a distant hill near the northern outskirts of the city. "That is my blessed alma mater, Mount Washington College for Ladies. I am visiting this weekend for our annual summer ball."

The sloth of these high-society Eastern customs never failed to bewilder Hugh. "In the middle of the afternoon?"

"With the recent unpleasantness, the school has imposed a curfew."

"A mission of mercy, you say?" Wallace asked.

Isabella Maria pulled a handkerchief from her sleeve and dabbed a tear. "A catastrophe has befallen us. With the war taking so many of our beaus away to the camps, we are left destitute of gentlemen to usher my so many classmates into the happiness and beatitude of society."

Hugh was eager to get away from the officious woman. "I am sorry for your predicament, but my brother and I cannot—"

"We are renowned for our punch. Cherries, ginger"—she winked at Wallace—"and a dash of the best rye ferment from the Chesapeake Bay." When Wallace's eyes flashed interest, Isabella Maria turned to Hugh and fluttered a light waft of her jessamine perfume in his direction with her fan. "Will you come to our rescue, Captain LaGrange, as I came to yours?"

Hugh tried in vain to escape her clutches. "We are due back—"

"Not until sundown," said Wallace, melting under the girl's flirtatious gaze, which darted back and forth between the two men.

"We have orders," insisted Hugh.

Wallace grinned. "We'll get the shoes. Plenty of time. Just an hour. You owe me, Hugh."

"Yes," Isabella Maria implored Hugh. "A mere hour of dancing and we will be forever in your debt."

Before Hugh could change Wallace's mind, Maria hailed a carriage and herded them to the opened door. Assisted inside, she sat between them. "Do you know the quadrille?" she asked Hugh in a coquettish challenge, tapping the tip of her parasol around his boot. "Or does your brother excel you in steps *and* valor?"

Hugh and Wallace climbed the steps with Isabella Maria and stood at the festooned entry to the Mount Washington College ballroom. Escorted inside, they stared with dismay at forty young ladies in hooped gowns adorned with fripperies and fobs. As if on cue, the belles turned toward them in greeting and fluttered their fans, creating an unsettling oscillation across the room.

There was not a man among them.

Hugh heeled a step back toward the doors. "We cannot be the only—"

Isabella Maria halted his retreat with her parasol. "You and your brother may deposit your *armes blanches* at the cloakroom."

Hugh pressed his saber to his leg for protection. "I will keep mine."

"You don't plan to dance with such cutlery swinging like the Sword of Damocles, do you?" she asked. "Why, you'll leave this floor bloodier than the road back to Washington when your General McDowell took on his retreat from Manassas."

"The battle ended in a draw," Hugh insisted.

She softened her tone. "How rude of me. You must forgive me, lording over you that tragedy. I was born with a sharp tongue, my kin tell me. I am prepared to concede that had Mr. Lincoln sent his best troops from Wisconsin, the outcome might well have been different."

Wallace unbuckled his gun belt for safe deposit. "See, Hugh, she has graciously apologized *and* accurately assessed our fighting prowess. Now, let's be introduced to our fetching hosts. Do you want word to get out that we offended the fine ladies of Baltimore? That could ignite another riot."

Hugh stood wordless, his jaw clenched.

Isabella Maria handed Wallace's belt to a black girl in the cloakroom. "Has your brother always been so skittish around the gentle sex?" she asked Wallace. "How did he ever manage to wrangle a betrothal?"

Wallace shrugged. "It's a mystery. Now, I, on the other hand, am known across north Wisconsin as the hoofer who has left more fiddlers prostrate than Davy Crockett at a Tennessee hoedown."

Isabella Maria turned back to Hugh with a taunting nod. "Captain, if you feel threatened by us Southern schoolgirls, you are welcome to reconnoiter the college grounds for artillery and breastworks. And Eliza here will guard your possessions with her life, won't you, Eliza?"

The black girl nodded blankly.

Isabella Maria caressed Hugh's forearm and led his hand to his belt buckle. He hadn't been touched so intimately by a woman since he said goodbye to Jennie. She whispered to his ear, "You have a reputation as an ardent Abolitionist. And yet you do not trust a Negress whose freedom you champion? If one didn't know better, one might consider you a hypocrite."

Hugh's muscles tightened, and he drew his head back stiffly. How did she know so much about him? True, his name had been in the national papers for his role in the Booth War. Even so, the lass seemed unusually well-informed. Goaded on by Wallace's insufferable smirk, he reluctantly relinquished his holstered Colt and saber in its scabbard to the black girl, who took the weaponry without so much as acknowledging him.

"Eliza, give Captain LaGrange the check token with his number. It will put him at ease."

The black girl dropped a token into Hugh's hand.

"Now, Lieutenant LaGrange," said Isabella Maria, kidnapping Wallace by the elbow. "It is Lieutenant, isn't it?"

Wallace shot a spiteful glance at Hugh. "Private."

"Oh, how unjust!" she said. "If wit and charm demand their merits, I am certain you will surpass your elder here in rank before the next shots are fired. I recall you mentioned a deprivation of spirits on your sojourn."

Wallace's eyes twinkled. "And I recall you mentioned rye punch."

Isabella Maria directed him with a dart of her blue-mascaraed eyes toward the object of his desire. "At the far table." She leaned to his ear to share a secret. "You did not attain this espionage from me. Our chaperon, Mrs. Kennerly, keeps a devoted watch over the recipe. She is rumored to stash a bottle of Dad's Hat on the sill behind the curtain." She stole a predatory glance at Hugh, who was still instructing the coat check girl on how to hang his saber without scratching it. She leaned even closer to Wallace and whispered, "Will you do me a courtesy in return?"

Wallace sucked his dry tongue as he scouted the curtain protecting the liquid treasure. "Your wish is my command."

"Slip a tumbler of the elixir into your brother's punch, too. I have known him for so short a time, but I fear the burdens of his rank have taken a toll on his chivalry. He'd benefit from Bacchus's embrace, don't you think?"

Wallace winked at her.

Having sent Wallace off, Isabella Maria walked to the center of the ballroom and clapped her hands. "Ladies, please welcome our guests from the nether frontier of Wisconsin, where they have strived to tame the savages for our security. Captain Hugh LaGrange and his brother, Wallace. Do show them the best of our Baltimore hospitality."

The young female students stared at the two Northern brothers as if wild bears had been led into their midst.

"Now, if you will excuse me, I must retire to the dressing room to change into my gown." Isabella Maria snapped her fingers at the small orchestra of young ladies at the north end of the floor. "Until I return for the toast, a song in honor of our danseurs, please."

Before the LaGrange brothers could manage another word, Isabella Maria glided toward the side door to the changing room and disappeared. The girls surrounded Hugh and Wallace and inspected them from head to toe.

The orchestra struck up "The Bonnie Blue Flag."

Isabella Maria reappeared at the side door. "Stop! Absolutely not!" The instrumentalists fell silent. "These gentlemen may be Yankees," she said. "But they are here at my invitation! Why not the 1812 Overture instead? No one here has a particular love or hatred of Napoleon, I presume?"

Hugh, grateful for her intercession, inched a bow. As the orchestra played the rousing number, complete with horns mimicking the boom of cannons, Isabella Maria batted her lashes at the brothers and retreated again to the changing chamber.

A student whose height barely reached Hugh's middle vest button sashayed up in her expansive hoop gown and offered the two Yankees cups of punch. "Made to your order, Captain."

That assurance perplexed Hugh. "To *my* order?"

"Ah, thank you, *mademoiselle*." Wallace accepted the cups, judged their respective aromas before choosing, and handed one to Hugh. After kissing the young lady's gloved hand, he savored a sip of the punch and sighed with approval. "Please send our compliments to Mrs. Kennerly on the superb vitality of the concoction."

"Oh, I will, sir, provided you offer me the first dance."

Wallace snapped his boots together and brought a hand over his heart. "General Beauregard himself could not keep me from it."

Hugh gazed dumbstruck at his brother and the belle.

"Please raise your glasses!" Isabella Maria had returned, wrapped in the most ravishing gown Hugh had ever laid eyes upon. She appeared like a white candle consumed in a flame of scarlet red, with a pleated valance baring her alabaster shoulders in a low décolletage, tailored to cover her impressive bosom and yet force one's eyes to linger there. Her silhouette tapered to her narrow waist and exploded outward to the hemline, and her luxurious auburn hair, no longer hidden by the foppish hat, had been braided and pulled back with strands falling around her ears. As she floated to the center of the floor, she towered over her admiring younger classmates, bringing to Hugh's imagination what Boudica might have looked like holding court with her Celtic daughters.

"Misery me," Wallace, awestruck, whispered to Hugh. "Carry us both out with the tongs."

Isabella Maria accepted a glass of punch from a Negro servant and motioned the two Yankees to open the afternoon ball. "My father, a hotelier, once heard a steamboat pilot give a toast, and he often repeated it in our home. I offer it now to you, the Brothers LaGrange, who will forever be remembered in the annals of Washington College for their chivalry and grace." The students applauded, and she raised her glass. "We have not all had the good fortune to be ladies. We have not all been generals, or poets, or statesmen. But when the toast works down to the babies, we stand on common ground."

Hugh broke into a smile. This alluring woman, he conceded to no one but himself, could launch a thousand more ships than Helen of Troy.

"Captain LaGrange, will you do us the honor of the first quadrille?"

Hugh's smile vanished into a grimace of panic. "I've never danced it."

Isabella Maria clucked astonishment. "No soldier should go to war without knowing the figures of the contredanses. I will make you this promise. What you learn today shall hold you in greater stead than any military formation drill." She took his hand and placed it on her wrist. "I will demonstrate. You follow."

Wallace's punch-spiking conspirator sidled up and led him to stand opposite Hugh and Isabella Maria. Two other couples of female students filled out the square. On Isabella Maria's signal, the orchestra performed a rendition of "Le Pantalon." She launched Hugh into a maddening maze of approaches, locking elbows, twirls, and separations—all designed to allow just enough intimacy with one's partner for a whispered challenge, but no time for a response. He and Wallace resembled two wobbling planets orbited by dazzling stars.

On the third locking of elbows with Isabella Maria, Hugh asked, "You have a worldly way. How old *are* you?"

She spun off to the next dancer without answering him. Three gyrations later, she returned. "The last man who challenged my age regretted it severely."

"How so?"

He watched her float off again. He was ready to give up on the entire exasperating exercise when she whirled back for the third time and lingered.

"When I was twelve," she said, "my father insisted I was too young to join the adults at a dinner party one evening. I ran out of the house in a huff, determined to prove my maturity."

"So, you pouted on the porch?"

"To the contrary. I saddled my horse in the barn, rode it into the house, and cantered it into the dining room. Before my father could so much as peep a protest, I announced to the guests: 'Well, is my horse old enough?'"

Hugh's jaw dropped.

Isabella Maria motioned for two students to take her place in the dance. She led Hugh to one of the towering ballroom windows overlooking the city. "As to my age, I'll give you a hint." Making sure no one was watching, she retracted the curtain slightly, revealing her name and the year of her graduation engraved into the glass.

He did a quick calculation. "Seventeen?"

She shared a devious smile. "The dean would have expelled me had he discovered it. I try to leave my mark on the world wherever I go. ... Have I left my mark on you, Captain LaGrange?"

Hugh felt the heat in his cheeks rise. He tried to divert her from the topic by running his hand across the pane. "This glass is hard. What did you use?"

She pointed to her neckband.

Hugh looked closer. "Is that ... a diamond?"

She nodded. "Given to me by an admirer before he went off to join General Johnston. Did you give your wife a diamond?"

He averted his eyes, ashamed. "I couldn't afford one on a teacher's salary."

"Tell me of her."

"She was one of my students."

"Scandalous. You robbed the cradle." Seeing him choke up, she said, "You miss her."

"More than you can imagine."

She reached behind her neck, unclasped the band that held the diamond, and pressed it into his palm. "War is hard on those left behind. Many say I possess the gift of clairvoyance. I fear your belle may not wait for you."

Hugh swallowed a gasp. The gall of this tart, telling him such a horrid thing to infect him with doubts while knowing he was only months' married.

She closed his hand around the precious gem. "Send this to her."

"I cannot. Wouldn't be proper."

"Please, as a gesture of gratitude for the joy you've given me and my friends today." She turned to the window and watched the setting sun. "How the time has flown. I promised not to monopolize you. I will call for your carriage."

Being a student of science, Hugh had no use for spiritualists and charlatans who preyed on widows. Yet he did not return the necklace, hoping it might rectify his failure to give Jennie a ring. He bowed and, catching Wallace's eye, angled his head to signal they should leave. Escorted to the door by Isabella Maria, he walked to the coat check and handed the token to the Negro girl. She returned the belts with the saber and pistols. Wallace savored another drink of punch, reluctantly bowed his farewells to the ladies, and followed Hugh from the ballroom.

Isabella Maria, her eyes tearing, called Hugh back. "Captain LaGrange, if I *have* left my mark on you, do remember that wounds heal with time."

At the Relay House encampment, Hugh and Wallace stood at attention in front of Colonel Paine and the other officers of the Fourth Wisconsin.

"The warehouse?" demanded the colonel.

"Empty," admitted Hugh.

"The quartermaster confirmed this morning that two hundred pairs of shoes were stored there. I sent you at nine. When did you arrive?"

Hugh hesitated. "Just before sundown, sir."

The colonel, baffled by the lapse in time, glanced at his adjutant.

Wallace, suffering the *katzenjammer* willies from the spiked punch, stepped forward. "It was my fault, sir."

"No," Hugh insisted. "I was in command."

"You'll write a detailed report," the colonel said.

Wallace persisted. "A local lady came to our aid when we were attacked—"

"Attacked?"

"By a bucket of offal."

"By god, man, you are both lucky to be alive," snarled the colonel.

Hugh intervened. "Sir, the lady asked for our assistance at an afternoon gala at the local women's college. I felt we could not refuse without giving offense."

The colonel marched back and forth, glancing with shared secret knowledge at his other officers. He stopped and sniffed the breaths of the two men for a taint of alcohol. "This temptress of yours. Did she give her name?"

"Isabella Maria."

Hugh heard a collective groan from the ranks.

The colonel dipped his chin. After a moment of vexed contemplation, he looked up at Hugh again and ordered, "Present arms."

Hugh came to attention and drew his saber from its scabbard. A ripple of laughter assaulted him. He followed the smirking eyes of the other men to the blade he held in his right hand, vertical at his left breast. To his horror, he saw that the exquisite engraved blade had been replaced by a slender, rusty farm scythe, hammered to fit his scabbard. The abomination rattled loose from the hand guard, held by a lone screw.

"Pistols," ordered the colonel with a tone of resignation.

Hugh and Wallace unbuckled their holsters and drew their Colts. The lacquered grips on both revolvers were glued to wooden facsimiles, hallowed out and filled with packed mud to simulate the weight of the original frames and barrels. Hugh bit tongue in a fury. That fork-tongued wench with the fake tears made the switch while she was in the dressing room. How had she managed it so quickly? He turned an accusing glare on Wallace, whose weakness was to blame for all of this.

Wallace kept his eyes forward.

"How many is that this month?" the colonel asked his adjutant.

"Twenty eight pistols. Ten swords. Fifteen cases of ammunition."

Hugh rocked to his heels. "We aren't her only victims?"

"You fell prey to Isabella Maria Boyd, the Secesh Cleopatra. She uses her given name for her marks. Her fellow traitors call her 'Belle.'"

"A spy? But she is only months out of finishing school."

"She travels freely across the lines."

"How?"

The colonel huffed. "By frequenting the bed of officers and politicians from Richmond to Washington. She secures the checkpoint passwords in exchange for her favors. Travels in consort with a Negro accomplice, a servant named Eliza. We've tried to arrest the accursed hussy, but she has admirers and friends at the highest echelons in both armies."

Hugh muttered a curse. *Southern strumpets.* Treacherous creatures, he was now learning, too late. Fair Northern ladies like his Jennie would never be capable of such perfidy, using their alluring wiles to steal and run weapons to the enemy. He vowed never again to fall for their evil enchantments and clever parlor talk. *They are the Devil's own handmaidens!* He pulled out the neckband studded with the small diamond she had given him and stared at its bevels. He laid the band on a stone and stomped on it with his boot heel.

The diamond disintegrated into powder.

Wallace cleared his throat and retreated, as if fearing his brother might leave him in the same condition as the counterfeit jewelry.

Paine stepped close enough for Hugh to feel the officer's breath on his neck. "So, let's tally up the damage. You disobeyed orders to requisition shoes. You're both half-soused on cheap Confederate gut rot. You unwittingly divulged our troop strength and location to a Southern agent. And you lost your pistols and saber, which will be put to deadly use against our troops." He turned his glare on Wallace. "Ever since you arrived, the discipline in this regiment has gone to hell. I'm starting to think you're a baneful influence on your brother."

Wallace lowered his head. "Sir, I accept full responsibility and—"

"Did I give you permission to speak?"

Hugh glared at Wallace to stop before he got them into more trouble.

The colonel shook his head at Hugh. "*You* should know better. If I had the authority—"

"You have the authority." Hugh reached to rip off the stripes on his shoulder and offer himself for arrest when the colonel reached into his own pocket, pulled out a letter, and handed it to him. Hugh feared the spiked punch was still bending his perceptions when he saw the signature on the letter.

Colonel Edward Daniels.

His academic mentor recruited a regiment of Wisconsin cavalry?

The colonel stuffed the letter into Hugh's breast pocket. "You and your miscreant brother have been transferred back West." The colonel walked away muttering to his adjutant. "The cavalry is the perfect landing for two horse's asses. Let's hope they don't lose their saddles to the lady Rebs, too."

15

LAGRANGE, GEORGIA
APRIL 1862

"Nannie, are you not feeling well?" asked Mary.

While the other women practiced their target shooting in Harris grove, Nancy sat several yards away on a log, rereading a letter from Brown. She wiped a tear and coughed back the swell of emotion.

"You've not shot yet. You're always the first on the range."

"What use is it?"

Mary leaned her musket against a tree and sat. "What has he written now?"

Nancy showed her the letter. "They transferred him from the Fourth to serve as commissary officer for cousin Alfred's brigade."

"A promotion! That is grand!"

"Brown is crestfallen. He will no longer fight aside Miles and Joe. Worse, he will now have to forage for onions and potatoes to feed others who win glory on the battlefield. All because he knows how to sign a requisition contract. It's not fair."

Mary took Nancy's hands and pressed them to her bosom. "Brown will be the most popular man in the army. Come suppertime, they will bow and sing songs in his honor for having gathered such a feast."

Nancy hesitated before revealing the more troublesome news. "Word of our militia has spread around the regiments in Virginia. The men tease Brown to no end that his wife outranks him. They are so cruel! They say I've shot a bull while he hasn't even seen a Yankee."

"I'm sure Brown takes it in stride."

Nancy hung her head. "We've become a laughingstock. Even here in town, they cheer us to our faces, but I hear their snickers."

"You must chase this darkness of the spirit. We all suffer it."

Nancy looked toward Broad Street and the row of boxwoods in front of Mary's columned home. Pack Beall planted them in December to celebrate the first Christmas for the Nancy Harts. Mary had begged her not to venture out that wet and chilly day, but Pack, the senior member of their troop, was visited with a premonition of death, and she resolved to leave something behind to grow in her memory. Pneumonia crept into her lungs that very night, and she passed three days later, their first casualty. On the day of her burial, the Nancies walked aside the hearse as the honor guard.

After Pack's death, the joy faded from those early days when the Nancies rejoiced over the design of their uniforms and planned grand parades. Their hopes for a swift end to the war had been dashed, replaced by daily reports of deaths and bloody battles. After suffering devastating losses, the Confederate government passed a conscription act and took even more men from LaGrange for the armies. New Orleans remained under siege, and two weeks ago, near Corinth, Mississippi, at a wilderness church called Shiloh on the Tennessee River, 23,000 men were wounded or killed on both sides, including the gallant commander of their Western army, Albert Sidney Johnston. In Virginia, the Federals, led by a blowhard named McClellan, landed at Yorktown and now threatened to capture Richmond. The Fourth Georgia and the Army of Northern Virginia were the last obstacles in McClellan's path. If Brown or her brothers fell in battle, they might end up in unmarked graves, never to see Troup County again.

Mary embraced her. "Darling, the others look to you for strength."

Nancy watched Leila toe the twine marking the firing line and shoot at the scarecrow in the field below. Her musket ball didn't land within ten feet. Nancy shook her head, despondent over their progress. "We've been coming out here twice a week for nearly a year. Caroline hits a beehive and sends us home with stings. Two window panes cracked. And the brush fire we ignited last September almost burned Henry Bottom's barn to the blocks."

"Yes, but—"

"Mary, it's my fault." Nancy turned to whisper her disappointment. "I raised their hopes, but I have offered them no means to improve."

"You are too hard on yourself."

She dropped her head into her hands. "What are we doing? Wasting time. With Peter gone, you have your hands full running his business. I must maintain Brown's legal correspondence. Caroline feeds half the town."

Mary tried to instill her with resolve. "You cannot abandon hope now. I doubted you from the start, I admit, but you've given those of us left here a reason to pull together." She pointed to the women on the firing line. "This is not a burden for them. They live for these shooting practices. It provides them a respite and instills them with a sense of control and purpose. The college has closed, and the younger girls need our guidance. You cannot take this from them. Not when morale is so low."

Nancy shivered with apprehension. Ten months had passed since she last felt Brown's embrace. His letters came less often now, a circumstance the local postmaster blamed on the incompetent Confederate mail service and the siege at Richmond. She analyzed and decoded each word, trying to extract his heart's genuine feelings from every serif and stroke of his pen. What if she were never to have children—she glanced at Caroline—or worse, become widowed? Was she fated to spend the rest of her life caring for Joe and Miles if they returned as invalids? Such fears wormed through her mind more and more these days, keeping her up at night. And there were the blank looks of the Negroes returning from the fields in the evenings. She saw in their hooded eyes what they were thinking. They surveyed the town as if calculating how many fewer white men remained to overpower if—

"I, too, have withheld some news," said Mary. "For fear it might upset you further. But with these misgivings you suffer, I feel compelled to tell you."

"What news?"

Mary glanced with concern at the other women who kept their backs to them, loading and firing. She lowered her voice. "Peter learned this morning that a gang of Yankee raiders led by a spy named Andrews infiltrated their way to Kennesaw. They captured several of our locomotives."

Nancy shot to her feet. "Kennesaw is on the outskirts of Atlanta."

Mary stood and walked Nancy a few yards away, farther out of earshot. "For now, keep this between us. We must not panic them."

"Where are the Yankees taking the engines?"

"No one seems to know. The raiders have been cutting the telegraph lines. Rumors are rampant, but—"

"If they head south, they could be *here* within hours."

Mary brought her kerchief to her lips to hide her fretting. "We have waited too long. The men who could instruct us on military drill are gone."

Nancy paced back and forth. "Not *every* man."

"Who?" Suddenly divining her plan, Mary scoffed. "He'll never do it."

Nancy studied Caroline on the firing line. She debated if she should play the trump card she had kept pocketed for an emergency.

"Whatever you decide," Mary said. "I will stand by you."

Masking her desperation and melancholy with an upbeat act, Nancy sashayed into Gus's apothecary and pulled a bottle of whiskey from her reticule.

Gus shot her the evil eye from behind the counter. "Whatever you're selling, I'm not buying."

She pressed a fist to her lips, feigning hurt. "Is that any way to greet a neighbor bearing a gift?" She lifted the bottle's label to his eyes for his inspection.

"Old Crow. Came in on the train this morning. I had to wrestle Clemmons Cunningham for it. I'm told this is General Grant's favorite."

He studied the bottle as if it were the Holy Grail. "I suppose I could sample—"

"Let's have a chat first." She placed the whiskey on the counter and scooted it just out of his grasp. "You'll never guess who I ran into this morning."

"Don't know. Don't care."

"Anna Wagnon."

Gus paled, and his hand flinched toward the whiskey bottle.

She pushed the bottle away. "Full of life and fun. She reminds me of myself when I was, what ... seventeen?"

Gus busied himself by wiping the counter. "I think I've encountered her."

She pulled out her fan and cooled herself. *"Encountered* her? Why, I'd hardly use that description." She turned as serious as a constable's interrogator. "Cut the blarney, Gus. I know you've been courting her for three months."

Gus threw the rag at the refuse hamper, riled that he had fallen for her honey trap. "So, what if I have?"

Nancy took a step back, posing put-out by his bluster. "May-November couplings have been known to blossom. Don't be so defensive. In fact, I was planning to put in a kind word for you."

Suspicious, Gus vetted her with one eye. "Why would you do that?"

She leaned over the counter. *"You* sent that telegram to the Atlanta newspaper announcing the formation of my militia. And you know what else I know?"

"I have work to do, if you don't—"

"You did it because you are secretly proud of us."

Gus harrumphed. "You are as daft as the first day I suffered your nonsense in that classroom."

"Nothing could please me more than to see you and Anna married in the Episcopal church. You being a vestryman there, how delightful! We ladies will play host to your reception at Bellevue."

"I haven't even asked her—"

"But we need a small favor."

"Of course you do."

She snapped her fan shut and ruffled it open again, just inches from his nose. "We want you to teach us how to shoot and drill."

Gus's jaw dropped, looking as astonished as if she had just demanded his first-born. "Absolutely not! I will not sully my name by becoming involved with that town nuisance you've concocted."

"I wouldn't ask, but you seem to be the last man in town who knows the difference between a cockhammer and a nipple."

Gus reddened, shocked by her coarse *double entendres.*

She locked the door and turned the "Open" sign to "Back In An Hour." She walked into his storage room and brought out a basket of his shirts, pressed and folded. One by one, she culled the shirts and flung them on the counter. "You think I haven't seen what's been going on behind this office for the last year?"

Gus turned his back and fiddled with his herb bottles. "I don't have a clue what you're bleating about."

She balled up a shirt and hit him in the back of the head. "I wonder how sweet Miss Wagnon might feel about a husband who keeps a Negro laundress as his concubine for afternoon dalliances?"

Gus spun and took another balled shirt in the face. He fought off a barrage of laundry. "Are you blackmailing me?"

She loaded up with her last round. "You've left me no choice. A proper gentleman would have offered his martial knowledge to us months ago."

"Outrageous!"

She let fly and landed the shirt on his head. "But, then, perhaps Miss Wagnon will welcome a ready-made family from such lofty pedigree. To share you with the mulatto daughter of President William Henry Harrison and be asked to help raise Marie's three children. Well, what bride would *not* be thrilled with that prospect?"

Gus flung the shirt off his face and glanced at the rear entrance, worried Marie Harrison, the laundress, might walk in any moment from her small lodging next door. Cornered, he proposed a compromise. "One shooting lesson."

"We'll start with one and see how it goes. This afternoon, at four. Don't be late." She grabbed the bottle of Old Crow as a hostage and walked out.

Under the shade of Harris grove, Gus limped across the single line of Nancy Harts and inspected the motley array of weapons they shouldered. Grumbling curses, he corrected their posture and feet alignment with rude taps of his cane. When he reached the end of their ranks, he pulled out a kerchief and wiped his perspiring brow while shaking his head at his enforced attendance.

Nancy stepped forward. "I wish to present Dr. Ware to our first annual grand review of—"

"Enough of the prattle!" Gus snapped. "Everyone here knows who I am. And I want it recorded in the regimental record that my participation in this accursed assault on gender propriety is being conducted under protest."

"So noted," said Nancy. "Protest litigated and denied. And for the *brigade* record, I move it be memorialized that the only reason we have agreed to suffer the foul moods of this town's most notorious galoot is that he is the only man left who can tell the difference between a bullet and a bellyache."

"I second that motion," shouted Leila. "All in favor say 'aye.'"

The Nancy Harts shouted, "Aye!"

Outraged, Gus moved to leave, until Nancy's extortive smile stopped him. Trapped in a cage of his own making, he wiped his dry lips and searched in vain for something to sate his thirst.

"Private Leila. Offer Instructor Ware here a drink from your canteen."

Leila stepped out of the line and unscrewed the cap. With a mischievous smile, she gave the canteen to Gus. He monitored her with skepticism, then risked a drink, as if half-expecting it to contain poison. Nancy winked at Mary, waiting for her plan to work its effect. Gus's eyes widened as he discovered the canteen's cool water spiked generously with the Old Crow.

"You were starting our first lesson," Nancy reminded him.

Gus took another gulp before reluctantly handing the canteen back to Leila. He wiped his mouth and ordered the women, "Ranks of two!"

Three minutes later, after much negotiation and debate, the militia agreed who should stand next to whom.

"We will now learn how to stack arms," said Gus.

Nancy screeched. "Stack arms? We don't have time for that, Gus. We need to learn to shoot *today.*"

"Stack arms!" Gus insisted.

Nancy set her fists on her hips. "Why on God's green Earth should we waste time building toothpick towers?"

"Because I don't want my arse shot off like my bull's jewels were!"

Nancy could not argue that point, and for the next twenty minutes, the women practiced a series of intricate maneuvers that involved groups of four handing off their muskets and broom handles to their mates and stacking them in free-standing pyramids. Once accomplished, they learned to unstack the weapons and distribute them back to their owners just as deftly. By the end of the exercise, the Nancies were grinning and slapping backs, thrilled that they had mastered the exercise.

"Not bad," said Gus.

"Come on, Gus," said Nancy. "Lincoln would wave a white flag if he saw us now."

Gus frowned at her overconfidence. "Do you remember your Herodotus, Captain Morgan?"

Nancy couldn't fathom what he intended by such a strange question. "Some."

"King Croesus."

"The one who turned sand to gold?"

Gus motioned Leila to bring over the canteen. "So they say. Croesus consulted the Delphic Oracle to learn if he would prevail against the Persians. You remember what the priestess told him?"

"Please enlighten us, O Plato of LaGrange."

Gus licked his lips from another gulp of water-cut whiskey. "'When a mule becomes leader of the Medes, then, oh Lord, it is time to flee.'"

Nancy waited for an explanation why *that* parable was relevant.

Gus paused just long enough for the women to step closer. He leaned into Nancy and said, "I'm not sure whether you or Mr. Lincoln is more mulish."

Mary moved to break them up before Nancy could land a fist. "Gus, come now. We can't have you insulting our commanding officer."

Rescued from a thrashing, Gus rearranged his lapels and removed his hat to smooth back his thinning hair, buying time to regain his composure. He motioned Nancy and Mary back to the ranks. "Lesson Two! Leila, step forward."

Leila came up and saluted him.

"Are you wearing gaiters?"

"Gus!" Nancy cried. "What kind of question is that?"

Gus ignored her protest. "Answer me, Leila."

"Yes, but—"

"With stockings, I presume."

Mary's mouth fell open. "Gus Ware! That is most inappropriate!"

"Take off a shoe," Gus ordered Leila.

The women glared at him as if he had gone mad.

"Avert your gaze," Nancy ordered him.

Gus turned his back while Nancy lifted Leila's skirt to her ankle.

"Is the stocking wool or cotton?" Gus asked.

"Wool," said Nancy.

"Are there wrinkles in the heel?" Gus asked.

Nancy removed Leila's shoe and examined the bottom of her foot while Leila leaned on Mary for balance. Nancy looked up at Gus, stunned to find a blister forming at the bottom of Leila's foot. "How did you know?"

"Smooth the bottom of the stocking and put her shoe back on."

With the operation accomplished, Gus admonished the women. "An army wins or loses a battle on the smallest of details. A regiment that marches twenty miles will lose a third of its soldiers to straggling. The primary reason they drop out of line? Blisters caused by the bunching of socks. You should wear cotton stockings while drilling. They absorb the moisture from the humidity."

Nancy and the women nodded with a newfound respect for Gus's military knowledge, however annoyingly delivered.

Gus examined the stacked weapons and picked out two muskets. "Lieutenant Heard and Corporal Poythress to the front."

His knowledge of their ranks impressed Nancy. The old rascal had been paying attention, after all. She signaled for Mary and Caroline to step forward.

Gus handed one of the muskets to Mary. "A Springfield smoothbore. Probably used by Private Heard's grandpa in the War of 1812. Anyone hazard a guess why it's called a smoothbore?"

"They named it after you?" piped Leila.

Gus endured their chuckles. "There are no ridges forged inside the barrel." He opened the cartridge pouch on Mary's belt and pulled out a round ball with powder wrapped in paper. He bit off the end of the cartridge, poured powder into the hammer pan, and dropped the rest into the barrel.

"My lord, Gus," said Caroline. "You don't expect us to do *that*, do you? Our teeth will be black as coal in a week."

"Of course not, dear sister. You can bring the scissors from your sewing kit and snip off the ends with care while hundreds of enemy bullets buzz your head. And when we put you in the grave, riddled with holes, we will say, 'But Caroline died with such white teeth.'"

The women laughed, except Caroline, who fixed on her brother with a vengeful glare. "I suppose you won't be hungry for supper tonight."

Gus raised his free hand in a plea for forgiveness. Having survived his sister's wrath, he removed the ramrod from Mary's musket, drove home the patched ball and powder, and replaced the ramrod in its slot under the barrel. "You must take care to pack the powder tight with the ball. Otherwise, the force of the explosion will dissipate in the barrel, and the fired ball will bounce through like a marble in a tin can."

The women covered their ears as Gus pulled the hammer back and took aim at the scarecrow in the field. He stopped, seeing them cowering in his periphery. "What in Heaven's name are you doing?"

"The shots are loud as thunder," said Aley Smith. "I wish to preserve my hearing for my singing career."

Gus's jaw dropped. "Your *singing* career? Do you plan on serenading the Yankees with dulcet lullabies? How's your singing career going to prosper if you've abandoned your weapon while a thousand Billies are shooting at you? Now stand at attention! All of you!"

Aley, appalled by his rudeness, fought back a tear. Yet she and the other women did as ordered, dropping their arms to their sides. Satisfied at last with their comportment, Gus took aim, bracing against his bad leg, and fired. The scarecrow's hat flew off from the hit. The women applauded the shot while Gus examined the sight notch on the barrel.

"Shoots high. I was aiming for its stomach."

Nancy had counted off the seconds it took for Gus to load and fire. "That was more than a minute. Surely we can do it faster."

Gus cut an exaggerated bow. "Why, by all means, General von Clausewitz. The greatest military minds of the last century have studied the drill, but enlighten us on your proposed improvement."

"Well, for one, I see no need to waste time by replacing the ramrod into its slot. We're just going to pull it out again a few seconds later. Why not just stick it in the ground?"

"Brilliant!" shouted Gus. "Let's see how *that* works." He handed the musket to Nancy and stepped five yards away. "You've just loaded it. Now, demonstrate for us."

Nancy bent to one knee, spiked the ramrod into the dirt next to her, and took aim. Reenacting a shot without actually firing, she shouted, "Boom!" She reached for the ramrod to imitate loading the musket again—

Gus stumbled at her on a jagged run, flapping his arms like a wild turkey.

Startled, Nancy leapt to her feet and retreated.

Without his cane, Gus fell in a clump on the spot she had just vacated, inches from the impaled ramrod. He plucked it from the ground and grinned at her. "Aren't you going to shoot me?"

Unnerved by his unprovoked assault, however instructive, Nancy threw the musket aside. "Unfair!"

"War is unfair!" Gus struggled back to his feet with Leila's help. "You think soldiers just stand in one place during a battle firing away at each other? There are charges and counter-charges! If you lose your ramrod, you might as well throw away your gun."

Nancy, steamed at being embarrassed in front of her troops, brushed the leaves from her skirt and shouted, "Brigade dismissed!" She picked up the musket, yanked the ramrod from Gus, and marched toward Mary's house. The other women retrieved their weapons and followed her up the hill, glaring at Gus over their shoulders.

Gus stopped Leila and begged another drink. Leila smiled and pulled the canteen strap from her shoulder. The canteen was nearly within his reach when she turned it over and poured the rest of the Old Crow on the ground. Satisfied with his look of horror, she ran off to catch the other women.

Gus shrugged and squinted at Nancy. She appeared to be practicing ramming a shot into her musket's barrel while in full stride up the hill's path. Her quickness in picking up his loading lesson impressed him. "You don't want to learn the Enfield rifle?"

Nancy, her mouth ringed with black powder, turned and fired a shot over his head. He ducked and fell to his knees. She drove the ramrod back into its slot. "You're right! Shoots high!" She resumed her angry march up the hill.

16

ST. LOUIS, MISSOURI
MAY 1862

The chaos playing out on the drill field appalled Hugh. More than a thousand men from twelve new squadrons of the First Wisconsin Cavalry ran pell-mell across the grassy plain, chasing a herd of nags driven into the Benton Barracks camp that morning by Oklahoma profiteering agents. Hugh was no expert at judging horse flesh, but even he could see these dregs were underfed and scarred with hide scabs from pulling gristmill wheels and mining trolleys. Some of the pitiful animals staggered and circled in fits, no doubt doped to pass muster.

"Not exactly the Camptown Races," muttered Wallace.

After just a week in St. Louis, Hugh already regretted his transfer. Last he had read in the newspapers, the War Department shipped their old regiment, the Fourth Wisconsin Infantry, across the Gulf to help capture New Orleans. And here he and Wallace sat stuck in another city rife with Secesh traitors who flimflammed as shopkeepers during the day and turned ruffians at night. He looked toward the bustling port on the Mississippi and imagined escaping. "When's the next steamboat leaving?"

Wallace comforted him with a mocking hand to his shoulder. "This is it for us, Hugh, unless you want to give the artillery a go. Welcome to your gory bed, or to victory."

"Something that tavern maid whispered into your ear last night?"

"Robbie Burns. A school teacher-turned-warrior like you should know his Scots poetry."

"Warrior? What a crock of hogwash. We haven't fired a shot at anything more sinister than a squirrel."

Wallace picked up a stick and drew slashes in the dirt to mark the battles they'd missed since volunteering last July. "Fort Sumter ... Ball's Bluff ... Bull Run ... Fort Donelson ... Mill Springs ... oh, and that dustup at Shiloh."

Hugh refused to take the bait. His brother knew how to get under his skin by recounting the campaigns fought by other armies and the promotions received by battle-tried officers. "Another word and—" Hugh turned to see a horse galloping toward them.

The bearded rider yelled, "Charles Darwin has shed more light on the workings of the world than all the theologians combined!"

That shout stirred a shiver of boyhood recall.

Perched atop a magnificent black Arabian, the arriving officer wore a dark blue campaigning jacket under a flamboyant fire-red cape, and he had pinned a metallic eagle to the brim of his black felt hat. The fellow seemed an awfully inviting target for enemy snipers. Hugh couldn't fathom who this Napoleon impressionist might be—until he saw the sardine-epaulet with a silver eagle on the rider's shoulder.

His old geology instructor.

Edward Daniels pulled to a halt and saluted the LaGrange brothers with a hairy grin. "The doctrine of Evolution has removed in every thinking mind the last vestige of orthodox Christianity. Darwin has not only stated, but demonstrated, the inspired writer knew nothing of this world, nothing of the origin of man, nothing of geology, nothing of astronomy, nothing of nature. The Bible is a book written by ignorance at the instigation of fear."

Hugh remembered the author of those claims from his lessons. "Ingersoll. You quoted him in your lecture on the *Truth in Rocks.*"

Daniels tumbled from his saddle with the nimbleness of a rheumatic gnome. He groaned from his sore thighs as he waddled up to embrace his protege. "You were always my best student."

Hugh lifted his hat and scratched his head, still trying to get accustomed to the eccentric geologist in a uniform. "Professor Daniels … I mean Colonel."

"Can you believe it? Together again on the Great Crusade for Negro Liberty. We will yet avenge Bloody Kansas. I wrote the governor requesting your return to me as soon as I received my commission. At last, we can finish what that buffoon Buchanan prevented us from accomplishing."

"You remember Wallace."

Daniels studied Wallace with a quizzical frown. He brightened from the shock of recognition. "Little Wally! Hugh brought you to class."

"He's grown a foot," Hugh said. "But he's still a brat."

Wallace cut an awkward salute. "Sir, it's my duty to report that my brother here would never have survived the war this long without my protection. A legion of scheming jezebels waylaid him in Maryland and—"

"The Colonel has no time for such nonsense!" Hugh snapped.

Wallace winked at Daniels with a promise he'd finish the story later.

Daniels walked his horse in a half circle to observe his regiment choosing their mounts in the field below. "Lads, I have drawn up plans for a campaign that will cleanse Missouri and Arkansas of the Secesh devils before month's end."

Hugh was skeptical the men could be ready. "That's only three weeks."

"Hannibal crossed the Alps in sixteen days."

"Yes, but—"

"With elephants."

Hugh feared his old mentor was conflating academic learning with military training. Most of his fellow troopers hadn't sat astride anything friskier than a plow horse, and many had volunteered for the cavalry only because their families were wealthy enough to pay the livery fees. Now, those few who managed to wrangle the animals with ropes didn't know how to saddle or mount them. Some led the horses to fences to use the top rail as a ladder. The sad, cracked saddles didn't have underbelly straps, so the recruits grabbed manes to hoist themselves up—only to slide straight to the ground. The spectacle resembled more a rodeo clown show than a cavalry drill.

"Fine soldiers, all," said Daniels, beaming with pride. "Good Republicans."

Wallace squinted. "Sir, what are they carrying on their lanyard clips?"

Daniels shrugged. "Broomsticks. We're still waiting for a shipment of sabers from Cairo. Should be here any day now."

"And carbines," said Hugh, hopeful.

Daniels shook his head. "The legislature requires patriots forming cavalry regiments to help foot the bill. I'm not a wealthy man. Besides, this war will be over soon." When Hugh slumped, disappointed they would fight without Spencer repeaters, the colonel tried to lift his spirits. "I have a gift for you."

"A gift, sir?"

The colonel reached into his breast pocket and displayed two epaulets with gold leaves. "Congratulations, Major LaGrange."

Hugh stared in disbelief at the insignias.

Wallace held an epaulet on Hugh's shoulder. "I must find a seamstress. I hear most of them frequent Kuhlage Tavern."

Hugh slapped Wallace's hand away and protested to Daniels, "Sir, I'm not a veteran of battle, but I've seen enough drilling back East to know those men aren't ready to fight."

"Then get them ready. We ride for Cape Girardeau." Daniels unclasped his dispatch haversack and pulled out several pamphlets. "Cavalry tactics manuals. I haven't had time to study them. One written by Poinsett. Another by St. George Cooke. They read like ancient Greek to me."

Hugh's interest lingered on a slender leaflet in the bunch, only a few pages of handwritten notes stitched together. "What's this?"

"An unpublished treatise by a Rebel colonel from Georgia named Joseph Wheeler. An officer in the barracks who knows him gave it to me. No doubt this Wheeler knave forced one of his concubine chattel to transcribe it, being as he is from that lazy plantation class of scoundrels. A shrimp of a man, they say, barely passed the height requirements at West Point."

"Where is Wheeler now?" Hugh asked.

"Last I heard, he rode with Bragg at Shiloh. Fightin' Joe—that's what they call him—is probably preoccupied with burial detail after Grant and Sherman left ten thousand of Sidney Johnston's slavers writhing on that field."

Hugh kept it to himself that thirteen thousand of their own comrades were felled there, too. He tucked the Confederate officer's manual in his breast pocket and handed the other tracts to Wallace for reading later. Perhaps they might learn something about the enemy's ploys and stratagems.

Daniels saluted the two brothers and mounted. "Oh, and Hugh."

"Yes, sir."

"You and Wally had best get to the corral and choose your war stallions."

Hugh scanned the drill field and saw only a few picked-over nags left.

"First come, first serve," said Daniels with a roguish twinkle in his eye. "You can leave your pay chits for the horses and saddles with my adjutant."

* * *

A cloud of dust trailed Wallace as he caught up with the regiment on the Old Bloomfield Pike, two hundred miles south of St. Louis. He saluted Hugh and Daniels and reported his findings from his scouting foray. "The Swamp Rangers are camped just across the river."

Blood rushed to Daniels's cheeks. Excited by the prospects of his first fight, the colonel stood in his stirrups and studied the low ground that sloped west toward the St. Francis River, a tributary that formed the border between Missouri and Arkansas. "You are certain?"

Wallace nodded as the troopers at the front of the column hung on every word of his report. "I cornered a ferryman in a piss-hole town there. He said that devil Jeffers guards a ford called Chalk Bluff."

"How many men are with him?" Hugh asked.

Wallace shrugged. "I saw maybe a dozen smoke chutes from their tents. I'd say a company, no more."

Daniels tacked his horse, manic for a charge. "By Jehovah's ghost, we've got them now! That whoreson of Delilah will feel the heat of Hell's eternal fires!"

"There's even better news," Wallace said. "Cotton fields along that river teem with slaves picking the bolls. We can free them."

The colonel slapped Hugh on the back. "Did you hear that, Hugh, my boy? When that slaver Jeffers surrenders, we'll force him to walk back to St. Louis accompanied by God's Chosen People singing spirituals. Give the command for the trot. Close up the ranks."

Wallace's report spread quickly down the column. The troopers hooted and unsheathed Bowie knives, spoiling for their first draw of Rebel blood.

Hugh refused to join in their celebration. Daniels hadn't afforded him sufficient time to drill the regiment on even the most basic maneuvers, and he had only skimmed Wheeler's manual of tactics. These greenhorns couldn't execute a column-to-rank-line formation, let alone a complicated oblique-left and oblique-right split on the flanks that would be required to encircle an encampment. They might outnumber the enemy, but the Rebel leader, William Jeffers, was a veteran dragoon of the Mexican War. Jeffers and his Secesh bushwhackers, though armed mostly with shotguns, pistols, squirrel rifles, and frog giggers, had terrorized the Missouri bootheel for more than a year. The man knew how to fight, and fight dirty.

Daniels, finding Hugh unconvinced, preached fortitude. "Lad, do not lose resolve at our hour of glory."

The familiar knot gripped Hugh's gut, his sure sign something was amiss. "Sir, our orders from General Marmaduke are to scout in Missouri only. Jeffers may have set his encampment across the state border to bait us."

Daniels huffed, annoyed at being reminded of his superior's demand they avoid entering Arkansas. "We are in hot pursuit. If every scofflaw is allowed to ransack towns and scamper off unscathed across the threshold, we will never be rid of them." He rode closer and studied Hugh. "What happened to my brave Free Stater who rescued Dr. Booth from that Milwaukee jail?"

Hugh dipped his chin to his chest, shamed by the suggestion he had become too tentative.

"The sun is setting," Daniels warned. "If we don't hurry, darkness will cost us our victory."

Hugh looked to Wallace for support in his plea for caution, but his brother slapped at his revolver handle to show his eagerness to get on with the assault. Outranked and outnumbered, Hugh snapped an order for his junior officers to relay the command. "By the Fours! On the trot!"

The officers sat motionless with blank stares.

"Damn it!" Their failure to remember even the simplest of preparatory commands exasperated Hugh. "Four riders in each rank! One horse width between ranks! When I call for the gallop, double the breadth between ranks, or the horses in the rear will balk at the hoofs of those in front! Is that clear?"

Ambivalent salutes answered his scolding.

Daniels hung back with his adjutant. "Godspeed, Major LaGrange."

As the other officers rode off to rejoin their squadrons, Hugh realized Daniels did not plan to lead the attack. Hugh glared an accusation of betrayal at Wallace for not supporting him in his protest against the raid. Finally, Hugh raised his hand to signal the advance.

Not one trooper moved.

The bugler displayed his horn to Hugh to complain that regimental protocol had been ignored. "Major, shall I play 'Charge?'"

"I think not." Hugh struggled to bottle his anger at the absurdity of the entire enterprise. "You see, Private, a loud tinny noise extended for several seconds tends to be counterproductive to a surprise attack." He snapped his reins to lead the column toward the Arkansas border.

Twenty minutes later, Hugh and Wallace reined up at the river, their mounts sweating and spent from the gallop to beat the setting sun. The column came staggering up behind them with all order of formation abandoned.

Hugh squinted into the dimming light to make out the Rebel camp across the water. Daniels carried the regiment's only pair of field glasses, but he remained at the rear, watching from afar. Best as Hugh could tell through the smoke haze, the Rebs had placed no guards on the heights. He held his champing troopers at bay while he cantered closer to the edge of the Chalk Bluff ford and its white clay beachhead. Rubbing dust from his bleary eyes, he scanned the breadth of the river and cursed. The ferry barge he hoped to use to transport his troopers to the enemy's camp sat moored on the far bank. Incensed by that lack of reconnaissance, he reeled on Wallace. "Did you not see *that* on your excursion?"

Wallace shrugged, but Sergeant Stephen Nichols, a tall Choctaw Indian, sized up their predicament and leapt from his horse without orders and dived into the river. Another private joined him. Before Hugh could call them back, they swam to the barge and floated it back to the Missouri side.

"How deep?" Hugh asked the soaked troopers.

Nichols shouted, "I don't think the horses can—"

A sharp crack echoed across the river.

Hugh felt a ball whiz past his ear. *They found us out.* The ground pinged with puffs from gunfire. He froze. The spooked horses reared.

"We can't stay here!" Wallace cried.

Hugh was about to lash out at Wallace for stating the obvious when he heard a groan. Behind him, his next in command, Lieutenant Phillips, spiraled in his saddle and fell. The officer rolled down the embankment and stopped near the hooves of Hugh's horse. Hugh dismounted and turned Phillips over. A ball had pierced his throat. Hugh searched the mash of his troopers thrown into disarray. Daniels was nowhere to be found. Should he call retreat? In his first action? *No. I'd rather die.* He shouted an order to dismount. "Every fourth man! Loop the horses! Companies A and B! Follow me on the barge!"

Those troopers not assigned to guard the horses dodged the Rebel fire as they scurried with Hugh to the riverbank. He and Wallace saw mud sacks on the barge used for ballast. They threw the sacks to the bow, hoping for some protection from the enfilade. While the two brothers rowed, a dozen troopers behind them leapt into the water and pushed the barge toward the far bank as they swam. Peppered by Rebel balls clinking off the sides, a young private huddling in the barge panicked, leapt to his feet, and fired his revolver at the Confederates hiding behind the trees. A bullet struck him in the thigh. He fell backwards and screamed. Wallace pulled a bandanna from around his neck and fashioned a tourniquet to stanch the trooper's hemorrhaging artery.

At last, the barge careened onto a submerged sandbar near the far bank.

Hugh dived into the waist-deep water and waved his pistol. "With me!"

His troopers fanned out and scampered up the hillside while shooting at the Swamp Rangers. The steep elevation caused most of their shots to sail over the Rebels' heads. In the woods on the crest, Hugh spotted an officer sporting a wide-brimmed slouch hat and swinging a dragoon saber while screaming orders. He wore stars on his collar.

Jeffers.

His hand shaking with anticipation, Hugh aimed his revolver and fired.

Jeffers ducked—the bullet grazed his raffish headgear. The Rebel commander glared a promise of payback while muzzle-loading his pistol, but before he could ram the ball home, the Wisconsin troopers converged on the row of brush held by the Missouri bushwhackers. Jeffers, in danger of being cut off, shouted for a retreat. He and his ruffians hightailed it to their horses and scampered off before Hugh could get off another shot. The Federal troopers chased them with a shouted volley of huzzahs.

Wallace, his face black from gunpowder, came running and held his brother's hand up in victory. "Go tell the Spartans!" The troopers, unfamiliar with the Herodotus verse, stared with incomprehension at Wallace.

Hugh shoved away his brother's hand, in no mood to revel after the melee. He walked across the debris searching for wounded and asked Wallace for the condition of his most competent officer. "Phillips?"

Wallace lost his grin and shook his head.

Colonel Daniels, rowed across the river by his adjutant, came bounding up the hill pumping his fist. "A brilliant victory! We did ourselves proud!"

Hugh's pulse still raced from the brief but ferocious ordeal. He asked for casualty reports. As the fingers of his sergeants went up with their counts, he turned and glared at Daniels. "Three killed. Four wounded. For what?"

Daniels bristled at the mutinous challenge. "War has its price."

Hugh turned away to avoid blurting a rejoinder that might be grounds for a charge of insubordination. With Hugh's submissive silence compelled, the colonel paraded back to the barge, shaking the hands of his troopers and reminding them to take what booty they found.

Inspecting the scattered tins and abandoned bed rolls, Hugh kicked dirt into the embers of a dying fire. Incensed by the needless loss of life, he muttered to Wallace, "The professor has his story for the newspapers back home. We'll leave this hardscrabble hole tomorrow and Jeffers will come take it back. Nothing changed here but a few graves and a letter to a widow."

* * *

As Hugh predicted, the Chalk Bluff campaign achieved nothing. Yet Colonel Daniels drove his exhausted regiment back north to trumpet his unsanctioned raid as if he had just matched Alexander's march to India. The professor's megalomania grew more outlandish by the day, and soon after their return to Cape Girardeau, he raided the city's pro-Southern newspaper, *The Eagle*, confiscating the printing presses and declaring himself the editor of a new pro-Union weekly that churned out Utopian sermons and lengthy hagiographies extolling his exploits. Daniels ruled this city of divided loyalties as a conquering monarch, imposing many of the same draconian policies that General Benjamin "Beast" Butler prosecuted in New Orleans. Yet his confiscation of property and burning of houses only caused the locals to stiffen their resistance. Secesh guerrilla fighters, secreted into the city by the Swamp Ranger Jeffers, terrorized those citizens who collaborated with the Federal occupation. Unfazed by the temporary setback at Chalk Bluff, Jeffers remained bent on revenge.

Daniels, feeling his oats after his hollow victory, decided to teach the stubborn marauder another lesson. That morning, the colonel ordered Hugh to form up the regiment on the fairgrounds facing gallows that had been erected in an hour. The planks held a dozen captured ruffians, their necks noosed, residents of the city that Daniels declared a nest of spies. The families and friends of the condemned Confederate guerrillas, summoned to watch the hanging on penalty of exile, stood around the gallows with their fists balled and faces defiant, itching for a brawl.

Daniels affected a dramatic arrival on a sleek white stallion impounded from the stables of a suspected sympathizer.

Hugh risked the colonel's wrath by suggesting a more measured response. "Sir, these men haven't received a trial."

Daniels fixed his determined gaze on the gallows. "Article Two, Section Two of the Constitution."

"What does that—"

"President Lincoln is your commander-in-chief. And I, as his proxy in this military zone of operations, exercise his powers."

"You've received no such orders."

"To your station, Major LaGrange."

Given no choice, Hugh climbed the steps to the scaffold and waited at the lever to drop the trapdoors on the colonel's command.

Daniels circled the fractious crowd and pulled from his breast pocket a page from the *Eagle*, published a month before he confiscated the editor's office. The paper had reprinted a letter, authored by a correspondent who identified himself as the Vicksburg Whig, from the *Memphis Daily Appeal*. The colonel held the page aloft and, affixing his reading spectacles, read from it aloud:

> "*A friend of ours who arrived here yesterday from Arkansas tells us a story, the correctness of which he vouches for, which shows that the genuine Yankees are perfectly willing and anxious to put the Negroes upon an equality with themselves. While the Yankee troops were in camp in Arkansas, Colonel Daniels, of the First Wisconsin regiment, became terribly enamored with a Negro woman belonging to David Goodloe, of St. Francis County. Although she was black as ebony, the Colonel proposed marriage, and in a short time he led her to the hymenial altar, and there the black-hearted dog took Miss Mary Goodloe for better or for worse.*"

"How was the spring plowing?" shouted a Southerner in the crowd.

Daniels twisted in his saddle, determined to find the source of that blistering aspersion. "Slander! I'll not abide it!"

"I see the light!" a woman cried.

Galvanized by that biblical utterance, Daniels hoped to bring the woman back into the Lord's righteous fold. "Madam, the Light of the Almighty, indeed. Come forward and attest your allegiance to the Union and—"

"That ain't the kind of light I'm seeing!" The woman grinned grimly and pointed toward the regimental barracks on the outskirts of the fairgrounds. "The flaming sword of St. Michael comes seeking vengeance!"

Hugh looked over his shoulder toward the ridge—the camp's fodder barn was on fire. "Company A!" he shouted. "To the bucket detail! At once!"

The company fell out and ran toward the barracks.

Seething at the sabotage, Daniels pointed an accusing finger at the woman who taunted him. "Your hands! Stained with innocent blood in this unnatural conflagration you have brought upon your sinful land!"

The woman refused to be cowed. "Your ape Lincoln started this war!"

Exasperated, Daniels ordered Hugh, "Proceed with the execution!"

On the platform, Hugh scanned the boiling crowd, listening for the hammer cocks of weapons and trying to find a way out of this predicament. He signaled Company B to fall out and march to the front of the scaffolding to form a buffer against the surging mob. The remaining companies fanned out behind the surly citizens to prevent them from escaping.

The jeering woman broke through the cordon of troopers and ran to stand below the gallows. "John Bennett!" she shouted at one of the noosed men. "You are my husband eternal!" She fixed an evil eye on Hugh, daring him to pull the lever. "I swear on the graves of my children, *you* will be cursed by every Southern woman who draws breath!"

"Enough threats!" ordered Daniels. "Major LaGrange!"

Hugh hesitated, flustered.

"Private LaGrange!" the colonel shouted. "Take over for your brother."

In the ranks, Wallace, driven by the colonel's threatening glare, reluctantly ascended the steps—

Hugh pulled the lever.

The twelve roped bushwhackers dropped to their deaths.

A collective gasp rippled across the crowd, punctured by anguished cries and muttered promises of vengeance.

When the dangling men suffered their last twitches, Daniels dismounted and ascended the platform. "Every man, woman, and child will swear loyalty to the United States of America! Refuse, and you will be punished as traitors!"

Hugh, standing next to the swaggering colonel, prepared to suppress a riot should the Southerners resist.

Only the newly widowed woman walked away, refusing the oath.

"Arrest her!" ordered Daniels. "Take her to the jail."

The sullen citizens held a grudging silence and nodded their agreement to the enforced oath.

17

LAGRANGE, GEORGIA
JUNE 1862

Church bells tolled that morning as Nancy hurried across the square to intercept Gus before he left his office for his home rounds. She caught him just as he inserted his key to lock up. "Gus, come back inside."

He pulled his watch. "Shouldn't you be in bed getting your beauty sleep?"

She herded him through the door and pulled the shade.

"You didn't have to come downtown to tell me why the bells are ringing," he grumbled. "They captured those Yankee raiders with the locomotive at Ringgold yesterday. The scoundrels will be hanged and—"

"Sit, please." She led him to the chaise used for his waiting patients. When he was off his feet, she searched the cabinets behind the counter and found the whiskey bottle he kept stashed next to a tumbler. She poured two jiggers into the glass and handed it to him.

He swallowed the drams as if meeting a dare. "If you think you can get me corned on this anti-fogmatic so I'll purchase those Enfields—"

She sat next to him, took his hands into hers, and drew a deep breath. "Gene is dead."

Gus's lips quivered. Several seconds passed before he could form the words. "Can't be. I read the notices at the courthouse this morning."

"Caroline received a telegram at the house addressed to you an hour ago. From your brother, Joe."

Gus struggled against his cane to stand. "I must go to her."

Nancy placed an arm around his shoulder to coax him back to the chaise. "Give her some time alone."

Gus rested his forehead against the knob of his cane, lost in grief over his younger brother's death. He coughed emotion from his constricted throat and whispered a hoarse lament. "Gene is the regiment's first loss."

She nodded through tears, ashamed of the relief she felt when she learned Brown and her own brothers weren't listed on that telegram. Brown now served with her cousin Alfred Colquitt's brigade, in the division commanded by General D.H. Hill, that much she knew from his last letter. As best she could gather from the rumors and newspapers, the Georgia regiments had marched north from Norfolk to join the army a few miles southeast of the Confederate capital in Virginia. There they were dug in to prevent a Union army of superior numbers under George McClellan from marching up the James River peninsula and capturing Richmond through its rear door. She tried to imagine what the LaGrange men must be enduring now, facing battle for the first time.

"Where was he killed?" Gus asked.

"At a place called King's School House."

Gus tipped his head and groaned, stung by the irony that Gene, the least studious of the Ware siblings, met his end near a classroom.

"Joe is making arrangements to have his body sent home." An extended silence fell between them, and she was at a loss how to console him. "I thought this war would be settled months ago. You are the only one in town who didn't predict a swift victory."

Gus pulled a kerchief to dry his eyes. "I came to know the Northerners and their character while I attended medical school in Philadelphia. They are not the dandies and codfish aristocrats the fire-breathers like Edmund Ruffin make them out to be. They can pull a trigger just as our lads can. And there are more of them than us."

She borrowed his cane to draw in the floor dust an outline of the state of Virginia from her memory of geography class. "Where is Richmond?"

Gus added details to her crude map by scratching dots to mark the capitals of the two warring countries.

"So close to Washington?"

He nodded. "Davis should have kept the capital in Montgomery. Even Charleston or Milledgeville are preferable. But Virginia has always enforced its preferences on us since the Revolution."

"Do you have confidence in our generals?"

He huffed. "We lost the best of our litter at Shiloh."

"Sidney Johnston? But what about Beauregard?"

"A flapping peacock."

"Joe Johnston, then."

"Wounded two weeks ago. Out of action."

This litany of disaster alarmed her. "Will we run out of West Pointers?"

"If we are fortunate."

"Who now commands the Army of Northern Virginia?"

"Davis's desk adviser. A man named Lee."

"Is he capable of turning back McClellan?"

Gus shrugged. "I doubt it. Lee's father was a rogue firecracker in war and a bankrupt in business. The son, Robert, had a commendable record in Mexico, but his lackluster performance in the recent western Virginia campaign gives me little hope."

The harsh reality of their predicament hit Nancy like a slap. If the Yankees captured Brown and her brothers at Richmond, Lincoln might imprison or hang them as traitors, along with President Davis and Senator Hill. Who would run the Troup County businesses and plantations? Would the Yankees dare come south and commandeer their homes, leaving them destitute?

Gus moved the tip of his cane a few inches to the left on her map of Virginia. "A savior may yet rise here ... in the Shenandoah Valley."

She estimated the distance from Richmond. "That must be at least two hundred miles away."

He didn't disagree. "You remember that eccentric artillery instructor who made a nickname for himself at Manassas?"

"Yes, Stonewall Jackson."

"He has been running three Yankee armies ragged between Staunton and Harpers Ferry."

"The Arsenal is there," she recalled. "Where John Brown was captured."

He circled his cane around that dot near the Maryland border. "Harpers Ferry is the key to defending Virginia. Jackson has kept the Federal forces in the Valley from joining up with McClellan. The newspapers call his men Jackson's Foot Cavalry."

"If this Stonewall Jackson is so brilliant, why doesn't President Davis give him command of all our troops?"

"Jackson is not a popular officer, from what I hear. He has marched his infantry more miles in less time than it took General Washington to reach Yorktown. I'm not a military strategist by any means, but if I were advising Davis, I'd order Jackson to steal away east under cover of night, join his forces with Lee's at Richmond, and strike the Yankees on the Peninsula before McClellan takes breakfast."

Nancy tried to visualize how such a plan might succeed. "That's a long way to walk. Wouldn't his men be too tired to fight?"

"You'd be surprised what the human body can endure when faced with annihilation." Gus fell silent again.

She sensed he was wallowing in the same old shame from not being with the Fourth Georgia. "Gus ..."

"I might have saved Gene."

"Perhaps the Almighty places some of us in reserve for more important tasks yet known?"

"I have been kept in reserve my entire life. I am mightily tired of it."

She felt his hand trembling in hers. "I have been too hard on you. You've always been a loyal friend and counselor. I will no longer hold you to my ill-made bargain. You have nothing to fear if you wish nothing more to do with my deluded tilt at windmills. I will disband the militia and—"

"You will *not* abandon that militia!"

"But—"

"If I can't fight, at least I can teach others." He struggled to his feet. "I won't allow Gene to die in vain. Tell the other women to be at Harris grove tomorrow afternoon."

"We should wait until after the funeral."

He waved off her plea. "Do you think the men of the Fourth take time off from the fighting to mourn?"

"No, but—"

"You must decide if you intend to lead a military unit or a social club." He limped to a bookcase, pulled out a dog-eared pamphlet, and handed it to her.

She read the title: *Rifle and Light Infantry Tactics.* "Written by General William Hardee in 1855." She thumbed through its worn pages of drills and drawings. Gus's handwritten notes filled the margins. "I've heard that name."

"Hardee commanded a corps under Sidney Johnston at Shiloh. His drill manual is required reading for all officers."

She saw the inscription and stifled a gasp. "Gene and Joe gave it to you."

Gus bit on his quivering lower lip. "I wanted to be a soldier from the first day I picked up a stick. They let me tag along when they drilled with the Home Guards. You'll have more use for it now."

She hugged him, her effusive affection causing him obvious embarrassment. Saluting him, she smiled through tears and walked out, clutching her precious gift to her bosom.

* * *

The next day, the Nancies, attired in black mourning dresses and gray militia shell jackets, marched in a column by twos down the path from the red schoolhouse to Harris grove. After studying the Hardee tactics manual for most of the night, Nancy learned enough field maneuvers to assign them positions in traveling formation. The tallest she placed on the right of the column. Accompanied by Leila pounding a dirge on a drum, she led the women, their weapons shouldered, toward the far end of the shooting line. Just as they had drilled that morning in the meadow at Ferrell Gardens terraces, each pair in the column wheeled left on her orders and fell into two long lines with the tallest of the pairs standing behind her designated mate. The women waited in silence, a somber determination replacing the gaiety of their past meetings.

She walked to front-center with a folded flag under her arm. "Some ridicule us as frivolous women who play at war while sipping lemonade and baking cookies. Gene Ware's death has brought us to a moment of decision. If we are to continue as a proper militia, we must accept the responsibilities that accompany such a grave undertaking. That means swearing allegiance to the duties and regulations that govern our brave men in the field. Should anyone wish to withdraw, no judgment will be held against you."

None moved.

Nancy released a held breath, gratified. "Order arms! Raise your right hands!"

The women dropped the muskets to their sides and raised their right hands.

"Do you swear you will bear true faith and allegiance to the Confederate States of America and that you will serve honestly and faithfully against all enemies or oppressors, and that you will observe and obey the President of the Confederate States, and the orders of the officers appointed over you, according to the Rules and Articles of War?"

"I do," the women replied in unison.

"And do I," said a voice behind Nancy.

She turned to find the source of that tardy vow. Caroline, veiled, clung to Gus's arm. Nancy rushed to hug her. "You needn't be here."

"This is where I belong."

Nancy felt a tug on her skirt. Leila drew her notice to the others maintaining ranks while weeping. Her voice cracking, Nancy ordered, "Fall out!"

The women stacked their muskets and ran to embrace Caroline. Most had not seen her since the news of her brother's death.

Nancy unfolded their militia's flag and offered a corner to Mary. "To honor our men who fall in battle." She and Mary unfurled the flag in front of Caroline. Embroidered onto its background were the words: *Eugenius Ware, King's School House.* Caroline slumped sobbing into Gus's arms as Nancy presented the banner to her. "We have voted you color bearer, if you will accept the role."

Caroline nodded through tears as she accepted the flag. When she regained her voice, she straightened and insisted, "Enough keening. Gene would not have wished it. We have work to do."

"I have paired you with Mary."

Mary took Caroline's arm and teased her old friend with her childhood nickname. "To the front rank with you, Pussie. You have always been an inch shorter than me, but I will always be your wise elder."

"Fall in!" As the women retrieved their weapons and reformed ranks, Nancy claimed her position at the front. "Today, we will learn close-order drill." She motioned Gus to her side, and he limped over and waited, as if expecting her to surrender an imaginary podium. She gave him a searching look. "What now?"

"The commander of the unit stands thirty feet behind the line."

Nancy's nostrils flared. "Certainly not! I will remain at the front with my brave soldiers."

Gus kept his finger pointed beyond the rear line. "Your duty, Captain Morgan, is to manage the formation as a teamster drives his draught horses. You cannot rein the carriage left and right if you are flouncing and prancing in *front* of the harnesses, can you?"

"Well, no, but—"

"Did you not read the manual?"

"I didn't get that far. You only gave it to me yesterday and—"

"Captain!" said Mary. "Permission to speak?"

"Granted."

"Should we return to the lesson?"

When none of the women came to Nancy's defense, she pouted her way around the end of the line to her enforced station at the rear.

Satisfied, Gus shouted his next order. "Sergeants!"

Andelia Bull and Augusta Hill raised their hands.

"You two will stand at the flanks." Seeing their faces droop with disappointment at being shunted to the hinters, he mollified them. "Very important duties. You are the bookends. Do you know what bookends do?"

Andelia bit off a sarcastic retort. "Keep the books from scattering?"

"Precisely! You anchor and protect our flanks."

Before the two sergeants could dispute their assignments, Gus looked beyond the heads of the women and found Nancy sulking alone. "Captain Morgan, *you* must keep the unit well-dressed."

Furious, Nancy elbowed her way forward and confronted him, nose to nose. "I remind everyone here every week of the time and place we meet. I pester the codgers for their weapons. I ordered lunches. And now you tell me I have to buy the fabric and stitch everyone's uniforms? *That* is the last straw!"

Gus allowed her rant to carry off into the trees. In a calm but firm voice, he deflated her complaint. "Dressing the line, *Captain* Morgan, means moving soldiers closer when a gap forms from dissipation or casualties."

Nancy reddened, mortified by her mistake.

Amid snickers, Gus motioned the women to open a path through the ranks for Nancy, now silenced, to return to her assigned spot at the rear. Next he came to Aley Smith and Sallie Bull, who stood side-by-side in the front. They moved closer as he tapped their shoes with his cane until their elbows nearly touched. He limped to the left flank and peered into the open space between the first and second ranks. "Thirty-three inches here!"

Mary squawked. "That is nigh impossible, Gus! We'll step on our skirts!"

Gus picked at the lint on his coat sleeves. "The manual is adamant on this point. There is a purpose for it."

Nancy marched around the left flank to confront him again. "The manual was not written for ladies. These foot and hip positions are impracticable. We have different anatomical demands."

Gus feigned astonishment. "Oh, you do, do you? I must have missed that lecture during medical school." He tapped on their hems. "Next time, get rid of the hoops!"

A collective gasp erupted around him.

Leila pounded her drum in protest. "How are we to catch the attention of gentlemen if we are forbidden to enhance our figures?"

"Do you see many gentlemen here?" Gus asked.

Leila heated her glare at him. "Absolutely none."

Flushing from the sly insult, Gus extracted one lady in the rear and took her place. Wielding his cane as a *faux* musket, he lowered it just above Ella Kay's shoulder in the front line. "If I stand too far behind her, the discharge from my barrel will deafen her. If I stand too close, the flash from the powder pan will leave her blinded. Thirty-three inches is the precise distance between pan and barrel end to avoid injury."

Nancy pondered the conundrum. "I have a solution. We'll place the best shooters in front. After *they* fire, they'll hand their empty muskets to the rear rank for reloading. The front shooter takes the second loaded musket from the rear and fires again."

The women nodded, impressed by her brainstorm, but Gus exaggerated a gawk with his jaw hanging. "I wonder why Napoleon didn't think of that?"

"Well, he was a man. Maybe his imagination was severely limited."

Gus bellowed, "What happens when the sharpshooters in front are hit first?" He answered his own question. "All you have left are the loaders who are your worst shooters!"

Nancy shrugged. "It was just a suggestion."

Gus hung his derby on the knob of his cane and ran his hand through his hair while recovering his composure. He lidded his greasy scalp again and limped back and forth in front of the women while continuing his lecture. "You must learn the maxims of infantry warfare. First rule. Mass your firepower for maximum effect. This is why you stand tight in ranks. You fire together by files. That way, you hit the enemy with a battering ram of balls."

"But the enemy stands in tight ranks, too," said Leila.

Gus leaned closer to her with a slant of contempt, as if she had just tried to patent the obvious.

Leila persisted. "And that makes them easier to hit."

"What *exactly* is your point?" he asked.

"It just seems both sides crowd together so both can get killed faster."

Gus's mouth moved, but no sound came forth.

Mary raised her hand. "The Creek didn't fight in ranks. They hid behind rocks and trees."

"And where are the Creek now?" Gus barked.

Mary took his point and made a buttoning gesture over her lips.

Gus slowed his breathing to calm and walked along the line of women, tapping their shoes to adjust their distances. "The best military minds of the centuries have installed these rules to allow soldiers in close quarters to wield their weapons and fire at the most rapid rate possible."

"But there are so many commands," said Nancy. "Can't we simplify them?"

Irked, Gus paced in front of their ranks. Suddenly, he stabbed his cane into the ground, blessed with an epiphany. "Think of musketry drilling as dancing. The quadrille requires many intricate steps, does it not?"

The women perked up and swished their skirts while curtsying to their muskets, as if accepting invitations to the floor.

Pleased with his brilliant insight, Gus added a strut to his faltering step. "Your weapons are your dance partners. You've always wanted to steal the lead from the gentlemen. Now is your opportunity."

Nancy clapped. "Let's give Gus's theory a try." She pointed at three stacked bales of hay set fifty yards a way. "Shoulder arms!"

"Wait!" Gus ducked and crouched. "Allow me at least to remove myself from the line of fire, for Jove's sake!"

The women giggled as Gus scuttered off to the side like a three-legged crab.

"Arms!" Nancy shouted.

The women brought the butts of their muskets to the ground between their feet. Commands of "Cartridge!" and "Rammer!" and "Prime!" sent them into their memorized ritual of loading. "Ready!" Nancy shouted. "Aim! ... Fire!"

Forty muskets rattled and flashed.

Gus lifted his racing-track field glasses and dialed in his focus on the bales of hay. He lowered the glasses and shook his head. He nodded for Nancy to bark the next order.

"At ease!"

Gus made certain the women shouldered their guns before he limped back to the front of his class. "Second maxim. Aim low."

Mary checked the notch on her barrel. "This sight must be off."

"The sight is fine," said Gus. "It's your education that's off."

"Gus!" Nancy scolded.

He refused to be dissuaded. "The muskets kick. You warriors of the gentler sex are, shall I say, less endowed with the necessities to maintain the level. Hence, you must compensate by aiming for the lower extremities of the enemy."

"Even if we adjust our aim?" asked Nancy, exasperated.

Gus averted his eyes. "I'm uncertain how detailed I should get on this subject, given the recent news."

"Do not patronize us, Gus," Caroline warned.

Finally, driven by their insistent glares, he explained, "If you aim at the legs and miss high, you will probably still kill the Yankee."

"And if our aim is accurate?" asked Nancy.

"You will maim him in the legs or the gut. And two soldiers will abandon the enemy's line to assist the wounded man to the rear. You will have disabled three combatants."

The women shared stunned glances, dazzled by his knowledge of combat.

"That's enough for today," said Gus. "We won't move to the next drill lesson until you perfect these maneuvers."

"What about bayonet exercises?" asked Nancy.

Gus stared at her with incomprehension. "Do you have bayonets?"

"No, but we could practice using imaginary ones."

"Is there a shipment of bayonets en route?"

"Of course not."

"Well, then, bayonet drills are a waste of time!"

Mary waited for the spittle from Gus's shout to dissipate in the breeze. Then she stepped forward and snapped open the button on her side holster. "Not for me." She pulled a kitchen carving knife.

The women gathered around Mary to examine the blade.

Gus chortled. "Mary, dear, are you going to attach your turkey machete with twine?"

"No need." Mary reversed the knife, revealing she had whittled its wooden handle to a small ball knob. She inserted the knob into the barrel of her musket like a cork into a bottle and stabbed the makeshift bayonet into the ground as if gutting a wounded Yankee.

The women applauded her ingenuity, and Gus's condescending grin vanished. Astonished, he stared at the plug bayonet.

After dismissing the women, Nancy sidled up to Gus and whispered to his ear. "No classes at the Philadelphia School of Medicine on kitchen cutlery?" She walked off with a satisfied smirk.

* * *

The next morning, Nancy entered Gus's office to thank him for the musketry lesson. She found Caroline's mulatto house slave, Marie Harrison, folding laundered cloths and storing them in a cabinet.

"Good morning, Marie. Is Dr. Ware in?"

Marie bowed. "No, missum. He's out on his calls."

She inspected the neatly stacked towels. "You take good care of him."

Marie looked at her hard, then cast her eyes down.

"Do you love him?"

Marie glanced up, shocked by the question.

"You can speak freely."

Marie hurried unloading the rest of the laundry. "He takes care of me. I take care of him. That's what the Good Book says to do, don't it?"

"I know how the men around here carry on."

"Yessum."

"I give Gus the Devil, but I have great affection for him. I hoped you might also feel more than duty for him, too."

Marie looked over Nancy's shoulder toward the window, as if fearful someone might walk in.

"What we share will never leave this room."

Marie straightened in defiance. "You speak of love, Mrs. Morgan? My momma told me no one ever knows their true feelings until they have the freedom to walk away. She was forced to share the bed of President Harrison. He claimed to have affection for *her*, too, until he decided having four bastard children by her in his household would look bad for his election. So, my brothers and I were sold to the Poythress family. I can't tell you what I feel for Dr. Ware because I don't know feelings no more. I'm just trying to keep my kin and me together. Now, if you will excuse me, Mrs. Poythress is expecting me back at the house."

Shaken, Nancy stood silently while Marie gathered up her laundry basket and disappeared through the back door.

18

Hugh and Wallace sat mounted at the mooring wharf watching a detachment from the First Wisconsin herd two hundred Rebel prisoners onto a docked steamer. The ragged and half-starved gaggle, rounded up after the month-long siege at Corinth, packed both levels of the paddle-wheeler. Bound for transport up the St. Francis River to Missouri, they were to be marched overland to Cape Girardeau and paroled or imprisoned at Cairo.

"Not a bad haul," said Wallace.

His brother always plowed around the stump, but Hugh shook his head at the folly of it all. Truth be told, their latest raid across the border into Arkansas—another unauthorized campaign launched by Colonel Daniels—had turned into a wild turkey chase with only a hundred nags and a few empty wagons to show for two months in the saddle. These butternut scarecrows would just be exchanged and allowed to scurry back to the Army of the Mississippi, handed over by Jeff Davis to that surly hypochondriac, Braxton Bragg. The rumor in these boondocks was that Bragg and Kirby Smith were scheming to invade Kentucky. The war might end with a Waterloo on a bluegrass pasture up there, and here *he* sat more than a year since volunteering, still on the wrong side of the Mississippi chasing razorback ruffians and driving cattle on forage runs.

Wallace licked his cracked lips. "Reckon they have a saloon on that paddler?"

Hugh turned and snarled at him. "By God, if you ever, through some divine error of accounting, arrive at the gates to Heaven, you will demand St. Peter divulge the bottle count before agreeing to admission."

"And you will demand the sourest lemon in Paradise to suck!"

"I should have left you at home."

"And I should have stayed with the boys in the Fourth!"

"I can arrange it."

"Who would launder your long johns? It took me an hour to scrub out your britches after that assault on Chalk Bluff."

Try as he might, Hugh couldn't suppress a smile. His brother had an infuriating talent for puncturing his rants. "I can't let you go. Not until we encounter a traveling circus so I can hire a replacement for the regimental court jester."

"You can have the glory, big brother. I prefer medals for jokestering and Saturday night hoofing."

Hugh fell into vexed thought.

"Not the Colonel again?"

Hugh slumped and nodded. "We will come under suspicion for this illegal excursion. Hanging those men in Cape Girardeau without trials and burning towns just because they're in our path."

"What would you have the professor do? Leave us to sit in the barracks and wither? At least he's a man of action."

"He's reckless. And he's begging for a court martial. This regiment is undisciplined. The fish rots from the head."

"We're cavalry. We scout and harass. That's our job."

Hugh set his jaw. "We're getting our asses kicked in every engagement."

Wallace studied him with concern. "You've been reading that Reb general's manual again. What's his name?"

"Wheeler."

"Is he some kind of Napoleonic genius?"

Hugh swept his hand across the Arkansas swampland and scrub brush. "We scatter our cavalry here and there, one squadron in this county, another in the next. Wheeler concentrates his horse for maximum impact. He has a free-wheeling colonel under his command named Forrest. I've been reading the papers about him. He's a slave broker and bounty hunter, but he breaks every rule and wins every fight. He maneuvers his troopers like infantry. At Shiloh, he charged a brigade protected by artillery. Scooped up one of Sherman's men who aimed a pistol at him and dragged the poor fellow onto his saddle to use as a shield. And at Fort Donelson, he refused to surrender and led his troopers across a half-frozen river to escape in the middle of the night."

"Then let's go after this slaver and give him a whipping."

"We haven't even been issued sabers or repeating carbines. We'd be the ones getting whipped, and hard."

Wallace spat a dry ball of dust. "What the hell would we do with sabers? Roast rabbits on them? You should chase that Charge-of-the-Light-Brigade nonsense from your head. In case you haven't noticed, our boys don't exactly have the dexterity of Genghis Khan on horseback. We're farmers. We walk behind harrow blades with reins around our necks. We weren't trained to chase foxes across Lord

Wellington's hunting parks. Nothing's gonna change, so why fret—" He was so engrossed in his argument with Hugh that only then did he see Lieutenant Eggleston standing before them. "What's the problem now?"

"Some of the Rebs are being cantankerous," said Eggleston.

"Let the pilot and his Navy detail handle it," said Hugh. "Our orders are to get them on the boat and return to Madison."

"Sir, the prisoners may start jumping."

Annoyed, Hugh dismounted and motioned for Wallace to follow him to the log pilings along the embarcadero.

Eggleston kept pace. "We've segregated them by rank, as you ordered. But their officers won't abandon one of the privates."

Hugh, exasperated, glanced at Wallace. "This right here is what I'm talking about. We're nothing but provost guards."

Wallace shrugged as they crossed the gangway. "But damn handsome ones."

Reaching the platform at the paddler's bow, Hugh confronted the pilot, who stood surrounded by five Confederate officers, identified by the stars on their collars. With them was a short, slender soldier whose ragged pantaloons, cut off at the shins, and dirty calico blouse suggested he was the private causing the disturbance. The stunted troublemaker kept the brim of his straw hat pulled over his eyes. Hugh demanded, "Which one of you is the ranking officer?"

A tall, patrician-looking man with a goatee and sad eyes stepped forward from the cluster of prisoners. "Major Maney at your service."

"What unit?"

"We are mutts from various litters. My comrades here and I hail from Cheatham's division. I apologize for the disruption, but I've sworn an oath to personally see this lad safely back to his mother."

Hugh studied the bantam private who kept his eyes fixed on the floorboards. Sure, the boy was young, but he had encountered plenty of Rebels his age. Yet something about this one seemed different. The shadow cast by the boy's drooping hat brim prevented him from getting a good look at his face. "Is he one of the Lost Princes of London Tower?"

The Confederate major smiled. "Ah, a learned man. 'The raven himself is hoarse that croaks the fatal entrance of Duncan under my battlements.'"

"I have no time to trade Shakespeare. Regulations for transporting prisoners require officers and noncommissioned men to be kept in separate quarters."

"Then, I'm afraid you have no choice but to shoot us."

Wallace intervened. "Hold on now."

Hugh glared at the obstinate Rebel major. His eyes shifted again onto the youthful private causing a ruckus that might derail his and Wallace's military careers. "Guards! At arms!" The sailors stationed along the railing brought their rifles to the ready, and Hugh drew his revolver. He rolled its cylinder and told the pilot, "I need your cabin for a few minutes."

The pilot pointed him toward the door. Hugh grabbed the young prisoner by the arm and dragged him into the cabin. The Confederate major and his fellow officers risked a step to intervene, but Hugh turned and cocked his revolver to halt them. "I *will* interrogate this prisoner. If he is a spy, you'll hang from those masts with him." Hugh shoved the private inside the cabin and locked the door behind him. "What's your name?"

The boy kept looking at his toes, refusing to answer.

"Son, I don't know what contrivance you're scheming, but I'll string up your benefactors out there, one by one, if you don't start talking."

"Anderson."

"Your regiment?"

The nervous boy glanced at the porthole as if looking for a means of escape. "Second Kentucky Cavalry."

"Get undressed."

For the first time, the boy looked up, startled. "No!"

"You're carrying correspondence. Lose those rags, or I'll cut them off you."

The boy backed into a corner. Hugh lunged at him and pulled off his straw hat, determined to check its band for messages. Shocks of thick black hair fell to the boy's shoulders. *Come, you spirits, that tend on mortal thoughts, unsex me here.* That verse—which followed the one from *Macbeth* quoted by the Confederate major—suddenly came to Hugh's mind. He backed away, now understanding why the Rebel officer was so protective of his charge. "My God ..."

The female prisoner clutched her arms around her chest. "Are you going to plunder me as the Canaanites did to the wives of Israel?"

"There doesn't look to be enough left of you *to* plunder."

She straightened and yanked her hat back. "You ain't seen the elephant. I can tell it from those soppy eyes. Still a virgin, ain't you?"

"A virgin?"

"I buried my husband at Shiloh! Dug the grave myself! Fought next to him until you Yankees riddled him in the Hornet's Nest. I figure I killed twenty just like you. Don't scare me. Go on and shoot me!"

"Simmer down. Take a breath."

The girl's coal-black eyes flamed with wrath. "I hope I'm there the first time you stare at the wrong end of ten thousand barrels. How's it feel knowing a Mississippi woman has done more fighting than you?"

Hugh kicked a chair across the floorboards and motioned for her to sit. He holstered his revolver and pulled up a second chair. "To be honest, it doesn't feel pleasant. I suppose I might learn a thing or two from you."

"I reckon you might. Damn lucky for you that Sidney Johnston caught his death bullet, or we'd be watering our horses in the Ohio River."

"Cavalry, huh?"

The girl nodded. "I was born on a horse."

"You ever encounter Colonel Wheeler?"

"Encounter him? Why, I made him breakfast while he and Bedford Forrest drew up plans to ride around Grant's right flank."

"What kind of man is Wheeler?"

"His kinfolk came from New England, but he managed to overcome that stain on his ancestry."

"I was born in upper New York and—"

"I don't give an armadillo's ass if wolves raised you inside the Liberty Bell. Do you want to hear my story, or not?"

Hugh raised his hands and nodded for her to go on.

"Now, the way Colonel Wheeler told it to me over greased grits, he picked up the name 'Fightin' Joe' from his youthful days chasing Comanches in the New Mexico Territory. But he's a cautious fellow, not one for the fancy play like Forrest."

"They get along, those two?"

"Like starved gators in a sack."

"Is Wheeler a skilled saberist?"

"He's a West Pointer. Whatever skills he picked up coon-gigging in Georgia were likely corroded by you Northern muggins."

"Is he right-handed?"

She pinned him with a suspicious eye. "You writin' a book?"

Hugh reached into his breast pocket and pulled out the Wheeler pamphlet. "I'm reading one."

She waved off those pages as useless. "You can't learn horse fighting from a primer. Heck, Forrest can barely sign his own John Hancock. You're doomed and deserve it."

Hugh studied her gaunt, sunburned features, trying to come up with a solution for what to do with her. He stood and stomped the dried mud from his boots. "I don't suppose if I found a dress on this paddler, you'd agree to put it on in exchange for a parole?"

She shook her head and folded her arms. "I've become partial to airy skivvies. The lice in tow keep me company."

Resigned to her stubbornness, he motioned her out. When the girl neared the threshold, he shut the door again. "What's your real name?"

She hesitated. "Amy Clarke."

"I'm sorry for your loss, Mrs. Clarke."

She looked away to brush tears. "You have a beloved?"

"My wife, Jennie."

"She did not accompany you to the war?"

A pang of guilt struck him. He'd not had the time to write to Jennie in over a month. "She's not a camp follower. An army is no place for—" He caught himself.

Her eyes pierced him with an accusation of imperfect love. "That's why we'll defeat you. Your womenfolk stay at home and knit. Ours will fight to the last death."

Hugh thought the boast absurd, but he decided it wasn't worth the effort to refute it. He motioned her outside. Wallace, with his revolver still trained on the Rebel officers, waited for a report on the interrogation. Hugh sighed and brought the prized prisoner to Maney. "From what Private Anderson has told me of his exploits, Major, I think you owe him a temporary promotion."

Maney's confused frown gave way to a relieved smile. Grateful for the compromise, the Rebel officer pulled the disguised private to his side and shook Hugh's hand. "If there is ever a service I can perform for you, Major LaGrange ..."

Hugh ordered the pilot, "Escort these men to the officers' quarters. If you have any grits on board, send a bucket with my compliments." He saluted them and walked down the gangplank.

Wallace tarried and whispered to the pilot, "And if you carry any spirits—"

"Private LaGrange!" shouted Hugh. "On the quick!"

Wallace, pouting, trailed his brother to the waiting horses.

An hour later, summoned by a courier to regimental headquarters, Hugh left Wallace and Eggleston at the dock to see the steamer off. He galloped the five miles to the courthouse in Madison, where Colonel Daniels had taken up residence in the judge's chambers. Hugh prayed orders had finally arrived transferring the First Wisconsin to the Army of the Tennessee under Sam Grant's command. The newspapers were full of reports that Lincoln and Halleck had devised a master plan to cut off the Sesech snake's head. Billy Sherman held a division ready to march from Memphis, and Rosecrans stationed his Army of the Mississippi in Corinth. This could be the blow to end the war. He was determined to be part of it.

He leapt off his horse and dashed up the steps, not pausing to share salutes with the headquarters guards lounging on the grounds. He yanked open the courtroom doors and found Daniels huddled over a table with his staff officers, sharing a bottle of whiskey. Strange, he'd never seen the colonel imbibe liquor. Daniels, eyes blood red, waved him up and asked the other officers for a moment alone with Hugh. They cut half-hearted salutes and departed the chamber, avoiding eye contact with Hugh. Daniels offered him a shot of the whiskey, but he declined. "What has happened?"

The colonel poured himself another round and downed it. "I should have listened to you."

"Sir, if this is regarding those Negro refugees you lost at Jonesboro—"

"I've been recalled to division headquarters. I must report to Memphis by sundown tomorrow."

"To join forces with Sherman. I'm certain of it."

The colonel pulled a letter from the top of a pile and slid it across the table. Hugh scanned it—he reread the last sentence: *To appear before a board of inquiry for your unauthorized incursion into Arkansas, violating direct orders to remain at your post at Bloomfield, Missouri.* The order was signed by General Frederick Steele, commander of the Military District of Southeast Missouri.

"My career as an officer is finished," said Daniels.

Hugh's worst fear had come to pass. "Take a skilled advocate with you. Lieutenant Eggleston has practiced law and—"

"I don't intend to contest the charges." The colonel turned and, slumping, braced against the railing below the judge's bench. "I am a man of science, not a soldier. I have been trained to assess soberly the facts of nature, to winnow them from the whims of preachers and the passions of warriors. And yet, in this mission, I have failed. For the year past, I fooled myself into believing I could command a regiment as a scholar commands a classroom. I have been petulant and domineering. I must now submit myself to the judgment of my superiors, a failing student whose dissertation has fallen short of the mark."

Hugh risked breaching the formality of rank to grasp his old professor by the forearm. In a low but comforting voice, he said, "You have always been a Utopian. A man of ideals, determined to reform the world."

The colonel's eyes flooded. "A fool."

"Was Thomas More a fool? The great father of Utopia? That is not how I remember your lesson on English history."

The colonel looked up and, through tears, smiled with gratitude for that comparison. "You remember."

"I also remember you telling me the great More was braver than any knight in King Henry's ranks."

The colonel nodded and straightened with resolve. "And now, like Chancellor More, I must go to my martyrdom." He opened a pouch and pulled out two shoulder straps that held silver oak leaves. "This has been too long in coming, Lieutenant Colonel Lagrange."

Hugh blinked hard. "I can't accept these. I won't aggrandize myself with your misfortune."

"You must. I'm leaving you in command. The regiment trusts you. When I'm formally discharged, you'll receive a full colonel's rank." He hugged Hugh. "Heavy is the head that wears the crown. Take good care of my boys."

Hugh fought back a cough of emotion as his old professor released him. He saluted and moved to leave. He was almost to the door when—

"Don't neglect Wallace," said Daniels.

Hugh turned.

"Your brother deserves a promotion, too."

"He's not ready. Too frivolous and carefree."

"He *is* ready. You can't expect him to stand by and watch as you climb the ladder of command while he lives in limbo, a private and yet the brother of the officer in charge. It will break his will."

"Then *you* promote him. It will mean more."

Daniels shook his head. "It must come from you. Don't wait long, or you will regret it."

* * *

"When the sun comes back
And the first quail calls
Follow the Drinking Gourd.
For the old man is a-waiting
to carry you to freedom
If you follow the Drinking Gourd."

As Hugh led the vanguard of the First Wisconsin south across the sun-cooked St. Francis River delta, a chorus of a thousand angelic voices echoed through the distant haze behind him. On the regiment's march from Madison, slaves working the cotton fields in their shoddies on both sides of Crowley Ridge dropped their gunnysacks and rushed barefoot to his column of troopers, crying and juba dancing and singing songs of freedom.

Their joy caused his heart to swell. Yet the Lord's blessings always came with burdens. He'd had no choice but to put the regiment on half rations to feed the growing throngs of refugees when he could least afford it. Four hundred of his men were ill with dysentery, most unable to mount, and the water in these brackish lowlands was putrid. Yet his orders from General Curtis were to hurry to Helena to join the defense of that port city on the Mississippi. Scouts expected the Confederate commander in the region, Earl Van Dorn, to attack it any day now.

He sighed. A week since Colonel Daniels's departure and already he wished his old mentor were here to counsel him. *Heavy is the head that wears the crown.*

With little forage in these godforsaken swamps, he decided that morning to divide the regiment. He ordered Eggleston and his Wallace to bring up the rear guard with the Second Battalion while he and the rest of the regiment rode ahead. Eggleston took the Negro refugees and the wagons carrying the sick to the river ferry at L'Anguille Ferry, just east of Marianna, where they would camp and cross in the morning. After the recent Union victory at Hill's Plantation, he felt confident one more blow against the Secesh forces in this region would secure Arkansas and open the way for the capture of Vicksburg.

As the sun eased into the western horizon, he rode past a columned plantation house. Through the dusky murk, he saw a girl armed with a carpet beater standing on its porch. She watched him pass with a wary eye, as if a lone sentinel, and she pounded the carpet, rolled out across the boards, with a vengeance. As he drew closer, he gasped. The girl could have passed for Jennie's twin. She had the same dark features, but he couldn't help but feel her unyielding glare carried a message from afar. He tipped his hat to her.

She thrashed the carpet again, never taking her condemning eyes from him. "Gone!" she shouted. "I'm gone!"

He shuddered from a foreboding. Was this the Devil at work? Did the girl truly look like Jennie? A wave of dread swept over him. Jennie's features were fading from his memory with each passing day. Shaken, he rode on, determined to escape the bewitching harridan. Was every woman he now encountered bent on toying with his sanity? He'd heard rumors that pagan voodoo witches traveled up the Mississippi from New Orleans offering to cast spells on Yankee invaders. He placed no truck in these superstitions, and yet … He palmed his feverish forehead. Had he contracted the yellow jack from the damnable mosquito-infested pools in this infernal—

"Colonel!"

He turned to find Captain Torrey galloping up with an elderly Negro man seated behind him. "Mister Jeremiah here came from L'Anguille Ferry," said Torrey. "I think you'd better hear what he has to say."

Hugh waited for the refugee slave to catch his breath.

"Massa, your brother's in a bad way. We and your buckras was attacked at the river."

Hugh figured the old slave had to be mistaken. "There are no Rebel forces in this area."

The Negro clutched his hat, bending and unbending its brim in a jittery tic. "They came on us from five sides, they did! We thought first it was soma your people. Got through them picket boys like lard. Hot fight!"

"Did you get a look at their flag?"

The slave nodded. "Had a big ol' star on it."

Hugh shot a disbelieving glance at Torrey. "Texas dragoons?"

"Likely Parsons's cavalry," said Torrey. "Aching to get revenge for the bloody nose those boys got at Hill's Plantation."

Hugh spurred to the chase. "Bring two hundred men!"

Hugh nearly ruined his horse on the eight-miles rush back to L'Anguille Ferry. He arrived with his troopers at the river to find a scene of devastation. The camp was strewn with dead and wounded, and the ambulances and supply wagons sat burning, emptied of the ammunition and rations. He searched the hills, but the Texans had vanished. He trotted closer to the river and reined up. By his estimate, a hundred black bodies lay in a pile—men, women, and children. Murdered in cold blood.

"Hugh!"

He searched for the source of that distant shout. On the far side of the river, Wallace swam while dragging a raft filled with wounded men. He leapt from his saddle and threw the reins to Torrey. Unbuckling his weapons, he dived into the river and swam to help Wallace drag the raft to the banks. They carried the wounded men to a small grove of swamp oaks for shade.

Wallace collapsed.

Hugh checked him for wounds. "Are you hurt?"

Wallace shoved away his pawing hands. "Just grazed."

Hugh scanned the clusters of groaning men. He saw the regimental surgeon at a butcher's table set in the grove, triaging the worst of the wounded for the saw. "How many did we lose?"

Wallace pushed up on his elbows, panting to catch his breath. "Seventeen killed. At least forty wounded. We can't find another thirty. Parsons's Twelfth Texas hit us. Outnumbered us three-to-one. Stole the run on our pickets. We thought they were local bushwhackers. Held them off for half an hour ..."

"Where's Eggleston?"

"Taking care of a body."

"Whose body?" When his brother didn't answer, Hugh grabbed him by the shoulders. "Tell me, damn it!"

Wallace lowered his voice, as if to lessen the shock. "They shot Reverend Densmore walking out of his tent. He was clutching his Bible."

Hugh kicked at the ground. *Those bastards murdered our chaplain?*

"They also stole the regimental desk and papers," said Wallace. "Along with a month's worth of mail from Memphis."

Hugh dropped to a knee. "This is my fault." He cursed himself for allowing Daniels to send the regiment so poorly armed into this godforsaken bonescape. "God damn Sam Curtis and those politicians!" He looked at Wallace with determination and vowed, "I will *never* let this regiment go into another fight without sabers and carbines."

Eggleston came running down the hill. Seeing that Wallace had delivered the tragic news, the lieutenant put a hand on Hugh's shoulder. "The lads fought hard. You'd have been proud. But one trooper deserves special recognition in your report."

"Who?"

"Your brother here. He swam that river thirteen times, towing that raft while under fire. We'd have lost a hundred more without him."

Hugh studied Wallace. Colonel Daniels was right. His brother *had* grown ten years in these last few months. He reached into his front pocket and pulled out a pair of wet epaulets, each with a single gold bar, the insignia for First Lieutenant. He flapped the dripping strips in the breeze and wrung the water from them. "I was planning to give them to you in Helena. You've earned them on this field."

Wallace levered to his knees and grinned at the shoulder insignias.

Hugh pulled him to his feet. "Get the wounded on the next steamer heading downstream."

"What should we do about the dead contrabands?" Wallace asked.

Hugh gazed across the river at the piled bodies of the escaped slaves who believed they had finally found freedom. "Bury them alongside our men. I intend to send a message to these murdering slavers. If they come back to dig up the coloreds, we'll be waiting."

19

LAGRANGE, GEORGIA
DECEMBER 1862

Nancy slipped into the upstairs bedroom of Caroline's house and whispered, "You've not slept. I'll sit with him for a few hours."

Caroline rose from a chair alongside the bed and hugged her. "His bandages need changing."

Nancy nodded and eased the door closed behind her. She inched the chair nearer to Lieutenant John Gay, who lay with his upper chest wrapped in strips of linens. She rested the back of her hand against his feverish forehead.

Her touch roused him from a fitful sleep, and he looked up at her with bloodshot eyes. "Nannie ... I should stand and salute."

She forced a smile, grateful he managed a sense of humor in his suffering. "You needn't salute me. At least not until I receive my general's promotion."

"Captain Morgan," he said, studying her. "If I had a nickel for every time I've reminded Brown that you outrank him, I'd have purchased his law practice by now."

She cooled a cloth in a basin of water and spread it across his brow. "You are cruel beyond measure," she teased.

"I'm keeping you ladies from your militia drills."

"You needn't worry," she said. "We've become such expert shots that we no longer require practice."

"I don't doubt it." He tried to smile, but the drool caked at the corners of his mouth impeded his effort. With his good hand, he skimmed his long fingernails along his rough jawline, feeling for how many days of beard he had grown. "I should like to observe the famous Nancy Harts on parade before I leave again for Virginia."

She stopped dabbing his forehead and dropped the cloth into the basin as a protest. "Leave? You are in no condition to go back and fight."

He found her hand and pulsed it to allay her distress. "I have a duty to your brothers and my friends in the Fourth."

She lowered the sheet to his stomach and inspected the blood-seeped dressings covering his left pectoral. "Do you have enough strength to lift your shoulder?" He winced as he propped against his right elbow, allowing her to place two more pillows under his neck and back. He tested his left arm and tried to raise it, but his damaged shoulder was too weak to elevate the hand more than a few inches. She eased him back onto his side. "Gus will be along this morning. If I don't get fresh bandages on you, he will screech at me for a week."

"Ol' Gus is more powder than shot."

She unwrapped the strips of linen from his shoulder and upper waist. After removing the last coil of bandage, she swallowed hard and stared at the exposed gash in his chest, searching for the "laudable pus" that Gus said was the sign of healing. The hideous shrapnel wound was dark as liver and three fingers wide. She brought a fist to her mouth to stifle a gasp.

"Gus says it's not as bad as it looks."

Determined not to break down in his presence, she disposed of the soiled bandages in a basket and cut new strips from a sheet boiled and hung out to dry. She sponged the wound and wrapped his chest with fresh dressings.

"You put Clara Barton to shame," he said through gritted teeth.

"Who?"

"A nurse from New England. Yankee prisoners at Sharpsburg spoke of the woman as if she were an angel. She drove a wagon with medical supplies into the battle and tended to the wounded while the balls flew all around her."

Nancy cinched the bandage and finished with the ghastly cleaning. Pressing her trembling chin to her chest, she fought the urge to flee the room.

"Nan, I'm sorry. I didn't mean to upset you."

She wiped her swollen eyes. "I sit here safe, wasting everyone's time with this militia foolishness."

"Never say that." He hesitated. "I swear you to secrecy on what I'm about to tell you."

She nodded, apprehensive.

"The fellows in the Fourth jest about you and your Nancies, but they take great pride in what you have accomplished. I once heard Miles lambaste an Alabama blowhard with the certainty that his sister could out-shoot him and probably out-march him, too."

Flustered by her brother's testimonial, she turned to hide another surge of remorse. "His opinion is not widely shared. A banker from Marietta traveled through town last week. He saw us firing our muskets and scolded us for being an abominable stain on Southern womanhood."

The blood rose in Gay's ashen cheeks. "Bankers. Leeches. The scoundrel was no doubt on his way to Mobile to receive a shipment of British Enfields to sell to our government and collect ten times what he paid." He angled toward the window, his eyes traveling to another place and time.

"John, what happened at Sharpsburg?"

"Leave that be, Nannie."

"I have to know."

He dropped his head back and grimaced.

"If I am ever to lead my women into ..." She couldn't imagine the horrors he refused to talk about, perhaps the kind she and her militia would one day have to face themselves. "I have a duty to prepare them."

The gaunt officer stared at the ceiling as if photographs of that murderous September day were flashing across it. "General Lee scattered his divisions across Maryland. He has a vexing habit of doing that, you know. General Jackson hurried up from Harpers Ferry to join us in the nick of time. That Yankee rooster McClellan is an overly cautious man, but he moved against us rapidly. It was as if he knew our dispositions and plans."

"The newspapers say the Yankees found a copy of General Lee's campaign orders wrapped around two cigars. Dropped by a courier."

His eyes widened. "My God. I was not told. Had we known ..."

She reached into her haversack for an old edition of *Harper's Weekly*, pilfered from Gus's stack. She opened it to a page of illustrations depicting the infantry charges near Antietam Creek. "Is this how the battle truly looked?"

Gay ran his finger over the raised imprint of the black-and-white drawings penned in haste by an eyewitness correspondent. "Fanciful, mostly, with none of the blood and gore." His attention lingered on a white, one-room church shown in the middle of the sketched battle. "I remember *this* place. A congregation that called themselves Dunkers owned it. Peaceful Christians who swore off war." He studied one illustration with such focused concentration that she feared he might slip into a trance. "*There* is where I fell." He pointed to a cross-hatched etching of a copse of woods bordering a patch of stalk rows.

"A cornfield?"

His breathing quickened. "Hell's acre, harvested by the Devil himself."

"We should discuss no more of it."

He persisted, evidently desperate to exorcise those bloody hours. "Colonel Doles positioned us to the right of this cornfield. Your cousin, Alfred, brought his brigade on the double to yoke with our flank." He recounted the clash with Hooker's Union corps. "We'd just set our coffee tins and flapjack pans over our fires. We'd been on the march and hadn't eaten since the morning prior. John Key shouted the order to fall in." He rubbed his stomach, beset by phantom pangs of hunger. "Your brothers were madder than hornets. Miles took one drink of his chicory mud and flung the rest toward the Yankees."

"Where was Brown?"

"Bringing up the commissary wagons. He tried to get us fed and restocked with cartridges before the firing started."

"How long did it take the regiment to get into line?"

"No longer than you can say, 'Here they come.' You'd be surprised how fast you can move when the Miniés are buzzing your head."

She studied the *Harper's Weekly* illustration and tried to imagine herself in the midst of all that. "Did you reach this cornfield?"

"A dozen times. Back and forth, we came and they came. Half an hour later, there wasn't a stalk left on that stretch. If those German pacifists plant corn there again, the ears will grow blood-red kernels."

She felt for a pulse near his windpipe, concerned he might hemorrhage. She risked another question. "Do you feel fear at such moments?"

"Hard to describe what I felt. It was as if I stood outside my own flesh."

"A hallucination of sorts?"

"Very much so, a vivid dream but more real. Suffering the most god-awful thirst. Faint from dehydration. Gulping for breath in the smoke."

"Gus said Dr. Young treated you while you were both under fire."

"I don't remember being hit. The last thing I recall ... I saw several of our men standing at a fence with their backs to me. Miles insisted there was no line to form. He ran along the fence and shook those poor fellows leaning across it to show me. They all fell limp. They'd been standing dead, propped against the rails. I awoke in an ambulance. The night of our retreat, it rained so hard the wheels kept sliding off into the mud. I prayed to die with every jolt from the potholes in that infernal road back to the Potomac. If I'd had a pistol ..."

Nancy bolted from the chair, fussing with the laundry.

"You should go to Brown."

She blanched from that suggestion. "In Virginia? To the front?"

"The Army will take winter quarters soon. Many officers bring their wives up to visit."

"I've never been north of Atlanta."

"He misses you terribly. And it would raise morale for Miles and Joe to see you." He patted the seat on the chair for her to sit again. "I have confided in you. Now, you must confide in me."

She sat, wary of what he might ask her.

He glanced at the door. "These past weeks, I've grown fond of Caroline."

"Fond?"

He drew a painful breath. "I've fallen in love with her."

"Do you mistake her care for love, John?"

"I have never been in the throes. How is one to know?"

She glanced out the window toward the Ferrell terraces, where she had walked with Morgan during her girlhood days when the world was so much simpler. "I fear love and war mock each other."

He struggled onto his elbow. "You think me unworthy of Caroline."

"I think you're the worthiest man in Georgia."

"Yet you hesitate to bless us."

She looked at the floor and the framed portraits on the walls, anywhere but at him, struggling to muster her thoughts into coherence. "The men of Troup County have suffered beyond measure. But we women left behind here have endured our own trials. Hardships that you will never understand. A deep bond has formed among us. It is a sisterhood in war that will never be broken."

"You make it sound as if you've taken vows for the nunnery."

"Caroline lost a husband when she was young."

"Frank Poythress, yes. I knew him."

"He died at twenty-three from the yellow fever. His illness came on so suddenly. Caroline spiraled into a black melancholy. Several months passed before she found the strength to leave this house."

"Is she not entitled to the happiness of another marriage?"

Nancy turned inward to search how best to protect two people she cared for deeply. At last, she found the fortitude to say what she knew she must. "Caroline cannot bear to reopen her wounded heart only to have it crushed again. If I'm to serve as your liaison in this bonding, promise me you will return to her."

"Nannie, none of us can presume to know God's destiny for us."

"Promise," she insisted.

He took her hand between his palms. "You have my word."

* * *

"I am green with envy." Nancy adjusted the nosegay in Caroline's hands. "You'll enjoy the advantage of the Christmas decorations to brighten your day. All I had was the mud stomped on the carpets by those election brutes."

"This is too much fuss," Caroline insisted. "It is unseemly."

"You deserve every admiring eye upon you," said Mary.

Nancy traded a conspiratorial wink with her as they assisted Caroline onto a measuring block to adjust her flounce and hide the frayed hem. Nancy had lobbied for a new wedding gown of silk and lace, but Caroline refused, choosing instead an old linsey-woolsey dress that featured a simple plaid of purple and gray to honor the fallen. Nancy pulled a few ringlets of hair from Caroline's severe bun. "Better."

Caroline cringed as she examined the adjustments in a hand mirror. "Nannie, I am not a Vestal Virgin."

"If you don't stop caterwauling," Nancy threatened, "we'll put you in your militia jacket and make you get married shouldering your musket."

The upstairs bedroom door in Bellevue mansion thrummed from a knock. The tip of a cane cracked it open. Gus peeked in. "The guests are waiting."

"You've given us the same update three times," snapped Nancy.

Gus tapped his cane against the door frame to imitate a metronome. "If you don't come soon, I may have to open another bottle of Madeira—"

"Has the lovely Miss Wagnon been escorted to her seat next to yours?" Nancy asked, reminding him she had not forgotten that, despite his courting of the young belle, Anna, he still pursued a secret concubine relationship with his sister's house slave.

Gus's pouched eyes narrowed with alarm. "She is here. Am I not allowed to invite a guest?"

"Of course you are, Gus. I was just being solicitous as to her every comfort. Should I ring for your sister's chambermaid—what is her name? Oh yes, Marie—to attend to Miss Wagnon personally?"

Gus reddened. "I'm just trying to help by reminding you of the time."

"And as always," said Nancy, "you are missing your mark."

Gus muttered a curse as he backed away, about to close the door to make his long trek back down the stairs.

"Oh, and Gus," said Nancy.

He stuck his bulbous nose through the crack again. "Yes?"

"Do *not* botch your sister's entrance into matrimonial bliss as you did my debut. Or I will give a lecture at our next drill on the history of friendly fire."

The door slammed, and the three women shared a chuckle.

"You are too hard on him, Nannie," said Mary.

"Nonsense," said Caroline. "He laps up the attention."

Nancy studied Caroline and sensed a sudden onset of sadness. "What oppresses you?"

Caroline walked to the window and gazed across Broad Street toward her house. "Do you think Gus will marry her?"

"Anna Wagnon?" asked Nancy. "He adores her."

Caroline brushed away a tear. "John plans to leave for Virginia when he recovers. If Gus weds, I will be alone again. I can't bear to think of it."

Mary rushed to her side. "You will never be alone."

Nancy joined in their embrace. "Mary and I will raid your pantry so often that you will pine for solitude."

Caroline smiled through tears. "I'd never manage without you two."

Nancy extracted herself from their hug and paced the floor, debating if she should raise a subject she had kept to herself these past weeks.

Caroline, perplexed, observed Nancy's bright disposition vanish. "Now I have cast *you* into a despond."

Nancy turned. "Do you love John as much as you loved Frank?"

"Nannie!" scolded Mary. "Such a question! And on her wedding day?"

Caroline, flushing, retreated to the dressing bench. "You cannot understand what it is to walk the streets and see people look at you with pity, as if your life is finished. ... I care for John. In time, I believe love between us can blossom. That is more than I ever thought possible after Frank died."

Nancy sat next to her. "He is more than worthy of you. I just fear ..."

"Fear what?" asked Mary.

Nancy turned aside. "This is the second Christmas we've endured at war. How many more years will we suffer sleepless nights, rushing out every morning to read the notices of casualties while our hearts break, over and again?"

Caroline snuggled closer to show she appreciated Nancy's concern. "I have steeled myself, knowing that I may lose John, as I lost Frank. We are no longer offered good choices and bad choices in this malevolent struggle. I think we must pray for solace from compromises that allow us to survive."

Nancy wiped the moistness from Caroline's eyes. "No more sad thoughts today." She kissed Caroline on the cheek and, arising, led the bride with Mary to the door and opened it. Gus, waiting in the upper foyer after another climb, blessed Caroline with an approving smile and offered his arm.

Nancy stood with Mary at the banister while Caroline and Gus descended the staircase and the other Nancy Harts sang a hymn of Zion in Caroline's honor. As Gus presented his sister to the guests seated in the parlor, Nancy stifled a gasp from an assault of memories. It seemed impossible she had made this same descent five years ago, a mere girl then, eager to announce her entrance to society. She pictured Brown's grinning face that night long ago as he stood near the door admiring her. Or was he ogling Sallie Reid?

This afternoon, alas, there were no such gallant young men in attendance. The armies had taken them all. The next several minutes passed in a blur: the exchange of vows; Lieutenant Gay, thin and drawn in his new dress gray uniform sewn by the Nancies, the left sleeve draped over his injured arm; the celebratory dances dispensed with for lack of partners; Gus's awkward toast to the newlyweds; the sparkle of past gatherings replaced by whispered talk of the failed Maryland and Kentucky campaigns and the converging of opposing forces in central Tennessee. She shuttered with a dark premonition: this would be the last of the gaiety in LaGrange.

A commotion erupted at the grand entrance.

The guests rushed from the parlor to greet two unexpected guests, Senator Hill and President Jefferson Davis. Both their arrival and physical appearance stunned Nancy. The two men looked tired and pallid, the lines in their sunken faces more furrowed than when she had last seen them. Mobbed for handshakes, Davis wobbled on his cane. She saw that the war had taken an alarming toll on him.

Senator Hill searched the parlor and beckoned Caroline into his embrace. "My darling, forgive me. I have accompanied the President on a tour of our forces in Tennessee and Alabama. We are en route to Savannah and have but three hours until our train leaves. I was told this was your wedding day. I pray for you all the happiness in the world."

Caroline curtsied. "I am so grateful to you, Senator, for allowing us the use of Bellevue. Nannie took the liberty to offer your home for the ceremony."

Senator Hill kissed her cheek and searched the guests. "Nannie! Come, let me buss you, too!"

Nannie grasped his dappled hands. "You do not come home enough."

Senator Hill brought Davis forward, and the president bowed to the ladies. "You have me to blame," he said, his voice hoarse and weak. "I cannot long be denied the Senator's wisdom." He studied Nancy as if trying to place her face.

Nancy came to his rescue. "We met in this very room years ago. I shouldn't think you'd forget my *faux pas* with the dance of the state flags."

"Ah, yes. You so reminded me of ..." Davis caught himself.

Nancy suspected he feared the mention of his first love might be misconstrued and conveyed maliciously to his wife, Varina, in Richmond. "A compliment I shall always treasure." She motioned up the groom to her side. "Mr. President, may I present Lieutenant Gay of the Fourth Georgia. He is on furlough recovering from his wound suffered at Sharpsburg."

Gay saluted. "An honor."

Davis shook Gay's good hand. "We are in your debt, Lieutenant."

"Sir, I am not the only soldier present. You should know one of the most dedicated fighting units in our Confederacy stands with you in this room."

Davis looked around, expecting to find more uniformed men.

"Mrs. Morgan here is captain of the Nancy Harts militia. The ladies of LaGrange have drilled twice a week since the start of the war. They are better shots than many men I have fought with in the Army of Northern Virginia."

Davis acted nonplussed as Nancy and the other women came to attention. He seemed uncertain of what to make of the report. Before he inquired further, the other guests pressed up to beg news of the war.

Nancy saw Davis stagger from the rush upon him. She supported him with a discrete hand to his back. Caroline spied the falter, too, and she motioned

Nancy with a dart of her eyes toward the bedroom upstairs. Nancy took the hint. "Ladies and gentlemen, the President is surely exhausted from his journey from Montgomery. If you will grant him a respite, I'm certain we can convince him to grace us with a few words before he leaves for the depot."

Led upstairs with her firm grasp on his elbow, Davis thanked her in a faint whisper. "I now recall why you reminded me of my long-departed Sallie."

She escorted him into the guest bedroom and shut the door behind them. "There is lemonade in the pitcher. If you wish anything stronger, I have learned the skills of the commissary officer from my husband." She shelved his top hat and helped him remove his overcoat.

He sat on the bed, slumping, and closed his eyes. "It has been a long three months. Atlanta. Marietta. Murfreesboro. Jackson. Montgomery. Mobile." She moved toward the door to leave him when he called her back. "Mrs. Morgan, is it true what the lieutenant said? About your militia?"

She colored, reticent to speak of what surely was to him a trifle. "I'd never claim to excel the Army of Northern Virginia in marksmanship, but the rest of his report is accurate."

Davis dropped his face into his hands. "Have we come to this? The flower of our womanhood now required to take up arms? We forfeit the very principles for which we fight."

She risked a step closer and resisted the urge to place a comforting hand on his shoulder. "I am often admonished that I am too brash for my own good."

He opened his pouched eyes and greeted her self-deprecation with a doleful smile. "Please, speak freely."

"Our militia is named for a patriotic woman who fought the Tories during the Revolution. You men give us too little credit for our part in civilizing this country. How many of us have defended our cabins from attack by savages? Is defending our towns from the Yankees any different?"

He pondered her point. "It speaks poorly of our military situation."

She had vowed not to add to his burdens by prying for information, but she couldn't ignore such an opening. She poured a glass of lemonade and offered it to him. "Are our armies in such dire condition?"

He took a sip and sighed. "May I count on your confidence?"

"Of course."

"The Federal forces in the West have designs on Vicksburg."

She nodded. "The Anaconda Plan."

He flashed surprise at how well-informed she was about military affairs. "You study the newspapers, I see."

"I do, although they can be less reliable than our own generals who often pass through town. An advantage from living on a rail line."

He stirred the lemonade as if reading his future in the swirl of the pith and pulp. *"My* generals on this side of the Appalachians claw at each other like roosters in a cockfight. I had no choice but to make this journey to enforce a semblance of discipline."

"Bragg."

He answered her with a knowing glance. "He is an old friend. Do you have officers under your command?"

"Nine."

"How do you resolve petty jealousies in your ranks?"

She sighed. "I am the last woman in Troup County to give advice on petty jealousies. If my ladies get their hackles up, I remind them of the dozens of menial duties I attend to, and I offer to resign the rank and relinquish the tasks to the most vociferous complainer. That usually does the trick."

He smiled ruefully. "You are fortunate in not having to deal with West Pointers and ambitious politicians."

"And you, sir, are fortunate in not having to wrangle a new class of debutantes with designs on the same gentleman." She hung his coat in the armoire and winked at him. "Rest your eyes for a while. I will have the servants pack a lunch and wake you when your carriage arrives."

* * *

The train chugged past a shell-pocked depot called Hamilton's Crossing, the last stop before Fredericksburg. Nancy retracted her mourning veil of black bombazine and studied the crude map of the Virginia environs that her brother, Miles, had drawn on the back of an envelope. She peered out the window and searched the wooded high ground to the left of the tracks for Prospect Hill, a knoll held by the Fourth Georgia during the bloody battle fought here two months ago. A gagging stench forced the passengers to bring kerchiefs to their mouths. In the open farm fields just beyond the rail embankment, hundreds of horse carcasses lay frozen in every imaginable pose of agony, their heads and legs poking out from three inches of snow to form a white menagerie of horror. Thousands of crude headboards marked the shallow graves of nine thousand Yankees. The Army of the Potomac had crossed the Rappahannock River just to the right of those tracks on pontoon bridges, only to be forced back within the hour.

This is the place.

The Slaughter Pen.

Joe was killed over there. She tried to weep, but she had spent the last of her tears on the grueling three-day trek by way of Knoxville and Richmond. Her deep pangs of guilt did not abate. While she celebrated a warm Christmas at home, her brother, Joe, had lingered in a hospital hut out in that field somewhere, dying from artillery wounds. The telegram arrived three days after Caroline's wedding. Strafed with tuberculosis, Miles resigned his commission soon after Joe's death and brought their brother's body home. Tormented by his battle experiences, Miles vowed to start a law practice in Valdosta, two hundred miles south of LaGrange and as far away from the war as possible.

A frigid blast of the February wind rattled the windows. *I have never been so cold.* She clutched her arms and regretted not bringing warmer clothing. An elderly woman sitting across from her shared a shawl draped over her legs. She nodded to the woman, grateful for the kind gesture.

"First time to Fredericksburg?" the woman asked.

"Yes, ma'am."

"A shame."

"I'm sorry?"

"I wish you could have seen our grand city before the Yankees plundered it. President Washington lived here, you know. The Northern savages turned his home into a stable."

The train slowed and shimmied into the outskirts of Fredericksburg. Every muscle in Nancy's body went rigid, and her hand flew to her chest. Brown had warned her of the destruction, but the bleak blocks of ragged frames and crumbled chimneys shocked her. The streets were strewn with ransacked garments, emptied wine bottles, smashed furniture—even the skeleton of a piano on a corner, used by the Yankees for a barricade. Two hundred yards beyond the train depot, the bridge that led to Washington lay destroyed, its empty piers rising from the Rappahannock like giant gravestones. On both sides of the tracks, soldiers of General Lee's army huddled around barrel fires, many without coats and shoes. "I was told we won the battle," she muttered. "Our men look more wasted than if they had been held in prison camps."

The elderly woman seemed grimly amused by her observation. "Where are you from, child?"

"Georgia."

"Ah, the fresh core of the rotting apple. What brings you north?"

"My husband is an officer with General Colquitt's brigade. He has requested my companionship during his winter quartering."

The train lurched to a jolting halt. The conductor announced this stop as the end of the line and reminded passengers that the route no longer ran to the Potomac. She assisted her feeble compartment companion from her seat and draped the shawl around the woman's shoulders. At the steps, the woman turned back and grasped her hand. "Enjoy your honeymoon."

Nancy thought it an odd remark, perhaps even a malicious one, but before she made sense of it, her eye caught sight of an emaciated officer waiting on the platform. His faded uniform was frayed and stained with mud and blood. Several seconds passed before she recognized Brown. Stunned by his frail and slovenly appearance, she hurried to the gangway door. A thousand thoughts raced through her head. Had she been so altered, too? Would he still find her attractive? Would they need time to return to intimate conversation? What accommodations had he arranged for her? Would they find the privacy to—

Brown stepped up and swept her into his arms. He pressed a kiss to her cheek and took a step back to examine her. "You are shivering, my love."

"I fear my toes are frostbitten. I will warm them in the carriage." She saw him hesitating with a downcast look. She glanced around and realized there was no conveyance waiting.

"We suffer deprivations here, Nan. An officer with a horse is considered fortunate." He whistled a half-lame mare to them.

"Where is your Arabian?"

He lifted her to the saddle. "Old Cane Break gave up the ghost during the Maryland campaign." He strapped on her baggage, climbed aboard the saddle behind her, and snapped the reins.

She eased into his chest, remembering how much she missed his embrace. "I am so tired, I may sleep a week in bed with you as my hostage." She waited for his approval, but he said nothing. "Brown ... there *is* a bed in the inn?"

"Did I describe General Lee's headquarters here in my letters?"

"No, but why—"

"A small tent."

"We'll have a cot, at least?"

Brown squeezed her tighter to warm her and kissed her frozen cheek. "For once, you'll be thankful I'm a mere commissary officer."

* * *

The next morning, Brown entered their tent carrying a steaming cup of coffee and a plate of biscuits and bacon. "Another foot of snow last night."

Nancy awoke and rubbed her eyes. "Where are we, exactly?"

"Rappahannock Academy. A few miles southeast of the city. There used to be a military institute on these grounds."

She sat up and, smelling the coffee's bracing aroma, shot a grateful but guilty look at him. "From real beans. You shouldn't have."

"You give me too much credit. It's a gift from General Colquitt."

She wrapped herself in the blanket and sipped the brew. "Cousin Alfred has always been so kind to me."

Brown sat next to her on the cot and fed her a strip of bacon. He grinned and kissed her. "I remember once feeding you chocolate-dipped strawberries like this. Where was it now? Oh yes, at the West Point social." His eyes twin-kled with mischief. "Sallie Fannie Reid made those confections, didn't she? So delicious, I can still taste them."

She playfully slapped his shoulder. "You can mark *her* off your dance card. Gossip has it she is quite enamored of that Watkins County gentleman who out-jousted you."

"William Grant?"

She nodded. "He rides with Bedford Forrest in Tennessee."

"Well, Captain Grant made the wrong choice for Queen of Love *that* day."

She blushed at his reference to their intimacy that night.

"How did you sleep?"

She couldn't hide a girlish smile. "You *know* how I slept."

"I have missed you so."

She rested her cheek against his. "Miles brought me your last letter. I spent hours reading it." She lifted her head and forced him to fix on her determined eyes. "Brown, I must know more."

He dipped his chin. "Nan, how will the grisly details help you overcome your grief for Joe?"

She turned aside, stung by his chiding tone. "You men witness so many deaths that you become numb to them. We women are held hostage to our imaginations, forced to conjure every instance of suffering and violence. Miles refused to open Joe's coffin. I never had a chance to say goodbye to him."

Brown sighed. "Burnside crossed the river in front of the city and also far-ther south. The Yankees found a marsh in front of our lines that General Gregg thought was impenetrable."

"The Yankees waded the swamp?"

Brown nodded. "We were ordered in from the reserves to throw them back. We hadn't been in a fight so desperate since Antietam. The Yankees got their artillery across the rail tracks, close enough to rake our exposed lines."

"That's when Joe was hit?"

He refreshed her coffee, trying to avoid the grisly particulars, but her insis-tent glare drove him to oblige. "Some of the men said Joe called out for Miles."

"And?"

"Miles staggered and fell to his knees, gagging for breath. He couldn't reach Joe. After the Seven Days campaign, Miles was diagnosed with the consump-tion. He should have gone home months ago, but he refused to leave Joe."

She fought back the grip in her throat. "How long did Joe live?"

"I found him the next day in a barn converted into a field hospital. His legs were ... gangrene had set in. He was slipping in and out of consciousness. I don't think he recognized me. He passed two days later."

She prayed her brother didn't linger in agony. "How many casualties did our army suffer here?"

"Five thousand. The Yankees nearly triple."

"And the Fourth?"

"The count is uncertain. Since leaving home, the regiment has lost more than four hundred men."

She turned inward, unable to comprehend such numbers. Bobby Smith. Sallie Bull's brother, Dolph. Gene Ware. Now, Joe and Miles. "If this war persists much longer, we will have no men coming home." She waited for him to counter that prediction, but he stood and turned his back to her. "Brown, what will happen to us?" He peeked through the tent's flap, preoccupied, and she persisted in her demand for an answer. "We have never kept secrets."

"There are rumors General Lee plans to invade the North come spring."

She leapt up to confront him. "How will *that* succeed? The Yankees drove him from Maryland last year. And he has lost a third of his men."

"The Army can't stay here through the summer. Northern Virginia and the Shenandoah Valley have been devastated. There's no forage for the horses, and I can barely scrape up enough pork bellies and flour to feed our brigade on half rations. An invasion would give our farmers time to plant a season's harvest."

She looked at the plate with the biscuits and felt a pang of guilt at eating so well while these soldiers around her were hungry. "At the Richmond depot, while waiting for my train, I saw a mob of women pounding on the government warehouses. They were shouting 'bread or blood.'"

"There are shortages in every war," he said. "It will pass."

"What if the Yankees invade Georgia?"

Brown regarded her as if she were daft. "They will never reach Georgia. They can't even get past Chattanooga."

Before she could press him, a bugler played drill call and a chorus of voices outside the tent sang:

> "We marched from western Georgia
> To the old Virginny land.
> Cap'n Nannie did assure us,
> She said we'd fight just grand."

Hearing her name, she looked at Brown with confusion.

> "We saw the Yankees coming,
> We heard them give command;
> To arms, to arms, they shouted,

And by your colors stand.
Cap'n Nannie, Cap'n Nannie,
Come out and show us how,
The Nancies load a musket,
And cause the Yanks to howl."

She threw on a coat and laced up her traveling boots. When she was presentable, Brown yanked open the flaps. Dozens of LaGrange men in the Fourth Georgia stood serenading her. "My Lord, so many familiar faces!" She rushed to them, grasping their hands and conveying messages from family members and friends back home.

Sergeant Joe Ware, brother of Gus and Caroline, ordered his men into formation. "Attention! Is this any way to salute an officer?"

The LaGrange men grinned as they fell in line for inspection.

Ware pointed at Brown. "You, too, Lieutenant. She outranks you."

Brown accepted the gibe with a grin and stepped into line.

Nancy adjusted a lapel here and checked a buckle strap there, but the rags the men wore appalled her. Finished with her inspection, she took her position at the center. "I've never seen a more handsome company. I promise when I return to LaGrange, you will all have new uniforms sewn by the Nancy Harts!"

The men cheered. "Don't send them to the commissary officers, Nannie," said John Key. "Those scoundrels are worse than the Yankee pillagers."

As Brown laughed, Sergeant Ware stepped forward. "Folks back home have been writing to us about the legendary marksmanship of our local militia." He pointed toward a scarecrow set up for a demonstration. "We were hoping you'd give us a show."

The men chanted "aye" until Nancy relented. She blushed and glanced at Brown, fearful of upsetting him, but he smiled and motioned her to the task. She walked to a stack of muskets and found an Enfield that resembled the one she practiced with at home. She extracted it from the stack without collapsing the other muskets, drawing whistles of admiration for her deftness. She threw a cartridge box over her shoulder, strutted through the snow with the eager men hurrying behind her. "Who has a watch?"

The men shrugged. "Heck, Nannie," said one. "Up here, we count off the seconds by calling out, 'One Yankee down, two Yankee down.'"

She brought the musket's butt stock to the ground between her feet, just as she had learned from *Hardee's Tactics,* and braced for the signal to start.

"Fire at will!" Ware commanded.

Nancy pulled a cartridge, bit off its end, loaded the hammer pan, and dropped the patched ball into the barrel. She whipped out the ramrod, drove the ball home with two plunges, returned the ramrod to its sheath. With her feet set at the prescribed angle, she braced against her back leg, lowered the barrel, and steadied its notch just below the scarecrow's belt. She took a steadying breath and pulled the trigger. She absorbed the kick and held the aim two seconds after the explosion, waiting for the smoke to clear.

The scarecrow's millinery—an abandoned Union kepi—lay on the ground with a smoking hole in its brim. The men cheered and threw their hats into the crisp air to celebrate her shot.

Nancy handed the musket to Ware. "Whose weapon is this?" When Ware admitted ownership, she playfully scolded him. "Shoots high."

A frown crossed Ware's face. "Why, look here, Nannie, you got the Yankee straight between the eyes."

"I was aiming for his belt buckle." She turned and addressed the men. "Every soldier worth his salt knows you aim low. Furlough canceled, Sergeant. Clean your barrel. You'd never cut it with the Nancy Harts. You remind me of a cantankerous doctor back in LaGrange."

Ware stood speechless as the men slapped their knees and laughed so hard that a couple tumbled into the snow—a roar echoed up from the outskirts of the encampment. "We gotta go, boys!" shouted Ware. "It's fightin' time!"

The LaGrange soldiers saluted Nancy and took off on a run through the snow, scooping up snow and forming hard balls. She turned to find two masses of men squaring off on the low ground. Alarmed, she turned to Brown for an explanation. "Are we attacked?"

Brown smirked. "You wanted to see the Army of Northern Virginia in action. Here's your chance."

Baffled, Nancy watched the drifted fields below as thousands of men formed opposing battle lines and unfurled their flags, preparing to charge. Officers dressed their ranks, and soon a battalion of cavalry came swooping down from the nearby hills and galloped across the no-man's-land. The horsemen unleashed a volley of snowballs against the infantry on the left and sent them retreating. Several soldiers on both sides fell to their knees and groped their bleeding heads.

"A snowball fight?" Nancy cried. "In *their* condition? Brown, they'll collapse from exhaustion, if they don't maim their eyes first!"

Brown grinned. "Builds esprit. Our lads are taking on the North Carolinians today. The winner has been promised a barrel of sour-mash whiskey."

Nancy, incredulous, walked closer to the crest that overlooked the snowball battle. The butternut lines formed, charged, and retreated across the white expanse. Those Georgia men who ventured too deep into the North Carolina lines were taken prisoner and escorted to the rear, pummeled by snowballs to the backs of their heads. She saw another Carolina regiment rush to the front and open haversacks filled with dozens of balls packed with ice. "Those Tar Heels are cheating! They don't have to reload!"

Brown shrugged. "That's the least of our worries. Your cousin, Alfred, put the sun in our faces. Our fellows will soon suffer snow blindness."

Nancy squinted into the white glare and found General Colquitt riding behind the Georgia lines and laughing as he gave orders for counter-charges. Her gaze scanned higher to the opposite ridge where a dour, long-bearded officer, crowned by a battered forage kepi, sat on a chestnut horse while watching the contest. From time to time, he ducked errant throws, tipping his cap with admiration for the arm strength of those men who reached him. She was amazed by how calm his horse remained under the assault. "Is that ... ?"

"Old Stonewall himself," Brown confirmed. "On Little Sorrel."

Nancy rushed across the snow to gain a better view of the famous general. He looked nothing as she had imagined. Every few seconds, he raised his right hand and pointed it toward the sky, as if mimicking a weathervane. "Why, Brown, I'd mistake him for a queer tinker if I passed him on a street."

Brown chortled. "A tinker who would outflank you and steal your artillery before you knew you'd been pickpocketed."

"What is he doing with his arm?"

"Rumor has it he believes the left side of his body is heavier than the right. He allows gravity to drain the blood down his arm to balance the humors."

"He must be crackbrained."

"You won't get an argument from me."

She watched with growing dismay as the North Carolina regiments pushed back the Georgians. "We are getting the worst of it."

Brown set his gloved fists on his hips, resigned to the outcome. "The boys won't take kindly to losing that whiskey ration."

She paced back and forth in the snow, agitated by the prospect of having to return to LaGrange to describe this humiliation for her Nancies. Something had to be done. She racked her memory for what she had learned about infantry tactics. Inspired by an idea, she turned to Brown. "Do you have an order book?"

"Yes, but—"

"Hand it to me." She took it, pulled the pencil from its sheath, and scribbled a message. "Take this to Cousin Alfred."

Brown stared gape-mouthed at her. "This is not time for letters."

"Hurry!" she insisted.

Brown shook his head, bewildered but resigned to her demand. He waved over a mounted courier to deliver the dispatch to General Colquitt in the field below. The courier saluted and galloped off into the snowball fray.

Nancy stomped her feet as if that would hurry the courier. She watched with anxious hope as the rider handed her message to Colquitt. The general read it and looked up at her. She nodded emphatically to encourage him to implement her suggestion. He grinned, saluted, and issued orders to his staff. The junior officers fanned out to the breaking Georgia regiments with new instructions.

"What did you tell him?" asked Brown.

"Battle of Cannae."

Brown frowned. "What in Heaven's name are you talking about?"

"I borrowed a copy of Livy from Gus's library awhile back."

"And?"

"Just watch."

The Georgia regiments in the center of the melee gave way and retreated in controlled order while the flanks held their positions. The North Carolinians, warbling the Rebel yell, hurled themselves into the melting middle of the Georgia line.

"We are whipped even worse," said Brown. "I guess you aren't the military genius you think—"

"Now!" Nancy shouted to herself.

The flanks of the Georgians swallowed up the charging North Carolinians, trapping them between two jaws, just as Hannibal and his Carthaginians did to the Roman legions during the Second Punic War. Surrounded and without a fresh supply of snow, the North Carolinians huddled together with their arms protecting their heads as the Georgia men, gathering up the pristine supplies of snow behind them, pummeled them into submission. Dozens, and then hundreds, of North Carolinian hands went up to surrender. Victorious, General Colquitt laughed and reared his horse to thank Nancy for the suggestion.

Brown stood dumbfounded. He shook his head in amazement as he offered his arm to return Nancy to their tent. All he could manage in concession was an anemic observation about her shivering. "You are cold again."

She lorded a triumphant smile over him. "Not as cold as those losers down there from Greensboro. Be sure Joe Ware delivers *my* dram of whiskey."

Escorted back, she glanced at General Jackson and his staff on the far ridge. She blinked hard and wiped the tiny icicle on her lashes, uncertain if her eyes had deceived her. *Did Stonewall just doff his kepi to me?*

20

CAPE GIRARDEAU, MISSOURI
APRIL 1863

On the drill field, Hugh walked across the ranks of his First Wisconsin troopers, inspecting their uniforms and weapons. Accompanied by Wallace and Major Eggleston, he heard whispers questioning why he had called them out after religious services on that frosty Sunday morning to stand in front of ten pine coffins. Camp deaths from dysentery and measles were common now, and the Army typically buried the dead with little ceremony. He stopped at the center to address the regiment. Accepting a small Bible from Wallace, he turned to Jeremiah 51:20 and read aloud: "'Thou art my battle-ax and weapons of war. For with thee will I break in pieces the nations, and with thee will I destroy kingdoms.'"

"Amen," the troopers muttered with little enthusiasm.

Hugh closed the Bible and recited from memory another passage, this one from the Gospel of Matthew. "For there is nothing hid, which shall not be manifested. Neither was any thing kept secret, but that it should come abroad." He lowered his eyes in silent prayer.

After a minute passed in this contemplation, a trooper stepped out the ranks. "Colonel, who exactly are we sending to their Maker?"

Hugh roused from his meditation and walked behind the row of coffins, pointing to each. "Today we bury Chalk Bluff, Scatterville, Gainesville, Greensboro, Jonesboro, Harrisburg, Wittsburg, Madison, West Prairie, Bloomfield, Greenville, and last, L'Anguille Ferry."

The troopers shuffled and shifted, baffled why he was reciting the skirmishes where the Rebels had bloodied them during the past two years. "Sir, you been into the whiskey?" another trooper risked. "We were told the taverns in town were off limits on Sundays."

Hugh motioned for Wallace to hand out crowbars. "Let us offer the dearly departed a last farewell."

Appalled, the troopers grudgingly obeyed and pried open the lids on the coffins. They gasped from what they discovered inside. "Dust thou art, Jeff Davis!" said one of the men as he pulled out a brand new Sharps carbine from among thirty rifles packed in the coffin. He waved the weapon over his head to show his comrades.

From the next pine box, another trooper plucked a sleek saber with a brass hand guard and leather grip. Its curved blade, much lighter than the heavy 1840 dragoon models they had been lugging, flashed under the sun. He brandished it with thrusts and parries. "And to dust thou shalt return!"

Cheers rattled every window in Cape Girardeau. At Hugh's smiling nod, the troopers broke ranks and rushed to the coffins. They pulled out their new weapons to admire and tossed their old muzzle loaders, shotguns, and swords into the boxes.

"Form up!" ordered Major Eggleston.

"We have Professor Daniels to thank," Hugh said. "He may be out of the Army, but he hasn't forgotten us. He pestered Governor Salomon and those skinflints in the Legislature back home until they ponied up."

"Huzzah for Colonel Daniels!" the men shouted.

Hugh handled one of the new carbines to demonstrate how it should be carried and fired. "These get off three shots in the time it took you to load and fire your old squirrel snappers. On the command of 'Order Arms,' raise the carbine in the right hand to waist level." He grasped the carbine with his left hand and connected its swivel snap to the ring on his shoulder lanyard. "The barrel hangs at your right side. Sabers hang on your left. Every man will drill until he can dismount and form picket and battle lines within ten seconds of the command."

"Colonel, permission to speak," said a trooper.

"Granted."

"Sir, you want us to fight like infantry? We ain't never done that and I don't reckon we ever will. Them generals, Curtis and McNeil, they just use us for screening and foraging. The war's done gone two years. Shiloh. Pea Ridge. Wilson's Creek. Donelson. Perryville. Corinth. And that's just on this side of the Alleghenies. Why learn these new tricks?"

"The Rebs at Corinth," Hugh said. "How did *they* fight?"

"I heard they dug in."

"Did they dig in at Bull Run and Shiloh?"

The trooper thought for a second. "I guess not."

"So, you're saying they changed their tactics." When the trooper shrugged, Hugh patted him on the shoulder. "I wasn't born a soldier. Most of us here weren't. I'm a schoolteacher. And because of that, I'm a fair learner of new lessons. The way I see it, this war is changing by the month, and changing fast. Our boys in the First Kentucky Cavalry have been chasing Bedford Forrest and John Hunt Morgan. Last year, they cornered Morgan in Lebanon. Morgan dismounted and posted his men in the buildings of the town. The First Kentucky charged in a scrum and was bloodied good. But those Kentucky boys learned quickly. Next time they found Morgan, they dismounted, drove that rapscallion out of the town, and routed him in the open field with a saber attack. Those Texas Swamp Rangers dismounted and fought on foot at L'Anguille Ferry. We've had our last bloody lesson. I don't need another one. Do you?"

When the men shook their heads, Hugh signaled for Wallace to grab a knapsack lying next to the open coffins. Wallace opened the sack and distributed pamphlets to the company sergeants.

"Cavalry Tactics," said Hugh. "Written by Confederate General Joseph Wheeler. Learn it by rote. Fall out!"

* * *

Two weeks later, Hugh climbed the ladder to a barn loft on the outskirts of Cape Girardeau. He stood at the open loft door and focused his field glasses on five thousand Confederate troops massing for an attack on the city's defenses. The armies of Earl Van Dorn and Sterling Price had been driven from Missouri, but a hothead named John Sappington Marmaduke, known for dueling fellow officers, had rounded up every bushwhacker and slaver left in Arkansas to invade Missouri. Marmaduke vowed to kill the Union general in command here, John McNeil, and give no quarter to their outnumbered Federal occupation force of three thousand. Scouting reports said Marmaduke rode with Hugh's old nemeses from Chalk Bluff, William Jeffers and his Swamp Rangers. Hugh figured that murderer Wild Bill Parsons was also with them, looking for revenge for the ruffians Colonel Daniels hanged here.

Wallace climbed the ladder to find him. "What's the plan?"

From his regiment's position along the Bloomfield Road on the left flank, Hugh watched Marmaduke's screaming regiments advance across a chain of small hills that led to an arc of Union forts. Behind him, panicked residents ran for a steamboat the mayor commissioned to take them to safety on the Illinois side. If Marmaduke broke through the ring of Federal fortifications, his First Wisconsin troopers would be pinned against the river with no escape.

"Hugh? The boys are getting antsy."

Hugh delayed issuing orders while he watched the Union artillery stationed on Fort B, in the center of their defenses, open up and send a thunderous boom echoing back through the city. Hissing Minié balls filled the air, sounding like a thousand beehives overturned. The big guns of a battery with the

First Nebraska Infantry raked the approach into the city, forcing the Rebels to halt and regroup. He spun the focus on the glasses tighter and barely made out a flag on the right Confederate flank. *That damn Texas star again.*

"Hugh, for God's sake!" Wallace shouted. "Are we going to sit here idle while those Rebs overrun the forts?"

Hugh turned with a grin. "That's Jeffers in front of us."

Wallace paled. "You can't mean to take them on *directly?* That's massed infantry out there."

Hugh debated the risk. He'd had only two weeks to drill the regiment on oblique attacks. Such a complicated maneuver would require his troopers to advance in a column of four abreast with sabers drawn, execute twenty-degree turns to the right, and align forward again in a new assault angle. All depended on his men hearing his commands and performing them in unison without hesitation. With the artillery pounding away on both sides, he'd have to lead the charge from the front and rely on hand signals. If the dust and smoke obscured him, the sortie could turn into a suicidal disaster.

His mind blanked with indecision. Was he losing his nerve? He didn't hesitate that day in Milwaukee when he broke Sherman Booth from jail. He had come an inch to being hanged for it, but never gave that a thought.

"Hugh, dammit, those Arkansas toothpickers out there are getting closer."

He raced for the ladder. "Order A, B, and D companies to dismount and form a line a quarter-mile down the Bloomfield Pike. You take them far enough up where they can get an enfilade angle on Jeffers's flank."

Wallace scrambled down the ladder to catch him. "What about you?"

"When you distract them with carbine fire, I'll hit Jeffers in the gut."

The dangerous plan stunned Wallace. "We're supposed to screen the city's flank. What if they break us?"

Hugh ran for his horse, took the reins from his adjutant, and put a foot in the stirrup. As his troopers waited for orders, he explained to Wallace, "Jeffers thinks we'll do what we've always done. Sit on the flank and watch the party. When's the last time Federal cavalry charged their infantry with sabers?"

Wallace shrugged and mustered his troopers. "Companies A, B, and D! Dismount! Unsling carbines! Form up with me!"

Hugh heaved into his saddle. The ground under him shook, pounded by the ten howitzers brought up by Marmaduke. He listened for the explosions and calculated the trajectories and locations of the Rebel battery. When he deemed the time ripe, he shouted to Major Eggleston, "Close Order!"

The mounted Wisconsin troopers formed up in a column, four abreast. Hugh led them on a trot across the Bloomfield Pike and veered them to the left, behind a hillock that rose just enough to keep them out of sight of the

Confederates. He cocked his ear for the distinctive ping of carbines, the sign that Wallace and his companies had engaged Jeffers's infantry. At last, hearing the distinctive *rat-a-tat-tat,* he ordered Eggleston, "Draw sabers! On my signal, prepare for Oblique Right! Then On Right into Line!"

Eggleston relayed the command down the column.

Hugh turned to assess the reaction. The men, perplexed, greeted the order with blank stares. He shouted, "Who wants to visit an old friend?"

His troopers waved their sabers overhead and shouted, "Huzzah!"

There it was again—the rattle of Sharps carbines, followed by screams. Wallace was on them full-bore now. Hugh signaled the charge and raced his mounted troopers over the hillock. On the gallop, he passed Wallace's men lying on the ground along the pike, pouring fire into Jeffers's flank. He searched the gray lines and found his old rival on foot, scrambling to reform his line at a ninety-degree angle to meet Wallace's attack.

From the corner of his eye, Jeffers spotted Hugh and his troopers rushing over the ridge.

"For Chaplain Densmore!" Hugh shouted with his saber angled over his head. "Remember L'Anguille Ferry!"

His Wisconsin cavalrymen took up the call for revenge.

Pressed on two sides now, Jeffers called for his confused infantry to turn again and take aim at the mounted troop.

Hugh swirled his saber and signaled for the Oblique Right. Rebel gunfire sprayed around him. Smothered in smoke, he couldn't see twenty feet in any direction. He had to trust his men had followed him to the right at twenty degrees. He counted off ten seconds and reined left again.

The smoke cleared. Just as Hugh had mapped out the tactic, before him stood Jeffers's confused rebels, looking around and wondering why the charging Federals had disappeared from their front. Hugh grinned at his troopers, who had performed the Oblique Right without a hitch. He pointed his saber forward and drove into the flank of the unsuspecting Rebel scrum. Both sides descended into a melee of swinging rifles and cutting sabers. Breaking from his ranks, he circled his horse and searched for Jeffers, determined to pay back a second debt, *that* from Lieutenant Phillips's death at Chalk Bluff.

There the bastard stands.

Hugh crashed into the Missourians and spurred for Jeffers. The Rebel commander aimed his revolver and fired. Hugh ducked—the ball whizzed past his ear. He shouted, "You murder men of the cloth!"

Jeffers cocked his revolver for another shot. *"You* hang shopkeepers!"

Hugh slashed at the slaver but missed his head by an inch. He reared his arm to hack again, but the snarling Jeffers backed away and called for a retreat. Before Hugh could give chase, the Confederate battery loosed a round of grapeshot canister. If he pressed the pursuit, he would expose his own flank to deadly artillery fire and risk envelopment by Marmaduke's men in the center. He cursed for failing to bag Jeffers and reluctantly ordered his column back to the Bloomfield Pike. On their galloping return, the mounted companies fought a rear-guard action, allowing Wallace's men on foot to fire their hot carbines while backtracking in good order.

After returning to the city's defensive line with only minor wounds, the Wisconsin troopers welcomed Hugh, grimed in gunpowder, with raucous cheers to applaud the daring maneuver.

"Form up!" Hugh shouted. "They may come at us!"

Wallace pointed him toward the river, where a steamboat filled with hundreds of blue-clad reinforcements pulled into the quay. "Looks like we're done fighting for the day."

From his command post atop Fort C, General McNeil observed the results of the cavalry charge on his left flank. "I think that old polecat Marmaduke is whipped. His swamp pirates prefer the hit-and-run to ten-pound balls whizzing around their noggins on the open field." He lowered his field glasses and, pointing to his left flank, asked Lt. Colonel Baumer of the First Nebraska Infantry, "What is that cavalry unit guarding the Bloomfield Pike?"

"First Wisconsin, sir. Colonel LaGrange's command."

McNeil nodded. "Remind me to mention him in my report. He fights like a berserker."

21

LAGRANGE, GEORGIA
MAY 1863

Nancy hadn't seen the town so excited since the LaGrange Guards paraded off to war two years ago. A telegram arrived that morning announcing the South's most celebrated heroine, Belle Boyd, planned to visit that afternoon on her grand speaking tour through Tennessee, Alabama, and Georgia. To give the Confederate Cleopatra a proper welcome, Nancy mustered her militia, clad in their gray shell jackets, at the train depot. Behind them, a crowd buzzed with more good news from the morning papers: General Lee won a decisive victory over the Army of the Potomac at a crossroads in Virginia called Chancellorsville. Lee sent his opponent, the latest in a long line of inept Yankee generals, a boisterous loudmouth named Joseph Hooker, retreating toward Washington so dazed that one correspondent described him as a duck clubbed in the head.

Nancy's spirits soared. The Shenandoah Valley was open now for the invasion into Pennsylvania that Brown predicted. Since the death of her brother, Joe, she kept her hopes in check; tragedy seemed to come with every victory. Yet this summer would be different, she was certain of it. General Lee would soon take the devastation to the Northern farms and towns and let those people suffer the sting of deprivation and destruction. Meanwhile, that drunkard Grant remained bogged down with his army of Abolitionists in the swamps around Vicksburg. One more hammer blow against the Yankees would force Lincoln to negotiate the South's independence.

A familiar rapping roused her from her thoughts: Gus's pecking cane. Even the cynical doctor was so intrigued by Miss Boyd's impending visit that he had closed his office for the day. He limped up to the depot with his new fianceé, Anna Wagnon, on his arm and greeted Nancy with trepidation.

Nancy curtsied to Anna. "You've had a salutary effect on Dr. Ware, Miss Wagnon. He has become a regular paragon of society in recent weeks."

"I wouldn't think of allowing him to miss the Siren of the Shenandoah," said Anna. "I do hope she tells us stories of her exploits."

Gus harrumphed. "Might be a welcome change to have a woman in town who can hit a target." He sneered at Nancy. "Perhaps you should challenge her to a match."

"If I take aim at a target today, it won't be with a gun." Nancy fingered his starched collar. "Miss Wagnon, surely you've not been laundering Dr. Ware's shirts? But how else to explain how pristine and pressed they appear?"

Gus's eyes rounded.

"Oh, no," said Anna. "His sister's house servant performs those duties."

"I must compliment her on such dedication to his needs."

A distant whistle blew. The locomotive from Montgomery churned into town and hissed to a stop at the depot platform. The Nancies, singing *Dixie,* formed a cordon to hold back the raucous crowd from rushing the caboose. A tall, slender woman in a black veil emerged from the exit door and stood at the railing. Holding a riding crop, she wore a black felt campaign hat with one brim pinned back to a white plume and sported a revolver tucked under her belt. The rest of her outlandish attire comprised a black mourning dress festooned with officer shoulder straps and a gold palmetto breast pin.

The crowd hushed, confused by her sepulchral appearance. The dignitary drew back her veil with a gloved hand, revealing an intellectual face framed by dark red strands of curls. She was not beautiful, thought Nancy, but beguiling with the intense glare of a hawk.

Boyd stood in a practiced stance, one shoulder drawn back, as if draped with a cavalier's cape. Her cobalt blue eyes scanned the crowd and, trained to find the leader in a pack, alighted on Nancy. "You must be Captain Morgan. And these the Nancy Harts of much acclaim."

The Nancies beamed and saluted. "Welcome to LaGrange, Miss Boyd," said Nancy. "We have a podium set up for you in the square—"

"I apologize, but I cannot stay." A groan of disappointment rustled through the crowd, and Boyd extracted a folded document from her sleeve and handled it with the care due a precious relic. "I received this dispatch yesterday in Mobile. General Jackson ... my good friend ... lies in state in Richmond."

Nancy regarded the stunned reactions of Mary and Caroline, uncertain if she had heard correctly. "Stonewall Jackson is dead?"

When Boyd confirmed the report, women shrieked and wept, and the few men present, elderly mostly, wrung their hands. "Word has not arrived here? Our own men shot him by mistake when he risked a night reconnaissance for General Lee."

"Yes," said Nancy. "But our newspapers said he was recovering."

"I am as distraught as you. His last words to me were to travel West. He promised me all would be well." Boyd grasped the railing for support.

Nancy rushed up the steps to assist her. "You should rest."

"I must reach Richmond before he is buried."

Nancy could not accept the hopes of her fellow citizens being so cruelly dashed. Searching for a way to accommodate Boyd's revised schedule, she saw the full coal bin on stilts aside the tracks. Struck by an idea, she climbed down from the caboose and whispered to Leila, "Bring the engineer here."

Moments later, Leila returned with the engineer.

"Where do you refuel?" Nancy asked him.

"Newnan."

"Delay your departure two hours here."

"Ma'am. I can't do that. I have a timetable."

"We'll supply the coal, no charge. You can cut your Newnan stop short."

"I've got orders."

"I'm a captain. I'll give you new orders." Nancy glanced at Gus, determined to sweeten the offer. "And Dr. Ware will provide you with a bottle of the finest medicinal whiskey south of Atlanta."

Gus's jaw dropped. He prepared to lodge a protest until Anna squeezed his arm to beg his compliance. Rolling his eyes, he tapped his cane to seal the bargain. When the engineer consented, Nancy helped Boyd descend the caboose steps, and the militia formed an escort into town, making sure the citizens did not pester their esteemed visitor for souvenirs or shared memories of the deceased general.

The ladies turned onto Broad Street and led Boyd into Mary's house. Nancy and Caroline positioned a chaise in the center of the parlor, removed Boyd's shawl, and eased her to sitting. Leila and Augusta hurried into the pantry and returned with a glass of sweet tea and a plate of deviled eggs and sliced apples. Outside, denied entry into the sanctum of the local sisterhood, Gus and the old-timers stewed, craning in vain to peer through the drapes.

Boyd accepted the refreshment with a sigh of gratitude. "You run quite a military operation here, Captain Morgan."

"Anything to ease your sorrow," said Nancy.

The women gathered around Boyd, some pulling up chairs, the younger members of the militia sitting on the carpet at her feet.

"I heard you shot a Yankee stone cold," said Leila.

"Leila!" scolded Nancy. "Miss Boyd has been through a trauma. We must allow her to rest her eyes."

Boyd clasped Leila's hand. "You remind me of myself, darling, before I went off to the academy in Baltimore. How old are you?"

"Seventeen."

"Why, just two years younger than me. I was your age when I put that slug into the Northern vandal."

The women inched closer, enthralled by the legendary confrontation, the account of which they had read in the newspapers.

"He earned it," Leila said. "That's what I was told."

Boyd lifted her leg onto the arm of the chaise, most unladylike, and unbuttoned her boots to soothe her feet. "We're soldiers, are we not? And these parlor gatherings are our campfires?"

Her refreshing informality put the women at ease. While Nancy drew the drapes to thwart the gawkers on the porch, Boyd's roaming attention fell on the staircase that led to Mary's upper floor. "It was July Fourth in my hometown of Martinsburg. Y'all would love it there. Most exquisite old oaks in God's creation. The Federals came stomping down our lone street, drunk as skunks and firing off their revolvers. A gang of them took offense to me flying the Stars and Bars from my bedroom window. They broke in and threatened to shoot my mother."

"Where was your pa?" asked Leila.

"With Stonewall's army. Ten miles away."

"You and your ma were alone?" asked Augusta.

"Alone as Old Abe in a whorehouse."

Nancy glanced at Mary, shocked by the coarse language. Mary shrugged, as if suggesting what harm done with no men around to witness the improprieties.

Belle removed her hat. "Those slobbering Yankees commenced climbing our stairs and yelling that they intended to burn my flag and replace it with their banner of abomination."

Leila rose to her knees. "What did you do?"

"I came to the head of the stairs and, in a becalmed voice, told them that every member of my household would die before we allowed that Lincolnite rag raised over our home."

Nancy fixed the stairs in her periphery and tightened her grip around an imaginary revolver, wondering what *she* would do if confronted with such an intrusion. "They kept coming?"

Boyd nodded. "They did."

"And you pulled your pistol," said Augusta.

"I did." Boyd built the tension by savoring a languorous sip of the sweet tea. "I could stand the effrontery no longer. My blood was boiling in my veins."

While all eyes trailed back and forth from the staircase to Boyd, she picked up the plate of deviled eggs and offered them around.

"Miss Boyd!" Nancy cried.

"Yes, darling?"

"What happened next?"

"Oh, I pulled our house pistol from behind my back and I shot that impudent scoundrel clean through the chest."

The women sat in patriotic silence, each in her own mind fingering that trigger and envisioning the satisfaction of sending the invader tumbling to the floor to contemplate his sins in a pool of his own blood.

"The other soldiers," said Caroline. "Did they assault you?"

Boyd culled through the apple slices until she found one to her liking. "They tried, but I offered my bosom for a target and declared, 'Only cowards shoot women! Now, shoot!' They didn't have the mountain oysters to do it."

"My lord," muttered Mary.

Boyd darkened and her neck flamed. "Those Yankees began yelling orders to burn my home. They set rubbish against its walls for kindling. I sent off one of our darkies to fetch the Yankee general. He and his entourage arrived seconds before their despoilers could commit their depredation."

"Did they arrest you?" Nancy asked.

Boyd lifted her wrists together to reenact her handcuffing. "Not only did they arrest me, they interrogated me like a common criminal. I told them a Southern lady had every right by law to defend her home against trespassers. I don't think they'd ever had a woman talk to them that way."

"They released you," said Mary. "How fortunate."

Boyd caressed the silver crucifix that hung from her necklace. "The Almighty protects the righteous. That's what General Stonewall always told me." She pulled a kerchief from her sleeve and dabbed her eyes. "My mama got married at sixteen. I lost four of my siblings to disease. I refused to surrender what little of my heritage I had left. Shall I be too ashamed to confess that I recall without one shadow of remorse the act by which I saved my mother from insult, perhaps from death? That the blood I caused to shed has left no stain on my soul and imposed no burden on my conscience?"

"No," said Leila. "You did right."

The women edged even closer to Boyd to show their allegiance, except Nancy, who looked toward Mary and Caroline with rising concern. She held no doubt regarding the virtue of defending one's home, but the casual and emotionless manner in which Boyd told the story left her questioning if the woman might not be sane.

"Enough about me," said Boyd. "Tell me about the famous Nancy Harts."

"We've been drilling and practicing our shooting for two years," said Leila. "Nannie here outgunned Joe Ware in a match at Fredericksburg. He hasn't lived it down."

Boyd studied Nancy with one eye narrowed. "Target matches are a sight different from shooting Yankees. You think you got what it takes?"

Nancy bristled. "We don't train for the pleasure of killing, Miss Boyd. We drill to prepare to defend our homes, just as you did."

"*Captain* Boyd. I hold a commission from General Jackson."

"And I hold a commission from the LaGrange militia."

"Fair enough." Boyd smiled thinly and surveyed the adoring women, as if eager to change the topic. "I suppose the men around these parts slander you for your vulgar and indelicate ways when you turn your backs on them."

The women cast their eyes to the floor and fussed with their pleats. "We live in two worlds," Mary admitted. "They expect us to keep their businesses operating and the town defended. Yet they look askance at us when we take on masculine responsibilities."

Boyd drew the revolver she kept tucked in her belt and spun its chamber. "Those Yankee cell guards in that Washington prison tried to shame me in the same way. They rained upon me every slander their weak minds could dredge. Circus freak. Sapphic abomination. Uranian grotesque."

Caroline broached what the others were thinking. "Did they take liberties?"

"A couple of the gamecocks tried," said Boyd.

"You fended them off," said Augusta.

"With ease. I advised them I was schooled in the art of Southern witchery. That I learned the African Voodoo powers from the Negresses and promised to curse their shriveling manhoods for the rest of their short days."

"They believed you?" asked Leila.

Boyd curled a vengeful smile. "They had their proof of my *bona fides*. How could any woman who is *not* a witch move back and forth across the lines and consort with officers from both armies?"

The women enjoyed deep, satisfying sighs and raised imaginary glasses in a toast, impressed with her cunning.

Boyd saw an old musket hanging over the fireplace in the pantry room next door. "How do you ladies procure your ordnance?"

"Donations, mostly," said Nancy. "We have a few Enfields, the rest are fowlers and hunting muskets."

"We must remedy that." Boyd looked for a test partner. "Leila, isn't it?"

"Yes, ma'am."

Boyd stood and motioned for Leila to do the same. "I'm an uppity Yankee officer walking the streets of your occupied town. Your assignment is to abscond with my revolver without me knowing."

Leila's eyes rounded. "How could I ever accomplish that?"

"You have an aptitude no Yankee can resist."

Leila preened. "I've tried telling Nancy that I possess a superior intellect and—"

"No," said Boyd. "School learning is an impediment. I'm speaking of your feminine wiles."

Leila's eyes widened. "You mean ..."

"I mean *precisely* that." Boyd adjusted Leila's bodice to enhance her bosom. "Now, I am the most eligible and handsome man at the dance, and you are the last debutante to find a courtier."

Leila reddened and glared at the other women. "Who told her?"

Surrounded by shrugs, Boyd chuckled. "I'm speaking in general terms, hon. You must so enchant the Northern intruder that he forgets everything else in the world."

Leila turned inward, pausing as if to consider how she would play such an unseemly role. Signaling her readiness with the twirl of her finger, she walked around the parlor and swished her dress to suggest the sway of her hips. She glanced at Boyd and dropped her eyes. Moments later, she inched up her chin with a come-hither look. "Sir, I fear you have placed me at a disadvantage."

Boyd played along, acting surprised. "Disadvantage? Madam, have I made your acquaintance?"

Leila moved intimately closer. "By those heated glances of yours, most anyone might think so."

"Would you do me the honor of this dance?"

Leila batted her lashes and took Boyd's arm to walk her to an open space on the floor. Boyd led her around the parlor in a waltz. After several rounds, Leila staggered. Boyd caught her before she could hit the boards in the swoon.

Nancy rushed to Leila. "Do you have the spins?"

With their anxious faces hovering over her, Leila flashed open her eyes and grinned. She produced Boyd's revolver from under the folds of her dress.

The Nancies backed away, astonished.

Boyd clapped her hands. "Well done, my budding Confederate spy! Now, how do you get out of the ballroom with it?"

Leila lost her smirk. She hadn't a clue.

Boyd lifted her own skirt past her knee to her upper thigh, exposing a garter fashioned into a holster. She palmed the revolver and slid it through a hidden slit in the pleats of her dress, a sleight of hand that took two seconds. The women gasped and applauded.

Leila turned to Nancy. "We must get garters like this."

Nancy suspected the garrulous Boyd possessed more than a little of the yarn-spinning burleycue in her repertoire. "We haven't held a ball in two years. And last time I checked, we have no Yankees walking the streets here."

"Not yet," said Boyd. "Never in my wildest dreams did I think I'd witness Yankees marching through Martinsburg. The plunderers have designs on Chattanooga and Charleston. Perhaps the Nancy Harts might one day go on a shopping excursion for superior weaponry."

"Even if those cities fall," said Nancy, "how would we pass through enemy lines?"

Boyd regarded the windows to confirm no one could peer in. Reassured, she reached into yet another hidden compartment of her dress and pulled out a frayed cloth folded with bands.

"How many pockets do you have in your crinolines?" asked Nancy.

Boyd winked as she untied the cloth that held a small cross with splayed traverses, painted red. The women leaned in to examine the artifact.

"What is it?" asked Caroline.

"The insignia of the Knights Templar," said Boyd. "More than once the Yankees have stopped me while plying my courier service for Generals Jackson and Stuart. I show them this and they allow me to pass. Do you have a Mason in town?"

Nancy nodded. "Gus Ware."

"Procure the talisman from him and fashion copies. Y'all should carry one at all times. Freemasonry transcends secular enmities and will extricate you from many a scrape." She examined the hands of several women, looking for jewelry. "Have you installed a method to communicate should an invasion come?"

Nancy shook her head, stricken by her negligence in failing to learn more about how the Yankees conducted themselves in war zones. As if by magic, Boyd produced a pocket watch on a chain from another slit in her gown and removed its casing to reveal an empty chamber for hiding messages. Assured the women now understood the value of such accessories, she walked to the window, drew back the drapes, and raised the pane. While the citizens outside rushed up expecting a speech, she lifted and dropped the window's bottom frame to the sill several times, creating a staccato of slamming noises. She pulled the drapes shut again and turned to assess if the women grasped the purpose of her demonstration.

The women shrugged, except Leila.

"Does your father work at the telegraph office?" Boyd asked Leila.

"No, but I've watched Gus send telegrams. That sounds like Morse Code."

Boyd kissed Leila on the head. "Bright thing, you." She explained to the others, "It was my only way of sending messages to my network of spies while the Yankees occupied us."

The women hailed the lesson in espionage with an ovation.

Boyd checked her watch and slumped. "I have lost all track of time. I have so enjoyed our conversation, but I must go."

"We will accompany you back to the depot," said Nancy.

"No need. You have been so very kind."

The women crowded around her, offering their farewells, and Caroline said, "Give our love and condolences to General Jackson's family."

At the door, Boyd turned and asked the ladies, "Would you allow me a moment alone with Captain Morgan?"

Mary hugged Nancy. "Take as long as you need. I'll walk Caroline home." With her back to Boyd, Mary whispered to Nancy's ear. "Don't let her bait you. She feels challenged."

The other Nancies departed, and Boyd closed the door behind them. After a hesitation, she said, "My suggestions ... I meant you no disrespect."

"Nor I to you," said Nancy. "I wish I had your pluck and daring."

"I wanted to share something more, but I thought it best the others not hear it, at least not from me."

"Yes?"

"When the Yankees invaded Martinsburg, I was tending to the ill and dying in our hospital. Their soldiers burst into the ward with their bayonets flashing and shouted threats and insults. Their gesticulations and language grew so violent and their countenances, inflamed by drink and hatred, were so frightful, I thought I had reached the end of my brief life. I nerved myself to petition the intercession of a Northern officer and appeal to his sense of military honor. I was fortunate that day, for the officer restrained his turbulent men, but it might have turned out differently. ... I've never recovered from the shock of that first encounter."

"Why are you telling me this?"

Boyd's intensity radiated from her stringent eyes. "I admire what you've accomplished with your militia. But I have seen war firsthand, with the dying and agonies and the blood flowing. You must never raise a gun against a Yankee unless you resolve to fire it." She grasped Nancy's hand to seal their bond in the military sisterhood and departed.

Nancy, shaken by the warning, stood at the door and watched as the adoring crowd escorted Boyd to the carriage.

22

CHICKAMAUGA CREEK, GEORGIA
SEPTEMBER 1863

"River of Blood," said Wallace.

Hugh ignored his brother's irritating musings as they led a train of supply wagons into a narrow valley bordered by Missionary Ridge and Chickamauga Creek. He thought nothing could be more remote than the windswept plains of Kansas, but these forested mountains in northern Georgia chilled him with a foreboding. Towering pines blotted the sun, turning the midday dark as dusk. He consulted his worn map to confirm they were still on the trail into McClemore Cove, a box-shaped corridor forged by Lookout Mountain to the north and Pigeon Mountain to the east. He studied the arching folds in the surrounding cliffs, a habit Professor Daniels had instilled in him as a geology student. The dolostone and limestone crags transitioned to a sandstone plateau pocked with caves and fissures that provided inaccessible lairs perfect for an ambush. Little wonder the Cherokee fought so hard to stay in these rolling hunting hills before President Jackson drove them west along the Trail of Tears.

"River of Blood."

"I heard you the first time," Hugh snapped.

"That's what the natives called that stream over there."

"You speak Cherokee now?"

Wallace pulled a flask from his jacket. "I speak the eternal language of the golden Tennessee nectar."

"Put that away."

Wallace took a swig and slid the flask back into his pocket. "While you were scribbling dispatches at Caperton's Ferry, I did a little reconnaissance at the local tavern. The Cherokee used this gully to trap the Shawnee."

"That Secesh hooch purveyor was just trying to scare you."

Wallace kept a wary eye fixed on the treetops for ghost warriors that might jump him. "He said cursed burial mounds lay along this buffalo trace."

"And you believed that tall tale?"

Wallace caressed his holstered revolver as he made sure the wagons weren't falling behind. "Ever since you promised me we'd be fighting the cream of the Rebs by now, I don't know what to believe anymore. But I don't care to linger in this haunted holler."

"I'll include your complaint in my report to General McCook."

"Just saying my piece."

Hugh knew he shouldn't be so hard on his brother, but he'd been in a foul mood since leaving Tullahoma, up in Tennessee. When General Rosecrans transferred the regiment from Missouri to the Army of the Cumberland, sweetening the move with his promotion to the rank of colonel, he'd hoped they would finally see some major action. Yet his usual misfortune in timing caused the regiment to miss the battles at Murfreesboro in January and Vicksburg in July. Now, Old Rosy had spread his divisions too thin and was scrambling to reunite them south of Chattanooga before Braxton Bragg could strike a blow. His Wisconsin men had been shunted from the main Army again, this time to guard his caravan of rations on a mystifying straggle south toward an oasis called Crawfish Springs. They had made so many retreats and turns in these infernal boondocks during these past two weeks that he'd lost his bearings.

And he thought military incompetence was confined to the forgotten armies west of the Mississippi.

A rapid thud of hooves chased the crows perching on the scarps.

He turned to find an officer dashing up in a cloud of dust. No older than in his late twenties, the gangly, loose-limbed rider had a freckled Irish mischievousness about him. His close-set St. Patrick's teal blue eyes crinkled at the corners and a long angular nose ruffled his hemp-colored mustache. "These must be the Fighting Brothers LaGrange." The officer doffed his hat and spurned the formality of Hugh's salute by shaking his hand instead. "Dan Ray. Second Tennessee. You lads have the dubious distinction of serving under my brigade command."

Hugh straightened in the saddle, relieved to discover a senior officer in the vicinity. "General Ray, at your service."

Ray motioned for the teamsters to keep the wagons moving as he rode between Hugh and Wallace in the vanguard. "Just *Colonel* Ray. Truth is, *you*, Colonel LaGrange, would be leading this brigade if I didn't have you beat by a few months in service time. May I call you Hugh?"

"Certainly, but—"

Ray reached across Hugh's chest to give Wallace's hand a firm grasp. "How is it having an older brother to give you orders?"

"To be honest, sir," said Wallace, "it ranks right up there with being tarred and feathered."

Ray laughed. "Could be worse."

"Exactly how?" Wallace asked.

"Hugh here could be shooting at you." Seeing them expecting an explanation, Ray lost his grin. "My brother Billy joined the Rebels. He serves in the Sixty-Fourth North Carolina." He chased the dispiriting reminder of family disloyalty with a slap to his thigh. "I've done some checking on you, Hugh. We have much in common. I grew up farming and teaching."

Hugh took an immediate liking to this colonel who had none of the paper-collar stuffiness and arrogance of the politician-officers and West Pointers. "I don't suppose you studied geology, too?"

"If by studying geology you mean cracking plows on every rock in Flat Creek, Kentucky, then I've earned my advanced degree."

"You followed old Daniel Boone through the Cumberland Gap."

Ray nodded. "My family pulled up stakes more than a few times. Wherever a barren plot of land could be found, we found it."

The colonel's hailing from the Bluegrass State piqued Hugh's curiosity. "Did you ever brush saddles with the Second Kentucky Cavalry?"

"I served aside those hell-raising boys with Minty in middle Tennessee. Why do you ask?"

"In Arkansas, we encountered a rather unusual prisoner from that regiment." Hugh fumbled for the best wording to pose his delicate inquiry. "You said you served aside those boys. … Were they *all* boys?"

Ray stared wide-eyed at him—and burst out laughing. "Don't tell me you had a run-in with the Kentucky Phantomess?"

"She told me her name was Amy Clark."

Ray slapped Wallace on the back to share his enjoyment in discovering Hugh's misadventure. "Amy Clarke. Sarah Bradbury. Frank Morton. She has more aliases than Jeff Davis has slaves."

Hugh reddened at being duped. "How do *you* know her?"

"She hid in my regiment for two months. And she wasn't the only gal. Francis Elizabeth Quinn, *that* fire-breathing hussy I'll never forget. She went by the name of Frank. I hated to see her drummed out. She was a better soldier than half my men."

Hugh, tormented by Wallace's cackling at his expense, muttered to himself. "That conniving harridan."

"You let her go, didn't you," Ray said.

Hugh shrugged. "She'd just buried her husband at Shiloh and—"

"She fed that catfish line to me, too."

"Line?"

"The Second Kentucky was never at Shiloh."

Hugh shaded another tinge of red.

"You Northern shavetails are beyond redemption," Ray said. "I grew up in the South and learned early on that a man must steel himself against the wiles of our women. They will boil you like a plucked chicken before you know the fire's been kindled."

"Oh, Colonel," said Wallace, thoroughly enjoying his brother's come-down. "I could sing you a ballad of a fetching belle in Baltimore."

"That will be enough," Hugh ordered.

Ray winked a promise at Wallace to hear the tale another time.

A distant rattle of carbine echoed up the cove trail behind them. A cannon boomed—the shot came from across the creek. Before the three officers could find a path around the line of wagons, a breathless corporal galloped up from the rear and saluted. "Reb cavalry are attacking our trailing wagons, sir."

"How far back?" asked Ray.

"Half a mile," the corporal said. "Several baggage caissons lost contact."

"Did you identify the unit?" Hugh asked.

The corporal shook his head. "The Second Indiana opened fire. With the dust and smoke, we couldn't see much."

"Not a flag, even?" demanded Hugh.

The corporal dropped his chin to his chest to prime his memory. "There *was* one flag. Something strange about it."

"Strange?"

"Smaller than most. A Reb carried it on his sword instead of a staff."

Hugh's heart raced. *Wheeler.*

His enthusiastic reaction perplexed Ray. "That means something to you?"

Hugh checked the cartridges in his revolver. "After Shiloh, the women of Augusta presented Joe Wheeler with a new battle flag as a gift. They made him a banderole to fit on a sword. Wheeler complained traditional battle flags were too heavy for cavalry."

"How do you know this?" Ray asked.

Wallace answered before Hugh could explain. "My brother here is obsessed with that butternut general. Reads every newspaper article about him he can get his hands on." He reached into his pocket and pulled out Wheeler's manual of tactics, which he kept next to his flask. "He makes us memorize this."

Ray borrowed Hugh's map to study the angling course of Chickamauga Creek, a hundred yards to their right. "If it *is* Wheeler, he'll try to cut us off from Rosecrans." He looked hard at Hugh with his fighting blood up. "Hurry your First Wisconsin troopers to the rear and hold them off."

Hugh hesitated. "Sir, if I may—"

"Yes? Quickly."

"I've studied Wheeler's tactics. He's predictable. He prefers to launch a feint attack and then hit where the enemy has depleted its line."

"What do you propose?" asked Ray.

"Send Lieutenant LaGrange and the corporal here back down the road with four of my companies." Hugh turned to Wallace. "You fight a rear-guard action. Keep the Rebs at bay for as long as you can, but don't fully engage."

"What are *you* gonna do?" Wallace asked.

"I'll take the other six companies upstream and find a ford. We'll cross, circle back, and catch Wheeler." Hugh looked to Ray for permission to carry out the risky sortie. Ray cut off a sharp salute to send them off.

Hugh led his contingent east along the Cove Road and searched for a crossing over Chickamauga Creek. A sign ahead, marked Davis Ford, pointed to a path overgrown with brambles. He spurred through the overhanging branches to an embankment. With no time to test the water's depth, he lashed his balking horse into the stream and dropped waist deep. He looked back to make sure his troopers held their carbines aloft and were managing the currents. The crossing was fraught with an uneven bed and whirlpools, but the plunge at least would dampen the dust from their approach to aid in the surprise.

He goaded his horse up the far bank and trotted toward a ridge. As his drenched column caught up, he dismounted and signaled his troopers to hold their position. He pulled out his field glasses and crawled to the crest, lying on his stomach to avoid detection. Two hundred yards off, a plume of dark smoke billowed above the ambushed wagons. A couple hundred of the Rebel cavalry had crossed the creek on foot and were giving Wallace a hot time.

To the east, atop a wooded knoll this side of the stream, a clique of gray-clad officers lazed on their grazing horses, shading and watching the action as if enjoying a theatre production. An adjutant held a small Confederate battle flag on a sword. Next to him sat a rider of slight stature with a cropped beard who received reports of the wagon skirmish from couriers.

Hugh blinked hard and squinted. Could that truly be Wheeler? The diminutive patrician looked no more threatening than an apothecary clerk, sitting slack against his cantle, unperturbed and giving directions with a fey wave of his hand. A gold wreath embroidered his collar. So, the rumors were true. The Confederate government promoted Wheeler to a brigadier. He counted off the number of horses in Wheeler's attack force and calculated his six companies

didn't have enough men to encircle the Rebels. Still, he might give the treasonous West Pointer a scare he'd not soon forget.

Time for long-overdue introductions.

Hugh ran back to his waiting column and mounted. "We've got the big
fish on the hook! By File on the Right! When we close at a hundred yards,
execute a Pivot Turn!"

The troopers, skeptical, exchanged murmured misgivings.

He understood their hesitation. He was asking them to perform a maneuver that would make their Oblique charge at Cape Girardeau look like gram-
mar-school hopscotch by comparison. His plan was to head toward a point east
of Wheeler and wheel ninety degrees. If they closed fast before the Confederate
commander and his staff became alerted, they might outflank the entire Rebel
cavalry, drive them into the creek, and grip them in a pincer with Wallace's defenders on the far side. He stood in the stirrups and shouted, "When we cross
that ridge, no yells! Draw sabers on my command!"

His cavalry formed up, four abreast. He signaled the assault. As they galloped over the ridge in tight formation, the only sounds to be heard were the
caws of disturbed ravens and the pounding of hooves. The men maintained
good order, each rank three horse breadths behind the one in front.

Wheeler and his entourage lingered on the copsed hill ahead, still unsuspecting, their attention fixed on the fight for the wagons across the creek. Hugh
took aim at a boscage of dead pines fifty yards east of Wheeler. Ten more seconds to pin him, he prayed. When his count expired, he shouted, "Sabers!"

A metallic rasp of sabers pulled from scabbards rang out.

All depended on his next order: The movable pivot. "Turn!"

Neighing erupted in the column, followed by curses and the grinding
of smashed leather. Wheeler spun in his saddle—he saw the Union column
thundering toward him, a hundred yards away. He glared at Hugh in the vanguard, risking capture to delay a moment more and identify the Yankee officer
who had crept up on him. Wheeler smiled, tipped his hat in admiration, and
lashed his horse north with his staff officers.

Hugh, leaning against his panting horse's mane to deflect the wind, whipped
its flanks to catch him.

Wheeler circled and laughed, taunting him.

The bastard! He mocks me? I'll put an end to that!

Hugh twisted in the saddle to order his troopers with him into the breach.
He reined up, stunned. His six companies—fifty yards behind—thrashed and
cursed, entangled in a mash of confusion. The inside riders of the column had
attempted an abrupt stationary turn instead of a gradual angling of five degrees for every five paces of advance. As a result, the outside riders lost contact

while those in the rear crashed into the troopers in front. Crimson with rage at being humiliated in front of Wheeler, Hugh galloped back to harangue them when a cheer on the opposite side of the creek stopped him short.

At the wagons, Wallace and his four companies repulsed the Rebel cavalry-men fighting on foot. Those Confederates, seeing Wheeler retreat, broke and waded back across the creek. Soaked, they untied their horses, swung up on their saddles while dodging carbine fire from two directions, and escaped into the forest.

Colonel Ray trotted to the banks of Chickamauga Creek and, grinning, saluted Hugh for routing the famous cavalry commander of the Army of Ten-nessee. "Not bad for a schoolteacher!"

* * *

Crawfish Springs was a tableau of Hell.

The next day, ordered by Colonel Ray to guard the main Federal hospital sta-tion, Hugh hurried his First Wisconsin Cavalry through the village built around a natural basin a hundred yards in circumference and known for the pitiful gush of water that bubbled up from its core. Along its muddy banks, hundreds of panicked Union soldiers huddled together to fill their canteens. White hos-pital tents and ambulances dotted surrounding hills, which were strewn with wounded men writhing in agony. The effect was a macabre oscillation of sound and ground that struck him with a nauseous vertigo.

He braced a hand against his pommel to steady himself. A pile of limbs sat next to each surgery tent. He noticed from their thumbs and toes that most were left hands and legs. The gruesome reason for this oddity dawned on him: These men had been so jammed in the ranks they had to angle their bodies, exposing their left arms to hold the barrels while taking stances with their left legs forward.

He rode to the largest tent, its flaps pinned open, and found a surgeon, in a blood-splattered apron, sawing off a leg. He brought his kerchief to his nose to avoid gagging from the stench of brandy, ammonia, and rotting flesh. Recover-ing his voice over the peppery grip in his throat, he shouted above the groans before the surgeon could order another victim lifted onto the table. "Who's in charge here?"

The surgeon refused to look up from his work. "The Devil, by my count!"

"Colonel LaGrange. First Wisconsin. I was ordered to report."

"Well, bloody here you are!"

"What's your name and rank?"

The surgeon, resembling a blood-streaked demon, marched from the tent wielding his dripping cleaver. "Glover Perin! Medical Director of the Goddamn Army of the Cumberland! And if you don't want *your* carcass on these boards, you'll get these wounded men on wagons and moving north!"

The surgeon's vehemence so startled Hugh that he reined back a step to prevent his horse from spooking from the flash of the saw. "Retreat? My orders are to hold this position. Who commands the defense of the hospital?"

"Look around! There's no one in charge! Rosecrans sent his last infantry divisions north toward Chattanooga and left this goddamn hospital too far from his lines! We're ten minutes from getting cut off!"

"You needn't worry about the Rebel cavalry. We can hold them—"

The blaspheming surgeon slammed his cleaver into the table. "Cavalry? Look over there! That's Bragg's entire army coming at us."

Hugh turned toward the southeast and squinted into the dusty haze for evidence the surgeon hadn't suffered a mental breakdown. The mix of smoke and mist slowly dissipated. A quarter mile away, a solid line of butternut infantry appeared, trampling toward him and led by cavalry. *My Lord.* That looked to be an entire division—and Joe Wheeler was leading it *here*. He'd never seen so many men marching in ranks.

He reined around and glanced north toward the only road out of the hollow. Hands shaking, he pulled out his map. By his reckoning, they were twelve miles south of Chattanooga. Two gaps offered the only escape past Missionary Ridge. If they didn't reach those passes before Bragg ... but where was Rosecrans and the rest of the Union Army? Would Old Rosy really abandon his primary hospital to the enemy?

Wallace formed up the companies just beyond the springs. Mobs of terrified Federal infantry retreating from the onslaught overwhelmed his battle line. He tried to rally the routed men, but they stampeded past him for the wooded ridges to the north. Caught in the eye of this maelstrom, he pointed Hugh toward Chickamauga Creek. "They're coming fast!"

Hugh struggled to focus. He hadn't slept for three nights and his brain felt like smashed peas. Should he obey orders to hold or trust his judgment? He saw no senior officers to consult. A drumbeat roused him from his confused stupor. To his left, a blue-eyed boy with wild shocks of auburn hair stood steadfast against the retreating waves. No older than twelve or thirteen, the lad beat a sad refrain. With a resigned calmness, he slung off the drum and kicked it into pieces, slamming its snares and tension rods against an oak tree.

Hugh galloped to the boy. "Get out of here!"

The weeping lad stared at the skeleton of his once-prized possession. "No Reb is gonna play *my* drum!"

A distant volley of musket fire zinged around Hugh's ears as he extended his hand. "Climb on."

The boy backed away. "I ain't deserting my fellas."

Hugh snatched him by the collar and pulled him to the saddle. "You can't help them here." With the boy clinging to his waist, Hugh rode toward Wallace and shouted, "Cover us! When I give the signal, follow me north!"

Wallace chased Hugh's horse with a slap to its flank. To his front, thousands of thirsty Confederates engulfed the far outskirts of the village, firing at the retreating Yankees and kneeling at the springs to slake their thirst in water tinged red with blood.

Hugh galloped to his idled companies on the far side of the springs. "Four men to each wagon and ambulance! Load all the wounded you can move!"

While every fourth trooper dismounted and formed a stretched picket line, the others galloped to the surgery tents and carried the screaming wounded to the wagons and ambulances. Hugh stationed his temporary headquarters on their escape road. He calculated how many minutes before Wallace's meager defensive line collapsed. The wind had picked up, and dark clouds formed over the mountains. He could feel an ominous change in the weather coming. The tree leaves were turning upward. He remembered his father telling him *that* was a sure sign of an approaching storm. If his guess was right, the temperature would drop that night, and the wounded left stranded on these fields would suffer, if they survived. With his rescue train finally set to roll, he galloped back to the surgeon who had cursed him. "We're out of time. Bring your staff."

The medical director shook his head. "We're staying."

"I can't allow you to fall into Rebel hands."

"I outrank you," the surgeon said. "Begone!"

Hugh scanned the tents and saw the other doctors standing defiant. How would he explain leaving them to be sent to prisons? Resigned to their decision, he asked the surgeon, "You have a message for General Rosecrans?"

"Tell that papist coward I will see him brought before a court martial!"

Hugh admired the mouthy surgeon's mettle and loyalty to his Hippocratic oath. He removed his riding coat from behind his saddle and tossed it to him.

The surgeon stared quizzically at the coat. "Hell, I'm sweating as it is."

"You're going to need it." With the drummer boy holding fast to his belt, Hugh galloped toward the rear of the wagons and directed his men to screen both sides of the road. "Move fast! Don't stop!" He signaled for Wallace to retract his pickets and cover the retreating caravan.

The teamsters lashed the draught horses toward the gaps, shouting for the stragglers to move off the muddy road. Trailing the wagons, Hugh found a flat promontory a half-mile north that offered a vantage of the retreat and the Confederate advance into Crawfish Springs in the vale below. The sun was inching toward the horizon. Another hour and darkness should halt the fighting. He tried to banish the screams of agony from the jostled wounded as the ambulance wheels hit the holes in the deteriorating farmer's lane.

Twenty minute later, afforded a moment's rest, he risked falling asleep in the saddle to close his eyes. He muttered, "I've never seen anything like this."

"Stones River was perty rough."

He was so exhausted, he'd forgotten about the boy on the saddle behind him. "You were at Murfreesboro?"

"Yep. Old Rosy gave 'em the bayonet on New Year's Eve. You know any other general crazy enough to keep fighting in a snowstorm? I reckon I can say I fought a battle that spanned two years."

"You're more of a veteran than me. What's your name?"

"Al Walton."

"Regiment?"

"Seventy-Fifth Indiana."

"You miss home?"

"Nah, I ran away twice. My ma wouldn't let me enlist, so I took matters into my own hands."

Hugh pulled out his field glasses and studied the dimming horizon toward Chickamauga Creek. All he could make out were clouds of musket smoke hanging low in the sky. "What happened out there today?"

The boy considered his answer with deliberation. "I'm not saying being a drummer don't have its profit. Gives me an alibi to loiter around the officers and eavesdrop on the dispatches. The fellas trade me pennies for information."

"I'll bet they do."

"Don't hold me to this with my palm on the Bible, but best as I could piece together, the Rebs hit us this morning with everything they had. Rosy was pulling brigades from our line to strengthen his left flank. We got yanked harder than a bull with his balls roped. John Bell Hood's Texans caught us near a pond. Lot of the fellas chose a bullet as the cost for a last drink. To sum it, I think we got our asses altogether kicked."

Hugh shook his head, convinced the colorful lad was now just spinning a yarn to impress him. "You pulling my leg because I haven't seen the elephant as many times as you?"

"Pulling your leg?"

"Hood is with Lee's Army in Virginia."

"I'm telling you what I heard and what I seen with my two Hoosier orbs. Them's were Hood's Texans. We captured a couple of those rattlesnakes before they sent us hightailing. They came in blowing gas about their Yellow Rose and the Alamo and Sam Houston until you can't take it no more."

"If that's true, then—"

"Yeah, you're slow, even for an officer, but you're catching on."

Hugh refused to believe that Robert E. Lee would abandon Virginia to come fight with Bragg. But what if Lee sent a division by rail through Atlanta and up the Chattanooga line?

"They'd have us outnumbered," said the boy, reading his thoughts.

The last of the wagons and ambulances passed, followed by Wallace and his weary troopers. Hugh prepared to join them on the retreat north when something caught his eye in the village below. He raised his field glasses and tightened the focus knob. An entourage of Rebel officers rode to the tent manned by the chief Union surgeon. One demanded the surgeon's overcoat. The other Rebs followed his example and went plundering from tent to tent, stripping the quilts and coats from the wounded Union men. *That son of a bitch!*

The Confederate officer mounted again, his arms wrapped around two piles of Federal-issued coats.

Wait, Hugh said to himself. He had seen that horse before. *Son of a bitch's son! That's Wheeler! His officers are stripping our men and leaving them to freeze?*

Before Hugh could stop him, Wee Al jumped off the saddle and ran toward the springs. "They ain't doing that to my fellas!"

"Come back!" Hugh shouted.

The boy ignored the order and charged down the hill, shouting threats.

Wheeler and his officers heard the commotion and glared up at the cliff. Recognizing Hugh from their earlier clash, the Confederate general halted his horse and waved his men forward to intercept the boy. Wheeler's adjutant grabbed Walton and prodded him, screaming, into their laughing midst.

Hugh pulled his revolver and fired at Wheeler, hoping to dissuade the general's officers from the thefts. The shot fell short. He watched helplessly as the Rebel officers herded Wee Al, yelling and clawing, toward a gaggle of Union prisoners being marched toward Chickamauga Creek.

Wheeler pointed at Hugh as if promising a future meeting.

Hugh reloaded and fired again, the only protest he could manage against the boy's capture. Wheeler grinned at his inept marksmanship.

Drawn by the shots, Wallace galloped back from the wagon caravan. "What in God's name are you waiting for?"

Hugh maintained his duel of glares with Wheeler. "I want that scoundrel down there bagged and delivered!"

"Not today," Wallace said. "General Mitchell found us on Dry Valley Road. He wants you to report at once."

That night, Hugh expected a reprimand for his decision to fall back from Crawfish Springs. Instead, Colonel Ray and General Robert Mitchell, chief of the

Army of the Cumberland's cavalry corps, praised him for his swift action in saving so many wounded. Mitchell laced his commendation with curses at Rosecrans for placing the hospital too far from their shifting lines. As a measure of his trust, Mitchell sent Hugh to Old Rosy's headquarters—on the right-center of the Union defenses—to secure the next day's orders for the cavalry's right wing.

Accompanied by Wallace, Hugh galloped the mile to the Widow Glenn's cabin, careful not to trample the shivering soldiers huddled in fitful slumber on the pasture covered by black frost. Many had thrown away their blankets on the march here in the oppressive summer heat, and now that howling wind he had forecasted came sweeping down the mountains, killing the chiggers and bringing with it an early winter that froze the water in the canteens. There was not a cloud in the sky to hold the day's warmth, and the celestials danced twinkling around the emerging harvest moon. He thought of home and the last crop-killing September freeze he had suffered on the farm as a boy. The corn and potato yields, stunted by spring floods and roasting summer droughts, faced ruin. That meant more hardtack and less meat in the rations.

The two brothers dismounted, and Hugh handed Mitchell's dispatch to the guards posted at the door. It didn't pass his notice that Rosecrans had set his headquarters near the Dry Valley Road, one of the two remaining routes into Chattanooga if retreat became necessary. Permitted entry, he and Wallace found the commanding general holding merry court inside the one-room cabin with his division and corps commanders. General Alexander McCook, a short plug of a Scotsman with smirking gray eyes and a furrowed brow locked in a sneer in search of a scuffle, led the other generals in a love ballad:

> "In that sombre chamber yonder,
> Father's taper still burns bright;
> Bending to his breast his aged,
> Care-worn face he prays tonight.
>
> Open wide before the righteous
> Lies the Talmud which he reads,
> And his child e'en is forgotten,
> Fore his God, and Israel's deeds."

Hugh shook his head at Wallace, alarmed and not a little put out. Bragg had driven them back several miles, and here these generals stood singing songs as if attending a West Point reunion and enjoying hot coffee while their troops slept on their arms with no fires. On a table, illuminated by a solitary candle, sat a map dotted with black and white wooden marbles, flattened on one side,

to show troop dispositions. Hugh craned his neck to glimpse the current brigade positions. The black marbles representing the Confederate units nearly
surrounded the white marbles. The Union defensive line on the left formed a
horseshoe a hundred yards from the LaFayette Road, the second escape track
north to Chattanooga.

Is this Army on the verge of destruction?

"Strengthen the left," said a voice from the corner of the cabin.

While the generals indulged in a second chorus, Hugh searched for the
source of that drowsy command, which went unacknowledged. In the shadows sat an officer with a close-cropped beard, tipped back on a chair and
resting his head, crowned with wavy salt-and-pepper hair, against the log wall.
His recessed blue eyes were lidded, but he was awake enough to mutter another suggestion that again fell on deaf ears. Every geometric angle of his
frame cut sharp and solid as granite: square shoulders, square jaw, square torso.
Hugh marveled at the man's calm temperament and realized from the acorn
badge on the hat perched atop his knee that this sleep talker must be General
George Thomas, the commander of the Fourteenth Corps.

A third chorus broke out and, as if on cue, again—

"Strengthen the left," muttered Thomas.

McCook, who commanded the Twentieth Corps, conducted his choral
quintet using his right index finger for a baton. He finished the ballad with a
rousing coda worthy of an Italian opera. Only then did Rosecrans, in a con-
stant state of nervous motion, see Hugh and Wallace at the door. The former
civil engineer from Ohio chomped on the stub of a cigar as he stared down his
hooked Roman nose at them with the red-ringed, offset eyes of a ferret.

Hugh saluted. "Colonel LaGrange and Lieutenant LaGrange, sir, of the
First Wisconsin Cavalry."

"Do your kinsmen make up the entire regiment?" Rosecrans asked, his sarcasm drawing laughter from his staff. "Or just the officer staff?"

Hugh noticed a lanky man not in uniform sitting on a stool near the fireplace. He was using the flat crown of his straw hat as a portable desk while
scribbling notes of the conversation. Was the fellow a newspaper correspondent? He'd heard the rumors that Lincoln had infiltrated a spy onto Old Rosy's
staff to report back on his competence. The scrivener nodded to him as if sharing his disgust with the mawkish proceedings.

Rosecrans flicked his ashes at Hugh's boots to reclaim his attention. "Colonel LaGrange seems not to be in a talkative mood tonight."

Hugh stepped forward, irked at being sleep-deprived and made the object
of this warbling martinet's jests. "No, sir. General Mitchell sent us for cavalry
dispositions on our right flank."

General Thomas, rousing from his nap in the corner, rocked his chair to all fours. "Where *is* our right flank?"

Hugh didn't take his meaning. "Sir?"

Thomas stood to shake the rheumy stiffness from his feet. "If you can show us our right flank on this map, Colonel, you will be the first officer tonight who has managed the impossible."

Hugh's jaw tightened. Were these West Pointers having sport with him? "Sir, we protect the gaps south of Missionary Ridge."

McCook, a foot shorter than Hugh, circled him and aimed his chin in a challenge. "Why were my orders not followed today?"

The ferocity of that unwarranted accusation drove Hugh to his heels. Colonel Ray had warned him about the banty McCook, who hailed from a famous Ohio family of fighters but was notorious for his zealous repatriation of refugee slaves to their Southern owners. He formed an immediate dislike for the noxious bully. "Orders, sir?"

"I told General Mitchell to keep his horse affixed to my infantry. He disobeyed me. You can tell him I intend to file charges at a court of inquiry."

Hugh now suspected *this* was the reason Mitchell sent him in his stead. He could not hide his revulsion at these generals still bickering over the day's confusion. "General, if I might offer a suggestion and—"

"A suggestion?" McCook stomped the boards with his boot heel to demand silence. "*You* wish to offer *me* a suggestion?"

"Sir, if we—"

"How dare you!"

Thomas moved next to Hugh. "Let the man speak, Alex."

Incensed by his rival's intervention, McCook expected Rosecrans to countermand the breach of protocol, but the fidgety commander shrugged, crossed himself—a Catholic habit when pressed on a hard call—and gyred his hand in a gesture for Hugh to finish his thought.

"Our cavalry is scattered halfway to Alabama. If you would allow us to concentrate our squadrons as Wheeler does—"

"Wheeler?" shouted McCook, his spittle flying. "You present *that* traitor for our emulation?"

Hugh was losing patience with this crowing rooster. "Wheeler holds Crawfish Springs and our primary hospital, with thousands of our wounded. Had we two regiments more out there today, we could have saved it."

Rosecrans confronted McCook. "Is this true?"

McCook glared a promise of revenge at Hugh for being called out in front of Rosecrans. "I had an unconfirmed report that Old Joe was causing mischief below Gordon's Mill. My guess is he pulled back across Chickamauga Creek."

"His cavalry still holds Crawfish Springs," Hugh insisted. "And our surgeons now freeze in his prison pens. I also saw Wheeler's men stripping the hospital tents of blankets and coats. Advance elements of John Bell Hood's division—"

"Hood?" cried McCook. "Have you been drinking, Colonel?"

"Sir, I received information that Hood may be here."

Stunned, the generals tightened their circle around McCook, waiting for an explanation of why this intelligence hadn't made its way to headquarters. To abandon so many wounded was shameful enough and to lose irreplaceable surgeons was unthinkable. But if Hood's Texans from Virginia *were* on the field, McCook's divisions on their right flank were in even worse trouble than any of them had previously thought.

McCook shot a concerned glance toward the fireplace, where the scribe warming himself flipped a page in his journal and started scrawling notes faster. The general picked up a marble from the map and rolled it with ominous dexterity in his right hand. "There's one way to find out for certain."

"And that would be?" Thomas asked.

McCook came up snarling face-to-face with Hugh. "Send the ambitious Colonel here on a night reconnaissance into Crawfish Springs and find Bragg's left flank."

"He'd have to cross Wheeler's lines," Thomas warned. "You might as well order him to ride straight to Libby Prison."

Wallace burned Hugh with a scolding glance for speaking out of line and risking their lives for a suicidal mission to win a spat.

The generals watched Rosecrans for his approval of the mission.

Rosecrans crossed himself and shrugged. "It's Mitchell's decision."

"Mitchell isn't here," McCook reminded him. "His Second Brigade, with the First Wisconsin, screens my right flank. I have the authority to order it unless countermanded."

When Thomas lodged no objection, Rosecrans shook his head and offered Hugh a humiliating opening to backtrack. "I won't allow an order sending you and your cavalry back in there, but if you volunteer to go ..."

Hugh realized he had walked into a trap. If he failed on this scouting sortie, his military career might stall. Yet he could not in good faith decline the mission on behalf of the regiment after proposing it. He was determined, however, to exact a price. "Willingly, sir ... with one request."

Rosecrans rested the knuckles of his fists on the map, reviewing the packed line of Confederate brigades stretching seven miles. Thousands would come thundering at him through those eastern woods in a few hours. Finally, shaking his head in resignation, he turned to Hugh again. "Well?"

"If we return, you'll fit my regiment with Spencer carbines. The same re-peaters that Wilder's troopers carry."

Rosecrans spun on him for his arrogance in attempting to negotiate terms with a major general. Yet, sensing the opinion in the room had turned in favor of the brassy colonel, the commander nodded his assent.

Hugh saluted and grasped Wallace's elbow to hurry him toward the door.

McCook stopped Hugh with an arm to his chest. "I expect a report by dawn." He curled a sinister smile. "Or not."

At midnight, Hugh and Wallace led two hundred troopers past the right flank of Alexander McCook's corps and turned south on the Crawfish Springs road, the only route back to the captured Federal hospital. Hugh had argued such a large contingent increased the risk of being detected, but Colonel Ray insisted he take another squadron from the Second Indiana for support. Hugh had ordered his men to leave their saddlebags and replace them with bundles of coats and blankets found abandoned from the retreat earlier that day.

A half mile south, he halted the column and cantered a few yards ahead, listening for Wheeler's cavalry. The moon was in its first quarter, offering little light, and both armies had banned campfires to avoid artillery shelling. He cocked his ear toward voices interspersed with the whinnying and braying of gathered horses, then voices.

Southern twangs.

Hugh returned and signaled that the Rebel cavalry was just down the road. Although they had brought burlaps sacks to muffle the hooves, he calculated a dash through the encampment would cost too many casualties. So, he re-sorted to his backup plan. On their retreat that morning, he observed the Chattanooga Creek ran a hundred yards west of this road, almost parallel. And the water level was low. Wheeler had likely anchored his left flank on the creek. If he and his men held to a sluggish pace in the water and hugged the bank nearest the Rebel encampment, their silhouettes might be shielded from view and their clopping dampened by the gentle lapping rapids. It meant a longer, roundabout ride to Crawfish Springs, but he saw no other choice. He fixed in his mind the direction of the North Star and, keeping it to his back, signaled for a turn right into the woods.

He navigated for the creek from instinct now, his visibility limited to ten feet ahead. Each trooper held branches to prevent the rider behind him being lashed. Counting off the seconds to calculate distance, he prayed his horse would smell the water and make for it. If spotted by Wheeler's pickets, they'd be caught in a turkey shoot. He conjured the smirking face of that foul-mouthed Caledonian gnome, Alexander McCook, and steeled himself with the reminder of how many of his troopers he could eventually save with those promised Spencer repeaters.

A minute passed in silent riding, and then he felt the ground descend. His horse splashed into water and stopped to drink. He gave the thirsty animal a moment and whispered over his shoulder to Wallace, "Turn left here."

Wallace relayed the order to the column. Two abreast, the troopers eased down the slope into the creek. Just as Hugh had trained them, each man grasped the tail of the horse in front and rode blind in freezing water up to their knees. The tactic prevented stragglers from straying off and also calmed the horses, minifying their whinnies.

Hugh hugged the neck of his mount to avoid being seen above the bank. One slip into a blind hole and a horse baying from a broken leg could doom them. His feet and calves were turning numb. To his left, above him, the drawling Tennessee and Alabama voices became more distinct. The jangle of bridle bits and saddle harnesses threatened to give them away. And then, as if the Good Lord Himself were looking over them, a Rebel fiddler in the camp struck up a tune, and Wheeler's men joined in, singing:

"Nearer, my God, to thee,
Nearer to Thee!
E'en though it be a cross
That raiseth me.
At the moment of death
My strength is from Heaven
God helping, nothing should be feared forever!"

When the crooned Rebel laments became more passionate, Hugh increased his pace to a trot. A second chorus struck up, and just as the fiddler plucked his ending strings, the rear of the column eased past the camp. He released a held breath. Silence filled the night again, but only for a few minutes. As he feared, the cries and screams of the wounded abandoned on the blood-soaked pastures to the east, near Lee & Gordon's Mill, pierced the darkness. Before leaving, he had ordered no attempts to stop and comfort the suffering and dying. They had only six hours to reach the hospital and return. Cruel as it seemed, a drink of water for a man bleeding to death could mean the loss of his two squadrons.

After trudging another half mile in the creek, Hugh came to a ferry raft tethered to a post on the left bank. He halted and made a striking motion at Wallace for a candle and match. He slid his riding cape over his head for a canopy as Wallace leaned in and lit the candle, allowing him to consult his map in the dim light.

Cave Spring Ford.

The road into Crawfish Spring should be a mile to the east. Hugh figured enemy cavalry guarded this ford, so he led his troopers another quarter mile south and ordered them to dismount in the water. One by one, they prodded their horses on foot up the bank. In the distance, hanging lanterns lit the interiors of the white medical tents around Crawfish Spring. After draining the water from their boots, he and his troopers mounted again and formed an approach line. When they closed within a hundred yards, he signaled a halt. He dismounted and, motioning for Wallace to join him, stalked the first tent.

Hugh searched the perimeter of the village overlooking the spring. Two Confederate guards stood stationed on the road. He drew his revolver and opened the tent's flap just wide enough to peek inside. The surgeon he confronted that morning stood over the table operating on an unconscious soldier clad in a calico shirt. A Rebel sergeant hovered over the surgeon's shoulder.

Hugh eased into the tent and brought the revolver to the sergeant's temple. "One word, and you'll be on that table having your brains stuffed back into your skull."

The sergeant raised his hands and nodded.

The surgeon, startled from his surgery, recognized Hugh. "What are *you* doing back here?"

Hugh stuck his head out the flap and motioned for Wallace to enter and gag their prisoner. Hugh peered through the tent's crack and asked the surgeon, "How many Rebs hold the town?"

"Three hundred, maybe more."

Hugh slumped. Too many of Wheeler's men remained in the vicinity to attack them and escape before the shooting alerted the main Confederate force. "And our wounded still here?"

"Fifteen hundred," the doctor said. "Wheeler sent the rest south."

"I'll get *you* out, at least."

"Did you bring ambulances?"

Hugh glared at the bonecutter as if he were daft. "Sure, I dropped a dozen wagons from observation balloons."

"Most of these men are in their last hours," the surgeon said, sneering. "They won't last five minutes on a horse. You'd only prolong their agony."

Hugh kicked at the ground and turned on the gagged Rebel, itching to take retribution with his fist. Checking his temper, he asked the surgeon, "What did Wheeler do with the other doctors?"

The surgeon resumed stitching the leg of the unconscious Reb on the table. "Marched them to the train station at Ringgold. Off to prison camps, likely."

"And he let you stay?"

"He paroled me on the condition that I treat his wounded."

"Let's go. Before the Rebs change the guards."

The surgeon ignored Hugh's order.

"Did you not hear me?"

"I took an oath," the surgeon said. "I'm not breaking faith."

"I risked the lives of two hundred men to get here."

The surgeon shrugged. "You can shoot me. You'd be doing me a favor."

Hugh glanced at Wallace, debating whether to gag the surgeon and drag him back to stand trial for desertion. When Wallace shook his head to protest the risk, Hugh turned to the Rebel sergeant and lowered his gag. "I'm not leaving without something for my effort." He cocked the hammer of his revolver. "Are those John Bell Hood's Texans out there?"

Prodded by the barrel, the sergeant nodded.

"Hood came with a division from Virginia?"

"Not just Hood." The sergeant grinned at the unsettling effect of his report. "Longstreet and the best damn corps in Lee's army."

Hugh couldn't hide his consternation. If true, that meant Bragg had another fifteen thousand men in those woods ready to smash against Rosecrans's right flank at dawn. "Earlier today, I saw an officer with Wheeler taking coats and blankets from prisoners." He dug the revolver into the fleshy underside of the sergeant's chin. "What's his name?"

The sergeant's eyes bulged.

"I won't ask again."

"Reed," the sergeant blurted. "Duff Green Reed."

"His rank?"

"Major. He's General Wheeler's adjutant. Don't judge us by him. He's a drunken reprobate. Reprimanded by our own officers for stealing personal property on prior occasions. General Wheeler told Reed to give the coats and blankets back, but the man is the Devil's dogcatcher."

Hugh studied the sergeant, judging his trustworthiness. "You Secesh boys made a clever deal with the surgeon here and saved hundreds of your own men's lives at the expense of our wounded. Now, I'm going to offer *you* a deal. I'll let you walk out of here on two conditions."

The sergeant stared at the threatening end of the barrel. "You have me at a disadvantage in the negotiation, sir, but I am listening."

"First, you'll find coats and blankets piled near the creek, a hundred yards yonder. You and your men will distribute them to our prisoners tonight."

The sergeant nodded.

"Second, you tell Wheeler that Colonel LaGrange of the First Wisconsin Cavalry will hunt his adjutant, Duff Green Reed, to the nether regions of Hell for the suffering he has inflicted on our wounded."

The sergeant brightened. "That message, sir, I will gladly relay."

Keeping his revolver aimed, Hugh backed out of the tent with Wallace. Cleared of the hospital tents, they ran for their waiting troopers, praying the Rebel sergeant didn't change his mind and sound the alarm.

Halfway to his horse, Hugh felt something hard crunch under his boots. He stopped and picked up the shards of a drum with the batter head dangling lug casings and tension rods. He looked around and saw the tree where Wee Al Walton of the Seventy-Fifth Indiana had smashed his drum that morning to prevent it from being stolen. He gathered the remains of the drum and stuffed them into his saddlebag.

"Same way back?" Wallace asked.

Hugh studied the clear horizon to the north and shook his head. "Old Joe won't expect unfriendly visitors from his rear. Let's take the road this time."

* * *

The next night, Hugh sat mounted with his exhausted cavalry, screening the road to Rossville Gap while the panicked remnants of Rosecrans's defeated Army retreated for Chattanooga. His First Wisconsin troopers had driven back Wheeler's assaults with three countercharges that day, affording the divisions on the Union right flank enough time to avoid being cut off and captured. General Thomas, the sleepy West Pointer, had held the center in his horseshoe defensive formation, long enough for Old Rosy—more dazed, as Lincoln said, than a duck knocked in the head—to reach a Chattanooga hotel and sleep in a featherbed.

And Alexander McCook?

Hugh wondered what syrupy lullaby that Highlander troll was singing to-night. He had received not a word of thanks for saving McCook's bacon after confirming Wheeler's position north of Crawfish Springs and discovering Long-street's corps on the field. But he wouldn't forget Rosecrans's promise to deliver those Spencer repeating rifles, if he had to walk to Washington and present the bill of goods to Old Abe himself.

"We'd best get moving north," Wallace told him.

"You take the regiment on up with Colonel Ray and the brigade," Hugh said. "I have one last task. I'll find you."

Before Wallace could ask for an explanation, Hugh hurried down LaFayette Road against the tide of defeated men staggering for the protection of Missionary Ridge. He stopped an officer with one of the shattered units and asked, "Any word on the Seventy-Fifth Indiana?"

"Reynold's Division," the officer said. "What's left of them. I saw those boys heading for Rossville Gap an hour ago."

Hugh threaded past wagons, drawing grumbles and curses from the tired and hungry infantry forced to give way. At last, he spied the battle flag of the Indiana regiment. He cantered over to the standard bearer. "Your commanding officer?"

The soldier pointed to a limping man with a bandaged head.

The exhausted officer turned and grimaced as he raised his battered and swollen arm for a salute. "Colonel John Pettit."

Hugh opened his saddlebag and delivered the remnants of Al Walton's drum. "This belongs to you."

The survivors of the regiment gathered around to view the tattered relic.

"Where did you find it?" Pettit asked.

"I served an hour with Private Walton. No braver man fought on those fields out there. He destroyed his drum to prevent it from falling into the hands of the Johnnies."

The Hoosier soldiers wept as Pettit held aloft the drum pieces. "What happened to the boy?"

"He refused to abandon his wounded comrades. Wheeler captured him."

Choking back tears, Pettit clutched the drum remnants to his chest and saluted again. "We are in your debt, Colonel."

23

LAGRANGE, GEORGIA
SEPTEMBER 1863

Nancy waited that morning on the depot platform with Gus and Leila, surrounded by porters and Negroes summoned from the plantation fields to carry stretchers and push carts. A dispatch had arrived a few hours earlier, warning the town elders to expect a train from Atlanta loaded with soldiers wounded at the battle fought a week ago near Chattanooga. She watched the hazy horizon over the tracks to the north, steeling herself for what she would soon encounter. "How far is Chickamauga Creek?"

"Two hundred miles," said Gus.

"Those poor men," said Leila. "Agonizing in those wooden seats along these ragged tracks."

"They won't be sitting," said Gus. "Most will lay stacked on cattle cars."

"My Lord," muttered Nancy. "Why are they bringing them *here?*"

Gus unscrewed the brass handle on his cane and took a swig. "Bragg suffered eighteen thousand casualties in two days. We don't have enough hospitals in the entire state to treat half that many disabled. So, Major Stout—"

"The Army of Tennessee's medical director?"

Gus nodded. "In his infinite wisdom, he has chosen LaGrange to serve as a major hospital center."

"Is the Army not sending its own surgeons and doctors?"

"Most of them still have their hands full at Chattanooga. We must make do until they arrive."

Gus appeared more agitated than usual. Nancy could always tell when he was holding something back. She hadn't seen him this rattled since the news came of Vicksburg's fall and General Lee's defeat at Gettysburg. "You're hitting that medicinal pretty hard."

"You would be, too, if you knew what was coming at us."

"What are you not telling us?"

"We'll be getting the worst cases."

Leila drew closer to Gus to shield the stretcher boys from overhearing his dire prediction. She whispered, "Why do you say that?"

"Bragg will keep those men most likely to recover near the front. The hopeless and maimed for life will be sent to the end of the rail line."

Nancy looked south, past the small stream used by the tanning yard. On the west side of the rail line to West Point, the darkies were clearing brush from a field and stacking headboards. "What are they doing?"

Gus snorted. "What do you *think* they are doing?"

She wrinkled her brow. "A cemetery? Why so close to the tracks?"

"You'll find out soon enough." Gus cocked his ear for the train. "The women are ready at the Methodist church?"

"All but Caroline. I insisted she stay in bed. She could give birth any hour now." Nancy considered it a small blessing that Caroline would not witness this dark day. Two months after Caroline's husband, John Gay, returned to the Army of Northern Virginia, she learned she was pregnant. Caroline and John had decided to name the child Eugene, be it a boy or girl, in honor of Caroline's fallen brother. Fate continued its tradition, following every joy with a tragedy, for news came a few days later that Brown's younger brother, Charlie, had been killed on the retreat from Gettysburg.

A locomotive's whistle blew in the distance, and Gus screwed tight the handle on his cane. "Now, the both of you listen closely. You have the strips of cloth I told you to obtain?"

Leila displayed the knapsack on her shoulder. "Red, white, and gray."

"Keep up with me. Ask no questions. I will move as fast as I can. When I pronounce the color, you tie that strip on the man's wrist."

"What do the colors mean?" asked Nancy.

"Did I just say no questions?"

"Calm yourself," Nancy said. "We're not your orderlies."

Gus took a deep breath to gather his composure. "Do not stop to converse with the men. Many will be dehydrated and suffering from thirst. We must get them to the hospital without delay. Others will be in the throes of delirium. They may mistake you for their mother or sister." He leaned into their faces to impart his next instruction with emphasis. "If you feel faint or become hysterical—"

"Hysterical? If anyone is on the verge of hysterics, it's *you*. Leila and I have attended a birthing. Take heed of your own overwrought emotions."

Interrupting them, the train screeched into the depot and hissed to a stop. Confederate guards, many in rags and barefoot, leapt from the roofs of the boxcars, unlatched the doors, and lowered the ramps. The stretcher-bearers hurried into the cars and carried out the wounded.

Nancy brought a fist to her mouth. Such a panorama of misery she could never have envisaged. The entire train shimmied and hummed with a strange red oscillation. Another moment passed before she realized the effect was created by the hundreds of wounded men, wrapped in fetid bandages, writhing and moaning as the stretcher-carriers loaded them onto the carts. Every contorted face turned to her, begging for relief. Is this what her brother, Joe, suffered? Thrown into a maelstrom of the damned and—

"Red!" Gus barked.

Nancy's hands shook as she tried to tie the crimson strip to a man's wrist. She couldn't help but notice his face was nearly blown off. The soldier looked up at her with a wan smile and tied the strip for her.

"Nannie!" shouted Gus.

Nancy extricated herself from another poor fellow's tremoring grasp. She looked over her shoulder and saw Leila crying. "Leave, if you must."

Leila wiped her tears and shook her head. The next several minutes passed in a blur of horror. Nancy imagined standing outside her body to dull the assault of emotions. She concentrated on Gus's commands, refusing to look at the pinched, importuning faces passing her. She glanced inside a boxcar and saw dozens of coffins. A name scratched on one pine box with printer's ink caught her eye. She circled back and squinted through the murk of the car's interior. Her heart seized.

Colquitt.

Gus stopped, exasperated by her lagging. "We don't have time!"

She crawled into the boxcar and held her sleeve to her mouth.

Gus backtracked. "Nannie, what are you doing?"

A train guard shouldering a musket walked up to her. "Ma'am, I have to ask you to leave this car."

"Who is in this coffin?" she demanded.

"I don't know," the guard said. "These here are bound for Columbus."

"Open it."

"Nannie!" shouted Gus. "He can't do that."

She refused to budge. "I'm a commissioned captain in the LaGrange militia. I'm ordering you to open the lid."

Gus grumbled curses as he signaled for the guard to help him climb into the car. "Get back," he ordered Nancy. He nodded for the guard to pry off the lid with his bayonet. Gus looked inside and his eyes flooded. Nancy moved closer to see for herself, but he held her back. "Your cousin ... Peyton."

Nancy collapsed to her knees.

Gus struggled to bring her to her feet. "We don't have time to grieve. Pull yourself together."

She wiped her tears and stepped from the car with the help of the guard and Leila. Gus followed her out. The guard prepared to hammer the lid shut when Nancy stopped him. "Gus, give me your pen and prescription pad."

He dug them out of his coat pocket and handed them to her. She scribbled a message on the pad: *Dearest Julia, my deepest condolences to you and Cousin Alfred. Love, Nannie.* She tore off the page, handed it to the guard to place in the coffin for Peyton's widow, and resumed her chapfallen duty with Leila.

Gus next came to a cart that held a boy, no older than eighteen by Nancy's estimate. Gus hesitated, as if undecided. The boy's features so resembled his brother that he could have passed for Gene's twin. The remarkable affinity startled Leila, too. Gus pulled the boy's pant leg up to his knee, revealing a black fetid mass on his calf muscle. He dug his finger into the festering wound and examined the pus. He wiped his finger on a rag and coughed. "Gray!"

The terrified boy watched as Nancy tied the rag to his wrist. He stared up at her, questioning what the color meant. "Ma'am?"

She turned away, unable to tell him, and the stretcher-bearers removed him. She delayed to watch where they were taking him. They laid him in the shade, alone, under a small grove next to the space the Negroes were clearing for the new cemetery. Only then realizing his fate, she grabbed Gus's arm and spun him around, nearly causing him to fall. "What are you doing for that boy?"

"His leg is gangrenous. He will die within the hour."

Nancy staggered until Leila caught her. "Can you not amputate?"

"I am one doctor. I must help those with the best chance to survive."

Nancy fixed on his darting eyes. "Have you ever performed an amputation?"

"I observed one in medical school."

"Do not give up on him, Gus," she begged. "That could be Brown or Joe condemned on some Virginia field to die."

Gus kept limping past the carts and barking out the colors. Hectored by Nancy's glare burning his back, he finally relented and called over a stretcher team. "That lad in the grove over there. Take him to my office." He turned to Leila. "Show them the way. I'll be there as soon as I can."

"Fetch my whiskey," Gus ordered.

Nancy hurried to the cabinet and pulled the bottle from behind a stack of books. She opened the cap and prepared to give a drink to the boy as he sat upright on a table in Gus's office.

Gus waved the bottle in his direction. "Not for him." He took a swig and placed the whiskey on the counter behind him. He rolled up his sleeves and slipped on a white apron. "Leila, in that cupboard, you'll find clean linens and a small vial marked *Belladonna.*"

Leila brought the vial and cloths, and Gus lowered the boy onto the table. He retrieved the scissors from his surgical case and cut away the boy's pant leg halfway up the thigh. The boy raised to his elbows and fixed on Nancy with desperation in his bloodshot eyes. "If I die, promise me you won't let them bury me in that patch along the tracks. I can't long suffer train whistles in my ear. I got ten dollars in my pocket that'll pay my freight home."

"What's your name?" she asked.

"Seth Coogler. Thirtieth Georgia. My folks have a farm in Macon."

She placed her hand on his forehead. "Gus here is the best surgeon in La-Grange. When you pass to the Almighty from old age in Macon, I promise they won't bring you anywhere near that railroad plot to be buried."

He eased back, reassured, and nodded for them to continue. Gus wrapped a tourniquet around the boy's thigh, just above the knee, and tightened the clamp screw. Satisfied the flow of blood was stanched, he measured out a tincture of the liquid and dropped it into the boy's mouth.

Nancy studied the label on the bottle. "Belladonna?"

"Beautiful woman."

"I remember *that* from your class. But what are you using it for *now?*"

"It's a powerful narcotic and anodyne." He monitored the boy's fluttering eyelids. "Given in too large a dose, well, I suppose you remember *that,* too."

Nancy regarded the whiskey bottle, then she shot Leila an alarmed look.

Gus placed two fingers on the boy's neck to test his pulse. "Son, can you hear me?" When the boy did not respond, Gus pulled a long scalpel from his case. "We have two minutes before the sedative subsides."

Nancy held the boy's hand for support.

"Don't do that," Gus ordered.

"You are a cold-hearted man—"

"If he wakes during the cutting, he will crush every bone in your fingers."

Nancy pulled away and tucked the boy's arm against his side.

Gus took a deep breath. "Leila, hold him by the shoulders. Nannie, you take a firm grip here on his upper thighs." When they were in position, he honed the scalpel on a small grindstone. "Whatever happens, do *not* let go."

The two women, ashen, nodded.

"Father in Heaven, guide my hands." Gus cut a chevron gash just below the knee. With forceps, he pried back the skin and muscle to expose the fibula and clamped the skin wings open.

Nancy looked across the table. Leila had closed her eyes.

"Stand to the side," Gus whispered. "When I release the clamp, the blood will gush." He drew the saw back and dug its teeth into the bone. The boy contorted and his muscles drew taut, but his eyes remained closed. Three more long saw pulls and the leg detached. Gus unscrewed the tourniquet. The stump spurted, splattering his apron. He dropped the leg into a bucket and snagged the arteries with an instrument that resembled a handled fishhook. He stretched the arteries away from the incision and knotted them, then gathered a handful of balled cotton gauze on the counter and padded the swathing into the base of the exposed knee. Unpinning the folds of skin, he slid them together and took a step back, wiping the beads of sweat from his forehead.

Nancy released a held breath. "Now what?"

"We wait." Gus wiped his bloodied hands on his apron and took a long pull of whiskey. He handed the bottle to Nancy and nodded for her and Leila to partake. "You've earned it."

Nancy hesitated and looked at Leila. They glared silent vows never to speak of it—and both downed hearty gulps.

*   *   *

The women watched as Nancy demonstrated how to change the swathing on Seth Coogler's amputated leg. "Gus says we must dress it every four hours."

"Is he running a fever?" asked Mary.

Nancy felt his sweating forehead. "It's so hot down here, I can't tell."

"These men are all gasping for air," Leila said.

Nancy wiped her brow with a kerchief as she surveyed the basement of the Methodist church. Fifty beds held soldiers suffering from wounds and illnesses that ranged from dysentery to pneumonia and typhoid. Boards covered the lower windows for lack of panes, and the trapped air was putrid from the smells of festering sores, chloroform, varnish, bedpans, and the carbonic acid that Gus had ordered for a disinfectant. Added to this mix of cadaverous misery was the smoke that wafted low along the rafters from the stovepipe oven set at the end of the chamber. The lavender water and lime whitewash the women applied to the brick walls did little to chase the foul miasmas. This church, unlike most of the edifices in town, had no crawl space for waste disposal. She was desperate to take their minds off their despair. "Leila, go fetch your harp. Set up near the door and play hymns for them."

Leila, eager for the relief from nursing duty, rushed up the stairs.

Mary raised Nancy from the stool at the side of Seth's cot. "Get some sleep. I've set up shifts. We'll each take twelve hours."

Nancy nodded, grateful. "First, bring the women up to the sanctuary. There's something I must tell them."

In the nave, Nancy prayed to the large cross hanging above the altar while Mary gathered the other Nancies and sat them by rank in the front pews. Nancy turned and braced against the handrail. "Gus tells me we will lose at least two or three men each day. More wounded are on the way. The churches and hospitals from Atlanta to Newnan are filled."

"How will we feed them?" asked Andelia Bull. "We barely have enough for our own families."

"We'll start by saving the rotting vegetables," Nancy said.

"What will we throw to the hogs?" asked Ella Kay. "If the animals starve, we'll have no meats cured for the winter."

Mary came to Nancy's side and counseled, "We must take each week as it comes. Our armies suffer much worse deprivation. Most of those poor fellows in that basement, if they survive these first few days, will confront disease from malnutrition. We'll instruct the cooks to make stew from dessicated beans."

Aley Smith raised her hand. "Many of them have the flux. Won't the stew make their stomachs worse?"

"It's a trade we must risk," said Nancy. "And it means keeping them drinking water. We'll set up a relay team to bring in buckets from the spring."

Leila hurried into the church with her harp.

Nancy motioned for her to sit in the pew next to Aley. "One thing more. We will strive to keep them as comfortable as possible, but we have an even greater duty." She hesitated and glanced at Mary for reassurance.

"Nannie?" asked her sister, Augusta. "What is it?"

"If we cannot save them, we must help them make a good death."

The women coughed back sobs.

"We stand in for their mothers," said Nancy. "When I visited Brown in Virginia, he told me most dying men speak of home and family. Be strong. Assure them of their heavenly reward. Read from Scripture, if they ask. Keep pens and stationery at the nursing cabinet should they wish you to write letters. Some will arrange themselves for death by folding their arms over their chests and closing their eyes to wait. Stay with them until their last breath."

Mary pressed Nancy's shoulder to hers. "Any of those men could have been our husbands and brothers. We will prepare them for the grave as if they were our own kin. Wash the bodies and call for the burial detail. Reverend Heard will offer services at the cemetery. You are welcome to attend—"

"That is not wise," said a stranger's voice.

Nancy and the women turned to find Gus at the entrance, accompanied by a tall, genteel-looking man clad in a pristine Confederate uniform. The stranger had compassionate, swimming eyes and a flowing white goatee.

"May I present Dr. John Erskine," said Gus. "General Hardee's corps surgeon. He has been detailed here to take charge of the military hospitals."

The surgeon bowed. "Dr. Ware has done a splendid job preparing for our arrival. I have asked him to stay on to assist me."

The women stood and curtsied.

"You said *hospitals,*" Nancy reminded him. "We are to have more?"

Erskine sighed as he walked down the aisle. "I fear I am the first to bring this burdensome news."

"We work day and night to manage this one," said Nancy.

"I have requested more staff from Atlanta."

"You advised against attending services for the departed," Mary said. "Why?"

The surgeon fussed with the brim of his hat. "The government is indebted to you ladies. And we hope we can count on your continued help."

"And yet you hesitate to answer us," said Nancy.

"In every town where we have set up military hospitals, our stalwart women have responded to the call. Many become attached to the patients. The unmarried ones, in particular. When these men ..."

"Die," said Nancy, impatient with his patronizing tone.

Gus tried to intervene. "Nannie, please."

"I can see Mrs. Morgan has no patience for nuances," said Erskine. "That is an admirable trait in a ward."

"Sir, you need not shelter us from hard truths," said Nancy. "We have seen firsthand the horrors of war."

Erskine smiled at her innocence. "Guard your hearts, please. I have seen too many—of both genders—crushed from disappointment and grief."

Mary intervened before Nancy could object. "Thank you for your wise advice."

Erskine bowed and moved toward the stairs with Gus to continue his inspection of the basement ward. At the sacristy door, the surgeon stopped. "Do any of you ladies, by chance, speak French?"

The women turned toward Nancy.

"I took two years of French at the academy," she said. "But I'm not fluent."

"I have been assigned a fascinating patient from a hospital in Atlanta," said Erskine. "I wonder, Mrs. Morgan, if I might introduce you to him."

"I will help in any way I can."

* * *

The next afternoon, Nancy called upon Dr. Erskine at the small house he had rented on Newnan Road. He escorted her into his temporary study, where she found a pudgy young soldier seated in a chair and staring blankly at the wall.

"Dash," said Erskine. "This is Mrs. Morgan. She has come to help me speak with you." The boy sat motionless and his eyes did not move. The surgeon raised his voice to rouse him. "Dash!"

The boy broke into a silly, inanimate smile but did not audibly respond. He stood and walked with a mechanical gait around the room, paying no attention to his surroundings. After several circumambulations, he returned to the chair and continued staring at the empty wall.

"He suffered a head blow at Murfreesboro," Erskine explained. "Left on the field for dead. He hasn't spoken since that day."

Nancy stepped closer to peer into Dash's vacant eyes. "Why did he stand and walk just now?"

Erskine pulled up two chairs and situated them in front of the patient. "He responds only to the nickname the soldiers in his company gave him. The medical reports say before his injury he was a lively lad, well-liked, a ship chandler's clerk in New Orleans. He has been in a dozen hospitals."

She sat next to the physician. "He looks well-fed."

"Don't be fooled by his rotund appearance. His feet are edematous and his body has an anasarcous tendency."

She shrugged. Those terms meant nothing to her.

"I'm sorry. I keep forgetting you are not a trained nurse. Fluids are seeping into his feet and body cavities. From where, I'm not certain."

"Can nothing be done for him?"

The surgeon turned Dash's head to reveal a slight depression on the right side. "The location of the blow. The occipital bone near the lambdoidal suture."

"You're certain it was a brain injury?"

"Could have been a congenital malformation, but given his history, I doubt it." He turned Dash's head again. "You see this protrusion on the left side? Suggests the force of a blow compressed the skull."

She suddenly felt nauseated.

The surgeon retrieved a pitcher from his desk and poured two glasses of water. He gave one to her and helped Dash drink from the other. "Perhaps I should not have asked you—"

"No, I will be fine ... but how can I help him?"

The surgeon stood and bade her to follow him out from his study.

Before departing, Nancy waved to the boy. "Goodbye, Dash. I'll visit you again." The patient gave no sign he heard her.

On the front porch, Erskine lit a cigar and drew a long puff. "I'm operating on him tomorrow with an instrument called a trephine. I will drill a hole in his skull and remove a small disk of bone to relieve the pressure on his brain."

She grasped the banister. "My boast about not needing to be coddled ..."

"No, no. I'd not think of asking you to assist me in the surgery. The medical report says Dash immigrated to New Orleans from Gascony, a province in France. Sometimes, memories from childhood, if accessed, can bring the mind back to the present. Should he survive the operation—"

"You want me to speak French to him."

He nodded. "It's a long shot."

Nancy leapt at the chance to put her two years of suffering Mrs. Hort's French declensions to good use. *"Bien sûr, docteur, je suis à votre service!"*

*   *   *

"Quels repas votre mère vous préparait-elle quand vous étiez petit?"

Dash, his head bandaged from the incision, did not respond to Nancy's inquiry about what meals his mother cooked him as a boy. With her French vocabulary exhausted, she looked around Dr. Erskine's study for a prop she might use to stir his memory. For ten days, she had held these hourly afternoon sessions, but the boy sat through them frozen with his gaze unfocused. She stood and walked to a small world globe that the surgeon kept on his shelf. Spinning it, she came up with an idea. She brought the globe to her chair and set its base in front of the boy. Perhaps a visual stimulus might succeed. She dispensed with the French and asked him, "Can you point for me where Gascony is?"

He didn't even blink.

She found the border between Spain and France and pointed to the region west of Toulouse. "I'll bet you lived in Bordeaux. I've been told the best wines come from that province. Did you pick grapes?"

No reaction. Her finger traveled up the globe and came to rest on a dot just north of Paris. "There! I've always wondered where it's located." She hoped her excitement would elicit a response, but he remained mute. "You've probably been wondering how our town received its name. Your countryman, the Marquis de Lafayette, traveled here during the last years of his life. Our land reminded him of his estate in France, the Château de la Grange-Bléneau. To honor the champion of freedom, the first settlers came up with LaGrange. Isn't it a grand coincidence that you—" The church bells rang out in a staccato.

The danger warning. Was the town being invaded by raiding cavalry?

She leapt to her feet, rehearsing the plan her Nancies had devised for mustering: Gather at the red schoolhouse on the Bellevue estate and distribute the muskets. That was ten blocks away. She'd have to retrieve the key—

The door flew open. Breathless, Mary cried, "The hospital's on fire!"

Nancy gasped. "Tell the others to fill their buckets and bring blankets. Meet me at the church."

"The boy?"

Nancy looked into his empty eyes. "Dash, stay here. I will return."

Outside, Nancy and Mary found the townspeople rushing from their homes and converging on the Methodist church. Black smoke billowed from the chimney that rose only a few feet away from the wooden steeple. The other Nancies came running from all directions and gathered in ranks in front of the church, awaiting Nancy's orders. Gus staggered from his office on the square and limped as swiftly as he could toward the commotion. The town's fire brigade—a few old men, boys, and Negroes rounded up from the kitchens—rolled up a wagon laden with a large tank of water.

Nancy dipped her bandanna in the tank and wrapped it around her mouth. "Wet your kerchiefs!"

As the women prepared to fight the conflagration, Nancy circled the church to locate the source of the fire. In the rear, she found Dr. Erskine and five orderlies on his staff hacking at the back door with axes.

"The basement!" said Erskine. "We have to get those men out."

Nancy froze. There was only one stairway down to the makeshift ward. The lower windows had been boarded up. Most of the wounded and ill could not stand, let alone walk. She shouted at her Nancies. "Pile the blankets at the door here. Then grab crowbars from the fire wagon! Mary, you take your company to the east side. I'll take mine to the west! Break open the windows."

"It's too dangerous," insisted Erskine. "The pressure from the heated air could explode the boards."

"We don't have a choice." Nancy motioned the women to their assignments. "If we don't get these open, you won't get through that back door."

Erskine hurried to the rear of the church to direct his staff into the breach once the window boards fell away.

Nancy and Leila pried at the plywood nailed over the first window. When Nancy loosened it, she warned Leila to stand back. With one more yank, she sent the board flying. Black smoke charged through the casement. In minutes, the other women freed their boards, giving the medical men at the rear door enough ventilation to enter. The fire brigade, armed with the blankets, rushed into the basement, carried out the wounded soldiers, and rested them on the grass.

"Give them water!" Nancy ordered.

The women spread out among the gasping men to slake their thirst and fan air to their blackened mouths and noses. Gus checked their pulses and administered what comfort he could offer. After several minutes, the smoke receded.

Erskine, grimed, climbed from the basement. "We got them all out."

Nancy pressed her wet kerchief against her nose. She descended the three steps and poked her head inside the back door. The ward was a charred ruin. She climbed back up and asked Erskine, "What caused the fire?"

"The stovepipe overheated." The surgeon scanned the suffering men strewn across the grass. "I have no place prepared to take them. The Baptist and Presbyterian churches are not yet equipped with cots."

"We will make do." Nancy called the other Nancies to attention. "Each of us will take three men into our homes."

* * *

A week later, Leila rushed into Nancy's house in the middle of the night. Careful not to disturb the wounded soldiers convalescing on the parlor floor, she tiptoed up the stairs, slipped into the bedroom, and shook Nancy awake.

Groggy, Nancy muttered, "Is there another fire?"

"No, but come with me."

Nancy had learned to sleep in her dress for emergencies. She fixed her hair and threw on her cloak. Leila refused to explain the summons but locked arms with Nancy and hurried her to Caroline's house. Fearing her friend had fallen sick, Nancy rushed up the stairs and bolted through the bedroom door. The town midwife stood in the corner, washing blood from her hands into a bowl. Caroline, pale and exhausted, lay in the bed. She opened her eyes at hearing Nancy's voice and smiled.

At the foot of the bed, Mary held a baby girl. "Eugene, meet your Aunt Nannie."

Nancy rushed to Mary and took the newborn into her arms. "She has John's chin." She smiled through tears at Caroline. "And your sharpshooter eyes."

"Will you induct her?" asked Caroline.

Nancy kissed the infant on the forehead. "Private Eugene, do you promise to defend LaGrange and never allow your momma to leave my side?" Seeing the infant smile and burp, Nancy brought her to her shoulder and patted the newborn on the back. "I hereby declare you a Nancy Hart Riflewoman."

A noise that sounded like a drunken woodpecker echoed up from the staircase. Moments later, Gus staggered through the door with his cane, out of breath from the climb. "I came as soon as I heard."

Nancy approached to offer him his new niece but then pulled the infant back. "Have you been into the medicinal tonight?"

"Give me my kin!"

The women chuckled as Nancy took Gus's cane, placed the child in his arms, and braced him with a firm hand to his bicep to steady him. The curmudgeon tried in vain to blink away tears of pride.

"We must thank the Almighty for this miracle," said Nancy.

"And," a man's voice rang out, "we must thank *you*, Mrs. Morgan, for another miracle." The women turned to see Dr. Erskine at the threshold. "I hope I'm not intruding. Gus asked me to come should there be complications."

"You are most welcome here," said Caroline.

Erskine stepped into the bedroom and ushered in a reluctant companion.

Dash walked into the light from the stairwell's shadows. He lifted his shy gaze from the floor and looked straight at Nancy, his eyes bright and playful. "*Bonsoir*, Madam Nannie."

Stunned, Nancy rushed to Dash and hugged him, thrilled to discover he had returned to his old self.

* * *

The next morning, before leaving for her nursing rounds, Nancy penned a letter to John Gay in Virginia:

Dearest John,

I write with joyful news. You are the father of a beautiful, healthy girl, Eugene. She resembles you in both features and spirit. I have never seen Gus so gushing. Caroline remains weak from the labor, but Dr. Erskine of General Hardee's staff assures us she will recover soon. She sends her love.

I am exhausted and must apologize that I cannot give this letter the length it deserves. The horrible battles near Chattanooga have flooded LaGrange with so many wounded men that you would barely recognize our town now. That drunkard Grant remains pinned down in Tennessee, but rumors say if he breaks General Bragg's siege, he intends to drive south in the spring. Do you believe Atlanta can turn him back? I know not what will happen to us if that city should fall.

Peyton Colquitt died from wounds suffered at Chickamauga Creek. Cousin Alfred, I suspect, has received the tragic news there in Virginia. Give him my heartfelt condolences.

I hope you are blessed with a safe and uneventful winter. Gus says next year will decide our fate. If Lincoln can be voted out of Washington, the Northern moderates may negotiate an end to this bloody war. Tell Brown I owe him a letter. Christmas will be gloomy. Gus has consumed the last of his precious Madeira, so there will be no traditional toast. He has not located another bottle, let alone a case, since the Yankees blockaded Mobile.

John, you are in our prayers. Almighty God looks over you.

Love, Nannie

P.S. The Methodist church caught fire. I warned the government functionaries sent here from Richmond about that old stovepipe, but they little listen to me. I suppose I complain too much. The steeple and nave were saved, but the basement is gutted. The Baptist and Presbyterian churches are to be hospitals, too, and the medical authorities say more buildings will be requisitioned.

24

Hugh hurried his First Wisconsin regiment toward a dark plume of ash billowing above the hills north of Chattanooga. He rode ahead and found the source of the pillage smoke. A mile east of the Sequatchie River bridge, eight hundred Federal wagons, many loaded with wheat and meat desperately needed in the besieged city, sat ablaze. Dismounted Rebel cavalrymen scampered around the conflagration like crazed rats, ransacking commissary sacks for food and trading their ragged butternut uniforms for new blue overcoats, trousers, and shoes. In the midst of this half-naked orgy of plundering, a party of Confederate officers tapped an upturned barrel and raised their tin cups in a celebratory toast.

Son of the Devil ... that's him.

The scouting reports were accurate. Joe Wheeler had crossed the Tennessee River with six thousand cavalry on a raid to cut Rosecrans's last supply line. The Army of the Cumberland, whipped at Chickamauga, now hunkered trapped behind Chattanooga's earthworks, starving and dispirited. Grant was on his way from Nashville to take command from Old Rosy, who cowered inside his hotel headquarters. If Wheeler succeeded in knotting the noose of the Confederate encirclement, Braxton Bragg could take his time pounding Grant into submission with his artillery atop Lookout Mountain and Missionary Ridge.

Hugh's pulse raced. One bold stroke here might ease the sting of the defeat at Chickamauga: Wheeler's capture. All depended on closing fast at three angles on the carousing Rebels before they escaped to their horses.

He raised four fingers to form his column into sortie formation. A section of the rail fence bordering the road lay fallen; *there* was the swiftest entry point. He sent Wallace to the right with two companies to cut off Wheeler's retreat to the Tennessee River and doubled the pace of his own advance to a trot. Fifty yards in, he split off Major Torrey with three companies to the left, signaling for them to target the leading wagons in the burning caravan. With a single line of troopers now following him, he drew his saber and called for the charge at the Rebel center on a full gallop.

Hundreds of sabers zinged, pulled from their scabbards.

Wheeler and his roistering officers, alerted by the Yankee yells for revenge, scrambled for their grazing horses.

Hugh took aim for the bantam commander and slashed at the Confederate pickets bouncing to their feet a few yards from the crossroads. He was past them before they could raise their muskets.

Wheeler pulled up into his saddle. Around him, his officers staggered and tried to mount, but their horses spooked, leaving several of his staff behind to be captured. Wheeler spurred into a frantic gallop north and glanced over his shoulder to identify the Union officer chasing him.

Hugh caught up and slashed at Wheeler's head, but missed. Wheeler angled to the far shoulder of his horse to deny Hugh another target. Hugh circled and came at the Confederate general from the other direction. A volley from pistols fired at him from returning Rebel cavalry stopped him short. He reined up, outnumbered, cursing at being denied his prize.

Wheeler tipped his hat as he escaped across the bridge.

Hugh, nodding with grudging admiration for his rival's deft horsemanship, returned to the burning wagon train to salvage what supplies the Rebels hadn't destroyed or carried away. He dismounted and, with saber still in hand, surveyed the damage. He stuck a finger in the tap hole of the barrel stolen by Wheeler and his officers and tasted its contents.

Whiskey. Those thieves were soused.

Wallace herded up a dozen prisoners. "They were too busy ransacking the liquor and packed uniforms to put up much of a fight."

"Are they talking?" Hugh asked.

"Talking? Hell, they're babbling without cease. I've got Bragg's plans for the next year, and half of Bobby Lee's."

"Send them to Chattanooga with a detachment." Hugh turned to check the northern hills beyond the river, ensuring Wheeler hadn't rounded to recover his captured men. "I'll clean up here and—" He spotted a Rebel cowering between two charred wagons while aiming his revolver. He rushed at the skulker and lifted his saber to strike when the Southerner raised his hands and fired off the round into the sky.

The Reb reversed his revolver, holding its barrel, and slurred, "I shurndah."

Hugh pushed the prisoner toward Wallace and stuck his nose between the charred wagons to check if others were hiding there. Behind him, a revolver fired. The bullet grazed his hat. Nearly brained, Hugh spun and swung his saber to defend himself, enraged the oath-breaker had reloaded his revolver on the sly.

The thrust slashed the man's upper lip. He dropped his revolver and staggered to his knees, wiping blood from his cheek. "You marred me!"

Hugh itched to take another swing. "You surrender and then fire on me? I should string you up!"

The prisoner lurched to all fours, swaying from the effects of the whiskey. "Kicked your negrah-lovin' asses at Crawfish Springs!"

Hugh yanked the foul-mouthed Rebel to his feet. Something about the scoundrel looked familiar. He shrugged it off and shoved the drunkard toward Wallace to be bound when he glimpsed the buttons on the prisoner's blue-caped mantle. *This is* my *coat!* He grabbed the teetering man and lifted him to his toes. "It was you. *You* stole this from our surgeon at Crawfish Springs." When the prisoner, cursing and thrashing, refused to confess the theft, Hugh drove him against a fence railing. "What's your name?"

The man glared a demand for silence at his fellow prisoners surrounded by the Wisconsin troopers.

"He's Major Reed," a Confederate private revealed. "We don't countenance what he just done."

Reed snarled. "Traitor! I'll have you drummed out and whipped!"

Another prisoner raised a middle finger to Reed. "You done pinched your last parcel of personal property, Reed." He told Hugh, "That cut you gave him is his first wound. He ain't a fighter. He's a swindler."

His memory refreshed, Hugh unbuttoned the officer's blue coat and stripped him of it. "Major Duff Green Reed. Adjutant to General Wheeler. I trust that sergeant at Crawfish Springs relayed my message?"

Reed's boozy eyes bulged. "LaGrange ... damn you *and* your Saber Brigade! You got lucky nabbing me. But you'll never catch Joe Wheeler."

"Saber Brigade?"

The prisoner who identified Reed admired Hugh's blade. "You fellas are the First Wisconsin, ain't you? Saber Brigade is what we named you after you saved your infantry on Snodgrass Hill. Most of your Northern bowlegs hide behind carbines, which ain't a fair fight. But you boys seem partial to those long frog giggers. How did you get past us that night at Chickamauga, anyways?"

Hugh answered the Rebel private while maintaining his loathing glare at Reed. "My guess is, we rode through your camp while your officers like this one were stone-drunk asleep."

Reed lunged at Hugh, but Wallace wrangled him back.

The Rebel private spat at Reed's feet and told Hugh, "I reckon your guess, Colonel, is pretty close to right."

* * *

Weeks later, after Wheeler escaped into Alabama having lost a third of his men on the raid, Hugh wrote his official report of the Anderson's Crossroads incident and submitted it up the chain of command:

> Hdqrs. First Regiment Wisconsin Cavalry,
> Winchester, Tenn., November 6, 1863
> Col. E.M. McCook, Commanding, &c.:
>   COLONEL: To your inquiry of this evening, I have the honor to submit the following report: In the charge of my regiment at Anderson's Gap on the 2d October, I had raised my saber to strike a Confederate officer when he called out, "I surrender," and passed behind me, discharging his pistol at me as he did so. The distance he had allowed me to pass enabled him to avoid any punishment, save a slight cut across the face, which I am told, however, will frequently remind him of his unmanly act. Subsequent inquiry proved the officer (who was captured) to be Major Reed, of General Wheeler's staff.
>   I sincerely regret the occasion for making such a charge against any person claiming to be a soldier, more especially from the fact that Confederate officers with whom the chances of war have heretofore made me acquainted, have always left me with a high appreciation of their courage and their sense of military honor.
>   I remain, colonel, most respectfully,
>
> O.H. La Grange
> Colonel, Commanding First Wisconsin Cavalry

* * *

"You're an elusive man," said Daniel Ray. "No wonder you crept up on Wheeler."

Hugh turned from his seated perch atop Lookout Mountain and pocketed a letter he was reading. He pushed to a knee to stand for a salute, but the colonel motioned him back down and sat next to him on the smooth boulder. Hugh shook his head and clutched at the air with his fist. "I had him in my grasp."

Ray smiled and raised his face to warm it under the sun. "I'll wager, at least, Old Joe isn't sleeping as well at night now."

Hugh sighed his disappointment and gazed south. The day was so clear he could see all the way to Ringgold, where Bragg had retreated with his stunned army after Grant drove him off these heights with a spectacular assault. The siege had been lifted and the trains, filled with supplies and ammunition, were running again into Chattanooga. He felt in his bones something even bigger was in the works. "If we'd had Grant at that creek instead of Old Rosy—"

"Yeah, and if the Rebs here had Bobby Lee, and if we had Lord Wellington, and if the Rebs had Julius Caesar. We can play that game until one of us reaches Joshua and his trumpets below the walls of Jericho."

Hugh gave up the argument with a sheepish grin. During these past two grueling months, he and Ray had become fast friends, sharing school lectures, farming memories, and hopes for the future.

Ray studied him. "You feeling pekid? You don't seem yourself."

Hugh waved off his concern.

"Maybe this will cheer you up." Ray pulled a document from his back pocket and read it aloud. "'I cannot speak too highly of the conduct and gallantry of Colonel O.H. LaGrange, First Wisconsin Cavalry. To his intrepidity in leading, and skill in maneuvering his regiment, is attributable in a large degree to the successful repulse of the enemy. Signed General Edward McCook.'" He grinned and handed the report to Hugh. "That sounds like a soldier angling for my job."

"Not for all the gold in California."

"Turn it over."

Hugh kept a suspicious eye on Ray, uncertain what scheme he was cooking up. He found an order written in General McCook's hurried script:

> *Effective this date, Col. O.H. LaGrange is hereby ordered to relieve Col. Daniel M. Ray and take command of the Second Brigade, Cavalry Corps, Army of the Ohio. Col LaGrange and the First Wisconsin Cavalry will report to General Sturgis by December 31, 1863, at Dandridge, Tennessee.*

Ray clasped his friend's shoulder. "I'm resigning."

"You're on the way to a brigadier—"

"I have the consumption. The doctors say they caught it early, but I'll always be struggling with it. I can't breathe as deeply as when I joined. Hell, the climb up this rock nearly did me in."

Hugh tried to force him to take the order back, wanting nothing to do with his friend leaving the Army. "Three months yet until campaigning season. If you lie low and regain your strength—"

"Louise is with child."

Hugh leapt to his feet and pulled Ray up to congratulate him. "Why didn't you tell me earlier?"

"I didn't want to hex the birth. She's supposed to deliver next month. She's been too weak to bring in the corn and hemp. I feel as if I'm abandoning you and the lads, but she needs me. I won't be much good to you anyway with shriveled lungs."

Hugh hung his head, distressed by the prospect of being abandoned by the one officer he most admired.

"I thought you'd be thrilled with the promotion."

"My enlistment is up in February. I'm thinking of heading out West."

"What about Jennie?"

Hugh's eyes watered as he patted the pocket where he'd stored the worn paper and envelope he had been reading. "I got a letter from her this week."

"She's always begging you to come home, sure. And you said she was upset when you passed up the last furlough, but—"

"She moved back to Minnesota to live with her parents and filed for a legal separation last month."

"My God, Hugh. I'm so sorry."

Hugh required a moment to recover his voice. "It's my fault. I didn't take the leave last winter because I knew she'd find me a different man than the one she married. I couldn't even summon the words to write her. We were so young when we got hitched."

"Perhaps if you sent your brother home to plead your case."

Hugh shook his head. "I haven't told Wallace. Can't bear to do it. He took it hard when we got word our father died last year. I think he felt guilty about leaving him on the farm."

"Who's taking care of your stepmother?"

"She went to her Heavenly reward three months after Pa passed."

Ray stared at the ground, as if debating the wisdom of his request for Hugh to take his place in command of the brigade, considering this tragic news. "I have a confession. I lobbied General McCook for you. Probably my fault. Didn't take much arm-twisting, though. He admires you."

"His slaver cousin holds a different opinion."

Ray smiled and nodded. "I have no right to ask this of you, given your losses. But I promised the mothers of those boys in the Second Tennessee that I'd look after them until this war ended." He couldn't finish.

Hugh looked south across the Chickamauga Creek valley and the Western & Atlantic rail line that ran through Tunnel Hill to Atlanta. He tried to imagine what Lincoln, Grant, and Sherman had in mind for their next strike against the Confederacy. Whatever their plan, he figured it would involve casualties and devastation on a scale that none had ever witnessed. What was the worst that could happen to him now? To die in battle might be a blessed relief from his cares. He had nothing to return to after the war, no wife or children or home. Lasting love was a fanciful dream. Perhaps the Almighty had put him on this Earth solely to help free the Negro race.

He shook Ray's hand to seal a promise to shepherd his new charges.

* * *

As the sun broke above the hoary horizon, Hugh rode across the dismounted ranks of his new command, the Second Brigade of the Army of the Ohio's cavalry corps. He blew rattling breaths into his cupped hands to warm them. Icicles festooned his frozen saddle, and the colic hobbled his malnourished horse. He and his troopers had slept on the frozen ground with no blankets, coughing in the darkness without fires. In the middle of January, most armies would be huddled in winter quarters, deeming it cruel and insane to fight in such miserable weather. Yet here he was, in the wilds of eastern Tennessee, ordered to hold this insignificant hill against two of the fiercest infantry divisions in the Confederacy.

All for a few fields of corn left on the stalks.

He took some solace in knowing that Longstreet's twenty thousand men, arising from their beds of leaves three hundred yards to the east, weren't faring any better. Both armies had been campaigning half-starved, and he observed in the prior day's fighting that many of the Rebs wore no shoes. General Ambrose Burnside, cocky after breaking Longstreet's siege of Knoxville, ordered the hornet's nest poked a few miles beyond Dandridge, along the French Broad River. Hugh cursed the stupidity of generals. Burnside was another fatuous West Pointer who, after slaughtering thirteen thousand of his own men at Fredericksburg, was shipped West to practice his butchery here. Those Southerners across that field might be walking skeletons, but he'd seen proof enough they were angry as hell at being hit in the winter for no good reason. And they weren't eager to return to Lee's army in Virginia to be heckled for losing the two most important rail hubs in Tennessee.

Wallace rode up and dropped a few roasted kernels into Hugh's hands. "I sent a foraging party crawling out before light."

"Has every man had some?"

"Yeah, but several couldn't keep the corn down."

"Dysentery?"

Wallace nodded. "We aren't exactly in fighting shape."

Hugh noticed the old epaulets still on his brother's shoulders.

Wallace shrugged. "I haven't had time to stitch on the new ones."

"If you don't want to be a captain, I can rescind the order and—"

"You see how the other officers look at me. Every time you get promoted, I step up the ladder, too."

"Because you've earned it."

"They don't see it that way."

"I don't have time to coddle your hurt feelings. In case you haven't noticed, we've got a swarm of Rebs on our flanks."

"Noticed? Hell, I've been in the front every mile we rode from Knoxville! I was led to believe we joined the cavalry, but all we do is fight, dismount, and walk and fight, dismount, and walk. I could have stayed with the Fourth and done this. At least then I wouldn't have to feed a horse."

Hugh played with the hammer on his revolver to keep it from freezing. "Instead of caterwauling, why don't you help me figure out how to defend this godforsaken protuberance of earth from Pharaoh's legions. I didn't ask for this command. McCook ordered me to take it and—"

A warbling Rebel yell stirred the crows from the woods to their east.

Hugh turned and saw a horde of scared rabbits and deer scamper out as if driven by dogs. Moments later, Longstreet's infantry division cleared the trees and marched toward him in assault formation.

God help us.

Hugh watched his pickets being driven back like shooed flies. The Rebels lowered their muskets and fired. Six kneeling troopers in their thin Union line dropped. He scanned the Rebel flags. Those were John Bell Hood's Texas veterans on him again. The Confederates had him outnumbered, and a fourth of his own force was unavailable, needed to hold the horses. To his left, he saw Israel Garrard's First Brigade crumble and give way after the first volley. If Longstreet took *this* high ground, he'd station his artillery here and control the cornfields.

As Wallace ran off to rejoin his company, Hugh shouted, "We are attacked!"

The Second Brigade troopers leapt to their feet and backtracked to their horses while firing. From across the hill, Wallace stared at Hugh, impatient for his brother's decision to stand or run.

Another Rebel volley dropped a dozen more of the Federals.

Hugh held his ground until his troopers were mounted and ready. As they waited for his command to retreat, he cantered to the center of his line, drew his saber, and reined his horse to face the oncoming infantry. "Charge!"

Wallace sat stunned. Seeing Hugh determined to drive back the Rebel infantry and hold the hill, he and his troopers pulled sabers and rode to the assault.

Hugh led them at a gallop into the teeth of Hood's regiments. The charge halted the Texans's advance. Hugh slashed at the surrounding Rebels, who grabbed at his reins and tried to pull him off the saddle. Having stunted the Confederate infantry's momentum, he signaled for his bugler to sound a retreat. Wallace and his company were the last to disengage.

Back atop the crest, Hugh ordered his troopers to dismount and form a curving battle line around the apex of the hill. He threw his leg over his saddle to join them when he saw a dozen of his men trailing behind, caught in no-man's-land. The Texans rushed at them, ravenous for revenge. Before Hugh could stop him, Wallace leapt back on his horse and led his company on a charge to rescue the straggling troopers. Too late to join his brother, Hugh ordered his kneeling men to give Wallace covering fire.

Wallace lashed into the onrushing Rebel infantry, fighting them off with his saber and firing his revolver. His onslaught was so reckless and unexpected, it gave the stumbling Federals lagging behind just enough time to scurry to safety. His mission accomplished, Wallace reined his horse into a tight turn to gallop back. He was halfway up the defended hill when the horse buckled and reared. Wallace, hit in the lower back, lurched in the saddle.

He fell—both armies ceased firing.

"Wallace!" Hugh ran to his horse and ordered two companies to charge with him down the hill. He struck the swarming Rebels with a frenzy of saber slashes and held them off long enough for three of his troopers to dismount and carry Wallace up the hill. Seeing his brother rescued, Hugh galloped back to his command position on the crest as the balls whizzed overhead. He searched for Wallace among the wounded writhing on the bloodied snowdust behind his line.

Major Torrey rushed up. "I ordered two men to take him to Dandridge."

"How bad is he hurt?"

Torrey hesitated. "He was conscious."

Shaken, Hugh struggled to focus his mind.

"Sir, are we to hold this ground?" asked Torrey.

Hugh searched below the rim of smoke to his left. Their costly sortie had given the First Brigade on the next knoll over time enough to regroup. "If we retreat, we'll leave the Pennsylvanians exposed. Send a courier to Colonel Jordan. Tell him I intend to defend this position until nightfall. Unless otherwise ordered, we'll retire at midnight and cover him with a rear-guard action."

At dawn, Hugh and his exhausted troopers reached Dandridge. The town was in chaos, filled with wounded men laid upon the street's walking boards. Ambulances sat in front of a two-story residence marked *Bradford-Hynds Law Office.* Hugh dismounted and rushed inside. The floor was filled with wounded troopers. He searched their faces but didn't find Wallace.

The brigade surgeon, in a bloodied apron, stopped him from rushing upstairs. "The shot pierced his liver."

Hugh braced a hand against the wall. "Will he live?" When the surgeon shook his head, Hugh required a moment to reclaim his voice. "How long?"

"Only God knows. I've seen men with such wounds expire within hours. Others hang on for weeks."

Hugh slowly climbed the stairs, gripping the railing. With a deep inhalation to steel himself, he pushed open the cracked door and found Wallace lying on his side with the sheets soaked in his blood. His brother's eyes, glazed from the lingering effects of the chloroform, turned toward him.

"The damned thing," Wallace muttered. "The one time you'd allow me a dram of whiskey, I no longer have the taste for it."

"This is my fault."

"For once, I won't argue with you." Wallace managed a weak smile. "It has always been your fault. I intend to bring you up on charges of malfeasance with St. Peter at the Gates. You promised me a Spencer carbine."

Hugh choked back tears. Even to the end, his brother played the jester.

Grimacing, Wallace turned serious. "You'll be the last of the LaGranges, Hugh. Your enlistment is up next month. Go home to Jennie and start a family. It's what Pa and Ma would have wanted."

Hugh pulled up a chair, debating if he should tell him about her letter ending his marriage. He and Wallace had never kept the truth from each other, and he didn't wish to live with the guilt from letting him die grasping at a false hope. Swallowing hard, he confessed, "Jennie has left me." Wallace tried to arise, but Hugh eased him back onto the pillow. "She wrote to me the week after Chickamauga."

Wallace's eyes watered. "You'll find another lass."

Hugh slumped and averted his gaze, ashamed of this, his latest in a string of failures. "After what we've seen together, I've been ruined for domesticity."

Wallace struggled to his elbow, determined to belie that prediction. Before he could manage the words, the door opened and Major Torrey entered.

"Orders from General Sturgis. We're to fall back to New Market at once."

Hugh nodded. "Prepare the men to ride. I'll be down shortly."

Torrey closed the door, and Hugh kept his eyes pinned to the floor, hoping for some way to avoid the next few moments. Reluctantly, he turned, only to find his brother had slipped into a feverish sleep. He caressed Wallace's blood-matted hair. "Goodbye, Wally. Forgive me." He burned his brother's face into his memory and walked out.

At the bottom of the stairs, the surgeon braced Hugh with hands to his shoulders. "I did everything I could. I'm sorry."

Hugh dug his fisted nails into his palms to avoid breaking down. "Longstreet will pull back to Morristown. He cares nothing for this town. He wants the cornfields, or what's left of them. You'll be safe here until I can arrange transports for the wounded and dead." He reached into his pocket for his order book, tore out a page, and scribbled a hasty letter against the flat of the wall boards. He folded the note and pulled out all the cash he carried, placing the greenbacks within the fold. He addressed the name of the recipient and handed the correspondence to the surgeon. "I would ask a favor."

* * *

Later that year, Wallace's embalmed body arrived in Ripon, transported by rail from Nashville to St. Louis and up the Mississippi by riverboat. With Hugh still fighting in Tennessee, Professor Daniels honored his former protege's request by presiding over Wallace's burial in Hillside Cemetery. Before closing the casket, Daniels read aloud an excerpt from the official report of the Dandridge battle, written by General Edward McCook:

> *I have to note among the casualties of the day the severe and danger-ous wounding of Capt. W. W. LaGrange, First Wisconsin Cavalry, who fell while leading his men in a desperate hand-to-hand fight. He was a young officer of distinguished bravery and great promise.*

Daniels rolled the commendation into a cylinder and inserted it into the barrel of a Spencer repeating carbine, donated in tribute by the troopers of General John Wilder's Lightning Brigade. The professor placed the carbine in the casket with Wallace and closed the lid.

25

DEMOPOLIS, ALABAMA
JANUARY 1864

Nancy and Mary walked along the carpeted hallway of the plantation mansion, built in the Steamboat Gothic style, and admired the European paintings on the candlelit walls: Lush nudes of Greek huntresses; panoramas of Italian harbors and rocky promontories; fountains depicted with such realism that Nancy could feel the splash of water against ancient stones. Major Ivey Lewis, an officer with the Jeff Davis Legion in General Lee's Army, called his home here, on the banks of the Alabama River, Bleak House, but she deemed that name most inapt.

She sighed as she savored the cedarwood scent diffused by the aroma lamps. Here she felt lifted by angels from the misery of the war and dropped into a fairy tale, if for only one evening. Everything about the setting was enchanting: torches on the dormers and gables cast romantic shadows across the vast porch; lanterns marked the winding path up from the dock where three paddle wheelers floated along the canebreaks; the misting rain pattered the steep-pitched roof—all conspiring to transport the guests back to happier times. In the grand room, the men stood in their dress grays and the ladies in their colorful ballgowns brought out from storage. She hadn't worn her debutante attire since that spring night at Bellevue eight years ago, but hard times now required breaking with tradition. It was a small blessing that the spartan diet demanded by the food shortages allowed her to still fit into it.

She and Mary came to a canvas in oil of a boy on his knees, reaching up to a towering man to beg relief from an inchoate horror. She shuddered—the agony in the penitent's twisted face reminded her of brother, Joe, dying in that Fredericksburg field hospital. She closed her eyes to chase a dizziness.

Mary supported her at the elbow. "Are you ill?"

"I'll be fine." The train ride to Montgomery and up the river on the paddler had been taxing. Mary had counseled against accepting Dr. Erskine's invitation to attend, but Nancy refused to miss the most anticipated social event of that winter: the wedding of William Hardee, the general whose tactics manual she had studied for three years. Mary acquiesced only because Nancy agreed to bring Leila and Augusta as compensation for never having made their debut at a LaGrange cotillion. Nancy regained her balance with a deep breath. "This painting is so overwhelming ..."

"Tobias and the Angel," said a female voice behind them.

They turned to find a petite, vivacious woman, not much older than twenty. She had sparkling brown eyes and a welcoming manner. Nancy recognized her as the maid of honor for General Hardee's bride. Earlier that evening, she had played an affecting sonata on the parlor piano.

"It's based on a drawing by Sogliani in Florence," said the lady. "One of my favorites. Major Ivey and his wife, Kate, commissioned it when they took the Grand Tour of the Continent."

"I'm sorry," said Mary. "I failed to catch your name."

"Ack! It is a pernicious habit of mine. I fall into conversation with strangers and forget they *are* strangers. I am Sue Tarleton."

"Tobias," said Nancy. "I don't remember that story."

Tarleton leaned toward them in a playful conspiracy. "That's because it doesn't appear in the King James Bible. Only in the Catholic and Jewish scriptures. Tobias is the son of Tobit. He meets an angel without realizing the divine nature of the encounter. A test imposed by the Almighty, I suppose." Her voice fell to a near whisper. "You didn't learn this from me, but the Major and Kate fancy themselves as heretics of a sort. Feast your senses upon this nonpareil house. No Greek Revival columns for them."

This Sue Tarleton possessed such a disarming warmth that Nancy felt they were already fast friends. "I am Mrs. Morgan, and this is Mrs. Heard."

"I know very well who you are. The famous Nancy Harts from LaGrange."

Nancy couldn't believe their reputation had traveled all the way to Mobile, until Tarleton burst into a giggle, and Nancy realized her assumption had been too grandiose. "I see you've encountered our two younger companions."

"Your sister, Augusta, and Leila are precious," said Tarleton. "And so effusive in their devotion to your militia. I think your defense of your town is to be praised from here to Richmond."

Nancy noticed she had a habit of rubbing her right wrist with her left hand.

"I've had neuralgia since childhood," explained Tarleton, detecting her concern. "When it rains and I stroke the piano keys too long, it flares. Letter-writing is difficult. But enough about my niggling maladies." She peered into the hall as if planning a dangerous sortie. "Have you met General Hardee?"

Mary demurred. "No, we wouldn't intrude—"

"We'd be delighted to make his acquaintance," said Nancy.

Tarleton locked arms with the two LaGrange women and led them toward the grand parlor. Nancy caught Mary looking hard at her, as if wondering if she had bribed Leila and Augusta to connive the introduction. Tarleton turned the corner and found General Hardee, a short, stocky man of fifty with stoic eyes and a gray goatee, holding court with several officers and ladies. "General, you must meet my new friends from LaGrange. Mrs. Morgan and Mrs. Heard."

Hardee bowed. "You ladies have traveled a long way."

"You do us a great honor," said Nancy.

"Mrs. Morgan is too modest," said Tarleton. "You two have much in common."

Hardee frowned, confused. "Indeed?"

Nancy realized that Leila and Augusta must have also blabbered to Tarleton about her admiration for the general.

Tarleton coaxed the other guests away. "Has everyone seen the Sebastiono painting that Major Ivey had delivered last month? Come, you will be dazzled." She winked at Nancy as she led Mary off with the others. Gently extracted from Nancy's side, Mary glared a warning at her to behave.

Left alone with Hardee, Nancy sensed the general was preoccupied. She had to assume he was troubled by the loss of Chattanooga. "You must be elated to find love again, General."

Hardee stirred from his retrospection and smiled across the parlor at his bride, Mary "Mollie" Lewis, the daughter of a Mobile cotton planter. "I thought I'd never again marry. I buried my first wife, dear Lizzie, with military honors eleven years ago. The Florida climate is poisonous. I should have sent Lizzie away from my posting, but she insisted on staying with me."

"Consumption?"

He nodded and stared into his snifter of brandy as if divining the future from its swirl and tinge. "I hope I've not bound Mollie to the same grief I suffered from the sudden loss of a spouse."

She noticed a slight palsy—battle tremors?—in his hand holding the short-stemmed glass. "None of us can know what the Almighty holds in store for us. We must live as if each hour is our last."

Hardee's weary eyes watered. "I was born in Georgia, but I never made it to LaGrange. I have received such endearing reports of your home city."

"You must visit us soon."

"Miss Tarleton said you and I have much in common."

For once, Nancy was grateful her sister and Leila had such big mouths. They must have told Tarleton about her study of the general's manual. The opportunity she had long wished was at last granted, but she verged on losing resolve. "A foolish comparison, really."

He studied her. "Speak freely, Mrs. Morgan. We are all brothers and sisters of the same cause here."

She glanced around to make sure no one was listening. "In your manual of tactics, General, you advocate close-order formations in battle. I have seen what the new rifles do to men. Would it not be better to fight the Yankees in smaller units that can move with stealth like the savages of the frontier do?"

Hardee's jaw dropped. "You've read my handbook?"

She lowered her gaze, fearing his judgment. "I've studied it every day since I received a copy." Withering under his hard inspection, she now regretted raising the issue. "I'm sorry. I should never have been so presumptuous."

"Inertia."

Perplexed by his response, she risked looking up and saw that a brightness had returned to his eyes. "Inertia?"

"The Army is beset by inertia. We West Pointers learn to march and drill a certain way, and we resist any changes in our traditions, even if it means reducing casualties."

"I've foraged a few Enfields. Teaching my militia how to load one after training them on smoothbores was like asking puppies to unlearn a trick."

"Militia?"

She debated the propriety of revealing more. "Most of our men are gone to the armies, so I decided we women of LaGrange should drill and learn to shoot. We've relied on your maxims for tactics."

Confounded, he led her toward a corner of the parlor. "Between you and me, my manual was a compromise. I had to provide a method for our officers to speed citizen-soldiers from columns and into the fields while maintaining formations. When the shooting starts, the infantry has no time to think. The impulse for green recruits is to scatter and seek shelter. The ranks cannot move in unison once soldiers with their blood up lose contact with comrades."

"From what I've read, and learned from the wounded men I help nurse, the armies grow larger and their weapons more accurate. Does not standing our men shoulder-to-shoulder in tight ranks increase casualties?"

He sighed and regarded her with a newfound estimation. "You understand the complexities better than most of my officers. You make a valid point on the benefits of open-order fighting. At Chickamauga, a Yankee cavalry brigade armed with carbines and trained to fight on foot held off one of our divisions for three hours."

"I'm told General Lee formed his final assault at Gettysburg into lines that stretched over two miles. That seems like slapping a bull's forehead with a burlap sack. Why do our regiments not charge the Yankee positions with narrow columns of deep ranks?"

He placed his brandy on the table and slammed his fist into his palm to demonstrate her idea. "Drive a nail with a hammer."

She nodded. "Would that not be more potent?"

He hesitated, as if about to convey a government secret, and lowered his voice. "The column assault has been considered. But to retrain our officers and men to fight in such an unorthodox manner would demand at least six months on the drill field. We don't have the luxury of time."

With that suggestion shot down, she broached another possibility that had long worried her. "General, have you fought a battle in a town?"

He retrieved his brandy and sipped while he thought hard on her question. "We were forced to fight in the streets at Corinth. General Lee sent Barksdale's Mississippi sharpshooters into Fredericksburg to contest Burnside's crossing of the Rappahannock. But it is not advisable."

She could not chase from her memory the awful destruction she had witnessed at Fredericksburg. "If the alternative is standing aside and watching your homes go up in flames? How would you defend a city?"

Searching for a prop to use as a plat map, he spotted an embroidered serviette on a lamp table and positioned it to represent the streets and blocks that invaders confront in urban warfare. "I would cut off as many avenues of entry for the enemy as possible. Funnel the Yankees toward the main square by leaving one route open using cotton bales, wagons, anything to form barricades. An advancing column is vulnerable to sharpshooters from windows and roofs. Defenders enjoy the advantage of familiarity with the plot. They can hide in the alleys and wynds to ambush the enemy's columns."

She nodded, sobered by the challenges and risks. How could she manage all *that* with only forty women?

"If there was ever a general who *could* defend a city, it is *that* fellow." Hardee glanced at the far corner of the parlor where an officer with shocks of unruly brown hair stood apart from the other gatherings of guests. A scar cut across his cheek. The fellow seemed shy and out of place and rarely looked up from his boots to scan his environs with his steel-gray eyes.

She recognized him as Hardee's best man at the ceremony.

"Mrs. Morgan, do you employ skirmishers in your militia?" Hardee asked.

"I have barely enough recruits to form two ranks for battle."

"But you *do* know the purpose of skirmishing?"

"To test the strength of enemy forces. And to warn of their approach."

Impressed with her comprehension of his manual, he kept a keen eye on the officer alone in the far corner. "I'd trade Old Bishop Pike and a case of whiskey to have *you* on my staff. ... I wonder if I might draft you for a reconnaissance that will involve a more tender skirmishing?"

She sensed whatever the general wished to ask of her had to do with that lonely officer across the room. "I am at your service."

"General Cleburne is my best friend."

She was astounded to learn that the forlorn figure was Major General Patrick Cleburne, known throughout the South as the Stonewall of the West. He had a reputation as a gallant Irishman beloved by his soldiers.

"I've never found him irresolute on the battlements," said Hardee. "Yet on the Field of Love, he requires a push."

She smiled with eager anticipation, now understanding her mission. "And the other target?"

"He has become smitten with Miss Tarleton."

"Does she reciprocate his feelings?"

"Given his innate reticence, I suspect she doesn't know his sentiments."

Nancy saluted. "Leave it to me, General."

He bowed. "I am grateful."

Nancy slipped away from Hardee and floated around the parlor, speaking with breezy ease to other guests so as not to give away the aim of her sortie. When she gained the prime position to pounce, she spun and regarded him with surprise, as if seeing him for the first time. "Why, General Cleburne, I'm told you carry a rainbow and a pot of gold wherever you march your division. And yet here I see you lurking in the shadows, hiding your treasures from us."

Cleburne's wide grin bared a gap where two front teeth had been knocked out, casualties from the same wound that left the scar on his cheek. He bowed. "I'm not much for social talk, ma'am. I usually get the slagging end of it."

She detected a lisp in his strong brogue. "We have that loathing of prattle in common. I would much prefer to learn how a private attains the rank of major general in only three years."

He blushed. "The luck of the Irish."

"The Irish may be lucky, but they are poor liars." She offered her hand for his kiss. "I am Nannie Colquitt Hill Brown. You command my cousin, Colonel John Colquitt. He has written so highly of you in his letters."

"A fine officer, he is. That makes you kin to ..." His eyes moistened, sharing her remorse over the loss of her cousin, Peyton, at Chickamauga. "I am sorry."

She feared she had already lost him to his Irish melancholy. "I've been told the Colquitts hail from County Down."

His gaping grin returned. "The land of St. Patrick."

"And the Cleburnes?"

"County Cork. My father was a doctor in Cork Town."

"You chose the military life instead?"

"I failed the medical exam. So, the British Army it was for me. And when Queen Victoria cashiered me, Arkansas took me in."

She found his shyness and Hibernian gift for cobbling words charming. "The medical profession's loss is our Army's gain."

His eyes darted from the floor to her face, never fixing on her smile for more than a fleeting moment. "From your lips to the Wee People's ears."

She couldn't help but be taken by this modest yet possessing man. There was something unworldly about him compared to other officers in their Southern armies. He carried none of their grandiloquence and brash confidence, but underneath his restraint she sensed the ferocious strength of the ancient Celtic warriors. She was more determined now to make the match that General Hardee desired. "Do you know *The Wearing of the Green*, by chance?"

"The ballad? Aye, I was weaned on it."

"You must sing it for us."

Panic filled his eyes. "I couldn't possibly."

"Come, I will sing it with you." She glanced across the chamber and found Sue Tarleton returning with her entourage, including Mary, from her tour of the hall gallery. "Miss Tarleton!"

Tarleton glided over to them.

"You have met General Cleburne, I trust?"

Tarleton curtsied. "Much too briefly."

"I have held him prisoner for the past five minutes," said Nancy. "The terms of his parole require him to sing with me my favorite Irish ballad. Will you do the honor of accompanying us on the piano?"

Tarleton glanced at Cleburne, looking for an indication of his wishes.

"If my ranking commander agrees," said Cleburne, his terrified eyes pleading with Hardee for a countermanding injunction.

General Hardee came to Cleburne's side and placed a paternal hand on his shoulder. "It is an order."

Nervously, Cleburne obeyed, and the guests gathered round as Tarleton sat at the piano. The dazzling object of Cleburne's affection glanced up at him with her slaying blue eyes and asked, "Do you have a preferred key, General?"

Cleburne shrugged and shuffled. "In the old country, we always started with a whistle."

Hardee put two fingers to his lips and sounded a middle C. Before Cleburne broke and retreated, Tarleton played a chord to launch him into the ballad. Nancy thrilled to see her scheming bear fruit. Cleburne stood so close to Tarleton with her blonde ringlets and lavender fragrance that he fought his distraction to remember the words. More comfortable with each verse, he crooned the anthem commemorating the Irish Rebellion of 1798, and Tarleton smartly picked up the harmony of the lilting tune.

> "O Paddy dear, and did ye hear the news that's going 'round?
> The shamrock is by law forbid to grow on Irish ground!
> No more Saint Patrick's Day we'll keep, his color can't be seen
> For there's a cruel law ag'in the Wearin' o' the Green."

Nancy joined in and gestured for the other guests to follow, calling for an amendment to the chorus verse. "This time, the Wearing of the Gray!" The serenaders clapped and sang with full hearts:

> "When laws can stop the blades of grass from growin' as they grow
> And when the leaves in summer-time their color dare not show
> Then I will change the color too I wear in my caubeen
> But till that day, please God, I'll stick to the Wearin' o' the Gray."

While the guests, eyes tearing, launched into another chorus, Nancy slipped away and stood apart to observe Cleburne and Tarleton share laughs and trade flirtatious glances. The Irish general placed a palm on Tarleton's shoulder, and, at a moment of pause from her playing, she touched her hand to his. Nancy glanced triumphantly at Hardee, and he saluted her for a skirmish well done.

Mary, monitoring the entire enterprise from the arched entry, came aside Nancy and whispered, "Remind me never to underestimate you again."

"Oh, I will remind you on the hour, every hour," said Nancy.

Mary angled her head for Nancy to look toward the refreshments room across the hall. "You aren't the only one slinging Cupid's arrows tonight."

Nancy found her sister, Augusta, and Leila flirting with a Confederate officer who sported a wild mustache and oiled curls of hair bouncing upon his ears. He looked twice as old as the two girls. "Who is that man?"

"General Ben Cheatham. He has taken quite a fancy to Leila. They have committed to a correspondence."

Nancy reddened. "I will put a stop to *that*."

"Nannie!" Mary tried to hold her back. "Leila and Augusta are not much younger than Miss Tarleton. You had no problem with sparking *that* flame."

"That bag of bones in there is at least ten years older than General Cleburne." Nancy escaped Mary's grasp and marched across the hall. "General Cheatham, we've not had the pleasure. I am Mrs. Jeremiah Brown Morgan. I see you've made the acquaintance of my youthful charges."

The general smirked at the veiled accusation and offered a half-hearted bow.

"Would you mind if I had a word with them?" Nancy asked.

"I hear them crooning my plainsong in the parlor." Cheatham smiled at Leila. "Remember, Miss Pullen, you owe me a letter."

Nancy steamed at the presumptuous general as he strode past her, close enough to brush his boots against her hemline with a shrouded threat. When she and Mary were alone with the two girls, she herded them into an adjacent room and closed the door.

"What is wrong, Nannie?" asked Augusta.

"Comport yourselves."

"*Comport* ourselves?" snapped Leila. "You mean deflect the interests of eligible gentlemen?"

"Nothing can come of dalliances with *him*," Nancy warned. "He's old enough to be your grandfather."

"I remember *you* throwing yourself at an older man."

"Leila!" scolded Mary.

Leila reddened a shade darker. "It's true, Mary! And you know it! She made excuses to visit Brown at his office. Connived meetings in the woods to have him curl up and show her how to shoot. And now she schemes to deny us."

"I had already been introduced into society," said Nancy.

"And *we* have not!" cried Leila. "Thanks to this infernal war!"

Mary begged, "Keep your voices lowered."

Nancy tried to calm Leila. "The town has not held a cotillion for you—"

"Because there are no marriageable men left in LaGrange," said Augusta. "You and Mary received your coming out. We will *never* have ours. You carry on with letters from your husbands. What do we have to hope for? Nothing."

"I know it has been difficult," said Nancy.

"You do not understand *how* ruinous this war has been for us," said Leila.

Nancy tried to mollify her. "The men will return when the fighting is done."

"They won't want us!" said Leila. "They will prefer the new class of debutantes. They will turn away from us and we will have no husbands. We will have no children. We will have no one to take care of us. You tell us not to become attached to the wounded men. They are *all* wounded!"

Nancy tried to bring Leila, sobbing, into her embrace, but Leila resisted.

"I *will* accept letters from General Cheatham. And you won't stop me." Leila stormed out of the room with Augusta.

Distraught, Nancy staggered and braced against a table. "This journey was a mistake."

Mary hugged her. "They have a right to be upset."

"I feel so old."

"Nonsense," said Mary. "You are twenty-three. You have most of your life ahead. Come, let's take fresh air on the porch."

Arm in arm, Nancy and Mary slipped past the singing guests and walked onto the veranda. The drizzle had eased, and the crickets chirped in the cane-breaks along the river. As they strode the covered promenade, Nancy withdrew into her tortured thoughts. Tomorrow, she would leave this refuge and return to the hospital ward and the dying men. The spring campaigning would soon start again. She prayed Brown be granted a furlough to come home before April, after which the Army would strand him in Virginia for the summer. There were rumors of a new prison being constructed east of Columbus, less than a hundred miles away. Thousands of enemy captives, guarded by a few home guards. What if those ravenous Yankees escaped? And so close to La-Grange? They'd make for the rail line, only a three days' march. The Negroes were growing more restless, too. Despite cautions taken by the overseers to stifle gossip and hide newspapers, the few darkies who could read spread the news of the war across the plantations. Would they revolt should the Union armies invade Georgia? That madman Lincoln was even putting the coloreds into uniforms and giving them guns.

The entire world was closing in on her. She rested her head on Mary's shoulder as they walked, their eyes cast down. "Dr. Erksine shared an observation on the train that haunts me."

"What did he say?"

"This winter, a rush of new patients has overrun the Virginia Insane Asylum at Staunton."

"And this concerns you ... why?"

"They are all women."

"Nannie, why dwell—"

"There are times I am numb with despair. ... Do you ever pray before you go to bed not to wake?"

Mary stopped and took Nancy's darkened face into her hands. "You must not give up. We have each other, Leila, Augusta, and Caroline. The women rely upon your strength and guidance. You mean so much to so many. Why, just tonight, you lit the match between General Cleburne and Miss Tarleton. Who else could have managed such a miracle?"

"Even in that moment, though ..." She dared not speak what she was thinking.

"Nannie, what is it?"

"I had a fleeting premonition of despair between them." She fell sobbing into Mary's arms.

"Mrs. Morgan?" said a soft, familiar voice.

Nancy and Mary turned and searched the dark veranda to find who had called out to her. Two murky shadows stood at the far railing, their silhouettes outlined by the mist cast from the lanterns on the grounds below. They came closer. ... *Sallie Fannie Reid.* Nancy quickly wiped her eyes.

Sallie brought forward the gentleman on whose arm she clung. "Our carriage was delayed. I didn't know you planned to attend the wedding."

"A last-minute invitation," said Nancy. "You remember Mrs. Heard."

"Of course. I'll never forget that wicked croquet stroke."

Nancy saw a ring on Sallie's finger. "You are engaged."

Sallie pulled her companion closer. "Captain Grant proposed this week."

"Congratulations," said Mary.

A long moment passed before Nancy recognized the tall man who had bested Brown in the jousting contest before the war. William Grant looked gaunt and liverish, a mere ghostly wisp of the adroit equestrian she remembered from the Tournament of the Rings. "I trust, sir, you are educating the Yankees on the art of the saber, as you once did for us?"

Grant managed a weak smile. "Health required me to resign my commission, Mrs. Morgan. Governor Brown has assigned me the task of helping construct the defenses for Atlanta."

"Defenses?" said Nancy. "You believe the Yankees will reach Atlanta?"

"We must prepare for all eventualities."

An uncomfortable silence passed until Sallie spoke again. "Mrs. Morgan, might I have a word with you in private?"

Mary took the cue. "Captain Grant, you must be parched. Allow me to show you the spirits tray and introduce you to the other guests."

Alone now with Nancy, Sallie said, "This is the first opportunity I've had to offer my condolences for your brother's death."

"Thank you."

Sallie kept looking at the folds in her gown, as if trying to pin together the words she had long rehearsed. "I also owe you an apology."

"Not at all."

"So much has happened these past three years. I've come to regret the petty jealousies of my youth. All of that seems so meaningless now. There are times ..."

"You need say no more. I was equally at fault."

Sallie fought back tears. "I am engaged to a wonderful man, and yet, with Captain Grant assigned to Atlanta ... I find myself bereft of purpose. I wondered if you might use another nurse in your hospital."

Nancy, astonished by the request, brought Sallie into her embrace. "You are most welcome to join us."

26

VARNELL'S STATION, GEORGIA
MAY 1864

Hugh read the dispatch from Colonel McCook again: *You can make a demonstration toward Dalton when you receive this, in order to attract the attention of the enemy and develop their force, but do not engage seriously if you can avoid it.* Attract the attention of the enemy? Develop their force, but do not seriously engage? What in Hell's name did *that* mean? Same cover-your-ass West Point gibberish from headquarters.

He scanned the arid ground ahead, burned brown by a drought and percolating with tiny whirlwinds and switchgrass tumbleweeds driven by a scorched wind. More pine scrubs and red clay, red clay and pine scrubs. There wasn't a hill within five miles to climb for a vantage of what lay before him. Wheeler was out there somewhere stalking him, he could feel it in his bones. If Bragg were still in charge of the Army of Tennessee, the Rebs would have pivoted by now and attacked. But Jeff Davis sacked the despised curmudgeon after his fiasco at Chattanooga and replaced him with Joseph Johnston, a cautious bureaucratic infighter who might still command the Army of Northern Virginia if he hadn't been wounded in the Seven Days' Campaign.

Imagine that. No Bobby Lee. One bullet changed the war.

A bandanna-masked courier rode up from the south, churning a red cloud behind him. "Sir, Lt. Colonel Stewart has driven the Reb pickets two miles toward Dalton. The outskirts of the town are within our reach."

"Any signs of infantry or entrenchments?"

"No, sir."

Develop their force, but do not engage seriously.

He tried to place himself in Wheeler's mind. What was the rascal up to now? Would he truly leave Dalton undefended? Scouts confirmed Johnston had dug in most of his infantry on Rocky Face Ridge, a finger-shaped mountain that guarded the rail line entering Tunnel Hill from Chattanooga and joining with the Knoxville tracks at Dalton. Perhaps Wheeler was away screening Johnston's left flank. Yet if the Confederate government lost the Dalton depot, reinforcements and supplies from Richmond would have to travel through the Carolinas and west by way of Atlanta, a journey doubled in time. No, Dalton was the jewel in the Georgia crown. Wheeler would not abandon it without a fight.

"Sir, what should I tell Stewart?"

Do not engage seriously, if you can avoid it.

Since the start of this campaign, Hugh had received orders filled with conflicting demands. Lincoln had recalled Grant to Virginia, and William Tecumseh Sherman, not Edward McCook, remained in overall command of this spring drive toward Atlanta. The red-haired Ohioan suffered a mental breakdown two years ago, and many in the Army thought Sherman crazy still, but from what Hugh had seen, Grant's fast-talking alter-ego was crazy as a fox. Sherman's strategy depended on pinning Johnston in place, flanking him, and forcing the Rebel army to retreat to the next city south along the rail line. Sherman rewarded bold and independent action. Hugh knew if he and his Second Brigade captured Dalton, and McPherson could get his corps around Rocky Face Ridge to Resaca, they would have Johnston trapped.

Do not engage seriously, if you can avoid it—*that* mealy-mouthed verbiage was *not* coming from Sherman. Hugh assessed the fighting mood of his dismounted troopers waiting aside their horses. Their expectant glares had become more mistrustful since Chickamauga. He suspected what they were thinking. Rumors circulated that after his brother's death, he had become emboldened and reckless, even welcoming martyrdom. McCook and General Elliott both cautioned him against riding at the head of his column in battle.

Jennie and Wallace were gone.

Yes, he *did* welcome death.

But he promised Dan Ray he would look after his brigade to the end.

"Colonel, we're losing the light," said the courier. "It'll be dusk in an hour."

He pulled his dispatch pad and scribbled an order for the lead regiments of his brigade: *Hold your position until I come up with the Second Indiana and First Wisconsin.* He tore off the sheet and handed it to the courier.

Thirty minutes later, Hugh reached a clearing bordered by an arc of pine woods two hundred yards to the south. He ordered four companies from one of his brigade's regiments, the Second Indiana, to dismount and form a single line on his left. Major Harden, trailing, arrived minutes later with the First Wisconsin, and he filed them into a single line on the right flank.

Lt. Colonel Stewart, in charge of the skirmishers, returned from his run across the field. "Should we keep driving them?"

Hugh pulled out his field glasses and searched the crease of woods in the distance. A few Rebel pickets traded potshots with his troopers, but they were too far off to do much damage. Above the trees, smoke gathered from the chimney stacks and locomotives in Dalton, only ten miles away. He could raise Old Glory over that treasonous city within the hour. "Let's clear the Rebs from that thicket and see what's on the other side." He signaled for his bugler to sound the advance, and he led his troopers across the clearing.

Halfway to the woods, he noticed the Confederate pickets had disappeared. Strange. They must have run off like rabbits for Dalton.

A shriek echoed on his flanks.

He turned to find two columns of Rebel cavalry, four abreast, galloping out from ends of the woods and leaping a morass of swamp mud. The mounted Rebels closed up and drew weapons. At their head rode a smallish man accompanied by a flag bearer.

He stood in the saddle to gain a better view. *That's Wheeler.*

The Confederate general smiled as if taunting him.

Hugh laughed. *By God, you are mine now.* He drew his saber and signaled for the charge. His single line of troopers rushed to the clash and drove into the melee. All around him, pistols fired and sabers slashed. The two mounted echelons crashed and splintered into a bedlam of smoke and yells. Men fell from their saddles, some dragged by the stirrups, others crushed under hooves. He searched for Wheeler and found the cavalry commander leading his butternut horsemen back to the woods.

He's getting away!

Hugh's fighting blood spiked. He rallied his troopers to him and chased the Confederate cavalry toward the thick pines. He came within reach of the Rebel stragglers—a brigade of Texas infantry stepped out into the clearing. He reined up ten yards from their musket barrels.

The Texans fired. His horse reared and fell.

Hugh leapt from his saddle to avoid being crushed. The back of his head pounded the ground. Concussed, he staggered to his feet and vomited. In a blur, he saw the Rebel infantry break ranks and run for him. Wiping his mouth, he scrambled across wounded men pawing at him and wrangled an abandoned horse. Groggy, he pulled into the saddle and lashed the shirking animal into a retreat. He reached the far side of the field and circled the rattled cluster of his surviving troopers. "In line!" he shouted. "Back in line!"

Those Federal troopers who could find unmaimed horses remounted and braced for another Rebel infantry charge.

Hugh reached for his scabbard to draw his saber. He had lost it in the fall. He pulled his revolver and circled it over his head. "Attack!"

His thinned ranks charged into the clearing and drove the Rebel infantry back to the woods. As a cheer went up, he looked to his left. A second regiment of infantry stood from their hidden positions and poured a deadly fire into his flank. The Rebels attached bayonets and scurried for the rear of his line. In minutes, he'd be encircled. He searched for Wheeler, desperate to get his hands on him, but the general had vanished in the lingering smoke. Outnumbered and no match for massed infantry, he was forced to signal the bugler to call retreat. His Union troopers, demoralized, reined back and galloped north.

Wheeler bolted from the woods with his mounted staff and led what looked to be an entire division of cavalry and infantry toward the dwindling Union brigade. The Rebels let loose with their savage yell.

Caught in the eye of the storm, Hugh ordered away those Federal troopers who had stayed behind to protect him. "Go back! I'll cover you!" He fired the remaining rounds in his revolver to buy them a few more seconds.

The Texans aimed their muskets at him and fired.

Strafed, Hugh's horse reeled and careened into a rail fence. The animal collapsed and pinned Hugh's left leg against a post. A sharp burning sensation shot up his spine. He fainted. When he came to consciousness, the Texans surrounded him. They levered the dead horse off his leg and dragged him from under it. The pain from the decompression in his thigh sent him out again.

* * *

Hugh awoke on a bedroll with a throbbing stab in his left leg. He yanked away a blanket and reached to find his knee and shin bone, praying his foot hadn't been amputated. The leg, still attached, had turned purple and swollen from hip to ankle.

"A bad contusion," said a drawling voice from the shadows. "You'll be bed-ridden for a few weeks, then on crutches. My surgeon assures me there should be no permanent disability."

With clouded vision, Hugh turned to find the source of that prognosis. In the dim light of a tent candle, he made out the delicate face of a short, genteel man with mellow eyes, delicate lips, and a boxed beard coiffed with thin sides. He raised himself for a closer examination and sank into the cot, flushed with shame. Joseph Wheeler had come to gloat over his conquest.

"It is a blow, I am sure." said Wheeler. "It could have been me prone and captured by *you* at Anderson's Crossroads. You have performed your duties as admirably as any man I have faced in this war."

Hugh turned away. "Do not mock me, sir."

Wheeler pulled up a chair.

Hugh noticed he limped. "You are injured, as well?"

Wheeler waved off the inquiry. "One of your Yankee balls found my ankle at Ringgold Gap. Half spent, fortunately." He plucked two cigars from his breast pocket and offered one to Hugh. "The tobacco will blunt the ache. I have learned this from experience."

Hugh accepted the cigar and allowed Wheeler to light it for him.

"How many horses have been shot from under you?" Wheeler asked.

"Six."

"Ah, you have some catching up to do. I'm at ten. The secret is to lean away from the direction your mount is falling. Easier said than done, but after much practice, it becomes instinct."

"How many men did I lose today?"

"I'm uncertain of your casualties, but we took a hundred and thirty prisoners."

Hugh closed his eyes, distraught, imagining how the West Pointers back at Sherman's headquarters in Tunnel Hill must be cursing his name.

Wheeler seemed to read his thoughts. "Your superiors believe you dead."

He opened his eyes. "How can you know that?"

Wheeler pulled a copy of a telegraph dispatch from his pocket and read it aloud: "'To General E.M. McCook. General, your note announcing the action of yesterday has been received. The enemy avoids showing his troops and batteries, making it necessary to be very cautious. If the death of Colonel La-Grange is beyond doubt, the loss of so estimable a man and gallant officer is to be greatly deplored. Yours, respectfully, W.L. Elliott, Brigadier-General and Chief of Cavalry.'"

How did Wheeler intercept a copy of the dispatch?

"Your telegraph cables are not as secure as General Sherman thinks. My engineers have tapped the lines at Ringgold." Wheeler took a long puff on his cigar and watched the smoke's trail. "I owe you an apology, sir. I'm told my adjutant was drunk at Anderson's Gap and took a shot at you after surrendering."

"It was not the first time I caught him in a base act."

"No?"

"I saw him steal coats and blankets from our surgeons at Crawfish Springs."

Wheeler slumped and nodded. "I tried to put a stop to the looting. The man is a fighter, but he cannot handle his liquor." The Rebel general studied Hugh as if debating a sensitive question. "That day on your approach with the wagon train to Crawfish Springs, you seemed to know my plan of attack."

Hugh pointed to his riding cloak hanging on a peg. "In the pocket."

Wheeler reached inside and pulled out Hugh's worn copy of the general's tactics manual. Wheeler shook his head. "I should never have published this."

"May I ask you a question?"

"By all means."

"Our reports say you confiscated several Spencer carbines from prisoners at Chickamauga. Yet we've faced none of your cavalry using them. Why?"

Wheeler sighed, stretching out his legs and crossing his boots. "I'd give my right arm for a thousand of those marvels with their proprietary ammunition. The rimfire cartridges used in their breech loading require special manufacturing. We don't possess that capability in our foundries."

An officer entered the tent. "Sir, General Hardee requests your presence."

"Tell the general I will be along shortly." When the officer saluted and departed, Wheeler tied the flap strings to prevent others from entering. He scooted his chair closer to Hugh and lowered his voice. "I will deny this if ever pressed, but we may not have the pleasure of meeting again. I'd forever regret not asking about your philosophy on cavalry warfare."

"Mine? I'm just a farmer who taught school on the side. I never rode a horse faster than a mule before I joined up. You're a West Pointer. You fought the Comanches in New Mexico."

Wheeler dipped his chin. "All an impediment to my learning, I fear."

Hugh raised onto his elbow. "The way I see it, both armies are misusing us. We scout and screen flanks and scour for forage. We should concentrate our cavalries into independent armies."

"Precisely!"

"Infantry with the speed of cavalry."

"I have petitioned our government for permission to adopt that very strategy."

"Why hasn't Davis agreed?"

Wheeler dropped his cigar stub and crushed it under his boot heel. "It's no secret we suffer from a scarcity of horses. And those we procure are siphoned off to the artillery. The Congress in Richmond forces my men to pay for their own mounts and livery when they can barely afford to eat."

"Bedford Forrest seems to get what *he* wants."

Wheeler huffed. "Forrest is an illiterate slave trader. He steals and hounds and goes off raiding on his own whims."

"You two don't get along, I take it?"

Wheeler hesitated. "You know of Fort Pillow?"

Hugh nodded. "Is it true?"

"I have only read accounts of the alleged massacre. You people have pushed us to the brink of terror by recruiting slaves into your armies and—" He stopped, evidently remembering Hugh's reputation as an Abolitionist.

"Would you recruit Negroes into your service if it helped you win this war?"

"Certainly not! It would violate every principle for which we fight."

"I hear Pat Cleburne disagrees with you."

Wheeler reddened. "Cleburne is a fine soldier, but he is an Irishman, only recently immigrated to our land. We will never arm the Negroes."

An uncomfortable silence fell between the two men.

Wheeler stood and pulled out his dispatch book. He wrote a note, tore off the page, and handed it to Hugh. "I have no influence over prisoner dispositions. But should you find yourself in harm's way, perhaps this commendation may be of some assistance."

*   *   *

A choking stench roused Hugh from a tortured slumber. He gazed up to find the Angel of Death hovering over him. Was his flesh rotting with his soul still clinging to it? He blinked the caked sleep from his sore eyes and turned his head, wincing, to make sense of his surroundings. Dozens of cots with men who resembled skeletons sat in rows on both sides of a long aisle. Many cried out in pain and begged for water. He ran his hand down his aching side to feel for his ballooned left leg. The lesions were wet with pus. "Am I dying?"

"The next forty-eight hours will tell," said a languid female voice.

He blinked hard. Not a harbinger from beyond the veil, but a slender woman, a year or two younger than him by his estimate, applied a poultice wrap to his wound. Only her alabaster skin and the white carapace collaring her cape broke the bleakness of her black garb. He lay in what appeared to be a converted cattle stable with stalls. "What is this place?"

"Camp Oglethorpe prison. This is what passes for its hospital."

He closed his eyes in despair and sank back. "How many of us are here?"

"More than two thousand."

He muttered to himself, "I've finally arrived in Hell, where I belong."

"Macon is only the Devil's antechamber, but twice as hot."

Baffled by the woman's bad-mouthing of her own city, he sensed a searing bitterness. "You have a harsh bedside manner for a nurse."

She glanced at the Rebel private posted at the entry and raised her voice for effect. "You Yankees do not coddle our boys at Camp Douglas in Illinois! You will get no special treatment here!"

The guard grinned, in full agreement with her patriotic outrage.

Hugh gasped from stale air laced with peppery decay. A dull throb seized his injured leg and sent a wave of nausea up his throat. He pulled the sheet across his body. His thigh had turned even darker. He had seen many of his troopers fall and develop such blistering abscesses. The Army doctors told him the blood coagulates to form clots that attack the heart. The murkiness in his head cleared, and the events of the past week came back to him now. He had been dropped from a stretcher while being transferred between trains in Atlanta. The fall had ripped open his scars. He nearly bled to death on the jarring ten-hour journey south in that crowded cattle car. "How long have I been out?"

The nurse rinsed a cloth and applied it to his forehead. "Two days. If we don't break this fever, Hell will be an ice cellar by comparison."

"Gangrene?"

"The skin is hardening. The muscles could turn slough if the circulation is not quickened." She massaged his upper thigh, pressing the malefic humors toward the knee. "I've applied a balm of white oat, garlic, and onions. If it fails to awaken the blood vessels, the fragrance will clear your nostrils, at least."

A laugh forced its way up his inflamed throat but died in a coughing fit. With her free hand, she pressed her palm against his chest to ease the rasping convulsions. He hadn't been touched with such intimacy since the night he said goodbye to Jennie. "Your black robe ... are you a nun?"

"A novitiate. I train to be a Daughter of Charity. I will take the vow after another year of service."

"How did you learn these medical skills?"

"I grew up around horses."

"You ride?"

"Before the war, my father bred thoroughbreds. For the North-South races."

Hugh studied her, amazed how one so young could gain so much practical knowledge. "My regiment has lost hundreds of horses to the glanders. Have you a remedy for *that* malady?"

She glanced at the guard again and raised her voice. "None that I intend to share with you."

He recoiled at her sudden turn of mood. What was it about this impulsive woman that rendered her compassionate one moment, only to flash hostile without warning?

She took a step back into the aisle and, as if on an opera stage, announced loud enough for the entire ward to hear, "I have done all I can. Your recovery rests in the hands of the Lord. Will you take spiritual counseling?"

Put off by her mercurial temperament, he snapped, "No."

She pulled up a stool and sat beside him as if he had just answered in the affirmative. She lowered her voice again. "You are not a man of faith?"

"Less so every passing day."

"Darkness of spirit impedes the body's healing."

"I have witnessed many a man swear his life to the Almighty in the morning and forfeit it to a bullet in the afternoon."

She looked into his eyes as if she were an ancient oracle casting a divination. "You have suffered a deep loss."

He turned aside. "My brother brought joy to everyone he encountered, while I offered only moroseness. And he was taken for no reason but my ambition to defend a worthless hill. .... If I die here, it will be a blessing."

"You will indulge me if I take a moment for my own contemplation?"

He pulled the sheet over his head. "Whatever you wish."

She retrieved a small Bible from her small knapsack, opened it, and read aloud: "'When there were gathered together an innumerable multitude of people, insomuch that they trode one upon another, He began to say unto his disciples first of all, Beware ye of the leaven of the Pharisees, which is hypocrisy. For there is nothing covered, that shall not be revealed; neither hid, that shall not be known. Therefore whatsoever ye have spoken in darkness shall be heard in the light; and that which ye have spoken in the ear in closets shall be proclaimed upon the housetops.' ... The Gospel of Luke. Two: Twelve."

He peeked out from under the sheet. "Am I to gain sustenance from *that* passage?"

"Think upon it with an open heart." She closed the Bible and handed it to him. "I wish it back. I'm permitted to return on Sundays. Until next week, do your homework. I have marked a second passage for our future study."

The guard walked down the aisle. "Time's up, Sister."

She stood and sighed with relief. "Praise the Lord. I could not bear another moment in the presence of these heathen Yankees." She took the grinning guard's arm for escort and walked with him toward the door.

Hugh tossed the Bible aside and pulled the sheet over his ears to drown out the groans in the ward. *What an infuriating shrew! An affliction to mankind, that initiate nun is.* Was she *trying* to fracture his fevered mind with that incomprehensible babble from the physician Apostle?

When there were gathered together an innumerable multitude.

No 'yea, though I walk through the Valley of Death?'

For there is nothing covered that shall not be revealed.

Furious at the cards Fate had dealt him, he picked up the Bible again. What nonsense did the nurse have in store for him next Sunday? She had marked with a ratty doily the passage for him to study. The apprenticing harridan was not only an inept spiritual counselor, she could not crochet worth a damn. Rather than feature a traditional snowflake gauze in a circular pattern, the doily was square and opaque, with only six small holes spaced at random. A drunken laundress could have managed better needlework. He removed the doily and scanned the first verse on the opened page. His eyes fell on Kings 2:20 of the Old Testament: *As for the other events of Hezekiah's reign, all his achievements and how he made the pool and the tunnel by which he brought water into the city, are they not written in the book of the annals of the kings of Judah?*

He huffed. *The Secesh nun in training is toying with me.* Kings. Pools. *If I survive, she will no doubt try to convert me with Scriptural justifications for slavery.* He'd gained his fill of these religious hypocrites in Kansas. He picked up the doily and shoved it back into the crease where he had found it. Look at that! She so lacks creativity she can find no sewing pattern other than a page from the Good Book. How sacrilegious, cutting a template along the edges of—

He examined the doily closer. The top hole in the makeshift bookmark hovered over a word: *Tunnel.* He glanced at the guard at the door watching him and set the Bible aside, feigning a lack of interest. Was the fever ague playing tricks with his thoughts? He waited several minutes until the guard turned his back to shoot his tobacco chaw at a spittoon. He quickly picked up the Bible, opened it to the same passage, and positioned the doily to line up its borders with the edges of the page. He memorized each word exposed by the holes.

Tunnel ... wall ... shadow ... middle court ... fifteen days ... far country.

He hid the Bible under his mattress and waved at the guard. "I need to piss."

The guard snorted. "Use the bucket."

"The nurse said I should walk to the latrine to build strength."

"Did she now? When did *she* become Jeff Davis?"

"I'd prefer to save others the trouble of emptying it."

"You're a regular Good Samaritan blue-belly, ain't you?" The guard pointed to the north door. "Out and to the left. You fall, you're dragging your own carcass back. Walk near the shoot line, you won't have anything left to piss with."

Hugh struggled up to sit. When his dizziness eased, he levered to his feet and staggered limping down the aisle. After an agonizing two minutes, he reached the open door and shielded his eyes from the blinding sunlight. When his sight adjusted, he staggered to a latrine fed by a trickling stream that served as the camp's lone water supply. As he relieved himself, he looked across twenty acres of baked red clay surrounded by a stockade. Denuded of vegetation, these former fairgrounds crawled with ragged, barefoot men, some stricken prone with disease and lost hope, others prowling like caged animals.

He could see only one way out, through thick oak-wood gates crowned by a towering arch. Snipers were posted every ten yards on the ramparts, and guards strode through the camp, harassing prisoners whenever the urge came over them. Above the drone of talk and groans, locomotives clanged and church bells rang outside. The stockade was near the rail yard, in the city proper. He stole a peek through the logs and saw the angry faces of Macon citizens thrusting fists and shouting curses at the prisoners for siphoning off their food supply.

Wall ... shadow ... middle court.

He scanned the stockade's perimeter. Against the far palisade stood a small blacksmith's station shaded by a ceiling of crude boards. A gang of emaciated men loitered around the shed as if attempting to obscure whatever was going on inside. Every minute or so, a prisoner carried out a small sack and dumped its contents onto the compost heap, mixing in the dirt with their feet.

Fifteen days.

The butt end of a musket dug into his back.

"You need one of your yellow friends to hold your johnson for you?"

He buttoned his fly. "I'm done."

The guard spat at his feet. "I'll put in a word with Old Abe for your medal."

"What date is it?"

"Filling in your dance card, are yuh?"

"My ma died in June. I was hoping to say a prayer for her on the day."

"It's the nineteenth. Now, get back inside."

Hugh stumbled toward the hospital door and fell.

The guard laughed. "I warned you. Start crawling."

As he struggled to his hands and knees, Hugh counted forward fifteen days: *July Fourth.*

* * *

"You're not bringing that cudgel in here," the Rebel guard said.

Standing at the entry into the ward, the apprentice nun who visited a week ago held a crutch. "I'm getting a man up on his feet today."

"He's already been up on his feet. Besides, one of these slackers could use it to coldcock me."

"The sooner I get these Yankees out of here, the less you'll have to worry you."

The guard slapped the blunt end of a shillelagh against his palm while he debated her point. Finally, he motioned her down the aisle.

The nurse walked along the rows and came aside Hugh's cot. Without asking his permission, she drew back the sheet, removed the bandage, and inspected his leg. She nodded with approval, finding the swelling and blackness receded. "Looks as if my spiritual counseling worked better than you gave credit." She leaned over his leg, acting as if she were replacing his bandage, and whispered, "Let's see, Colonel LaGrange, if you can stay on a crutch better than a horse." She shot him a smirk. "Or, is that *two* horses?"

The blood drained from his cheeks. "How did you know—"

"Save your strength." She monitored the guard as she helped Hugh shift his feet to the floor. "You have admirers of high station. I don't know why anyone should want to rescue an officer so careless that he gets himself captured, but General Sherman seems to think you're worth ten Confederate generals."

With her help, he stood. She positioned the crutch under his left armpit and raised the rest pad another notch.

"Get the geddyup on!" the guard shouted.

The novitiate turned and glared at the brutish Reb. "I must adjust the height. It will take us a lap to the door and back to find his measurement."

The guard studied her with suspicion. Finally, he waved her on.

With their backs turned, the nurse held Hugh's elbow as he took a few cautious steps.

"Who are you?" he whispered.

"Did you do your homework?"

"Yes, but ... how do I know you aren't a spy planted by the commandant?"

"You don't. You'll have to trust me."

"The last two women from Dixie that I trusted conned me like riverboat gamblers."

She timed her answers so the prisoners on the cots they passed could not overhear. "Not all of us here are Secessionists."

He stopped, stunned. "You mean—"

"Do not lean your full weight on the crutch!" she shouted at him, evidently for the guard's benefit.

At the far end of the aisle, the guard sat on a cracker box with legs crossed, enjoying Hugh's struggles. "The Yank whiner givin' you trouble, Sister?"

"Nothing I can't handle with a whip," she replied over her shoulder.

The guard chortled, amused, and slapped his thigh.

The nurse lifted Hugh's chin to straighten his posture and assist his balance. She whispered, "We work in the shadows."

"So, all of this religious business is a cover for—"

"I will still take the vow in a year, whether I wish to or not."

He looked hard at her, demanding an explanation.

She relented to his insistence. "My brother fights with General Grant. In the First Alabama Cavalry. Say nothing of it to—"

"Sixteenth Corps? Those men were at Vicksburg."

Her eyes darted nervously around the ward. "I've received no news from him in two years. My father and most everyone else in this city shun me for being a Unionist. My husband ..."

"You're married?"

She turned away to hide a surge of emotion. "He abandoned me when the war started and left for California."

Hugh reached for her hand to comfort her, but she recoiled, reminding him with a sideways glance of the guard's presence.

"He's gettin' the hang of it!" the guard shouted. "Bring him on back now. He'll be out there with the other Hoosier hogs in the slop in no time flat."

She tightened her grip on Hugh's elbow and whispered, "Fall."

Hugh stared at her, confused. Under her robes, she kicked his good foot. He took her painful hint and crumpled to a knee, sending the crutch flying.

The nurse shouted at the guard, "Help me!"

Annoyed, the guard ambled down the aisle, twirling his club and taking his time. He yanked Hugh to his feet.

"He is far from healed," the nurse said. "Two more weeks, at least."

When they reached his cot, the guard dropped Hugh onto the thin straw mattress and waited, as if expecting remuneration for his effort.

The nurse glared at the impertinent guard. "I will say five Hail Marys for your soul tonight."

"That won't buy me a shot at McKinney's tavern. Or a poke."

"You blaspheme often?" she asked.

The guard glared menacingly at Hugh, evidently wondering if the nurse had developed a soft spot for the Yankee officer. He waved it off and walked back to his station, rattling the cots with his club to torment the other ill prisoners.

The nurse sat on a stool next to Hugh. She picked up the Bible and opened it to the doily bookmark. "You understood the passage I assigned?"

Hugh nodded, uncertain where this coded messaging was leading.

The nurse watched the door. When the guard was preoccupied with digging jerky from the few teeth that remained in his mouth, she removed the doily from the Bible and, turning to another page, replaced the template with a new doily hidden in her sleeve. Under her breath, she warned, "The sentries here are from the Augusta militia. They do not know me. But if they are replaced by Macon men, I will be suspected and likely denied entry."

She made a move to leave until Hugh grasped her wrist to delay her a moment more. "What's your name?"

"It's best you not know."

"I must."

She hesitated. "Lizzie Andrews."

"And your brother?"

"John Dean."

"I will do what I can to find him for you."

Her eyes flooded. She pulled her veil over her face, stood, and walked past the smirking guard.

That night, after the sentry postings changed, Hugh opened the Bible to the page Lizzie had marked. Aided by the light of the full moon through the small window above him, he placed the new doily in position atop the page and read the revealed words: *Your ... invocation ... camp ... day ... of ... independence ... boat ... river ... freedom.*

* * *

Hugh counted the charcoal markings he had scratched on the boards under his cot. Fifteen mornings had passed. Today was the Fourth of July. Was he strong enough to make the attempt? He sat and lifted the kerchief cover from his tin cup to examine what remained of his weekly ration, a pint of cornmeal mixed with ground cobs and what maggots he could find. He gulped the mash, this time without needing to hold his nose. He counted it a small blessing that his sense of smell had become so dulled by the stench here that he had acclimated to the odors of urine and rancid flesh.

He monitored the morning's switch of the ward guard. Yesterday was Sunday, but Lizzie didn't come. And that Devil's bastard who tormented him for the past two weeks was also gone. In his stead, a rough-looking cracker grabbed the club from its hooks and walked across the rows. When the new guard came to the foot of his cot, Hugh risked asking, "The nurse did not make her rounds yesterday."

The guard slammed his club into Hugh's shoulder. "Maybe she got sick of tending to murdering negrah lovers."

He staggered to his feet to defend himself. "She promised to discharge me."

"Ain't my call."

"My cot could go to another who needs it."

"Walk out. I don't give a damn. But you ain't coming back in."

He gathered his meager belongings, including Lizzie's Bible, which he had promised to return. He tied them in the sheet and slung them over his bruised shoulder. He limped on his crutch toward the door at the far end of the ward, trying not to cry out from the pain. At night, he had practiced crawling when the others were asleep, planning for this day. At the threshold, he turned back. "Those bells I keep hearing ... are they from a Catholic house of worship?"

The guard pressed his hands together in a mocking gesture of prayer. "You planning your funeral, Yank?"

"They remind me of home."

The guard spat a jet of tobacco juice. "Church of the Assumption."

"You've got a lot of churches here?"

"Enough to have the Almighty on *our* side. Now, move it."

He lurched past the door into the prison yard. That replacement guard knew too much about Macon to be from Augusta. With Lizzie's covert mission compromised, she probably had been reassigned to another hospital. Or had she been setting him up all along? He had hoped for one more coded message from her with details of the escape plan, but now he would have to react by instinct. The other prisoners stared at him as he staggered through the camp. Some saluted, others winked and nodded. *What did that mean?*

The stockade gates opened, and a contingent of Rebel officers walked in to take the morning's roll call. The prisoners lined up in silence. As the names were shouted out, one prisoner, a captain of German descent, yelled "Herzog" and waved over his head a tiny United States flag he had stitched from rags. He began singing *The Star-Spangled Banner.* The other prisoners, cheering and joining in, broke ranks and swarmed the patriotic Herzog. They lifted the mutinous captain on their bony shoulders and paraded around the yard.

"Happy Fourth of July, boys!" the German captain shouted.

The prisoners, tears flowing, started a rendition of *America.* The Rebel officers backed away toward the gate, alarmed by the spontaneous demonstration.

In the distraction caused by the commotion, another prisoner sidled up to Hugh and whispered, "We'll wait for you."

Before Hugh could ask what *that* promise meant, the prisoner disappeared into the cheering throngs. Five Yankees dragged an empty hogshead barrel into the center of the celebration to use as a soapbox and hoisted the chaplain of the Fourteenth Connecticut regiment atop its lid. The chaplain raised his hands for prayer. The Confederate officers released held breaths, trusting the demonstration was now tamped down—until the chaplain thrust his fist to the heavens and shouted, "The Lord Almighty saith, 'the multitude of thy enemies shall be like small dust, and the multitude of the terrible ones shall be as chaff that passeth away! Yea, it shall be at an instant suddenly!'"

The prisoners chanted a chorus of "Amens!" and began beating on boards and singing *The Battle Hymn of the Republic.*

When the Confederate officer in charge signaled for his sentries walking the ramparts to ready their muskets, Hugh searched the wall behind him and located the blacksmith's shed. A dozen prisoners were scrambling in and out of the lean-to, paying no notice to the celebration.

"And now," the chaplain shouted. "Who among you wishes to hear a speech by Colonel LaGrange of the legendary Wisconsin Saber Brigade? Scourge of Old Joe Wheeler! Horseman of great repute!"

Invocation.

As the prisoners let loose with a thundering call, Hugh realized Lizzie had tried to alert him to prepare a speech to give cover for the tunnel sappers. Before he could think of three words to patch together, his fellow prisoners lifted him atop the barrel vacated by the chaplain and handed up his crutch. At a loss what to say, he remembered a memorization lesson that Professor Daniels had assigned him in school: General Washington's address to his freezing troops at Valley Forge. Could he still recite it? He straightened, as best he could on his weakened left leg, and announced, "Men, I bring you words of faith and fortitude from your beloved general!"

"You talked to Grant?" asked a prisoner.

"Not Grant! From General Washington! Beyond the grave!"

Confused, the prisoners hushed, wondering if this Wisconsin colonel was a brick short of a load. Then, the prisoner who had whispered to him earlier shouted from the rear of the throngs, "If Colonel LaGrange says Old George is with us, by god, Old George is with us!"

The other prisoners cheered and placed their hands over their hearts.

Hugh saw the sentries growing restless, but he pressed on. He closed his eyes to aid his memory and recited to his rapt audience:

> "'The Commander-in-Chief again takes occasion to return his warmest thanks to the virtuous officers and soldiery of this Army for that persevering fidelity and zeal which they have uniformly mani-fested in all their conduct. Their fortitude not only under the common hardships incident to a military life but also under the additional sufferings to which the peculiar situation of these States have exposed them, clearly proves them worthy of the enviable privilege of contending for the rights of human nature, the Freedom and Independence of their Country. The recent Instance of uncomplaining Patience during the scarcity of provisions in Camp is a fresh proof that they possess in an eminent degree the spirit of soldiers and the magnanimity of Patriots.'"

He looked down at their spectral faces, fearing he had lost them, but they were hanging on his every word. He continued with Washington's inspiring message, invoking perseverance, glory, freedom, peace, prosperity, love, gratitude, and patience with scarcity of provisions, all delivered with energy-draining passion while he tried to catch an occasional glimpse toward the blacksmith's shed.

After twenty minutes more of this improvisation, he finished, plum out of speech material, and braced for the sound of musket fire. Hearing only coughs and murmuring, he looked down at the ragged men pressed around him. They were crying.

The stockade gates swung open.

A Confederate battery rolled three howitzers into position and aimed them to sweep the entire camp. The commandant, Captain Gibbs, accompanied by thirty armed Rebel infantrymen, climbed atop a cannon and straddled its axle to be heard. "There will be no more speeches."

As the prisoners hissed and edged toward their captors, Hugh lowered to his knees and climbed down from the empty hogshead cask. He moved to defuse the tense standoff when a hand grabbed his bicep and pulled him back into the mash of jeering prisoners. Before he could protest the rough handling, two prisoners ushered him toward the blacksmith shed while elbowing a path through the surging mob. Thrust inside the shed, he was met with a handshake from a Union officer. "I'm Captain Kellogg. We've sent twelve men out. You'll be the last. Can you crawl with your wound?"

Hugh tossed his crutch. "I'll die trying."

The captain nodded, impressed with his grit. "Make your way to the river. There is a sorghum barge waiting for you. It'll take you down the Ocmulgee to Altamaha, then on to the sea at Darien."

The captain's tunneling crew brushed away dirt to reveal a gunnysack that covered a trapdoor. They lifted the lid to a shaft, angled at forty-five degrees and just wide enough for a man to slither in. The captain rubbed bacon grease on Hugh's ragged shirt and pantaloons to decrease the friction. On the far end of the stockade, the jeers reached a crescendo. Warned it was now or never, Hugh abandoned his bundle and lowered into the hole, feet first.

"Six feet down," the captain said. "Then toward the river."

Hugh hesitated. "The nurse in the hospital who helped me."

"She's safe."

Hugh came back up, reached for his bag, and retrieved the Bible that Lizzie had loaned him. He tucked it inside his shirt and descended again. Loam sifted into his face as he elbowed his way deeper into the darkness. Above him, he heard the trap door snap back into place. He counted off his progress by the number of times his forearm reached forward and pulled him.

After ten minutes, his feet hit bottom, and the walls eased enough to allow him to turn and crawl headfirst. He soon became dizzy from the effort. To ward off his claustrophobia, he recalled his spelunking trips as a boy with Professor Daniels. Central Georgia, he remembered from his geology studies, sat on the border between the Piedmont and Coastal Plain geographic regions. The soil here was clay-laced with small pores loaded with iron oxide. Caves were prevalent, and the ground was notoriously unstable. He'd once been told of a Rebel skulker at Vicksburg who fell into a sinkhole so deep they couldn't find enough rope to pull him out. Poor fellow probably died of—

His scalp scraped a board. Was this an escape hatch? On his back, he retracted the board, wiggled his head out, and enjoyed his first gulp of stench-free air in a month. When his eyes adjusted to the harsh light, he looked up to the blue sky.

Ten musket barrels loomed over him.

The corporal of a Rebel patrol laughed and poked at Hugh with a knife, rousting him from the hole like an oyster from its shell, and sniffed Hugh's greased shirt. "Smells like breakfast, boys."

27

LAGRANGE, GEORGIA
JULY 1864

Exhausted from her long day in the hospital ward, Nancy sat at the writing desk in her bedroom and thumbed through the mail, mostly unpaid invoices from Brown's moribund law practice. She treasured this liminal time of the evening when the stirring machines shut down at the tanning yard and the tree frogs barked in the marshes of the Chattahoochee. These and other sounds of her childhood she missed most: The "roh-roh-roh" squawks of the Poor Joes in the hatching quags; the taps of the redheaded woodpeckers against the cedar trunks in the Ferrell terraces; and the rhythmic swish of gallberry bush brooms sweeping the verandas along Broad Street.

She lit a lamp and lifted the window. The church bells chimed, as they did now at every sunset, the town's declaration of solidarity with the besieged citizens of Atlanta. Each day brought more refugees south and with them dire news. Grant had driven General Lee's Army into the trenches at Petersburg. Adding insult to the disheartening events, the newspapers reported a clever Union colonel named Upton employed a novel deep-column attack—the tactic she had broached with General Hardee—to break through the lines at Spotsylvania Court House and crush General Doles's brigade with the Fourth Georgia. Earlier that week, President Davis replaced John Bell Hood with General Johnston as commander of the Army of Tennessee, a decision that reeked of desperation. The soldiers loved Uncle Joe, and he had done everything possible to impede that butcher Sherman, but the politicians in Richmond insisted he be sacked.

While Hood clawed and scratched to save Atlanta, Confederate medical authorities increased the number of military hospitals in LaGrange from one to five, confiscating the Baptist and Presbyterian churches. The wounded and ill men she cared for in the Methodist church basement were moved to Smith Hall, her old classroom building at the academy. If the groans and cries of pain from the wards weren't dispiriting enough, the streets around the courthouse square were now filled with grumbling, daily complaints, and arguments of homeless families, grifters, bounty hunters, and deserters driven from that devastated stretch along the Chattanooga railroad from Ringgold to Marietta. In the new cemetery near the depot, two hundred fresh headboards sprouted, many with no identification. The chaplains offered last rites now with such frequency that their monotone incantations seemed but one long, unbroken repine.

She dropped her face into her hands, desperate to chase these never-ending reminders of destitution and death. She couldn't bear to think of what might happen if Atlanta fell. Would the ravenous Yankee Army burn south along the rail line? She had to trust the Texan Hood, one of General Lee's top lieutenants, would never allow their last train connection to Montgomery and the beating heart of the Confederacy to be severed.

A knock came at the door. "Missus Morgan? We've got the pickings."

She wiped the weep from her eyes. "Come in, Dash."

The young soldier from Gascony whose senses she helped revive by speaking French walked in holding a bowl filled with black and persian walnuts. He proudly displayed his haul. "We done good, I think."

"You did." She heard a staggering noise in the stairwell. "Is that Seth?"

"Yes'm."

"Tell him to come in. He needn't be shy."

Seth Cooger, the boy soldier from Macon whose leg Gus amputated, hobbled to the door on his crutch. He opened the flap to a sack strapped over his shoulder to show her his cache of gooseberries, muscadine grapes, and pawpaws. "You was right about that patch of fescue behind Ol' Man Culbertson's barn. It's a veritable paradise of drupe delights."

"We even saw a rabbit," said Dash. "Figurin' we go back and introduce ourselves with a trap tomorrow."

She winked at them. "Leave some eatings for the widower, now, and don't go stealing from his garden. He's prouder of that than anything he's got left."

"Yes, ma'am," said Dash.

"Take those berries and nuts to the pantry. I'll wash them and bring them to the ward in the morning. You two may win a medal from the surgeons yet."

Dash and Seth doffed their hats and backtracked to the door. "I almost forgot." Seth reached into his pocket and pulled out a small envelope. "Mrs. Gay asked me to give this to you."

Nancy tossed the envelope on the pile, figuring it had been delivered to the wrong house. "There's plum cake in the cupboard. Help yourselves to a slice."

"Thankee, ma'am!"

She offered a prayer of gratitude to the Almighty for sending such blessings at her lowest moments. She wasn't much older than Dash and Seth, but she had grown fond of them in a maternal way. The two boys became fast friends and moved around town as if one organism. Dash hadn't fully regained his mental capacities and remained childlike, but he provided her invaluable assistance and legwork while Seth looked after him. They'd become so popular with the wounded men, cheering them with jests and pantomimes, that she assigned them odd jobs such as scavenging for edibles and cleaning the bed pans.

Her spirits renewed, she returned to the mail. She examined the envelope forwarded by Caroline and saw it was postmarked *Culpeper, Virginia.* Inside it, she found a letter from Caroline's husband, John Gay:

May 6, 1864
Dearest Nannie,

Yours of the 26th Apr came to hand yesterday. I was in line of battle when I received it, not more than three hundred yards of the enemy who shot at every head raised above the pile of logs we used as breast works. Yours contained so much Christian advice & wrote in such warm spirits &c. that I concluded the letter of yours the most appropriate letter for the occasion I ever saw. God Bless you, dear Nannie. I hope your prayers may be answered.

John

She hurried to a stack of newspapers and opened a *Southern Confederacy* edition from that week in May. She gasped. The Wilderness. He had been in *that* horrid place? And two months had passed. Was he still alive? She cursed the slowness of the governmental postal service. Should she show the letter to Caroline? She knew from John's correspondence that he kept details of the battles from Caroline for fear they would distress her. Yet he shared every hardship with *her*, as if she'd understand what a soldier endured. She had come to know him well enough to decipher when he was low in spirit.

A walnut shell bounced off her back. The boys were playing battle again. Without turning from her desk, she admonished them. "Dash, one piece of plum cake only. We must save the rest for the wounded men."

Another missile smacked her waist, that one an entire walnut.

She erupted to her feet and spun. "Dash, I have no patience—"

In the shadows, a rail-thin officer, grinning from ear to ear, stood at the door fingering a handful of nuts.

"Brown!" She rushed to his arms, scattering the nuts.

He kissed her with the pent-up passion of six months. "My little squirrel. Hoarding for winter."

She pressed him to her bosom. "What are you doing here? I must tell Mary and Caroline and Gus and—"

"No. I can only stay the night."

She pulled away, stricken. "The night? Have you deserted?"

He brought her back into his embrace. "I have been detached to find wheat and corn for the brigade. I must be on the train for Macon in the morning."

She sank at that news. "I haven't had a letter from you in weeks."

"We were detailed to Florida to counter a Yankee invasion at Jacksonville. General Lee has called us back to Virginia."

She caressed his shoulders and arms. "Darling, you are wasting away." She rushed out the bedroom and returned moments later with a large slice of plum cake. "It's all I have."

He bit off a mouthful. A frown of concern crossed his face.

"Cornmeal," she confessed. "We haven't had flour for months."

He forced a smile. "It is the best morsel I have tasted since you cooked me those fritters in Fredericksburg. Fried up with love."

"I will see if Caroline has any meat and—" He grasped her hands and eased her toward the bed they first shared on their wedding night.

"Come, hold me. That's all the nourishment I need."

She helped him slip off his boots. They lay together.

"Brown," she whispered. "Tell me Cousin Alfred hasn't sent you here to impress our grain reserves." When he didn't answer her, she pleaded, "We have barely enough to serve one meal a day to our men in the hospitals."

"Lee's Army is starving."

"What happened to the loads of rice Governor Brown requisitioned?"

"Never reached Virginia. Probably molding in some North Carolina warehouse. The trains break down with such frequency now that it's a miracle any edibles reach Richmond."

Alarmed, she levered to her elbows. "We are nearly out of salt. How will we cure the ham hocks for the winter? The Yankees destroyed the brine works at Darien."

"Tell Gus to have the Negroes scrape the smokehouses and leach the dirt."

"And what are *they* to eat to find the strength?"

"They'll manage."

She sat up, not convinced. "A gang of hungry women armed with knives and pistols rioted in Columbus."

"You needn't worry about mobs harassing LaGrange. You and your Nancies will drive them off."

Was he making light of her militia? "Hunger riots are erupting across the state. If we can't feed our families ..."

Brown sighed. "Nannie, allow me one night of respite from this burden. I have no answers for you *or* General Lee."

Dispirited, she lay her head on his chest. "It is the fault of the planters."

"Planters? They are our friends. And my clients."

She slid him a knowing glance. "You think I don't see what goes on down-river at night? They've been shipping cotton on barges to Apalachicola. Picked from fields that should have been planted with corn." She sighed and listened to the Negroes singing in their field cabins on the outskirts of the town. Their hymns these days seemed louder and more passionate. "Brown, is God punishing us with this war?"

"From what I've seen, I doubt Providence gives a good pin who wins it."

"The preachers assured us the Bible gave us sanction."

"They also said we sin against the slaves by imposing excessive labor, extreme punishment, withholding necessary food and clothing, neglect in sickness or old age. I don't see many of our countrymen taking *that* admonition to heart."

She felt him studying her, as if questioning what had happened to the naïve, carefree girl he married. She dared not reveal that she had earned a lifetime of practical education these last four years about the greedy depravity of human nature. There were profiteers and speculators in their midst, willing to fill their bank accounts while the soldiers fought and died on empty bellies.

"You are still the most beautiful belle in Troup County."

For this night, at least, she vowed to chase her worries. She curved a girlish smile. "On the subject of beautiful belles, remind me later to tell you of the new friend I made at General Hardee's wedding." Before he could inquire further, she reached for his hand and brought it to the buttons on her dress.

* * *

Nancy had no time to brood over Brown's departure. Three days later, Sue Tarleton and her sister, Grace, arrived from Mobile with Mary Hardee, hoping to rendezvous with General Cleburne. The shy Irishman, who had finally found the courage to propose, promised to take a few days off from the campaign and rush by train to LaGrange to marry Sue. Yet that madman Sherman pressed the Army of Tennessee so hard from Resaca to Kennesaw Mountain that Cleburne couldn't be spared even a night away. Now, "my gallant Pat," as Sue called him, remained trapped in Atlanta, fighting the Yankees with John Bell Hood. Fearing she'd never see Cleburne again, Sue reluctantly returned to Mobile after two weeks of waiting, but not before forming a deep bond with Nancy and the LaGrange women.

This morning, Nancy climbed the steps of Smith Hall. New concerns burdened her now. The younger, unbetrothed women in her charge were becoming attached to the convalescing soldiers. Several of the Nancies had already suffered broken hearts when the targets of their affections died or returned to the armies. Leila, in particular, worried her. General Cheatham broke off his correspondence, as Nancy expected, but Leila had barely recovered from that disappointment when she fell for a smooth-talking officer from the Twenty-Fourth Alabama named Rutledge Parham. Recovering from a shoulder wound, Parham was an entertaining fellow, often dressing up as a Chickasaw chief and recruiting other musically inclined men in the ward to form a minstrel band. They pounded on makeshift drums and played branch flutes while parading along the rows of hospital beds. The captain's intentions were true, she believed, but he was no proper courtier for Leila. She felt she must intervene. Yet after their argument at General Hardee's wedding, Leila now rebelled against any advice offered.

Nancy entered the ward in the main hall and found several nurses and patients hovering around a bed at the far wall. Had a patient died?

"Nannie, thank goodness you are here," cried Sallie Fannie Reid.

"Should I call Gus?"

"No, no. We have a new arrival. You will be thrilled." Sallie locked elbows with Nancy and hurried her down the aisle. During these past weeks since the Demopolis wedding, they had become close. Sallie had thrown herself into the nursing work, organizing a hospital in West Point and traveling to LaGrange on Tuesdays and Saturdays to offer respites for Mary and Caroline, who found her hands full with ten-month-old Eugene.

Sallie brought Nancy to the head of a bed that held a stocky officer of middling stature. He resembled the portraits she'd seen of Napoleon, if the French emperor had possessed deep-set, gray-marble eyes and an impressive black mustache waxed to long, dangerous points. Two crutches leaned against the wall, and the sheets had been pulled back, revealing the general's left leg amputated at the knee. Sallie moved in to introduce her, but the general was regaling the staff and convalescing soldiers around him with a stem-winding story, so Nancy winked for her to wait.

"The Yankees came scrambling up Missionary Ridge like rats released from a sack!" The general raised his shoulders higher against the wall to be heard by all. "We held our ground, but those Louisiana boys on each side of us melted away. I drew my pistol to stem the tide when I buckled."

"That's when they got your femur, General?" asked a wounded soldier.

The general nodded. "I left it on the highest mountain in Tennessee! How's that for getting a leg up on the Yankees?"

The nurses and patients howled with laughter, impressed by his bravado in the face of tragedy.

"You never hear the shot that's destined for you. No use ducking, that's what I tell my brigade. Sound has a peculiar aspect in battle. Up Kentucky way, ol' Don Carlos Buell couldn't hear the cannons booming just a few hills from his headquarters. But downwind, thirty miles off, the Lincolnites in Frankfort were soiling their britches from the thunder. 'Acoustic shadow' is what they call it. I reckon Joshua must have used it with his trumpets before the walls of Jericho."

"Tell that story again about the Fighting Bishop!" begged Leila.

The general twirled the points of his mustache. "Well, now, my good friend, Leonidas Polk, held the distinction of being the only general on both sides who was also an ordained church elder. Killing mixed with preaching can be a tricky business. We rose up to charge a Yankee stand at Perryville when General Cheatham yells, 'Give 'em hell, boys!'"

His audience inched closer, many already knowing the punch line.

"So, the Fighting Bishop's blood was up, but he had sworn as a man of the cloth never to curse. His men waited for a rousing sendoff like General Cheatham's blast. General Polk, reddening from exasperation, shouted, 'Give it to 'em, boys! Give 'em what General Cheatham says!'"

The ward erupted again with back-slaps and chortles.

The general dipped his head and made the sign of the cross over his heart. "God bless the Fighting Bishop's soul."

The others hushed, honoring a moment of silence for the Confederate corps commander killed by Yankee shrapnel earlier that month at Marietta.

Sallie broke the silence. "General, may I introduce Mrs. Morgan."

The general's eyes widened with delight. He reached for his crutches and struggled to get out of bed.

"General, please," Nancy begged. "There is no need."

He coughed harshly as retrieved his crutches and stood. He straightened into a military posture and saluted. "Brigadier General Robert Charles Tyler at your service, Captain Morgan."

Nancy blushed, astonished he knew her rank. "Sir, I fear my ladies here have been telling tales out of school."

"Not at all," the general said. "Best as I can tell, you've kept this town from falling into Yankee hands for three years. Very commendable."

She eased him back to the bed and onto his pillow. "We've never been graced here in the hospital with the presence of a general. Are you suffering complications from your surgery?"

He wiggled what remained of his left leg. "No, this old stump is healed. The bone cutters tell me I've got the water in the lungs now."

"Pneumonia?"

He nodded. "Nothing serious."

She told Leila, "Prepare the General a cup of honey tea, and steam a compress for his chest."

"Now, don't fuss over me," said Tyler, bent with another coughing fit.

"We're going to spoil you, General. Now, take an hour off from the stories. You must rest."

"God bless you, Captain Morgan."

She waited until his eyes fluttered into sleep. Then she walked Sallie away from the other women. "I have an assignment, if you will agree to it."

"Anything to help."

"The General will steal the heart of every unbetrothed lady here within the week. I need someone who is attached to take personal care of him. When his breathing improves, we'll find a proper private home for his convalescence."

Sallie smiled. "Leave it to me."

* * *

A month later, General Tyler recovered enough strength from his bout with pneumonia that Nancy agreed to give a treat to her militia women and the wounded soldiers in the wards. The stewards rolled the general in a wooden wheelchair from his new residence of convalescence, the home of Captain Francis Frost on Greenville Street, to the drilling ground below Bellevue. There, under the shade of the grove and surrounded by an applauding crowd, including Gus and his wife, Anna, the Nancy Harts marched down the old path in column formation from the red schoolhouse and split off into two ranks to confront their scarecrow targets in the pasture field.

Nancy brought her militia to attention and ordered them to about-face. She warned Tyler, "General, we haven't practiced much these last months. You must forgive our rustiness."

Tyler, attended to by Sallie Reid, doffed his hat. "A finer array of sharpshooters I've not seen since Shiloh."

Nancy took her position behind the ranks. "First line! Present arms!"

The women turned the lock plates on their muskets to face forward.

"Load!"

The women planted their musket butts between their feet, withdrew the ramrods, and drove the balls home. Nancy prayed for no embarrassing mishaps. Since Chickamauga, they had drilled only twice a month to conserve ammunition and because Mary and Caroline were preoccupied with families and the younger women consumed by their nursing duties. After those infrequent firing sessions, she asked Seth and Dash to harvest the spent balls to be reused. She watched their every move for slip-ups. To her relief, the women remembered their maxims from General Hardee's manual. When Leila, the last to finish ramming her ball into the barrel, indicated her readiness, Nancy shouted, "Dress left!"

The Nancies took a step left and touched elbows.

"Aim!"

They angled their muskets into firing position.

"Fire!"

Sharp cracks, followed by the shrill zing of balls, cut the air. When the smoke cleared, the eager crowd leaned forward to check the results. The scarecrows were decimated. The appreciative spectators burst into applause.

"Well done, ladies!" said Tyler. "Captain Morgan, you and Dr. Ware have trained your charges well."

Nancy beamed, and Gus bowed to another round of claps.

The general motioned for a steward to bring his crutches. He lifted himself from the wheelchair and hobbled to the firing line. He stopped in front of Leila and examined her musket. "Darling, you are a wee thing. This old blunderbuss weighs as much as you do."

"It's all I got, General."

"It's all most of us got," he said. "But we know tricks the Yankees don't." Leaning on one crutch, he rested the musket atop the pad of his other crutch and instructed the attentive women. "Wherever you can, use a fence rail or a wall for support. I had my brigade carry socks filled with dried beans. You rest the barrel on the beans, and the stock nestles in like a baby in its crib. Takes the strain from the joints."

"What if we have to shoot in the open field?" asked Caroline.

The general returned Leila's musket. "It's difficult, I'm not denying it, but you have to relax your musculature when you aim and fire." He motioned for Leila to give his advice a try. "Hon, take aim at that Yank scarecrow."

Leila sighted her empty musket at the target.

The general pinched a coin from his pocket and balanced it on the end of her barrel. "Give it a dry run."

Leila pulled the trigger—the barrel bounced, and the coin dropped.

"I can do it!" cried a girl's voice.

The general and Nancy turned to find the source of that boast. Standing next to Sallie Reid, a pig-tailed lass, no older than twelve, raised her hand.

"Well, child," said the general. "State your name and rank and come on down here."

"I'm Sarah Potts. Sallie's friend from West Point."

The general grinned at Sallie. "Does Miss Reid shoot, too?"

"She don't cotton to guns," said Sarah.

The general kept his admiring eye on Sallie. "We may have to change that predilection." He handed little Sarah the musket and placed the coin on the barrel. "Are you planning to shoot as an Alabamian or a Georgian today?"

"My Pa's place sits ten feet from the border. At home, I shoot from Alabama and I hit my target in Georgia."

The general guffawed and winked at Sallie. He promised Sarah, "If you can dry-fire this boomer without dropping that half-dollar, I'll give it to you."

"I'd rather have the musket."

The general grinned. "You trying to skin me?" When the girl held a determined look confirming she was dead serious about the prize, the general glanced at Nancy, who agreed to donate the gun. "If you keep that coin aloft, Captain Morgan and I will give them both to you."

Sarah took a wide stance, aimed the musket, and nodded for the general to place the coin on the barrel. She took a long breath and pulled the trigger. The coin didn't move. She flipped the barrel up and sent the coin flying into her hand.

The Nancies whistled and applauded the feat.

The general, impressed, pulled his pocket knife and etched the girl's name into the stock. "Sarah here has done some boar hunting."

"Yessir."

"Her trick is controlling her inhalations," said Tyler. "Draw in air for five seconds. Hold for three. Settle your sight and pull the trigger. If you hold your breath longer, you'll tense up." He scanned the ranks of women for a second candidate. "Who else wants to try? Captain Morgan, I haven't seen you shoot."

Nancy tried to beg off, but the spectators hooted for a show. Surrendering to their pleas, she pulled her favorite Enfield from the stacks, loaded the musket, and leveled its barrel, nodding for the general to place another coin near the sight notch.

"Cheek against the stock," the general whispered to her ear. "Easy pressure on the trigger."

She drew a deep breath and counted to five. At the apex of her inhalation, she fired. The smoke cleared. The coin remained on the barrel.

The spectators cheered.

"If I spend more time around you Nancy Harts, I'll go bankrupt." Tyler retrieved the coin and flipped it to Nancy.

She reached to catch the coin and clutched her stomach, attacked by a spasm of nausea.

Caroline and Mary rushed to her. "Nannie?" Mary said. "Are you ill?"

Gus limped over and palmed her forehead. "No fever."

Nancy covered her mouth with a kerchief. "I am so sorry, General. I must take my leave."

"Not at all, Mrs. Morgan." Tyler motioned for his stewards. "My fellows here will wheel you home."

Nancy objected to using his wheelchair, but the general insisted. The Nancies followed Caroline, Mary, and Gus up the path in a concerned procession behind the wheelchair. When they reached the Heard house, Mary and Caroline helped Nancy climb the stairs to the bedroom. Nancy sat on the bed and lunged for the bedpan. She knelt and vomited. Mary held her head over the pan while Caroline called for Gus, who waited on the stairs. He limped inside, checked the dilation of Nancy's eyes, and glanced with suspicion at Mary and Caroline.

Caroline fixed a glare of interrogation on Nancy. "Is there something you haven't told us?" When Nancy didn't respond, Caroline shoved her brother out the door. "Gus! Downstairs! Now!"

Baffled by his exile, Gus backed away and closed the door behind him.

Mary asked Nancy, "Did you miss your monthly time?"

"Yes, but..."

Caroline and Mary hovered over her.

Under their judging glares, Nancy revealed, "Brown was home last month."

Their jaws dropped, and Mary demanded, "How did we not—"

"One night. He insisted I tell no one."

Their dismay melted into joy. They brought Nancy to her feet and hugged her. Caroline, long a self-described soothsayer of fetal gender, placed her hand to Nancy's stomach. She closed her eyes. "A boy."

While Mary and Caroline scurried around the room making plans for the announcement, Nancy slumped on the bed, overwhelmed by a sudden wave of dread. How would she care for an infant alone *and* command her militia?

28

CHARLESTON, SOUTH CAROLINA
AUGUST 1864

A Confederate provost guard shoved Hugh, blindfolded, into a cell. The door locked behind him. Two hands caressed his head, and he recoiled. Someone untied the kerchief covering his eyes. He blinked hard, trying to make out his surroundings in the dim light.

"Welcome to the Six Hundred Mortals," said a man's voice.

A shell burst in the distance and rattled the floorboards. Ducking from being startled, Hugh rushed to a barred window and found smoke billowing up from a burning church steeple, two blocks away. In the barren prison yard three stories below, a brick enclosure marked the boundaries, and a gallows stood at the far end. He turned, his eyes adjusting to the dark cell. Several dozen prisoners stood along the wall as if formed up for morning drill.

The man who had spoken to him saluted and held out his hand. "You must have riled Stonewall Jackson's ghost to get sent here."

Hugh accepted the handshake. "Where are we?"

"Charleston jail. I'm Willard Glazier. Captain, Second New York Cavalry."

"Hugh LaGrange."

As the other officers stepped closer to examine Hugh's sun-burnt features, Glazier grinned at their discovery. "Colonel LaGrange, stalker of Fighting Joe Wheeler. Reports about you have reached the Army of the Potomac."

Hugh waved off that claim. "The prey got his claws into the stalker."

"You stand before men who deem it no dishonor to be overtaken in battle."

"Hear, hear!" the officers said.

Another cannonball exploded, landing even closer. Hugh looked through the barred window toward the mansion rooftops and churches. He made out the shoreline of an island across the harbor. "*Our* forces are shelling us?"

"We've become pawns in a long-running game." The captain pulled a spoon from his pocket and drew a map of the Charleston peninsula in the grime.

"Two months ago, the Reb general placed in charge of the city confined five of our generals and forty-five officers in warehouses within range of our heavy guns on Morris Island."

Hugh feared where the story was heading. "And Washington retaliated."

"Secretary Stanton ordered fifty Secesch officers transferred to the island as human shields. So, the Rebs herded six hundred more of our officers into the range of the guns. General Grant then upped the ante by landing six hundred more Rebels on Morris Island. There they sit, and here we sit. Rumor is the Reb officers are starving themselves rather than swear the oath of allegiance."

Hugh cursed the escalating standoff. "Martyrs to the slaver cause."

Glazier shrugged. "The pig-headed planters in these parts have beatified the imprisoned Rebs as the Immortal Six Hundred."

"And hence, *we* are the Mortal Six Hundred." Hugh paced the cell. "Cannon fodder for the stupidity of politicians who think themselves generals. Do our officers on Morris Island know the Rebs hold us in their range?"

Glazier led him back to the window and pointed toward several charred city blocks. "If they do, they don't care. We've had three fires erupt in adjacent buildings within the last week. If our gunboats strike a direct hit on this oversized brick kiln, the Rebs will probably leave us here to burn."

Weary from his forced march from the train depot, Hugh found a spot along the wall and sat. The officers around him also slumped to their haunches, some slipping into sleep, others staring with vacant eyes into the dimness. As miserable and dangerous as this place appeared, he knew he should be grateful. After being caught in the tunnel trying to escape from the Macon prison, the Rebels had staked him to the ground for ten hours as punishment. The Confederate commandant there, Gibbs, slated him for Andersonville with the other digging conspirators when, through a mysterious intervention, he was pulled off the southbound train at the last minute and transported here to Charleston.

Blessed sleep. At last, he could slip off and—

A *rat-a-tat-tat* noise came from the other side of the thick brick wall. *What is that infernal tapping?* He slid the brim of his hat over his eyes.

Rat-a-tat-tat. Rat-a-tat-tat.

He pressed his ear against the wall. Were there rats gnawing inside the crawl spaces? He followed the tapping along the bricks until he came to a door. He turned the knob, determined to corner the varmint—

"Colonel," Glazier warned, "that leads to the quarters for the enlisted men. The Rebs will shoot you if you mingle with them."

"They can shoot me, then." Hugh creaked open the door and discovered emaciated men lying in their own urine and feces. Some looked up at him with blank stares. He returned to the officers' cell, retrieved a lantern on a hook, and threaded his way back through the enlisted prisoners. With his sleeve pressed to his nose, he followed the rhythmic tapping to a shadow in the far corner. He knelt and brought the light to a pair of small hands banging on the back of a tin plate with sticks. A boy, malnourished to the bone, kept tapping. Hugh lifted the boy's battered hat to get a better look at him. "Wee Al?"

The drummer boy from Chickamauga stared vacantly at him, not recognizing Hugh's wild, bearded features. Suddenly, his glazed eyes widened. "Colonel LaGrange?"

"How long have you been in here?"

"I done lost count. Where are we again?"

"Charleston."

"You sure? I think this is Florence."

"You were in Camp Sorghum?"

The boy nodded. "Andersonville and Libby 'fore that."

Hugh balled his fists in a fury. Were the Secesh bastards so sadistic they intended to force the lad to endure every murder pit in the South? He helped Al across the cell while careful not to step on the other prisoners.

Glazier stood at the door. "If the boy comes in, the Rebs will thrash us."

"He didn't desert his comrades at Chickamauga. I won't desert him now. Am I not the ranking officer here?" When Grazier conceded that point with a nod, Hugh came up with a solution. "I'm promoting the boy to lieutenant. If the Rebs have a problem with *that*, you can all blame me." He placed Wee Al on straw and brought a tin cup of water to his lips. "You're going to stay alive. That's an order."

"Why bother?" the boy said. "There ain't another Reb prison will have me."

"I didn't ride through Joe Wheeler's entire division at night and rescue your drum, only to have you keel over on me now."

The boy enlivened. "You found my drum?"

"Your Colonel Pettit has it. Strung together again and ready for battle. He's waiting for your return."

Lieutenant Wee Al of the Seventy-Fifth Indiana struggled to remain standing long enough to salute his new commander.

* * *

A few weeks later, a plaintive melody that sounded chanted by angels roused Hugh from a fitful sleep. He rubbed his eyes and listened as the chorus above him became stronger in the night:

"When I enlisted in the army,
Then I thought 'twas grand,

Marching through the streets of Boston
Behind a regimental band.
When at Wagner I was captured,
Then my courage failed;
Now I'm lousy, hungry, naked,
Here in Charleston jail."

He looked around the desolate cell. Most of the other officers had been paroled, but he continued to refuse the oath to sit out the rest of the war. He stood and, leaving Wee Al sleeping on the floor, edged toward the door to find the source of the singing. The Reb guards had warned him not to stray from the cell except during mess hours, but he found no one posted at the stairs. Barefoot, he climbed the steps, taking care not to creak the boards, and reached the top floor. He entered the open door. More than a hundred Negro men, half-starved and clad in rags, sat swaying while they sang:

"Weeping, sad and lonely,
Oh, how bad I feel;
Down in Charleston, Car'lina,
Praying for a good square meal.
If Jeff Davis will release me,
Oh, how glad I'll be,
When I get on Morris Island,
Then I shall be free."

He realized these men had been separated from the white prisoners and held on the top floor because the heat here was the most unbearable. He began singing with them, picking up the lyrics. The black prisoners turned and, noticing him, fell silent and crawled backwards, fearing punishment.

One colored prisoner found the courage to speak. "We disturbing you, sir?"

"Not at all. I haven't heard Heaven's dominions testify with such passion since I was a young conductor for the Underground Railroad." He offered his hand to their senior officer. "Hugh LaGrange."

Those prisoners who could manage it staggered to their feet and saluted. "Sergeant Johnson," the officer replied, identifying himself. He was reluctant to take Hugh's hand because of Southern laws here. "We know of you, sir. You sprung Mister Booth from that jail in Milwaukee."

"How did you learn about that caper?"

Johnson signaled for two of his privates to watch the door. Assured it was safe to speak freely, he explained, "Well, see now, Joshua Glover was a friend of mine. Friend of many of us here. You and those Republican fellers stopped that fugitive hunter from dragging Joshua back in chains to Missouri. We ain't none of us forgotten your help."

"What unit are you men in?"

"Most of us are with the Fifty-Fourth Massachusetts."

"Robert Shaw's regiment."

"Yes, sir. We lost Colonel Shaw in the assault on Fort Wagner."

"That was last July. They've kept you holed up here for fourteen months?"

Johnson shrugged. "Some think we was the lucky ones. I ain't so sure."

Hugh remembered reading the tragic account of the Fifty-Fourth Massachusetts in the newspapers. "On the parapets at Wagner ... is it true?"

Johnson's eyes watered. "We was stuck in no-man's land all that night. The Secesh dragged hundreds of us over their earthworks and beat us. Those not clubbed to death were marched here. They're planning to sell us."

"They ain't selling me!" shouted a voice from across the cell.

Hugh saw an elderly Negro man holding a hammer at a window sill. "The guards allow you to arm yourself with that forge thrasher?"

"Allow? The city scions force me to come in here and work at night. My sight is poor enough, I got to drive pegs in the dark?"

Johnson brought the man with the hammer to his side. "Robert Vesey. His family has lived in Charleston for generations. He's a fine carpenter—"

"Architect!" Vesey corrected. "Just like my pap was." Vesey led Hugh to the barred window. "Down there, on Reid and Hanover Streets, my progenitor, Denmark Vesey, built the African American Methodist Episcopal Church. One Sunday, the gendarmes dragged him out with thirty-five of our congregants and strung them up on false charges they was fomenting a slave revolt. They burned the church. Nothing left but ashes!" He trembled as he recounted the desecration. "I want you to be my witness, Colonel. Before I meet my Maker, I *will* rebuild that church and reclaim my pap's good name!"

"I believe you will." Hugh walked across the cell and examined those men who were too weak to stand. "How much do they feed you each day?"

"One handful of cornmeal," said Johnson.

"That's half the rations we get. No meat?"

"Not unless you count the rats."

Hugh knelt next to a prisoner who looked near death. He raised the man's ragged pant leg. Fresh bruises marred his ankle and calf. He looked up at Johnson. "They beat him?"

Johnson unbuttoned his shredded shirt and revealed scars on his back from whippings. "We all get the treatment, sooner than later."

Outraged, Hugh tried to raise the dying soldier on the floor. "We have to get this man to the hospital."

"Sir, that's where he got his thrashing."

Hugh stared with disbelief at Johnson. "The guards did *this* while the medical staff watched?"

"No, sir. The surgeon performs his own cruelty. That bonecutter in the ward downstairs is the Devil's deputy."

Hugh bolted to his feet. "What's this surgeon's name?"

Johnson hesitated. "Sir, he exercises his boot on the whites, too. I'm not sure you want to—"

"His name," Hugh demanded.

"Todd."

Hugh threaded a path through the men to the door. "Guards!"

Two Rebel guards woke from their slumber on the floor below. They clambered up the staircase with their muskets cocked and found Hugh staring at them on the threshold of the Negro prisoners' cell. "Hell are you doing here?" asked the taller guard. "You'll get the lashes for this!"

"I demand to talk to the surgeon. Where is he?"

"Sleeping in his office."

"Get him up here."

The second guard sneered into Hugh's face. "You're new here, so maybe you ain't been educated on the rules. We give *you* the orders."

Hugh came nose-to-nose with the smart-mouthed yokel. "If I'm ever called to testify at a military tribunal about the conditions and treatment in this stink-hole, do you want me to say it was *you* two crackers-for-soldiers, and not that surgeon, who kicked these men to death?"

The guards pondered his threat. Finally, one ordered Hugh, "You stay here." He pointed at the other prisoners. "And you negrahs get back on that floor."

Hugh nodded for Johnson's men to comply with the order. Satisfied there was no breakout imminent, the guards backed down the stairs. Minutes later, they returned with the surgeon, a paltry man wearing spectacles over his savage black eyes and sporting a ragged goatee. He looked shriveled by the gravity of his evil, with his walnut-shaped head, twined by a few combed-over strands of greasy hair, too small even for his stunted torso, and his rotted teeth yellowed from a steady diet of cigars and whiskey.

"I'll hide-switch the Ethiopian who dragged me out of bed—"

Hugh seized the surgeon by his coat collar and slammed him against the wall. The Negro prisoners erupted to their feet and formed a protective circle around Hugh to prevent the guards from intervening. Hugh's face was so close to the physician's panting mouth that he could smell the laudanum on his breath. "Did you beat these men?"

The physician struggled to escape Hugh's elbow pressed against his neck. "Do you know who I am? Dr. George Rogers Clark Todd! The brother of the woman who beds that ape of yours in Washington!"

Hugh searched the surgeon's dilated eyes, hooded from the effects of opiates. Could this reprobate truly be the brother of Mary Todd Lincoln? "Do you know who *I* am?" When the surgeon couldn't place his face, Hugh revealed, "A founder of the Republican Party! So, by my calculation, I'm the man who put President Lincoln in the bed with your sister up there in Washington!"

The surgeon struggled to signal the guards to fire at Hugh.

Hugh wrestled Todd in front of him to use as a shield. "Listen up, you filthy slaver! If you abuse another man here again, I will muster Saint Michael's army of archangels against you!"

The surgeon croaked a grim laugh. "You're just another stinking Yankee officer. I've buried hundreds of you. What makes you so special?"

The guards fixed bayonets, prepared to stab their way into the cell.

"Hold off!" Hugh shouted at the guards. He gestured with his chin toward Johnson. "In my back pocket."

Johnson kept a close watch on the guards as he reached into the pocket of Hugh's trousers. He pulled out a folded letter.

"Show it to George … Rogers … Clark … Todd here."

Johnson unfolded the letter and held it in front of the surgeon's face. Todd skimmed it. His bespectacled eyes rounded when he came to the signature.

Hugh pressed him with a snarling grin. "I'm told Jeff Davis is quite fond of General Wheeler."

The physician stopped struggling and looked for a way out of his predicament. Trapped, he muttered a concession. "It won't happen again."

"These men go on full rations. You will order it as a medical necessity."

A guard protested, "Hell, *we* ain't eatin' as it is."

Hugh tightened his grip on Todd's collar. "*Full* rations."

Todd lowered his head, as much a concession as he could muster. The Negro prisoners opened their protective circle, and Hugh shoved the physician toward the guards. When the three Confederates hurried from the cell, Johnson softly clapped to resume their singing, now with appreciation and hope:

"Then we laugh long and loudly,
Oh, how glad we'll feel,
When we arrive at Heaven's doorstep,
And eat a good square meal."

Amid grateful nods and whispered thanks, Hugh walked to the door. He turned back and pointed at the proud carpenter. "Any chance a Wisconsin Abolitionist might preach a sermon in that church you're going to build?"

Vesey pinched his shoulders back and raised his hand to channel the Holy Spirit. "You bring the fire, Colonel, and I'll bring the brimstone."

* * *

Hugh, on a losing streak, shook his head in defeat. "You've been feeding your prize thoroughbred here your hardtack. Let's go two out of three."

Wee Al lined up his champion racing louse, a nit he had trained since picking it from his head two days ago. He placed the louse on his metal plate and knelt to it at eye level, waiting for the starter's call. "Come on, Braxton. Run like you ran down Missionary Ridge."

Hugh whistled to send the two lice off the blocks. Al angled his plate, and Braxton leapt to an early lead. Hugh watched in disbelief as his louse merely wiggled in place. As the boy's louse crossed the finish line, Hugh sighed and, lifting Al's plate to pour another thimble-full for his winnings, felt his fingers burn. He looked at the lone window and realized the boy had been heating his plate under a beam of harsh sunlight. "You cheating Hoosier ragamuffin!"

Al scampered away from his reach and—

The cell door clanged open. "Colonel LaGrange."

Hugh turned to find a Confederate general flanked by two officers.

"You're being exchanged."

Hugh stood. "I'm not changing my mind. I won't take the oath."

The general stepped inside. "Yes, you've made that clear. I am Sam Jones. Commander of the Department of South Carolina."

"So, you have no more use of me as cannon fodder?"

"You would have done the same, had you been in my position."

"No, I would not."

"Let's go. Sherman has agreed to release two of our officers for you."

"Two?"

"Your General Elliott made the mistake of revealing in the negotiations that you were more valuable to him than Murat was to Napoleon. We had the leverage. To be frank, I'm still not sure we're getting the better of the bargain."

"Who are your officers my government is trading for me?"

"You'll find out soon enough."

Hugh saw Wee Al had a stricken look of being abandoned. He brought the boy to his side. "I won't go without my lieutenant here."

Jones weighed if Hugh was bluffing. Shrugging, he nodded his agreement to the boy's release.

Hugh retrieved the Bible that Lizzie had loaned him and placed Joe Wheeler's folded letter in a crease. He wrapped his arm around Al's shoulders and, following the provosts, led the boy out of the jail house. They dodged jeers and debris thrown by angry citizens as a tumbrel took them to the harbor, where the Rebels boarded them on a small steamer and pulled anchor.

Halfway to Morris Island, a Union gunboat pulled aside the steamer and lowered its gangplank. Hugh stood with Al at the railing, gazing at the first full-sized American flag he had seen in three months. He waited for the Confederate officers to be brought forward on deck for the exchange.

No.

On the far end of the plank stood Duff Green Reed, Joe Wheeler's adjutant, who tried to kill Hugh after surrendering at Anderson's Crossroads.

Hugh backed away. "I will *not* be exchanged for that maligner!"

Reed glared vengeance at him from across the breach.

"Orders, sir!" shouted the Union officer in charge of the transfer.

Hugh pushed Al toward the gangplank. One of the Confederate officers ran across the boards, leaving Reed still standing on the Union boat.

"Come, Colonel LaGrange," the Union exchange officer insisted.

Reed, presented his chance to retaliate for his capture and humiliation, snorted a challenge at Hugh. "Are you afraid to face me in the field again?"

Hugh itched to send the scoundrel plummeting into the water. "General Wheeler apologized to me for your acts of dishonor."

Reed flushed. "He would never bring such ignominy on me!"

"He also said it wasn't your first reprimand. I'm betting you'll never see him again."

Reed aimed his chin, taunting Hugh to rush across the boards and throw the first punch. "I'll have my name restored by you when this war is over." He staggered toward Hugh, sneering and butting Hugh's shoulder as he passed.

When the Confederate provosts took Reed aboard their steamer, Hugh saw his protest was in vain. He reluctantly walked onto the deck of the Union gunboat, and the sailors raised the gangplank.

29

LAGRANGE, GEORGIA
NOVEMBER 1864

Gathered in the red schoolhouse for their weekly meeting, the women of the militia hovered over Nancy's shoulders as she scanned the headlines in the *Daily Intelligencer*, the only Atlanta newspaper of Southern loyalty still covertly published since the city fell. With the telegraph lines cut and the rail tracks destroyed above Jonesboro, the citizens of LaGrange had for weeks relied on wild rumors and panicked reports from refugees.

"Thank God," said Nancy, scanning the bold type.

Caroline rocked swaddled Eugene in her arms. "What has happened?"

"That fire-breathing butcher left the city," said Nancy. "Sherman has taken his army of locusts east."

The women gasped and hugged, thrilled by the news.

Leila pressed her hands together in prayerful gratitude. "We are safe, then. He is not coming south for us."

Caroline borrowed Mary's spectacles to read the rest of the account. "Sherman is even more a madman than everyone says. General Hood will destroy him in the open. Where does the Yankee fool think he will find food?"

Nancy displayed a map in the paper that traced Sherman's expected route to the sea. "Savannah."

Leila paced the room with rising excitement. "General Tyler told me Sherman's supply line from Chattanooga was stretched to its limit. The Yankees will have no choice but to live off the land. They will starve."

Mary noticed Nancy didn't join their celebration. "What concerns you?"

Nancy reread the next two paragraphs. She looked up, paled. "General Hood has taken the Army of Tennessee to northern Alabama."

The women hushed from disbelief, until Mary insisted, "That can't be. President Davis would never abandon Georgia to the deprivations of Yankee deserters and plunderers. Senator Hill would not allow it."

Nancy simply could not understand Hood's strategy. Two Union armies in Tennessee awaited him if he invaded north. He must have hoped to draw Sherman into a trap, but the Yankee general called his bluff. General Cleburne would have gone with Hood. She had to send a letter to Sue Tarleton at once to alert her. She looked up and saw the others staring at her with worry.

Caroline spoke what the others were too afraid to say. "The Yankees left behind a garrison to guard Atlanta. We have no force of any significance in the state to protect us should they send raiders down the rail line."

"We will increase our drills," said Nancy, trying not to show her alarm.

Leila stopped pacing. "Increase our drills? We work ourselves to exhaustion in the wards as it is. When will we find the time? And *you* shouldn't be standing an hour in the heat."

"I am perfectly fine," said Nancy. "Stop fussing over me."

"God help us," muttered Aley Smith. She had opened the newspaper to the second page. A look of terror passed over her as she read the dispatch aloud:

> *"'Yankee stragglers are terrorizing Cobb County and parts surrounding. A private named Lane from the 100th Ohio Volunteers was found guilty of raping Miss Louisa Dickerson of Marietta. Nor is this an isolated incident. A Yankee scoundrel, Bradburn, of the 145th Indiana showed up drunk at the house of one of our Southern ladies and demanded, in his crude Northern vernacular, a diddle. Near Burnt Hickory, two debauchers from the 7th Indiana Light Artillery broke into the cabin of James Smith and, claiming military authority, lured his wife into the woods. Mrs. Smith said the Yankees threatened to frig her right then and there.'"*

Caroline glanced out the window to make sure none of the house slaves were lurking. "If the Negroes get wind of Hood abandoning us ..."

Nancy stood and walked to the fireplace to collect her frantic thoughts. She stared at the crackling logs. "Leila, ask Seth to put another lock on our armory cabinet here. We'll hide the keys in the flower pot at the Bellevue gates."

"What about the gunpowder?" asked Andelia Bull.

"How much do we have left?"

"A small barrel," said Leila. "Enough for maybe a dozen shots each."

"I'll pester Gus to mix us more. He can requisition saltpeter from the medical commissaries. He tells them it's for treating the rheum."

"We don't have many cartridges prepared," Mary reminded her.

"We'll roll ten each night before we sleep," Nancy ordered.

The women nodded, accepting their assignments with renewed determination.

With both Sherman and Hood gone, Nancy debated which route into the town was now the most vulnerable. "If an enemy approaches—deserters, Yankee marauders, Negro gangs—we have no way to receive a warning. We'll set up a relay for messages with the women in Newnan and West Point. They can send their Negro boys running—"

"You trust the darkies?" asked Mary.

Before Nancy could insist they had no alternative, a hard knock rattled the door. The women backed away, alarmed. Nancy signaled for the muskets to be distributed. When they were armed, she cracked the door open.

A bright-eyed man in an over-sized businessman's coat and baggy pants stood at the threshold. Nancy guessed him to be no older than twenty. He nervously regarded the armed women, doffed his gray slouch hat, and bowed. "Mrs. Morgan?"

"Yes."

"I am James Edward Hanger, medical inventor of Staunton, Virginia."

"I'm sorry, have we met?"

"Dr. Augustus Ware of your acquaintance referred me." The man reached into his breast pocket and produced a calling card scribbled with Gus's signature. "He said you would be most interested in my wares."

Nancy set her jaw and mulled over the various ways she would get even with Gus for subjecting her to another of his pranks. He never tired of sending the endless arrivals of quacks and potion pushers to pester her. "I apologize for the misunderstanding, sir, but I am only a volunteer at one of the hospitals in town. I have no requisition authority."

When she moved to close the door, he blocked it with his boot. "Ah, you are too modest, Mrs. Morgan. I have asked around this bucolic burgh. You are universally regarded as the *de facto* mayor."

"And *you* are too kind, but we are engaged with pressing matters and—"

"A race."

"Sir?"

He glanced around the room at the scowling women fingering the triggers on their muskets. "Who among you is your fastest Atalanta?"

"You mean runner?"

He pistoned his elbows back and forth as if to mimic an ancient Greek competitor on the Olympic track. "I propose a match. I will walk, and the sprinter of your choice may use any mode of ambulation she wishes. If she prevails, I will never darken your doorstep again."

Nancy sighed. She figured the quickest way to get rid of the buffoonish hustler was to let his jest play out. "Leila!"

The women stacked their muskets and followed Nancy, Leila, and the peddler into the yard. Leila kicked off her shoes, eager to put the intruder in his place. She lifted the hem of her dress just above her ankles and settled into her stance for a fast start. "To that tree." Nancy set their finish line thirty feet away. "One ... two ... three."

Leila jumped to the lead, but the pushy peddler hung with her, fast-walking as if he had waged a race like this a thousand times. She staggered toward the tree, clenching her rustling folds. The huckster kicked into a higher gear at the finish and beat her by a nose. Leila bent to catch her breath while the man stood over her, not the least winded. He offered his arm and escorted her back to Nancy and the disappointed women.

"She is to be commended," Hanger said. "One of the most nimble competitors I have yet to encounter on my journeys."

Nancy glowered a reminder at Leila that she was no longer as young and spry as she constantly insisted. She told Hanger, "We promised to hear you out. But you shouldn't be crowing about your skill in walking. Any of the ancient galoots in this town could manage what you just did."

"Ah, but could they do it with one leg?"

Only then did Nancy notice the row of gilt buttons on the outer seam of the man's voluminous left pant leg. Hanger unclasped the baggy pantaloons to reveal a prosthetic limb made of barrel staves, metal hinges, and rubber tendons. The lower half of the contraption was designed to slide up over the stump below the thigh, mimicking the joints and allowing for the knee and ankle to bend without flopping around. The effect produced a natural gait.

The women gasped in amazement as Hanger removed the leg and displayed a cone-shaped socket that reached halfway to his hip. He demonstrated the flexibility of the artifice while balancing on his good foot. The women rushed around him to examine the marvel of engineering.

Nancy asked Leila to bring out a chair from the schoolhouse. She helped Hanger sit. "Sir, I owe you an apology."

"Not at all, Mrs. Morgan. If I could take you and Miss Leila here on the road as my assistants, I could sell a hundred more legs a day."

"What possessed you to design such a blessing?" asked Caroline.

Hanger basked in the glow of their admiration as he turned over his *carte-de-viste* to reveal several testimonials from satisfied customers. "I studied engineering at Washington College in Lexington. When the war came, my two older brothers volunteered for the cavalry. I wanted to join them but wasn't old enough. So, the local militia assigned me to guard duty near our railroad. First time I ever saw the Yankees, they brought a cannon up and fired at me. I have the dubious honor of being the first amputee of this war."

"The Almighty's ways are mysterious, sir," said Mary.

"Truer words were never spoken, madam," said Hanger. "As I dragged my bleeding body into a hayloft to hide from the enemy that day, I felt sorry for myself, caught in the grip of despair. I vowed to the Lord that if, in His infinite wisdom, He spared me, I would devote my life to His work of healing. I got right tired of that wooden peg they attached to me, so I dreamed up a replacement the Almighty Himself might fashion."

Nancy turned to Leila. "Go fetch Seth at the ward."

Mary gathered the other women even closer, as if sensing what Nancy had in mind. "Mr. Hanger, can we offer you tea? I'm afraid we don't have sugar."

"Much appreciated."

Aley Smith retrieved the pitcher and poured Hanger a glass.

"How did you manage to reach us this far south?" asked Nancy.

Hanger enjoyed a long, refreshing slurp. "No Yankee army can keep me from my mission. I have been visiting our hospitals from Richmond to Atlanta. The railroad guards don't find me much of a threat."

Nancy ran her hand across the hinges of his prosthesis. She could tell by the smooth shaving and precise fit of the moving parts that Hanger was an artist who valued his craft as much as Da Vinci treasured his inventions and artwork. "How long does it take you to cobble one of these together?"

"Three months. I employ a company of disabled veterans to help me in my shop in Virginia. The work must be done by hand. I have a backlog of orders, and delivery time depends on the rail lines remaining open."

"I can see you take great pride in your work." Nancy lifted a plaintive look at him. "I suspect the legs are prohibitive in cost."

"I take barter these days. Richmond money is worth less than kindling."

Leila returned with Seth on his crutches.

Hanger brought a finger to his chin in thought, evidently understanding at once what Nancy intended. "We can give it a try. But I strive to fit each apparatus to precise measurements."

Nancy knelt and untied the knot in the pant leg under Seth's stump so that Hanger could examine the amputation.

Hanger pulled off his prosthetic and slipped it on Seth. "Not a bad match." He motioned for Seth to try walking without his crutches.

Seth took several steps without assistance. He turned to Nancy with tears.

Nancy glanced at the other women with a silent plea, and they nodded. She told Hanger, "We'll gather what we own of value and you can decide on your trade."

Hanger waved off her offer. "I don't take payment until I deliver and the patient is satisfied."

"We wish to place an order for two."

He reacted with pleasant surprise. "Of course. I'll need the other fellow's measurements."

"You'll have them before you leave. The second leg is to be a gift for a dear patriot." She pointed an admonishing finger at Seth and the other women. "Not a word of this to General Tyler. We'll tell him we're taking measurements for a wooden peg."

*   *   *

As General Tyler drove their carriage across one of the two bridges that spanned the Chattahoochee River, Nancy caught her first glimpse of the fort constructed atop the highest hill in West Point to guard the railroad approaches. The unimpressive earthworks were nothing like the sophisticated defenses she had observed at Fredericksburg. A lone square of raised dirt, only forty feet in width, had been bolstered in haste by a palisade of stakes on the south wall and a surrounding ditch, ten feet deep and fifteen feet wide. The ramparts were so primitive they lacked banquettes for defenders to stand on and fire down the hill. Though she dared not express her dismay to the general, she had gained enough military acumen over the past four years to realize this so-called citadel was nothing more than a slaughter pen.

"I've withheld some news from you," the general confessed.

She tightened the shawl around his neck. "Are you sure you're not chilled? Gus gave me firm instructions you are not to—"

"I received orders this week from General Hood to take command of the defenses here. I am to hold West Point at all costs."

She was horrified. "You are in no condition to accept such an assignment. The pneumonia could worsen."

He shrugged, stifling a cough. "What is the disease called? The old man's blessing?"

"You are *not* old, and I've seen too many young men die from pneumonia. I assure you, the affliction is no blessing. And how does General Hood expect you to command this post hobbling on one leg?"

The general winked. "He commands the entire Army of Tennessee with one leg and one arm."

She folded her arms and harrumphed, disgusted with the utter stupidity of governments and armies.

"Mrs. Morgan ..."

"Call me Nannie, at least. Have we not become friends?"

"Of course." He smiled with empathy for her distress. "I acknowledge my return to duty may seem a selfish stubbornness, but did you not meet with the same resistance when you persisted with your militia?" When she gave him a sideways glance, he reassured her. "You needn't worry over me. I have no intention of allowing the Yankees to capture these bridges. I've requisitioned a thirty-two pound Parrott gun and two twelve-pound howitzers from Columbus. I plan to place them at the corners of the fort. That should provide us effective coverage."

Nancy counted a dozen men manning the miserable little station. "You surely can't expect to defend the town with so few soldiers?"

"I've requested transfers from the militias and guard detachments at Andersonville and Macon."

She scanned the higher environs northwest of the town and saw several stately homes within musket shot of the fort. "Will those houses not be in the line of fire?"

The general sighed. "Some may have to be dismantled."

Nancy slumped. She knew many of the families who resided here. Sunny Villa, the plantation abode of Sallie Fannie Reid, sat across the river, and Sarah Potts, Sallie's sharpshooting friend, lived a few hundred yards to the east of the hill. The fort sat smack in the backyard of Louisa Griggs's columned home.

Seeing her so distressed, Tyler promised, "I will do all in my power to save the abodes."

Thankful for his intercession, she sighed. "What will become of us?"

He gazed south while deflecting her question. "Did I ever tell you I almost became a king?"

"What?"

"Well, perhaps not a king, but at least a *conquistador.*"

"You toy with me, General."

"Not at all. Before the war, I was an adventurer of sorts. You've heard of William Walker?"

"The filibusterer?"

"I served as Walker's senior officer." He grinned at her astonishment. "We came within weeks of establishing a new American state in Nicaragua. It was a paradise."

"What denied you your dream?"

He shrugged. "The old-line conservatives in the country chased us out. But I have never forgotten those cooling breezes and lush forests. If we fail here, Nannie, I intend to take a frigate back to Nicaragua, or to Brazil. Establish a new Confederate country where Lincoln can't harass us. You and your husband should join us."

She couldn't fathom leaving LaGrange, and she wished to speak no more of it. The sun was dying fast; they still had more than an hour's journey back north. "The temperature will drop soon. I'll catch Hades from Gus if I return you with your cough worsened."

The general delayed turning the carriage around. "I have a confession. I didn't ask you to ride out here with me for the sole purpose of inspecting the fort, though I value your opinion. May I confide in you?"

"Always."

He struggled to find the words. "Because I will be here in West Point directing the strengthening of the defenses, Miss Reid has found accommodations for me. She has generously offered to oversee my convalescence."

Nancy felt a pang of the old jealousy return, but she chased it, knowing Sallie held the general's best interest in mind. "We will miss you terribly, but you must do what you think best."

"I will return often to LaGrange. You ladies cannot be rid of me that easily. I still have more yarns to spin."

"You will be welcome any time."

He dropped his gaze and lowered his voice. "There is something more."

She sensed he was troubled. "Please."

"I have formed a deep bond with Miss Reid."

Nancy caught her breath short. "You mean ..."

"I love her."

Nancy tried to hide any evidence of emotion that might cause him to think her judgmental. This was her fault. She asked Sallie to give special attention to the general to spare the hearts of the unattached girls. Never in her wildest dreams did she expect him to fall for a betrothed woman, even one as charming as Sallie.

"I have placed you in an untenable position."

"General ... Sallie is spoken for."

"Captain Grant, yes. I have made every effort to avoid the impropriety, but I am tortured beyond relief."

"Has Sallie ..."

"Shown reciprocation? I would never be so bold as to ask her. Yet there have been indications. A touch here, a look there. I've never excelled at translating the social gestures." He studied her. "Has she expressed feelings for me?"

Nancy silently repeated the adage about good deeds always punished. She tried artfully to dodge his question. "Sallie and I have become friends, but when we were younger, we were rivals for the same gentleman. I doubt she would share her innermost passions with me."

"If she should ask ..."

"I will attest without hesitation that you are one of the most gallant and chivalrous men I have ever had the honor to know."

* * *

Nancy spent the next week mired in melancholy; it required all of her strength just to get out of bed. General Tyler's transfer to West Point had struck her harder than she expected, and the hospital ward was gloomier without his boisterous stories and unflagging encouragement to the wounded men. She thought nothing could bring her lower until a knock pounded at her door that morning. She threw on her dress and hurried down the stairs, praying it was not a courier with a casualty list containing Brown's name. She opened the door to find General Hardee's wife, sobbing and clutching a letter. She led Mary Hardee inside and brought her to a chair. "What has happened?"

Mrs. Hardee handed her the letter. "From Sue Tarleton ... General Cleburne is dead."

Nancy's legs threatened to fail. She reached for the arm of another chair, staggered into it, and read the letter through tears. "John Bell Hood murdered him and five more of our generals in Tennessee?"

"At a town called Franklin. Sue says the charge was downright suicidal." Mrs. Hardee's faced pinched with raw anger. "That madman Hood was always jealous of poor Pat and my William."

Nancy gasped at the second paragraph of the letter. In a ragged hand, Sue wrote that she had been walking in her garden in Mobile when she heard a boy delivering newspapers shout that "her Gallant Pat" had been killed during an assault on the Union breastworks. "Sue fainted on the spot. ... Oh Lord, I wish she were here for us to comfort."

"She has vowed not to leave her bedroom for a year."

Nancy folded the letter and returned it to Mary Hardee, feeling utterly helpless. The tragedies came rushing in daily now. Brown was somewhere in Virginia or North Carolina, fighting God knows what Yankee army. Caroline's husband, John Gay, wasted away in the trenches of Petersburg with what few Troup County men survived in the Fourth Georgia. The governor had called up Mary Heard's husband, Peter, to the auxiliary guards. General Hardee was desperately trying to hold off Sherman from advancing to Savannah. Half of Georgia lay burnt to the ground, and nary a man with four working limbs could be found in LaGrange.

She felt a kick of protest in her womb. She rubbed her stomach and begged her unborn child's forgiveness for bringing it into such a broken world. She sat in agonized silence with Mrs. Hardee, both lost in their grief, and then muttered through tears, "Will it never end?"

30

NASHVILLE, TENNESSEE
MARCH 1865

As Hugh's train rolled into the state capital, the earthen redoubts of Fort Negley appeared on the city's southern outskirts where, three months earlier, General Thomas had thrown back the Army of Tennessee.

John Bell Hood is bent on destruction.

Hugh never could have imagined such devastation four years ago. His interrogation of Confederate prisoners confirmed that the irascible Texan, enraged by what he perceived as insubordination by his division commanders, had ordered the reckless assault at Franklin out of sheer spite. That madness cost Hood six generals, including his most effective, Patrick Cleburne. A sane man would have retreated and regrouped, but Hood, embittered and heartbroken at his rejection by a Richmond woman half his age, staggered north with his dispirited army and rammed his battered head against these Nashville battlements and the Army of the Cumberland.

Hugh glanced east toward the Carolinas and wondered what Joe Wheeler was thinking about these Confederate catastrophes. His old nemesis was now the only barrier between the city of Charlotte and Sherman's army. Grant's right-hand man had cut himself loose from his supply lines and had marched his army of gritty Westerners three hundred miles across Georgia to Savannah, living off the land and burning everything in his path. Hugh repeated the prayer he had offered every night in prison: *Before it ends, give me one more match with Wheeler.*

He pulled the War Department dispatch from his pocket and read the cryptic order again: *Report to the headquarters of the Army of the Cumberland in Nashville immediately for reassignment. Your regiment will follow under Colonel Harden's command.* He felt certain he would be sent East to serve under General Judson Kilpatrick. Sherman knew he understood Wheeler better than any cavalry officer in the West. Yes, he would soon capture Fighting Joe and make amends for his humiliating capture at Varnell's Station.

The sun broke through the clouds and flashed a reflection of his drawn face on the window pane. Three months of imprisonment had aged him a decade. Deep worry lines furrowed his forehead, bags hung on his high cheekbones below his eyes, and specks of gray peppered his flowing auburn hair. After his barber stop in Hopkinsville, all that remained of his unruly prison beard was a flowing mustache that terminated in waxed upturned points. The quartermaster issued him a new uniform with his old measurements, but the trousers and campaign sack coat dwarfed him. Perhaps it *was* best that Jennie never see him again. Four years of killing and suffering had hardened him beyond recognition. He was not fit to be a domesticated husband or father. This war was grinding to an end, and he had no plans for the rest of his life.

The train screeched into a depot teeming with Union soldiers loading wagons and making preparations for the next campaign. Something big was in the works. He stepped onto the platform, and a contingent of cavalry troopers, commanded by a sergeant, saluted him. Without a word of welcome, the officer escorted him across the street to the St. Cloud Hotel and led him through the lobby to the saloon. The sergeant announced his arrival.

A uniformed man of slender build stood at the bar with one boot resting on the railing. He turned with a glass of whiskey in his hand and offered a toast. "The Murat of the Union cavalry returns from his Egyptian captivity."

Hugh didn't recognize this officer with a light complexion, a twinkle in his blue eyes, and a handlebar mustache and goatee. On his shoulders sat the two stars of a brevet major general. He didn't look any older than twenty-five. How had he gained such a lofty rank? Hugh had developed the ability to size up soldiers at first encounter. This general, he estimated, was ambitious, quick-witted, always in the right place with the right people. Clearly, he didn't suffer fools.

As the other officers raised their glasses, the general grinned even wider and grabbed a bottle from the bar. Detecting Hugh's skepticism, he quipped, "Yes, I am just weaned from the nursemaid's breast, but a fine breast it was." The officers laughed, evidently accustomed to such witticisms. Their informality and camaraderie impressed Hugh and put him at ease.

"I'm afraid we have no French wine for the Marishal." The general offered him the bottle. "Will Tennessee bourbon donated by the Jackson family from the Hermitage cellar suffice?" As Hugh offered his tumbler to acknowledge the good-natured needling, the general poured two fingers of whiskey while studying him. "We've never met."

"No, sir."

The general extended a hand. "James Wilson."

"From the Army of the Potomac. You rode with Sheridan at Cedar Creek. Did you steal Grant's saddle? To be punished and sent out here?"

Wilson winked. "I prefer to believe Sheridan grew jealous of my superior horsemanship. You're a geologist, I'm told."

"I dabbled in the science."

"Odd vocation for a cavalryman."

"To be honest, when I joined up, I couldn't tell a cantle from a pommel."

Wilson and his officers chortled, lifting their whiskeys in shared commiseration. Wilson spun his finger around the rim of his glass. "I was trained as a topographical engineer. Sherman admired the proficiency with which I shoveled horse shit, so he assigned me to the Cavalry Bureau in Washington to reassess our tactics." He took another sip. "I don't suppose you have an opinion on that subject?"

"On horse shit or our tactics?"

Wilson laughed. "Has there been much of a difference?"

Hugh debated how forthcoming he should be. "Last time I offered advice, General McCook used my jaw to light his match."

"You can speak freely here."

The informal confidence exuded by this young general convinced Hugh he could trust him. "We scatter our cavalry. Screening. Foraging. We could be more effective as a separate force. Hit deep into enemy territory without being chained to infantry. A shock troop that could hit and run."

"No supply train? How would we feed our troopers and mounts?"

"John Hunt Morgan raided across Indiana and Ohio for three weeks with a few green apples in his forage pouch. Bedford Forrest commands his cavalry like infantry. Wheeler rampaged across Tennessee, plundering our wagons. We could live off the land as Sherman did below Vicksburg."

Wilson motioned for his officers to shutter the windows, and then he confirmed with his adjutant, "Guards are posted?"

"Yes, sir."

With the room secured, the general's adjutant retrieved a transport tube from his saddle bag. He removed a regional map of Alabama, Mississippi, and Georgia and tacked it to the boards. The other officers gathered around it.

Wilson put a hand on Hugh's shoulder and pointed his attention to Gravelly Springs, an Alabama town southwest of Nashville. "When the floodwaters recede, I'm taking three divisions across the Tennessee River. Thirteen thousand troopers deep into the underbelly of the Confederacy. No infantry. Only a few wagons for ammunition. Each division will bring one battery of artillery."

Hugh traced the fording route. "Northern Alabama is defended by—"

"Bedford Forrest."

He suddenly comprehended what Wilson was proposing. "He'll draw you in and try to starve you, then gnaw at you like a rabid polecat at night."

Wilson raised the lid on a portable humidor and passed the box around. He lit his cigar and puffed it hard. "Did you ever go spelunking in your geology days, Colonel?"

"More times than I wished."

"I can sum up what little I remember of the caving science in one maxim."

"And that is?"

"If the hole is dangerous and narrow, go in through the front, keep crawling head first, and come out through the rear."

Hugh glanced at the map again. "You don't mean to—"

"I hear the magnolias in southern Georgia are a sight to behold this time of year." Wilson ran his finger down the map, pausing at Selma and Montgomery, before tracking east to the Georgia border.

Hugh assessed the reactions of the others to determine if they thought the raid as daring but reckless as he did. To a man, the officers grinned at the chance to launch the wilding expedition.

Wilson flicked his ashes to the floorboards. "I intend to split off three thousand troopers and send them on a parallel route north of my main force to capture the bridges over the Chattahoochee River and the last operating rail line from Atlanta to Montgomery. If we succeed in this thrust, we'll cut the war short by months and save thousands of lives. To command this auxiliary force, I require an officer who thinks quickly in the saddle and acts with boldness. But if you feel your lecture on cavalry tactics should be relegated to theory—"

"Why me?"

Wilson gestured for a dispatch from his adjutant. He read a passage from it aloud: "'In your consolidation, whatever you do, see to it that LaGrange retains his brigade. For nearly two years, he has proved himself one of the very best cavalry officers in the Army. If this mission is completed, I desire to add my personal request for his promotion to brigadier general.'" Wilson took a long puff on his cigar. "Signed, General George H. Thomas."

The commendation stunned Hugh. He thought the sleepy general who advised Rosecrans to stand firm during the evening council of war at Chickamauga had long since forgotten him.

Wilson enjoyed Hugh's surprise. "Seems I'm not the only wet-eared officer who collects admirers in high places. I've looked into your record, Colonel. One matter gives me pause."

Hugh straightened. "I take full responsibility for my capture—"

"No, not that. I'm told you failed to keep a commitment to your old regiment. We can't have such a dereliction."

Hugh searched his memory for what malfeasance he might have committed against his First Wisconsin troopers.

Wilson signaled for his officers to open the doors to the saloon. "Do you know what Napoleon said he prized most in an officer?" When Hugh shrugged, Wilson circled him. "He had to be lucky. Are you lucky, Colonel?"

That question stung Hugh. This war had cost him his mentor, his wife, and his brother, and he had suffered for months in Confederate prisons. He was alive, but the last thing he considered himself was lucky.

"Let's find out how lucky you are."

On the general's signal, a guard opened the door, and two privates carried in a pine crate and pried open the lid. Wilson reached into the crate and pulled out a new Spencer magazine-fed carbine. He cranked the lever guard and pulled the trigger, repeating the motion rapidly until—

"One minute!" his adjutant shouted while watching his pocket watch.

Wilson tossed the carbine to Hugh. "Twenty rounds off in sixty seconds. That's twenty slaving butchers who were at Fort Pillow sent to the grave. Every trooper in your brigade will be armed with one of these. So, the question I pose to *you*, geologist LaGrange. Are you ready to hammer a tunnel through the subterrane of Old Dixie?"

Hugh grinned as he fingered the lightning-fast cocking lever of the magnificent weapon. "Sir, I'm told Joe Wheeler was born in Augusta. You think he might be getting homesick?"

Wilson took another puff on his cigar, tossed the butt into a spittoon, and walked toward the door. "Let's damn well hope so."

31

LAGRANGE, GEORGIA
APRIL 1865

"You are as beautiful as on the night Caroline and I prepared you for your debut," said Mary.

Nancy knew Mary was fibbing. She turned in front of the mirror, checking the stitching on the panels that Mary had sewn onto the sides and waist of her dress to hide her growing womb. Almost eight months pregnant now, she felt large and unsteady, even with the corset. Assaulted by another wave of despair, she gripped the edges of the dresser.

Caroline rushed to her side and pinned a strand of curls that had fallen from her bun. "These stupors are to be expected. My eyes were puffy for weeks from crying before I had Eugene."

Nancy sighed at her reflection in the mirror. Her hair was thinning, and a few more filaments of worry gray had sprouted. "Nine years ago, you two were giving me more dangles. Now you hide them."

Mary embraced her and pinched her cheeks to draw color. "The men will look to you for courage."

"And to whom do *we* look for courage?"

"We've always looked to each other," said Caroline. "And we always will."

Nancy feared she lacked the strength to confront what awaited her in Bellevue's grand parlor. Selma and Montgomery had fallen earlier that week to a horde of Yankee cavalry, and thousands of refugees and freed slaves were retreating east along the rail line toward West Point. The Northern marauders were burning everything in their path. To defend his pitiful fort, General Tyler had rounded up storekeepers, boys, survivors from the Selma siege, and wounded men from the local hospitals. Despite her pleas to stay, Seth and Dash insisted on going with them. This ragtag company of recruits would depart that very night for what she feared was a doomed mission. Yet she vowed not to let them leave without one last soirée, a reminder of better days.

"Nannie," said Mary. "They are waiting downstairs."

"Have the prosthetic legs arrived?"

Caroline and Mary shook their heads.

Nancy slumped. If General Tyler and Seth must go to war again, she had prayed they would fight without crutches, but it was not to be.

She studied a small glass inkwell on the dresser. Senator Hill had thrown its companion stand at Alabama firebrand William Yancey on the floor of the Senate in Richmond. What had become of their dreams for victory and unity? All had now fractured into bickering and recriminations. Savannah was lost, surrendered to Sherman without a shot fired. Hood's army lay scattered and crushed. The telegraph lines were cut below Atlanta, and the trains ran no farther north than Newnan. She hadn't seen a newspaper in weeks. Was Brown in Virginia? Was he even still alive? Was John Gay with him? She preferred the mayhem of the battlefield to this wretched isolation and lack of news. How could she bring a child into a world of such madness?

A cane tapped at the door.

She opened it. Gus stood on the stairwell, waiting to escort her, just as he had on the evening of her coming out. She brought her sleeve to her mouth to stifle a cry from the rush of memories.

He offered his arm. "I have always wished a chance to make amends."

Followed by Mary and Caroline, Nancy took his elbow and emerged from the bedroom. Her militia, some dressed in their old cotillion dresses, modified and worn against tradition due to the scarcity of fine fabric, stood in ranks on the footing below. Sallie Fannie Reid, draped in that same red gown that once so enraged Nancy, waited with them, along with the young West Point sharpshooter, Sarah Potts. Accompanied by Leila on the harp, the women sang the song they had opened every militia meeting with during the past four years:

> "Mid pleasures and palaces though we may roam,
> Be it ever so humble, there's no place like home!
> A charm from the skies seems to hallow us there,
> Which seek through the world, is ne'er met with elsewhere.
> Home! Home, sweet, sweet Home!
> There's no place like Home!"

Gus brought Nancy down the stairs without a misstep. She kissed him on the cheek, raising a blush, and whispered, "You will always be my first champion." Gus staggered against his cane, choking back a cough. She steadied him with a hand to his back. "For our brothers, Gene and Joe, tonight."

Gus nodded, tremoring, and escorted her into the grand parlor. The Nancies and the two West Point women filed in behind them. The candles in the windows were lit, an extravagance Nancy had demanded. At the far end of the room, standing in the flickering shadows, stood the officers of the new West Point garrison, attired in their frayed gray uniforms.

General Tyler, his collar speckled with stars, stepped forward on his crutches and bowed. "To the grand ladies of LaGrange, we are forever in your debt." He brought his officers to his side. "May I present my staff? Captain Celestino Gonzales, a dear friend from the First Florida regiment. His family has a long and renowned history in the Spanish defense of Pensacola."

Gonzales, a tall, dark-skinned Catalan, bowed with élan. "The General speaks too graciously of me."

Tyler introduced the other officers. "Lieutenant Louis McFarland, formerly of General Maney's staff. Lieutenant William Slatter of the First Tennessee. And I believe you know Major Rutledge Parham of the Twenty-Fourth Alabama and Colonel James Fannin of the Georgia Reserves."

"You are all most welcome here." Nancy brought to her side the wife of Senator Hill. "Let us express our heartfelt gratitude to Mrs. Hill, who generously offered Bellevue for the occasion."

"Hear, hear!" the guests said.

Dash, recruited as a server, passed around trays with glasses of muscadine wine, the only spirits Nancy could find. With the Yankees approaching, she dared not rely on the Negroes for loyal servanting for fear they might abscond with the general's plans for the West Point defense. She raised her glass in a toast. "To those we have lost. They will never be forgotten."

"Never," said General Tyler.

Nancy glanced at Gus and nodded a prearranged signal.

Gus cleared his voice. "Ladies and gentleman, Mrs. Morgan has drafted me for dance-call duty. I am a novice at the profession, so I beg for your patience. Miss Pullen will play the harp. And if we can impose upon Miss Reid to take a turn at the piano? Shall we start with a contredanse?"

Gus tapped the beat with his cane as the men found partners and the ladies lined up opposite them. Unable to join in because of his infirmity, General Tyler came aside Sallie and asked permission to stand at the piano while she played. Nancy signaled for Dash to bring a chair for the general. Sallie struck the chord to launch the dancers into their progressions.

After several tunes, including a rousing waltz, Sallie beckoned Aley Smith to her side. "I am monopolizing the keys. Nannie has often told of your talent. Please play for us."

Aley retreated a step, astonished. "Miss Reid, I'm a novice compared to you."

"You took Professor Chase's instruction, didn't you?"

"Yes, but—"

"You will do grand." Sallie turned to her admirer sitting next to her. "General, will you excuse me for a moment? I must freshen up."

Tyler held onto the top of the piano to pull himself up on his good leg. He pleaded, "Do not be long."

Sallie offered the piano bench to Aley. She threaded through the mingling dancers and, looking over her shoulder for an opportunity when the general was not watching, hurried to Nancy and whispered, "A word alone?"

Nancy observed her glancing worriedly at the general. When he was distracted, Sallie took her by the hand and led her through the foyer to another room. She closed the door behind them. "In the carriage on the way here, General Tyler professed his love for me."

Nancy feared this moment might come.

"Did he give *you* any indication of his sentiments?" asked Sallie.

Nancy was torn. How could she answer without betraying the general's confidence? "I saw from his warm manner he is smitten with you."

"I am betrothed!"

"Do you ... have feelings for him?"

Sallie turned aside. "I don't know what I feel. I care for him deeply, but—"

"But what?"

"This war has confused everything."

Nancy gathered Sallie's hands into hers. "You remember General Hood's fate after he fell for Buck Preston?"

"Miss Preston withheld her conflicted emotions for months—"

"Until it was too late."

Sallie burst into tears. "I cannot send him into that fort with a broken heart. It destroyed General Hood. He lost the will to live."

"And General Cleburne paid for it with *his* life."

"What must I do, Nannie?"

Nancy saw nothing but hurt arising from whatever she counseled. "You must search your heart and follow it, no matter the consequences. That is all anyone can ask of us, to be true and forthright in our affections."

Applause echoed from the parlor. They hurried back in and found Rutledge Parham on one knee before Leila. Nancy's worst fear for Leila had come to pass.

"Nannie!" cried Leila. "Major Parham has proposed to me!"

The room waited to hear Nancy's reaction. She glared at Parham, trying to divine the trueness of his feelings, but the officer refused to meet her eyes.

"Nannie?" said Leila. "Will you not bless the union?"

Nancy could not bring herself to challenge the overture on the night this officer would leave to fight for their safety. She had to be satisfied with a veiled warning. "Major Parham, if you marry a Nancy Hart, you answer to all of us."

Parham gave her an uncertain nod.

The music struck up again, and the festivities continued, but Nancy sensed the mood darken as the night progressed. There was a desperation in the air, a palpable resistance against allowing time to march on. She scanned the parlor and listened as the conversations turned more serious; the glances became more earnest and the subtlest gestures more pronounced.

In the corner, sitting apart from the others, General Tyler engaged in animated conversation with Sallie, who wiped her eyes. The general took Sallie's hands and pressed them into his, and she laid her forehead on his shoulder. He reached for his crutches. Gus signaled for the music to stop as the general limped to the center of the parlor and waited for silence. The guests, hushing, gathered around him.

"Alas, ladies and gentlemen," said Tyler. "The time has come for my staff and me to depart for West Point. We have many preparations yet to make. I can never repay the generosity and kindness shown to me, to all of us, by you grand ladies of LaGrange. You will remain forever in my heart."

Sniffles and whimpers erupted, followed by patriotic acclamations.

The general lowered his head until the room silenced again. "I would be remiss if I did not recognize two ladies in particular who have comforted my convalescence. Mrs. Morgan, you are as stalwart a leader as any commander I have had the privilege to serve aside."

Nancy, struggling to hold back tears, pressed her folded hands to her breast in a gesture of affection.

Tyler asked his adjutant, Lieutenant McFarland, to retrieve two items from his carry bag hanging on the foyer's cloak rack. The lieutenant returned with a pair of spurs and a gold-capped cane. Tyler offered them to Sallie. "Miss Reid, you have nursed me to health. I look forward to attending your wedding to Captain Grant, but should I be unavoidably detained, I hope you will accept these gifts as a memento of ... of our abiding friendship."

Sallie sank into a chair, undone.

Finding her too distraught to speak, the general placed the gifts on the table next to her. He swept the room with his watering eyes as if to burn into memory every face around him. "May I ask one last indulgence? Captain Gonzales here is a singer of great renown in Pensacola. Would you permit him to close the evening with my favorite song?"

"We would be honored," said Nancy.

Gonzales retrieved a mandolin he had placed at the foot of the piano and came aside the general. "When Napoleon invaded my native country of Spain, many *señoritas* took up arms as their men fell at the barricades. The bravest of them was Agostina, the Maid of Saragossa. Agostina replaced her lover at the cannon when he perished. So impressed were the *generalissimos* with her courage that they promoted her to a lieutenant of artillery, gave her a uniform, and took her with them to Cádiz. There she inspired our people to fight against the hated dictator of France."

"Down with dictators!" cried Leila. "Lincoln with them!"

When the approving shouts died, Gonzales placed a hand to his heart. "With your permission, I will perform for you the *Suspira Por Antequera,* the ballad sung by my family when they left Andalusia years ago. It brought comfort to General Tyler and me over many a campfire during our campaigns together in Nicaragua. On this night, I dedicate it to you, the *valiente Agostinas* of LaGrange." He strummed a chord and sang:

> *"Suspira por Antequera,*
> *El rey moro de Granada;*
> *no suspira por la villa,*
> *que otra mejor le quedaba,*
> *Sino por una morica*
> *Que dentro en la villa estaba*
> *Blanca, rubia a maravilla,*
> *Sobre todas agraciada"*

Tyler joined him in the next stanza, and they sang the rest of the ballad in English:

> "He sighed but for a Moorish maid,
> That lived a captive there,
> With bonnie face and rosy cheeks,
> The fairest of the fair.
> Her sixteenth year had come and gone,
> Her seventeenth year now smiled;
> More than his eyes he loved her well,
> Had loved her from a child.
> His words were mingled with the tears
> That burns within my heart,

Red with the wounds that pain my breast,
Pierced with a golden dart.
Thou gavest me this answer sad:
That writing could not save;
Then Almeria I will give
To be thy ransom brave.
To Antequera I will go."

When the two officers finished, the guests stood in silence, prisoners to their own prayers and dashed dreams.

Tyler bowed and led his staff to the door.

Nancy rushed after him. Desperate to delay him a moment more, she risked the intimacy of placing her hand on his against the handle on his crutch. Tyler smiled at her with his eyes full of heartbreak, kissed her gloved hand, and limped out.

Still recovering from his departure, Nancy found Sallie standing alone in a corner of the parlor, her back turned. She hurried over to comfort her. "I will have Seth drive you back to Sunny Villa in Caroline's carriage."

"Thank you. The General offered to take me, but ..."

"You needn't explain." Nancy glanced over her shoulder at the other women offering their goodbyes to the soldiers. She led Sallie out of earshot. "Do not place yourself in danger when the Yankees arrive."

"You are a fine one to talk."

"I'd ask a favor, if you find it possible."

"Anything."

"Send a rider to warn us what's coming up that road."

Sallie hugged her. "God bless and protect you, Nannie."

32

Morning church bells rang in Easter Sunday as Seth and Dash scrambled up the hill with the other recruits and hurried through the sallyport of Fort Tyler, the name given by West Point residents to the redoubt. A half-mile southeast, along the Chattahoochee River, hundreds of refugees from Selma and Montgomery crowded around the town's train depot, desperate to reach Macon before the Yankee raiders arrived. Yet with the rail lines destroyed above Newnan and east of Columbus, the locomotives and the boxcars filled with cotton bales sat idle.

Colonel Fannin brought out two muskets from the small gunpowder magazine built in the center of the fort. He tossed them to Seth and Dash. "Join the others on the east rampart."

Seth wiped the dust from his rusty smoothbore. The gun looked as if it hadn't been fired in years. He glanced around and estimated there were only two hundred and fifty defenders, mostly boys, old men, shopkeepers, invalids, and convalescents. "Colonel, when are the rest coming?"

Fannin gave him a handful of cartridges. "This is all the help we're getting."

As the colonel moved on down the line, Seth brought Dash to his side at the earthen wall, which barely reached their shoulders. He looked northwest toward a white-columned house that sat forty yards from the fort. In the valley, a girl stood on the porch of a nearby cottage watching the battle preparations. "Hey, Dash, ain't that Sarah Potts? The gal from the soirée?"

Dash grinned and waved at her. "Halloo, Sarie!"

Sarah held up her prized musket to show she was ready for a fight.

"Somebody oughta tell her to skedaddle." Seth called out to Fannin. "Colonel, that cabin ain't cleared!"

Fannin shrugged. "The family won't leave."

Seth shook his head at the stubborn ignorance of civilians who had never seen a bloodbath. He wiggled the balky hammer on his musket and muttered to Dash, "This ain't what we signed up for."

"Maybe there won't be many Yankees."

Seth shot a ball of sputum over the wall and watched it land in the dry moat. On the sloping approaches below, a few trees had been felled to serve as abatis, but he reckoned those wouldn't slow a cow from getting at a patch of grass. "Yeah, maybe. It'd be the first time, though."

The bugler sounded assembly, and General Tyler limped on his crutches into the fort. Behind him came his adjutant, Lieutenant McFarland, Captain Gonzales, and a dozen cannoneers furloughed from Waite's South Carolina Battery and the Point Coupee Battery from Louisiana. His face drawn but determined, Tyler saluted the huddled defenders and led his artillerymen around the perimeter. He assigned four men to the Napoleon twelve-pounders at the northwest and southwest corners and eight men to the thirty-two pound Parrott siege boomer at the southeast corner overlooking the bridges. Satisfied with the deployments, Tyler staggered to the mast in front of the powder magazine.

"Attention!" shouted Gonzales.

The men kneeling under the walls looked at each other, confused, many unfamiliar with military protocol. A few stood, followed by the rest of the defenders. Major Parham raised their new battle flag, sewn by the ladies of West Point and gifted to the general earlier that week.

"I know each man here will do his duty," said Tyler. "Your mothers, wives, and daughters depend on us. If we fail to hold this position, Macon and Columbus will be lost, and with them, our Confederacy. Should I fall, Captain Gonzales will take command. Some of you have never faced battle. Today, you become soldiers. Your grandsons and granddaughters will tell stories of your valor. I have never been prouder of a command. God be with you."

As the ragtag defenders waved their hats and cheered, a barefoot boy in torn pants sneaked into the fort and tried to fall in without being noticed.

Tyler spotted him. "How old are you?"

The boy saluted. "Eight, sir."

"Your name?"

"Alexander Anderson."

"You're too young, son."

The boy collapsed in tears. "The Yankees killed my brothers."

Moved by the boy's keen disappointment, Tyler called him forward. "I have a mission for you. You see that hill to the north? I need you to serve as my watch there."

Dash whispered, "I thought the Yankees were coming from the southwest."
Seth shushed him.

Tyler wrote a dispatch in his order book, tore out the page, and handed it
to the boy. "I hereby promote you to Major Anderson. Now, off you go."

Thrilled, the boy ran out, unaware he was being sent from harm's way.

Seth cocked his ear to hear Tyler give orders to McFarland.

"Lou, take twenty men and set a skirmish line across the Opelika Road."

McFarland hesitated. "These houses around us may present a problem if
the Yankees get close."

"I can't destroy them. The folks here have been too kind to me."

McFarland answered with a reluctant salute and turned to choose his skirmishers. He came to Seth and saw his crutches. Passing him by, he pointed to
Dash. "You come with me."

Seth protested. "Sir, Dash here ain't exactly—"

"I don't have time to argue. Now!"

Hugh led the Seventh Kentucky and First Wisconsin regiments on a trot east
along the Auburn pike. He halted his column and listened to the distinctive
bursts of Spencer carbines erupting beyond the line of cottonwoods ahead.
He had learned to gauge the intensity of an engagement by the rapidity of distant firing. The advance elements of his cavalry brigade—the Second Indiana,
the Fourth Indiana, and the Eighteenth Indiana Battery—had likely run into
a Rebel skirmish line, a mile off by the echoes. He surveyed the abandoned
cotton fields and spotted a slave cabin near a small creek. His method of reconnaissance had become so habitual he didn't need to issue the order.

Colonel Harnden of the First Wisconsin detached three troopers and sent
them to the cabin. They returned with an elderly slave who sprouted tufts of
white hair around his ears. The frightened Negro kept glancing around as if fearful his overseer might spy him riding with a white man.

"Good afternoon to you, sir," said Hugh.

The slave stammered, but no sound came from his lips. He seemed unable
to comprehend being spoken to by a superior in such a polite manner.

"Today you are a free man, compliments of President Lincoln."

The old slave slid from the trooper's horse and dropped to his knees to kiss
the earth.

"What awaits us up ahead?" asked Hugh.

The man wiped his eyes and climbed back to his bare feet. "Georgia, massah. That be Georgia."

"The town?"

"West Point. The rails meet in there."

"Is it defended?"

"I heard tell they built the Walls of Jericho on the highest hill to guard the town depot."

"How many bridges?"

"The railroad crosses the waters on the north side. There's the wagon span a few blocks south that leads to Kings Gap Road."

Hugh checked his watch: 1:30 p.m. This report matched his expectation. His Hoosier regiments had been trading sporadic fire in West Point for two hours. If the retreating Rebels intended to put up a final defense, it would be here, at the most important connection in the last rail artery of the deep Confederacy. His troopers and horses were exhausted from helping General Wilson break the siege at Selma and driving two hundred miles east. Wilson had taken his main body of cavalry toward Columbus, leaving him to split off to the north with 3,700 troopers and destroy the railroad and bridges along the Chattahoochee. They needed a day's rest, but his Indiana regiments, always ready for a fight, had found one. He reached to shake the elderly black man's hand. "You have a family?"

"Yessuh."

"Once we get those hills cleared of the Rebels, you bring your kinfolk into town. We'll see you and yours safe to a refugee camp."

"You be careful now. My son seen the Seceshers strappin' gunpowder to the bridges."

Hugh tipped his hat, grateful for the warning.

Seth risked inching his eyes above the redoubt. All around him, blue-clad troopers with carbines jumped off their horses and took positions behind trees and the nearby houses. On Ward's Hill, a half-mile to the west, the Yankees unlimbered a battery of howitzers and began lobbing screaming balls into the fort. The shelling was getting heavier by the minute. Seth glanced over his shoulder and saw Dash scampering back from the Opelika road, followed by McFarland and the skirmishers. Yankee cavalry flashing sabers was on their heels. The entire valley looked like a sack of angry blue hornets had been emptied over it.

Come on, Dash! Run like hell!

Inside the fort, Tyler limped from wall to wall, shouting encouragement. "Don't waste your shots, lads! Let 'em get closer before you pull!"

A Confederate swabber lifted his head to aim his twelve-pounder. He fell backwards. A bullet hole pierced his forehead.

Five hundred yards with those repeaters. Can't come close to that. Despite the general's order to be frugal with the ammunition, Seth loaded and fired his smoothbore as fast as he could to give Dash cover, but the Yankees were snapping off five shots before he managed one. *Damn it, Dash! Just keep headin' north. Don't come back in here.*

Dash dived into the ditch and clawed his way up the embankment.

With carbine bullets buzzing overhead, Seth pulled him over the wall to safety. "You shoulda kept running to Macon."

Dash sat shaking against the rampart.

"You alright?" asked Seth.

Dash, eyes glazed, didn't answer.

Seth hugged his buddy, distressed to find Dash had relapsed into his old trance. "We'll get you back to Miss Nannie. You stay put here."

Outside the fort, McFarland fired one last shot with his pistol at the pursuing troopers. A Yankee bullet grazed his chin. To Seth's amazement, McFarland turned, removed his hat in a dashing gesture, and bowed to the Yankee marksman. Assured the last of his skirmishers had returned to the redoubt, McFarland scrambled up the sloping parapet and leapt into the pen.

Tyler limped to his adjutant. "How many of them are out there?"

McFarland angled his shoulder to prevent the volunteers from hearing his report. "A brigade, maybe more."

The color drained from Tyler's face.

"General!" shouted Fannin at the south wall. "They're trying for the bridges!"

Tyler hurried as fast as he could on his crutches to the big Parrott cannon at the southeast corner. He squinted down its thick black barrel to check the aim. "Wait until the Yankees close within a hundred yards of the river."

Hugh galloped into West Point and halted his column two blocks from the river. He calculated that rangy siege gun on the redoubt to the north could reach the entrance to the railroad bridge. Around him, glaring eyes of angry residents peeked out from behind curtains in the windows. He couldn't remain long in such a vulnerable position before his troopers became targets for sniping from the balconies and rooftops. He clicked open his pocket watch. Dusk would fall in a few hours. If he didn't make a move soon, the Rebels in that fort might escape during the night.

A scout rode up after reconnoitering the bridges. "The Rebs have them ready to blow."

"How many guards?"

"I saw three cavalrymen on foot."

Hugh shielded his eyes in the haze. His dismounted Hoosier troopers were making slow progress up the slopes to the redoubt. They had the fort surrounded, but the Rebels were staging a spirited defense. How many men did the Secesh have inside that pen? A thousand, maybe more? He couldn't wait for his

Indiana boys to storm the hill. He had to take the bridges by surprise before the enemy cavalry destroyed them, or they would all be trapped on this side of the Chattahoochee for days. Determined to gain a foothold by taking aim at the wagon bridge first, he motioned up a courier. "Tell Captain Beck to concentrate his fire on that Parrott gun."

The courier saluted and rode north.

Hugh waited on the deserted street with his Fourth Indiana troopers arrayed in a column behind him. When Beck's artillery bombardment intensified, he ordered his bugler to sound the charge. He galloped up Gilmer Street and turned right at Kings Gap Road. At the wagon bridge, three Rebel cavalrymen stood watching the fireworks over the redoubt. Caught flat-footed, they rushed to their horses just seconds before Hugh was on them. With the bridge now open, he lashed his horse toward the far entry.

Nearly halfway across, he discovered several planks missing.

Are the charges set here?

With no time to inspect the trusses, he drove his horse over the gap and landed with a punishing thud. His troopers followed and secured the eastern approach. Leaving a company to disarm the powder charges, he wheeled back to make the jump again and return to the western side of the river.

Inside Fort Tyler, Seth saw the Yankee cavalry crossing the wagon bridge. There was no escaping to Macon now. He watched as the heaving Tyler cranked the elevation screw on the Parrott gun while two Louisiana men lifted a thirty-two-pound ball and rolled it into the barrel. The general pulled his field glasses from their case and monitored the bridge.

The crew itched to yank the lanyard.

"Steady, lads," said Tyler. "Only on my order."

Hugh patted the neck of his snorting horse, praying it had one more leap in its exhausted legs. He spurred toward the bridge's gap and went airborne.

A boom echoed in the distance.

His horse managed the jump with only inches to spare. He whispered "well done" to its flaring ear—a ball from the Parrott gun crashed onto the bridge and bounded across the planks. The missile smashed into the horse's forelegs. The animal bawled and crumpled.

Thrown, Hugh landed hard on the boards.

Lt. Colonel Lamsen of the Fourth Indiana galloped to him. He dismounted and lifted Hugh to his feet. "Are you hurt?"

Hugh, dazed, shook his head. Lamsen waved up a trooper and ordered him to relinquish his horse. Bruised but with nothing broken, Hugh grimaced as he pulled into the saddle. He saw his first horse had suffered a broken leg. He pulled his revolver and put it out of its misery with a shot to the head.

A courier from the Second Indiana met him at the western entry of the bridge. "Major Hill is wounded."

"Is it serious?"

"His leg may have to be amputated."

Hugh coughed back the grip in his throat. Ross Hill was his favorite officer. If the popular Hoosier lost a limb for that useless mound of Georgia clay up there, some Rebel slaver would pay dearly. "Return to Captain Beck. I want hellfire rained down on those guns up there."

Seth dropped his head in despair. A forlorn hush fell among his fellow defenders as they watched the Yankees flood across the wagon bridge. The Federal battery was now throwing balls into the fort twice as fast, and twenty men lay wounded and dying along the interior of the walls. There was nowhere to shelter them. Next to him, Dash sat on his haunches, shaking in terror.

Amid the groans of the wounded, General Tyler limped from parapet to parapet, offering encouragement and reminding his dwindling force that home lay just beyond the river.

Old Man Camp, the owner of the local hotel, screamed and reeled back from the wall with both eyes shot out. Another whizzing ball crashed into the mast at the powder magazine, cutting it in half and dropping the battle flag. Seventeen-year-old Charlie McNeill, one of Seth's ward mates, found a handful of nails, bit on them with his teeth, and climbed the splintered mast. Two men tossed him the fallen half of the pole. As balls zinged around him, McNeill cobbled the mast together and hoisted the flag again.

Seth set his hat on his ramrod and lifted it over the rampart to draw fire. After several shots pinged around him, he popped his head above the wall, long enough to see the Yankees inching closer up the hill—there were hundreds more. Yankee sharpshooters had invaded the surrounding houses, climbing to the top floors and now firing into the redoubt. He called to McFarland, who crouched three men down the line. "Them shooting from those windows are gonna get us all killed!"

McFarland nodded and crawled to Tyler to plead their case. "We have to send fire into those houses before we lose our cannon crews."

Tyler tried to assess the danger from the Yankee sharpshooters, but the ramparts blocked his view. He pulled a lady's kerchief from his pocket and stared at it, as if recalling precious memories the memento held for him. Seth watched as the general pressed the cloth to his lips. Was it a good luck talisman? Clutching the kerchief between his palm and crutch pad, Tyler limped toward the sallyport.

"General, come back!" pleaded McFarland.

"No!" Gonzales shouted from the west parapet.

Seth watched in disbelief as Tyler ignored their warnings and limped out of the fort. The general stood on his crutches in front of the wall and calmly surveyed the sharpshooters in the windows and on the roofs.

Seth shook his head. Does he *want* to die?

A bullet slammed into Tyler's chest. He staggered—a second bullet splintered his right crutch. He fell and lay motionless.

Seth begged him to rise. "General, back in here!"

Fannin and Rutledge rushed out, dodging carbine fire, and dragged the unconscious general back into the redoubt. At the creaking flagstaff, Gonzales knelt over his old friend and felt for a pulse in his neck. The defenders stopped firing to pray he was still alive.

Gonzales, ashen, looked up and shook his head.

Seth stared through the sallyport at the dirt soaked with the general's blood. The strangest of thoughts then came to him: Here on the border, General Tyler took a bullet in Alabama and died a second later in Georgia. What would they write on his certificate of mortality? Strange how the mind works when death closes in. He couldn't get over the fact that he had fought here for the only officer in the war who straddled two states during his moment of casualty. Damned if that didn't sum up this entire sorry enterprise.

"Captain Gonzales!" shouted Fannin. "Your orders?"

Seth figured surely now the Floridian would burn those houses. Gonzales had been begging Tyler to raze them the entire damn day. Yet the captain shook his head, as if comradeship and chivalry prevented him from countermanding his dead friend's wishes to save the only property still owned by these good folks of West Point rendered destitute by the war.

Hugh stood behind a cottage near the fort's west rampart and waited for the Rebel survivors to surrender. The Eighteenth Indiana's battery bombardment had disabled the three Confederate cannons, but no signal of capitulation came. The sun hurried toward the horizon; it was now a race with darkness.

Impatient, he had no choice but to order an assault and bridge the ditch surrounding the fort. He nodded for his men to pry planks from the houses. When his engineers were ready, he shouted to his troopers huddled on the sloping ground around the fort, twenty yards from the walls. "Two-weeks' furlough to the first man over those parapets!"

The troopers, carrying planks, scrambled to the ditch and dropped their makeshift bridges into place. Those men behind the engineers screamed as they rose up and charged across the boards.

Seth heard a bloodcurdling cheer below the wall. *They are coming.* The Yankees hurled fused shells into the fort, but he and the surviving defenders tossed the grenades back into the ditch. Out of ammunition, he threw rocks.

Gonzales ran toward the sallyport to shove the palisade gate against the opening to block it. A sniper's bullet ripped through his chest. He collapsed, gasping. Fannin dragged him back inside and laid him next to Tyler's body.

"He gonna make it?" cried Seth.

Fannin shook his head.

A defender pulled a white kerchief from his pocket.

McFarland aimed his revolver at the man. "Drop it!"

Hugh cursed as his troopers stalled in the ditch below the ramparts. He abandoned the protection of the house and, dodging fire, charged into the dry moat. He scanned his ducking troopers and saw Sergeant Nichols, the towering Choctaw Indian who had been with him in the First Wisconsin since the first day he saddled a horse. "Nick, show the boys how it's done!"

Inspired by his commander's confidence in him, Nichols screamed an Indian war yell and clawed up the dirt parapet. The troopers followed him.

Seth looked up to find the tallest Indian in God's Creation standing over him with saber drawn. Moments later, hundreds of Yankees lined the top of the ramparts and aimed their carbines and revolvers into the pit.

Fannin, seeing the cause was hopeless, pulled out his white kerchief and waved the rag to surrender.

Hugh climbed atop the wall and gazed into a scene of death and misery. "Who's in command here?"

Fannin and McFarland arose from their knees and stepped forward. "I am Colonel Fannin. This is General Tyler's adjutant, Lieutenant McFarland."

"Where did the others escape?"

"Sir," said Fannin. "There are no others."

"Don't lie to me. How many men defended this fort?"

"Two hundred and fifty."

Stunned, Hugh examined the powder magazine where Gonzales lay mortally wounded next to Tyler's riddled body. He motioned up two troopers. "Take this officer to that house over there. See to it he receives immediate care."

Rounded up with the others, Seth hung tight to Dash while the Yankees marched the Rebel prisoners out of the fort.

As Gonzales was carried away, Hugh stood over the bloodied corpse that had reclined aside the dying Floridian. The Rebel officer's collar bore the three stars of a general. Next to his body lay shards of two broken crutches and a bloody kerchief. He bent to examine them—a bullet whizzed a foot over his head. "In Hell's name!"

The Yankee troopers ducked behind the walls.

"Came from near that house over there," said Harnden.

Fannin said, "Colonel, no man in my command would violate a surrender."

Hugh searched the upper windows of the nearest house for the sharpshooter who tried to kill him. He ordered Harnden, "Take a dozen men and flush out that sniper. Bring him to me."

An hour after dusk, Hugh's staff officers escorted him toward the house that had provided cover for the Rebel sharpshooter. His adjutant gave him the casualty report: Their force suffered seven men killed and twenty-nine wounded. The Confederates, who fought with less than a tenth of the men at his disposal, lost eighteen killed and twenty-eight wounded. Hugh had been in hundreds of fights during the past four years, but none so lopsided in numbers and strength of weapons and yet so fiercely contested.

Led into the parlor, he found Ross Hill, with a bloodied stump, lying on a chaise. A local doctor stood over the major, replacing his bandages. Hugh dropped to a knee and grasped Hill's hand, relieved to find him alive. "You will have one less foot to kick that lazy Hoosier farm mule you always complain about."

Hill managed a wan smile. "I am indebted to Dr. Means here. I'd not be alive without him."

Hugh recalled hearing that name during his interrogation of the Rebel officers. "You are the mayor of this town?"

"Yes, sir."

"You understand I must destroy the rail depot and warehouses?"

The physician hung his head and nodded.

"I'm told the government commissary here holds seven hogsheads of sugar, two thousand sacks of corn, and ten thousand pounds of bacon. I will place these under your jurisdiction to help feed your residents."

The physician looked up, stunned. "You are most generous, Colonel."

"The prisoners will be held across the river. Tomorrow, I will take them on to Macon." Hugh searched the faces of the other injured men in the parlor. "One of the Confederate officers in the fort suffered a grievous wound."

"Yes, Captain Gonzales," the surgeon said. "He is upstairs, unconscious. My wife tends to him, but he will not live through the night. General Tyler's body is being prepared in the other bedroom for burial."

"I am sorry to hear it," said Hugh.

Harnden, carrying a confiscated musket, prodded in a powder-grimed girl who struggled against his grasp. "We found her."

"Found *her*?" asked Hugh.

"The sharpshooter."

"That shot came from more than a hundred yards away! You're sure?"

Harnden nodded. "She was carrying a cartridge case and reloading."

Hugh circled the girl. "How old are you?"

"Old enough to shoot a Yankee who trespasses on my property."

Her fearlessness impressed him. "Your name?"

"Sarah Potts."

Hugh turned to the physician. "She lives here?"

Dr. Means nodded. "Her mother and father are deceased. Her stepfamily sought shelter in Long Cane yesterday, but she insisted on staying."

Hugh saw no contrition in the girl's hard glare of hatred. "You pick up a weapon and fire it in war, you'd best be ready to suffer the consequences."

She sneered at him.

"Should we burn the house?" Harnden asked.

Hugh stared the girl down, and she stared him up, refusing to flinch. He sighed and shook his head. "Remove the hammer on the musket and let her go. Make sure she doesn't tail me and brain me with a rock." He tipped his hat to the physician and walked toward the door.

"You defeated us here!" the girl shouted with raw fury. "There's an army up the road you *won't* defeat!"

The girl's prophecy perplexed Hugh. He hadn't received reports of another Confederate force in the region. He shrugged off her claim as bluster.

Sallie Fannie Reid had stood for hours watching the battle from the porch of Sunny Villa mansion, which sat on the east side of the river. Fires lit the night sky over the bridges, and plumes of pillage smoke billowed from the rail depot, carrying the stench of burning cotton and scorched leather. The Yankees were destroying the ammunition warehouses, rail yards, locomotives, and boxcars.

Several hundred blue-clad troopers galloped onto the plantation grounds and set up camp around her house. She saw from the pitiful band of prisoners being herded across the river that Fort Tyler had fallen. She hurried to the gate and searched out the Yankees tying their horses to the surrounding trees. "Is there a graduate here from the West Point Military Academy?"

A young lieutenant dismounted. "I am, ma'am."

"Sir, I know you are a man of honor, for I have made the acquaintance of many such officers from that place."

"How can I be of service?"

"If you will post a detail of protection for my father's house, I will offer it as a hospital for the wounded."

"I accept your offer."

A loud boom echoed across the river from the northwest heights of town, shaking the ground.

"Is there still fighting?" she asked.

The officer shook his head. "That was the powder magazine in the redoubt. Colonel LaGrange ordered it exploded."

The smoke dissipated, and she could see the far promontory had collapsed into a crater. Was General Tyler still there? The lieutenant prepared to remount when she called him back. "The commander of the fort. Is he among your prisoners?"

"Killed in action."

Sallie struggled to hold back the tears, fearing if she revealed her friendship with General Tyler, the Yankees might burn Sunny Villa in retaliation for his determined resistance. When the officer rode out of sight, she fell to her knees, sobbing.

That night, exhausted by grief and lack of sleep, Sallie tended the wounded men from both armies who lay in Sunny Villa's rooms, bringing them water and cleaning the blood from their limbs. She glanced out the window and saw dozens of prisoners from the fort being led into a makeshift stockade on College Hill, a few hundred yards to the north. The temperature was dropping, and the dejected men stood huddled together, shivering inside the unsheltered pen. She hurried to the pantry and stuffed a sack with what biscuits and ham she had left. After gathering all the quilts, she left the house and approached the Yankee guards. She gave each a ham biscuit. "May I offer the prisoners food and coverings?"

The guards, grateful for the food, nodded.

Admitted entry, she distributed the blankets and biscuit sandwiches to the ragged Southern men. After emptying her sack, she moved toward the gate to return to the house when, in the murk, she glimpsed a familiar face. "Dash?"

The boy, blotched with gunpowder and blood, did not answer. He stood staring at the night sky.

She took his blank face into her hands. "Poor Dash," she whispered. "What have they done to you?"

"That you, Miss Sallie?" asked a familiar voice.

She turned toward the shadows.

"It's me, Seth Coogler." He moved closer with his crutches.

She remembered him from the hospital ward. "Thank God you survived."

"Dash is back to his old ways."

She drew them a few steps away from the guards. "I must get a message to Mrs. Morgan in LaGrange."

Seth barely had the strength to stand on his lone leg. "I ain't much good to you."

She turned to Dash. "You remember Miss Nannie?"

Dash's eyes sparked.

She struggled to remember her French, which wasn't nearly as proficient as Nancy's. "*Nannie est en danger. Je dois l'avertir.*"

Dash nodded—Dr. Erskine's old memory trick worked.

She brought Dash to the Yankee guard. "This boy is suffering a fever. He may die if I don't tend to him here in the house."

"You a nurse?"

"I work at the hospital in town. Ask any of these men."

The guard saw the prisoners nod to affirm her claim.

"I will bring him back in the morning," she pleaded. "I promise. This is my home. I will not abandon it."

The guard chewed on his ham biscuit. Finally, he allowed her to pass.

She led Dash up the porch and into the house.

After an hour passed, Sallie smuggled Dash to an outbuilding set behind the main house. She whispered to him, "Follow the moon in the sky. A mile north, you'll come to a cabin owned by my father's overseer, Mister Dansby. Tell him Sallie Reid wishes him to ride to our nearest cavalry detail. They must warn the women in LaGrange the Yankees are coming tomorrow."

He nodded to show he understood his assignment. "Warn."

She sent him off. "Dash, run fast. And get back here as soon as you can."

33

LAGRANGE, GEORGIA
APRIL 17, 1865

The next morning, shouting outside roused Nancy from her bed in the Heard home, where she had stayed the night. She awakened Mary, and together they rushed downstairs to discover the cause of the commotion on Broad Street.

A Confederate cavalryman galloped through town, warning residents to flee. "The Yankee devils burned West Point! They're heading this way!"

Nancy flagged him to a stop. "How soon will they be here?"

"Before sundown."

"General Tyler?"

"Dead."

Nancy clutched Mary's hand. "How many Yankees are there?"

"Enough of 'em to send these homes up in flames. Get out!"

The southern sky was darkening. Were those rain clouds or smoke heading in from West Point? What happened to Dash and Seth? Was Sallie Reid's plantation destroyed? Before Nancy could ask if any of the Fort Tyler defenders had escaped and were coming to help defend the town, the rider sped off toward the square.

"Nannie?" Mary asked. "What should we do?"

She had planned for such an attack a thousand times in her mind, but now with the danger so real, the moment overwhelmed her.

"We must ring the muster bell," Mary said.

Nancy hurried with Mary to the old schoolhouse on the Bellevue grounds. She found the spare key under the porch urn. Inside, she pulled the bell rope to clang the warning call for their militia to gather. While they waited for the other Nancies to arrive, she and Mary opened the armory cabinet and counted the muskets and bags of cartridges. They hadn't drilled in two months, and the guns were dusty and in need of oiling. She piled the cleaning rags on the desk.

Leila, breathless from her run, arrived first, followed by Aley Smith, Andelia Bull, and Nancy's sister, Augusta. "Is there word from Rutledge?" Leila cried. "Is he alive?"

Nancy handed Leila a musket to clean. "We don't know."

Caroline rushed in cradling her child, and soon forty women, their faces stricken with fear, closed on Nancy.

"West Point has fallen," she said. "General Tyler is dead."

A stunned silence filled the room.

Leila looked to the older women, expecting them to take up the muskets. "Why are we waiting?" When Nancy glanced at Mary, wondering what she thought best to do, Leila pressed her. "Nannie! You've prepared us for this!"

"She's a month from giving birth to her first child," scolded Caroline. "She must think of her family."

Leila reddened. "*Her* family? We have *all* lost family! Some of us *have no* family because of this war. Augusta and I never made our debut. And now you're telling us we should just stand by and watch our homes burn?"

Nancy couldn't bring herself to look at their pinched faces. Lightheaded, she retreated to the window and raised the pane for air.

Frightened by the shouted recriminations, baby Eugene wailed. Caroline patted her back. "Nannie, I will not raise this child as a refugee in a burned-out tenement in Atlanta. This town is as much a part of us as the blood that runs through our veins."

Nancy's emotions were running amok. One moment, she felt indignant, the next, frightened. She gazed across the street and watched the stiffening breeze blow through the boxwoods that Pack Beall planted in 1861, two days before she died. The trees had grown tall and stout. Pack didn't live long enough to see what she accomplished with the militia, but Nancy had never forgotten what Pack told her on that deathbed: *Do not raise their hopes, Nannie, only to dash them.* For four long years, they carried the name, the Nancy Harts. If they caved now, they would be forever humiliated and censured as hypocrites, their grand plans to save the town ridiculed as the folly of foolish women. She drew a deep breath and turned. "We will stand and fight."

Nancy noticed Aley Smith hanging back, lost in her thoughts. "Aley, if you have qualms, no one will hold it against you if you choose not to join us."

Tears rushed to Aley's swollen eyes. "My little Robert is sick. If something happens to me ..."

Nancy embraced her. "You must stay with him."

Mary handed out the muskets and powder.

"We'll muster in front of Mary's house at three o'clock," said Nancy.

"Where do you plan to fight them?" asked Leila.

Nancy found a nub of chalk and drew a crude map of the town on the old blackboard. "The Yankees will come up the road from West Point. They'll likely split off onto Vernon and Broad. There aren't enough of us to defend both streets. We'll form up here on College Hill, next to the gardens. It's the highest ground before they reach Bellevue and our homes. Remember your drill commands. Don't give in to your nerves and fire before my command. If our first volley doesn't turn them back, we'll retreat in good order, as we've practiced, and take up a second position behind the Bellevue fence."

The door opened. Gus limped in with his musket.

Nancy realized what he intended. "No."

Informed of the West Point calamity, Gus gripped the musket with his hands shaking from rage. "I don't intend to be the only man left in this county who never fought the bastards. I'd rather die."

Nancy understood his determination to shed his shame, but she couldn't allow him to fight. "Gus, you've done more for the folks in this town than most soldiers. We can't risk you getting killed or wounded. If we get hurt, you're the only doctor left who can take care of us. Besides, you've taken an oath to do no harm."

"Nannie's right, Gus," said Caroline. "Go wait in your office. We'll send word if we need you."

Gus slumped and fought back tears. He moved toward the door.

"Gus," said Nannie.

He turned, hoping she changed her mind.

"Is that an Enfield?"

He nodded. "Bought it from one of the wounded men in the ward."

"You've been holding out on us."

"I thought I'd be called up to the reserves and—"

"Leave it."

Hugh halted his column of weary troopers on the outskirts of the next town north from West Point. The sun was dropping fast; he calculated they had two hours before dark. He had hoped to make another ten miles, but the two hundred Confederate prisoners slowed his progress. Even though this dusty pike was quiet, that mouthy girl's curse kept gnawing at him. *There's an army up the road you won't defeat.* What had she meant by that? The dispatches from General Wilson confirmed the scattered Rebel reserves all around here had been sent to Columbus for a last stand. Yet he suffered the same nagging sense of foreboding the day his brother, Wallace, died. "Colonel Harnden!"

Harnden rode to his side. "Yes, sir."

"Send a scout to see what's up ahead."

Harnden signaled a Wisconsin trooper to gallop up the pike, leaving a cloud of dust. Minutes later, the scout returned with a perplexed look.

"Well?" asked Hugh.

"Colonel, I don't know how to tell you this ..."

"Why don't you try using the English language your mother taught you."

"The entry into town splits into two streets."

"And?"

"A militia guards it."

Hugh tried to make sense of the report. His interrogation of the prisoners at Fort Tyler confirmed every man and boy within fifty miles who could lift a rifle had been at West Point. Sherman cut the rail line running south from Atlanta. How could a militia have mustered anywhere near here without his scouts noticing?

"They're all women."

Hugh ransacked the trooper's saddlebag for whiskey. "If you've been drinking, soldier. I'm in no mood."

"No, sir, I'll swear it on Scripture," the trooper said. "They're armed and formed up in ranks."

Hugh set his jaw in anger. Two hundred old men, boys, and convalescents had cost him a day, and now a mob of Secesh women would delay him again? Wilson would skin his hide. He reined into a turn and rode to the line of bedraggled prisoners. "Anyone here been in that town ahead?"

Colonel Fannin and Major Parham kicked forward the mules he had given them to ride. "It's my home," said Fannin. "And Major Parham here spent time in one of its hospitals."

Hugh pulled a map from his pocket. "What's its name?"

"LaGrange," said Fannin.

The Federal troopers behind Hugh chortled, convinced the Confederate officer was running their colonel in circles by claiming the residents renamed the town in his honor to save it.

Hugh reddened. "Do you wish to walk to Macon?"

"With respect, Colonel," said Fannin. "My hometown has held that name long before either of us was born."

Hugh saw the Rebel officer was serious. "And who are these armed women?"

"The Nancy Harts," said Parham. "They've been drilling for four years."

"You find this amusing?"

"No, sir," said the Confederate major. "Those women will fight. I'd bet my parole on it."

"Why are you so sure?"

"The girl I'm betrothed to is with them."

Hugh was determined to get a look at these Southern Amazons. He signaled his column forward. When Fannin and Parham kicked their mules to return to the other prisoners, Hugh called the Rebel officers back and ordered them to ride with him. "Just in case any more of your womenfolk find it necessary to take a shot at me."

His pace slow and cautious, Hugh kept his gaze on the rise ahead until he came to a lush garden, a paradise of color: delicate pink and snow white dogwoods and brilliant ivory magnolia blossoms wafted sweet, if unsettling, fragrances. A company of his troopers dismounted to form a battle line on either side of the street. They marched through the garden and trampled the flowers and trimmed bushes. Hugh trotted closer to inspect a labyrinth of boxwoods planted in the form of a giant harp with an inscription: *God is Love.* He had never seen an oasis so peaceful and inspiring. He ordered his troopers, "Get out of that garden!"

Perplexed by his newfound concern for Rebel lawns, his men made their way around the groomed flora. A rumbling of voices and whistles erupted from his column. He turned back north—he wasn't certain if he trusted his eyes. A hundred yards off, across Broad Street, two ranks of women stood shoulder to shoulder. He estimated at least forty of them.

A woman pacing behind the ranks, in the position of command, shouted, "Attention!" The women dressed their two lines until their elbows touched.

Hugh's jaw dropped. He had seen veteran soldiers on the field form up with less precision.

"Load!" the lady commander shouted.

The women pulled their ramrods and drove home their cartridges.

Hugh yanked his horse back a step, convinced by their determined glares they were preparing to fire. He ordered his dismounted troopers to halt. Without taking his eyes from the armed women, he asked Parham, "Who is their commanding officer?"

"Mrs. Brown Morgan. She goes by Nannie."

"Does she have a rank?"

"Captain."

The women raised their muskets and took aim.

"Steady, men!" Hugh shouted. "Do *not* draw your weapons!" As his nervous troopers fanned out on foot and sought cover behind trees and fences, he cursed under his breath. He had stumbled onto an overturned hornet's nest and couldn't see a way out. Wilson expected him in Macon in two days, and there'd be hell to pay if he arrived late. His orders were unequivocal: destroy every town that refused to surrender and the homes of Confederate government officials in his path. Yet if he fired on these women, he would be remembered in the annals of infamy as a murderer of women, and he could face a court-martial. Should word spread across the South that a Union army massacred the wives and daughters of Confederate soldiers, the public outrage might compel Lee and Johnston to prolong the war. *Colonel O.H. LaGrange, responsible for thousands of needless deaths.* On the other hand, if he backed down, he would become a laughingstock in the North, chased off by a rabble of Secesh women. The newspapers would have a field day at his expense.

He studied the tall female officer commanding the militia. "Parham, tell me more about this Morgan woman. Can she be reasoned with?"

"She's stubborn. A little like you, I reckon, from what I've witnessed."

Hugh didn't appreciate the comparison. "If I send you up there, will you give me your word to return?"

"If you give me *your* word I won't get shot in the back."

Hugh nodded. "Go on, then. Tell her I want to talk."

Nancy stepped in front of her ranks and shielded her eyes from the sinking sun, trying to identify the unarmed man in butternut rags shuffling toward her on foot up Broad Street.

"Rutledge!" Leila dropped her musket and rushed up to hug her fiancé.

"Corporal Pullen!" Nancy shouted. "Back in line!"

Leila turned from Parham's embrace, stunned. "You cannot deny me this!"

"In line!" demanded Nancy.

Caroline and Mary gestured for Leila to obey. With a sullen glare, Leila pulled herself from Parham, picked up her musket, and returned to her post.

Nancy waited for the shifty Alabama captain to explain his approach. She kept one eye on the mounted officer down the street. "Did that Yankee send you here to scare us into surrendering?"

"Now, Mrs. Morgan, Colonel LaGrange has treated us well."

"Did he treat General Tyler well?"

"That wasn't the Yankee's fault. General Tyler ... why, he was hellbent on dying atop that hill."

"What did you say the colonel's name is?"

"LaGrange."

The blood rushed to Nancy's temples. "He mocks us! The impudent North-erner rides into town and thinks he can steal our name as a title of conquest?"

"No, ma'am, that's his actual name."

"Rutledge wouldn't lie to us, Nannie," insisted Leila.

Nancy glanced at Mary and Caroline, skeptical of Parham's report. She turned back to him. "What does he want?"

"To talk to you."

"I have nothing to say to him."

Caroline risked angering Nancy by questioning her decision in front of the other women. "Shouldn't we at least hear his terms?"

"You mean like the citizens of Atlanta heard Sherman's terms?"

"Ma'am," said Parham, "whatever you decide, he ain't gonna wait long."

Figuring the Yankee colonel had negotiated hundreds of surrenders, she knew she couldn't outsmart him. The women stared hard at her. Would she put their lives at risk without first hearing the Yankee out? What if he was laying a trap, stalling until his men surrounded the town?

"Nannie," whispered Mary. "It'll be dark directly. If we have to fight, we won't be able to see them in another hour."

Nancy nodded for Parham to convey her acceptance. "Tell him to come forward. We will lower our muskets if he comes here only with you."

Parham tipped his hat and hurried back to the Federal column.

Incredulous that anything like this could be happening, Hugh dismounted and walked his horse north a hundred yards closer with Parham at his side. He came before Nancy and her ranks and doffed his campaign hat. "Captain Morgan. I am Colonel LaGrange."

Nancy was taken aback, not only by the salutation formally acknowledging her rank, but by the colonel's imposing stature. She had expected an officer much older. He was one of the tallest men she had ever seen. His wild shocks of brown hair and flowing mustache brought to mind the drawings in the library books of Celtic warriors who fought Julius Caesar. Yet she saw a sadness in his intelligent eyes, and his weathered features suggested none of the brutality and bloodthirst she had presumed from the Northern aggressors. "Sir, we are prepared to defend our town."

Hugh surveyed their embittered glares. "I have no doubt of it. You and your ladies could do damage enough with the fire in your eyes."

Nancy raised her shoulders and braced her stance. He was trying to sweet-talk her, and she would have none of it. She noticed him admiring the columned homes that bordered the street.

"We find ourselves at an impasse, Captain Morgan. I have my orders."

"And we have ours," snapped Leila.

Nancy glared at Leila. She turned back to the Yankee colonel. "Do your orders require the burning of our homes?"

He hesitated. "If the residents resist."

"You'll have to kill us first."

Hugh studied the brim band of his hat, as if the answer to his dilemma lay hidden there. "'Advantage is a better soldier than rashness.'"

Nancy recognized that verse. It came from *Henry V.* This Yankee officer was a learned man, but she refused to allow him to lord his education over hers. She countered his Shakespeare verse with one of her own. "'And the victory is twice itself when the victor brings home full numbers.'"

"*Much Ado About Nothing.*" He smiled. "Did you study it?"

"I performed it." She angled her head toward the building across the street. "In that college hall. The one you intend to burn."

Hugh rubbed his stubbled chin, swallowing the hard truth that this woman was a formidable opponent. He saw that he would make no further progress toward Macon on this day. Somehow, he had to get through the next twelve hours without all hell breaking loose. "May I propose a compromise?"

Nancy braced for treachery. "What manner of compromise?"

"A truce for the night. If you stack arms, I give my word no harm will come to you or your homes while we seek some accommodation to our dilemma."

She yearned to confer with Mary and Caroline, but she knew that hesitation would betray weakness. The Yankee troopers had taken up positions on Vernon Street, a block south. There looked to be thousands of the bluecoats. If they fought here, she would have to re-form her ranks closer to the town square to prevent them from surrounding her. Yet such a retreat could leave their homes on Broad Street exposed to pillage and destruction. Would this man with the sad eyes fire on her militia if they lowered their guns? She risked trusting him and dropped the butt of her musket to the ground. "On your honor."

Hugh doffed his hat again, grateful. He mounted and prepared to ride back to his waiting troopers.

Nancy ordered her women to "about face" and form a column to march to the schoolhouse and stack muskets. In her periphery, she glimpsed the doors to Smith Hall and its auditorium. Her Shakespeare ripostes with the Yankee officer gave her an idea. She turned and called to him, "Colonel LaGrange!"

Hugh reined his horse into a turn. "Yes, ma'am."

"We haven't much variety of food left us here, but would you allow us to serve you and your staff supper this evening?"

She heard murmurs of protest from her ranks.

Hugh sat looking at her, stunned. "That is most generous."

"Shall we say in three hours? Major Parham will give you directions to the Heard house."

"I will not cook for those murderous Yankees!" shouted Leila.

While the women stored their muskets in the schoolhouse, Nancy watched the Union troopers set up camp on the Bellevue grounds. She scolded Leila, "Keep your voice lowered."

"Leila's right," said Caroline. "We barely have enough to feed ourselves and our own wounded men?"

"We will make do," said Nancy. "I have sweet potatoes and grits. I'll badger Gus to requisition whatever meat he can find from the hospital commissary. Augusta, you'll be in charge of baking biscuits."

"With what?" her sister asked.

"You and Andelia knock on doors. Tell folks I need anything they can spare. It will be a late supper, but if we hurry, we can still manage."

"Have the slave women do it," insisted Augusta. "This is beneath us."

"They can't be trusted now," said Nancy. "And the Yankees will not abide being served by them."

Mary had never been more furious with her. "What gives you the right to offer my home for entertaining those men who killed General Tyler and Captain Gonzales? Did that colonel charm every ounce of honor and propriety from you? I won't abide it!"

Nancy pleaded for them to hear her out. "I have a plan."

"*What* plan?" asked Leila. "Cut their throats during dessert?"

Nancy paced in a circle. "Do you remember the play we put on after the college burned?"

Caroline rolled her eyes. "What does that have to do with—"

"*She Stoops To Conquer,*" said Mary.

The women hushed, trying to comprehend what Nancy was proposing.

"We've lost the war on the battlefields," said Nancy. "But we can still win the war for their memories."

"What in Heaven's name are you talking about?" asked Leila.

"What is the best revenge we have left?" When the others shrugged, Nancy pinned them with a look of fierce conviction. "We will put on such a performance tonight that they will never forget the strength, dignity, and charm of a Southern lady. Even in this hour of our darkness, we will remain so unbowed and enchanting in our desolation that their wives and sweethearts will forever fall short in comparison."

"Like a Trojan horse lodged in their hearts," said Leila.

The women smiled with grim determination.

"Hurry," said Mary. "We have much to do."

Promptly at 8:00 p.m., Nancy opened the door to the Heard home and found Colonel LaGrange and his five regimental officers, accompanied by Lieutenant McFarland, Major Parham, and Colonel Fannin, the Confederate officers among the Fort Tyler prisoners. "I have brought more guests," said Hugh. "I hope we will not overburden you."

The unexpected gesture ruffled Nancy's cool facade. Was this courtesy to his prisoners a ploy to soften her up for the negotiations? "They are most welcome." She summoned one of her militia members, Ella Kay, from the kitchen. "Ella, call upon Colonel Fannin's wife and invite her to join us for dinner?"

Ella curtsied and hurried to the Fannin residence down the street.

"Forgive our attire," Hugh said. "We ride without our dress blues."

"If you will forgive us ours," said Nancy. "We have sent most of our fabric to our shivering armies."

Hugh and the officers removed their hats as she led them into a dining room arranged with a long table set with Mary's best china and lit by candles made of jars wrapped with corded rags mixed with cow fat and boiled berries. The Nancies stood against the walls and stared daggers at the Yankees. Leila, astonished to see her fiancé allowed to attend the meal, moved toward him, but Nancy glared a warning at her to remember her military decorum.

"Colonel LaGrange," said Nancy. "Please sit at the head."

Hugh bowed as he took his assigned seat. Forced to improvise because of more guests, Nancy ordered additional settings and chairs brought in. She then led the men to their places, strategically placing them between Mary, Caroline, and her lady officers. She had banished Gus to the hospital for the night, fearful he might offend the Yankees with his sharp tongue. When everyone was situated to her satisfaction, she took her seat at the far end of the table. The younger members, including Leila and Augusta, stood stewing behind her, drafted as servers.

Ella returned with Julia Fannin. The Confederate colonel's wife could not believe what she was seeing. She rushed to the empty chair next to Fannin with tears streaming down her cheeks and pressed a kiss to her husband's lips. "Thank God you are alive."

The Yankee officers lowered their heads in silence, uncertain of the protocol for such an unprecedented gathering. On Nancy's signal, Leila and Augusta retreated to the sideboards in the pantry and returned with platters filled with thin slices of smoked ham sassed with persimmon, stewed sweet potatoes thickened with bacon-drippings gravy, corn fritters, and baked Indian meal pudding. She hoped the men found the meal tolerable. She and the Nancies had never cooked for themselves, and their house slaves had fled to the Federal contraband camp on the edge of town. With their cupboards so bare, they had to make do for spicing with onions, leeks, and grated lemon rinds.

"I must apologize for the meager offerings," said Nancy.

Hugh closed his eyes to savor the aromas. "Captain Morgan, I can speak on behalf of my officers, we have not enjoyed such a bountiful repast since leaving home."

Leila ladled servings of the sweet potatoes. She plopped a dollop the size of a walnut onto Hugh's plate, almost splattering his shirt. She moved on to Major Parham's plate and loaded it.

"Leila," said Nancy sternly. "Colonel LaGrange is not on a jail diet."

Leila grudgingly retraced her steps and dropped another helping of the sweet potatoes on the Yankee colonel's plate while Augusta filled their glasses with blackberry wine.

As soon as all the guests were served, Nancy said, "Colonel LaGrange, would you offer Grace?"

"Ma'am, this is not my home."

"We follow rank here, Colonel. Please."

Hugh lowered his eyes. "'Almighty Father, if it is Thy holy will that we shall obtain a place and name among the nations of the Earth, grant that we may be enabled to show our gratitude for Thy goodness, by our endeavors to fear and obey Thee. Bless us with wisdom in our councils, success in ...'"

Nancy sensed him pausing from embarrassment. She recited the next line in the invocation for him. "'Success in battle.' We know General Washington's Prayer, too."

McFarland came to Hugh's rescue. "'And let all our victories be tempered with humanity. Endow, also, our enemies with enlightened minds, that they may become sensible of their injustice, and willing to restore our liberty and peace. Grant the petition of Thy servant for the sake of Him whom Thou hast called Thy beloved Son. Nevertheless, not our will but Thine be done. Amen.'"

"Amen," said the officers.

The younger women remained silent, glaring at the Yankee officers.

Nancy watched with relief as the men ate with vigorous appetites. For what seemed an eternity, not a word was spoken. She looked across the table at Colonel LaGrange, and he met her scrutiny with a vexed admission suggesting he was no Henry Clay as a conversationalist. She pitied the man. These Northerners clearly were not versed in the fine social arts. She signaled Augusta to pour the colonel another glass of wine to loosen his tongue—

"Major Parham here called your militia the Nancy Harts," said Hugh. "Was Hart your maiden name, Captain Morgan?"

A smile crossed Nancy's face before she could suppress it. "A coincidence only. Not unlike your last name, Colonel LaGrange."

Hugh frowned, confused.

Nancy had told the story a thousand times. "A newspaper gave us the title. Nancy Hart was the wife of a Revolutionary War soldier in Wilkes County. While her husband was off fighting, she defended their farm and sometimes joined our Patriot army."

"She fought in the ranks?" asked Hugh.

Nancy nodded. "At the Battle of Kettle Creek. One night, while she was alone in her cabin with her daughter, six British soldiers arrived on her porch and demanded she cook for them. She agreed. But while she plied them with corn liquor, she secretly slipped their muskets through a crack in the logs. By the time they discovered what had happened, she held them at gunpoint with several muskets in reserve."

The Union officers listened to the story with growing alarm.

"Nancy Hart was cross-eyed," Caroline explained. "But she could still hit a fly on a log from a hundred yards."

"Yes," said Hugh. "I'm learning that girls from these parts learn sharpshooting in the cradle."

"Lots of practice," said Mary, pointedly.

Glancing at his concerned officers, Hugh asked, "What happened to the British soldiers?"

Before Nancy could reply, Leila answered him, her voice quivering with raw anger. "The dullest of the bunch lunged at her. She shot him dead between the eyes. The others surrendered. When their menfolk came home, they strung the invaders up on the nearest oak tree."

The Union officers returned to their meal as the mood grew tense. They quickly cleaned their plates and placed their napkins on the plates. Nancy feared Leila's embittered finish to the story had ruined their chance at saving their homes. She despaired of repairing the hard feelings—

"The gardens we passed," said Hugh. "They are unique in my experience."

Nancy released a held breath, grateful for the change of topic. "The pride of our town. Thanks to Mrs. Fannin here and her family, the Ferrells."

"I wonder ..." Hugh paused. "The day has been long, and you and your ladies have labored hard for us, but if you feel up to it, Mrs. Morgan, would you show me those gardens?"

The other Nancies traded appalled glances at the disgracious solicitation: a Yankee officer asking a married Southern woman to stroll with him at night and unattended.

Hugh felt the ladies' sneers as accusations of an act worse than adultery. In an attempt to make amends, he added, "Perhaps Colonel Fannin and Major Parham could escort us with Mrs. Fannin and Miss Pullen?"

Leila's jaw dropped another inch.

"The gardens are less appreciated after dark," said Nancy.

Hugh lowered his head and nodded, accepting that his brazen request had crossed the line of propriety.

Nancy stood. "But it would be my pleasure."

"Nannie!" Mary protested.

Before Mary and Caroline could stop her, Nancy walked from the dining room and waited at the front door. The junior Yankee officers offered their thanks for the meal, bade goodnight to Hugh, and mounted their horses tied to the gate to return to their camp.

Nancy stood with Hugh as the other women lingered in the dining room, unable to comprehend her scandalous betrayal. "Leila, are you and Julia coming?" she asked. "Or do you intend to leave me unchaperoned?"

Left with no choice, the two younger women grasped the arms of their Confederate beaus. They descended the veranda steps and walked along Broad Street behind Hugh and Nancy. As the group approached the gates to Bellevue, the child in Nancy's womb kicked a protest. *You shame me, too?*

"This mansion?" Hugh asked. "Who owns it?"

Nancy turned and saw the two couples had fallen several paces behind, lost in their own impassioned conversations. Returning to his question, she hesitated to divulge the truth about Bellevue for fear it would doom her favorite place in the world to the flames. Seeing him intent on an answer, she risked the revelation. "Senator Ben Hill's home."

"Ah, yes. Built by slaves, I assume."

She studied him, trying to read his intentions. "He is a good man."

"Does any good man wield a whip against another human being?"

Her heart sank. She had hoped to find him a Unionist who cared little about the Negro question, but he had just revealed who he was, an Abolitionist. She had no response to satisfy him. "You Northerners lord your moral superiority over us. But you have your own sins of equal depravity to answer."

"Such as?"

"Last July, your General Sherman abducted four hundred of our women and children from the mills at Roswell and shipped them North across the Ohio River. We treat our slaves better than you treat those poor people. Many have died of neglect and starvation."

"That is preposterous."

"Ask the butcher Sherman when you next see him. He will confirm it."

Hugh walked the next twenty paces or so in silence, clearly vexed by her accusation. "Before my capture near Dalton, I met a group of Northern ladies at General Sherman's headquarters. The start of the war had stranded them here, in Georgia. They told me Senator Hill was helpful in gaining their safe passage through our lines."

Nancy's eyes teared up as she glanced at the lane to Bellevue—maybe for the last time. "I came out here."

"Came out?"

"Into society."

He seemed increasingly perplexed by her Southern customs. "I've encountered several folks named Hill since crossing into Georgia. Is everyone here related?"

She smiled. "Nearly."

"A doctor in West Point. Means was his name, if I remember. He introduced his wife to me. Her maiden name was Hill."

"My cousin, Celestia."

"She and her husband cared for my favorite officer. He lost a leg there."

"I lost a brother at Fredericksburg," she snapped. "My favorite brother." She immediately regretted that hostile retort. She sensed him pulling away.

They reached the entrance to the Ferrell gardens, and she led him into the maze of trimmed shrubs. A full moon cast a shadowy light, and the hundreds of fires from the Yankee encampment on the outskirts of the town flickered, filling the grounds with ghosts. Having for the moment lost their escorts, she risked a more indecorous question. "Are you married, Colonel?"

"I'm not sure how to answer that."

"Surely you would know?"

He drew a deep breath of air laced with the aroma of yarrow. "Two years ago, I received a letter from my wife. She ... she wrote she had moved back home to Minnesota and would file for a divorce."

"You haven't been home since the war started?"

He shook his head. "To be honest, I have no home."

"No family?"

"I lost my brother in Tennessee."

Her own rush of emotions angered her. How could she have sympathy for this Yankee colonel who had killed so many of her Southern countrymen? She fought the urge to take his hand to console him. These many months, she had felt sorry for herself, but now she wouldn't trade places with this lost soul who had experienced so much violence, death, and loss. She understood his pain and feared what this war had done to her own marriage. Would Brown also come back a changed man? Had she become so accustomed to independence and making her own decisions that she was ruined for him?

They came to the boxwood shrubs sculpted into the words: *God Is Love*. Hugh pondered its biblical message. "I've encountered many ladies of your region during these past four years, and each time I have been left baffled, if not literally disarmed. What is it with the fairer sex here that differs so from our women?"

Having not met a Yankee before this night, Nancy had never been posed such a strange question. Oddly, it thrust her back to her childhood. "My grandmother was the strongest woman I've ever known. She could go from dawn to dusk stirring the meals over the pot while preaching the Word of the Lord. Yet once a year, she retreated to her room and locked the door for days. We called it 'Granna Colquitt Taking To Her Bed Again.' The men knew not to disturb her, lest they raise the demons. I'll let you in on one of our secrets, Colonel. I came to understand she took to that bed because it was the only way she could exert her authority over a world that underestimated her."

Hugh stopped to consider if her anecdote meant something more. "Would you have fired on me today?"

"Would you have fired upon *me?*

"I asked first."

She resumed their stroll. "I grant but one secret per Yankee."

He smiled and nodded.

Nancy's thoughts lingered on those sculpted words in the boxwood shrubs. "I've walked past that message a thousand times but never questioned it until now. If God *is* Love, then is it heresy to believe He also caused all of this war's destruction?"

"Are we mortals not agents of our own shortcomings?"

She circled the labyrinth with him. "General Hardee's surgeon told me a story that has long haunted me. Years ago, your General Sherman, while attending the Military Academy in New York, fell in love with a Georgia girl from Bartow County. She did not reciprocate his passion and told him her reason: 'Your eyes are so cold and cruel. I pity the man who ever becomes your foe. Ah, how you would crush an enemy.' Sherman, devastated, replied, 'Even though you were my enemy, my dear, I would ever love and protect you.'"

Hugh shrugged. "Sherman is not the first jilted man."

"Last year, so I was told, Sherman crossed the Etowah River and came to a beautiful old mansion near Cass. You Yankees were about to burn it when Sherman heard a distraught old man cry out how glad he was Miss Cecelia wasn't there to see it destroyed. Sherman asked the old man if that was the home of Cecelia Stovall of Augusta, and the man confirmed it was, but informed him she had fled to Atlanta. Sherman ordered the house placed under guard and its belongings protected."

"Did Sherman ever see Miss Stovall again?"

"No, but he left a note with instructions for the old man to deliver it to her when she returned."

"What did the note say?"

She had committed the words of Sherman's note to heart. "'You once said that I would crush an enemy, and you pitied my foe. Do you recall my reply? Although many years have passed, my answer is the same. I would ever shield and protect you. That I have done. Forgive all else. I am only a soldier.'"

Hugh turned aside.

"Colonel LaGrange, is there no one who has ever protected *you*?"

His eyes watered. He did not answer her.

"If so, *there* is your home."

He stood silent for an extended moment and turned toward the couples trailing them on the garden path. When the two Confederate officers and the other women caught up, he said, "Colonel Fannin, please escort Mrs. Morgan home. I will send a member of my staff to retrieve my horse."

Parham and Fannin, confused, waited for an explanation. When none came, Fannin reminded Hugh, "Sir, we are your prisoners."

"I have paroled you for the night. I believe you to be men of your word. Report to my headquarters at dawn."

The Confederate officers saluted, stunned by his trust and generosity.

Hugh tipped his hat to Nancy. "Thank you for the meal and the tour, Captain Morgan."

Nancy watched him walk off into the night after offering no indication if he intended to burn their homes.

* * *

The next morning, drawn by the sharp stench of smoke, Nancy and her militia women rushed onto the porch of Mary's home. Nancy's heart sank. Dark plumes billowed up from the warehouses near the train depot. The heavy clops of cavalry horses echoed up Broad Street. Colonel LaGrange, riding at the head of his column, turned the corner and halted in front of the Heard home. Alongside his troopers rode the captured Confederate officers on mules. Nancy struggled to fight back tears. Had the Yankee colonel tricked her? Their own muskets were in the schoolhouse, too far away to retrieve.

Hugh doffed his hat. "Ladies, we must take our leave."

"Colonel, you mean to burn the entire town?" asked Nancy.

"The warehouses and train depot. I have spared the lumber factory because it fashions coffins. The foodstuffs in the commissaries have been placed in the jurisdiction of your mayor."

Her voice cracked, "And our homes?"

"They will not be touched."

Caroline, holding her child, dropped to her knees in relief.

The other Nancies wept and embraced.

Nancy struggled to stay composed. "Our weapons?"

"I have no discretion in that regard," said Hugh. "My provost must confiscate them."

"Marauders and deserters perpetrate mischief in these parts," Nancy said. "How will we defend ourselves?"

Hugh motioned for his dispatch book from his adjutant. He scribbled an order, tore the page out, and handed it to her. "The muskets will be stored under guard in the courthouse. Should you or these ladies in your charge come into harm's way, present this to the provost. He will send word to me."

Nancy coughed back the clutch in her throat. "Thank you."

The other Nancies, sobbing, rushed to the Confederate prisoners and gave them packages of food for their hundred-mile march to the prison camp in Macon.

"Attention!" commanded Nancy.

The LaGrange women shuffled into ranks along the street.

Hugh surveyed the magnificent homes along Broad Street one last time. He wheeled his horse to face the Nancies and, tapping its haunches with his spurs, reared it a few inches. With practiced precision, the horse's head swung low and descended into a deft bow. He drew his saber and touched its point to his boot's toe in the traditional cavalry gesture of respect.

The Nancies returned his chivalry with a salute.

Hugh shared a glance of mutual understanding with Nancy, as if thanking her for something she had said to him that night in the garden. Breaking off, he reined his horse east and trotted away.

Nancy dismissed her exhausted women to their homes. Alone now and overcome by a wave of despair, she stood watch until the Yankee colonel vanished in the haze on the road to Macon.

EPILOGUE

GEORGIA
MAY, 1865

Nancy stood with her militia, veiled in mourning black, at the burned ruins of the LaGrange depot. They waited in silence as one of the last functioning locomotives in Georgia staggered into town on the repaired tracks from Newnan.

Three days after the Yankee cavalry left town, news arrived that General Lee surrendered in Virginia on April 9—a week before the battle at West Point. General Tyler was the last general killed in the war; he, Captain Gonzales, and the other defenders buried at that redoubt had died for a cause already lost.

Nancy had not heard from Brown in months. She prayed he was in North Carolina with the survivors of General Johnston's Army, which surrendered to Sherman at Benton Place a week after Appomattox. President Davis, captured by Federal cavalry near Irwinville, sat in a Virginia prison cell. Senator Hill made it home to Bellevue, only to be arrested. She feared the North, outraged by Lincoln's assassination, would demand both men be hanged. Due to give birth any day now, she had intended to disband the Nancies weeks ago, but one last duty called. She held firm to Caroline's arm to support her as the train screeched to a stop.

The door to a boxcar slammed open.

Nancy's brother, Miles, and Colonel Fannin, paroled at Macon, climbed into the car and lifted a coffin to the gangway. Joined by Gus Ware and three disabled veterans of the Fourth Georgia, the pallbearers carried the pine box to a waiting grave in the Confederate military cemetery near the tracks. Nancy, Caroline, and Mary, accompanied by their fellow militia members, walked behind the coffin in procession.

Every blessing is followed by a tragedy.

As they entered the cemetery and stepped around the fresh mounds of dirt, Nancy rested her head on Caroline's shoulder. She must be strong for her friend.

A week after their homes were saved, news arrived by courier that Caroline's husband, Lieutenant John Gay, had died from wounds suffered at Fort Stedman during General Lee's last attempt to break out from the Petersburg siege trenches. Caroline insisted that John lie forever with his comrades here, rather than with her in Hillview Cemetery.

The mourners gathered around the coffin as the chaplain spoke a few words. Nancy, lost in her thoughts, did not hear them. When the chaplain finished, she called her women to attention. Clutching her small Bible, she stepped forward to speak her piece before the dirt was shoveled into the grave. She pulled back her veil and opened to the Book of Ruth. Telling the story of Ruth in her own words, she said, "During a time of famine and desolation, Israelite women lost their men. One of these widows, Naomi, was forced to leave her family in Moab. Naomi told her sisters and daughters-in-law not to follow her to an uncertain future. But one woman, Ruth, refused to abandon Naomi."

Sallie Fannie Reid came to her side to give her strength.

Nancy read aloud the biblical Ruth's vow from the verse. "'Entreat me not to leave thee, or to return from following after thee. For whither thou goest, I will go. And where thou lodgest, I will lodge. Thy people shall be my people, and thy God my God. Where thou diest, will I die, and there will I be buried. The Lord do so to me, and more also, if ought but death part thee and me.'"

Surrounded by sobs, Nancy closed the Bible and looked toward the homes and church steeples of her beloved town, offering a silent prayer of gratitude for their survival. She turned to Caroline, Mary, Leila, and her sisters-in-arms to affirm Ruth's vow to them. "Wherever *you* go, I will go, and wherever *you* live, I will live. Where *you* die, I will die. May the Lord punish me if anything but death separates you and me."

The Nancy Harts saluted their last order.

* * *

Hugh rode into Macon and halted in front of the Catholic Church of the Assumption. With the war over, he and his First Wisconsin troopers had been ordered north to be mustered out in Tennessee. He glanced across the rail yard at Camp Oglethorpe prison, now abandoned, and spat a farewell to that damnable place. Before leaving, he had one last mission, his most formidable yet of the war. He debated the wisdom of what he was about to—

"May I help you?" An elderly priest stood at the opened rectory door.

Hugh drew a deep breath. "A Daughter of Charity lives here?"

"Sister Elizabeth, you mean?"

His heart raced. "Yes."

"What business do you have with her?"

"I wish to return a book."

The priest narrowed his suspicious glare. After a hesitation, he disappeared into the rectory. Moments later, he came out with Lizzie Andrews in her robe and bonnet. Lizzie's eyes widened when she saw him.

Hugh tipped his hat. "Miss Andrews."

She blushed. "Colonel LaGrange. I feared you perished in Charleston."

"How did you know I was sent to Charleston?" When she merely shrugged, he pressed her for an answer. "Someone intervened on my behalf to transfer me from a train bound for Andersonville."

She stole a worried glance at the priest. "God works in mysterious ways."

"With more than a little help from His angels." Hugh reached into his saddlebag and pulled out the Bible she had used to convey the coded messages to him in the prison. "I couldn't go North without making good on your loan."

She stepped forward to take it, but the priest moved in front of her and accepted the Bible on her behalf. "You may leave now."

Hugh peered over the priest's shoulder to ask her, "You took the vow?"

"Next month," she said.

He studied every flicker of her eyes, trying to read her. "This Bible has been a source of great comfort to me. I found particular inspiration from Leviticus Eleven. I commend those verses for your immediate contemplation."

Before she could ask why *that* passage so moved him, the priest herded her back into the rectory.

Moments later, confined to her small room, Lizzie sat on the cot and opened the Bible. Dried blood and mud stained its pages. She turned to Leviticus to find the verses the Yankee colonel had cited:

> *And the LORD spake unto Moses and to Aaron, saying unto them: Speak unto the children of Israel, saying, These are the beasts which ye shall eat among all the beasts that are on the earth. Whatsoever parteth the hoof, and is clovenfooted, and cheweth the cud, among the beasts, that shall ye eat. Nevertheless these shall ye not eat of them that chew the cud, or of them that divide the hoof: as the camel, because he cheweth the cud, but divideth not the hoof; he is unclean unto you.*

What did *that* mean? Did the Yankee come back here just to make jest of her with a passage about cloven hooves? In a huff, she reached up to shelve the Bible, but she paused and opened it to the passage again. Struck by an outlandish notion, she hunted for the last doily she had used as a code template in the prison camp. She found it in the crease between the last page and back cover. A couple of fresh holes appeared to have been carved into the doily and previous holes stitched closed. She placed it over the page with the Leviticus verses and copied the letters revealed by the interstices in the knitted cloth:

M—A—R—R—Y—M—E

Slamming the Bible shut, she quickly exchanged her habit for a calico dress, packed a knapsack, and swept past the priest in his office. She shoved open the rectory door and found Hugh waiting on his horse. She threw her knapsack to him and ran for his outstretched hand.

He lifted her onto the saddle and kicked the horse north on the road toward Tennessee. Leaving Macon, they passed hundreds of freed slaves, some working the same fields under white overseers, others huddled in the contraband camps, starving and ravaged by disease. The South didn't look much different to him than it did in 1861, save for the charred mansions and the fresh graves in the cemeteries. Had the war accomplished anything in raising up black Americans? Was Professor Daniels's dream of a Utopia for the races all for naught? Had Wallace died in vain?

"You would never make a spy," Lizzie whispered to his ear. "You forgot the question mark at the end of your coded message."

"Scripture has question marks? I thought the Almighty was all-knowing."

"If you think the Almighty is all-knowing," she said. "Wait until you have a Southern wife."

Hugh hid a smile. "I should warn you. I have no home. I haven't got ten dollars to my name. I'm leaving the only profession I've known for the past four years. And I've been a miserable failure at understanding women both above and below the Mason-Dixon Line."

She tightened her arms around his waist. "If you can ride us out of Georgia without getting me shot, I'll overlook your many other faults."

Hugh intertwined his fingers with hers and sent the horse into a gallop.

☙

AUTHOR'S NOTE

After the war, the Nancy Harts disbanded. Their exploits might have disappeared into the mists of history had Leila Pullen Morris, the youngest member of the militia, not given a speech in 1896 commemorating her comrades to the United Daughters of the Confederacy. By that time, Leila had long since broken off her engagement to Major Rutledge Parham and had married James Allen Morris, a businessman from Pennsylvania.

Six weeks after her confrontation with Colonel LaGrange, Nancy Morgan gave birth to a boy, Charles. Her husband, Jeremiah Brown Morgan, surrendered to General Sherman in North Carolina and returned home to practice law until his death in 1884. Nancy died in 1910. She lies buried not with Mary Heard, Caroline Gay, and the other Nancy Harts in the town she helped save, but in Decatur, Georgia.

Dr. Augustus Ware raised two families, one covertly with Marie Harrison, his sister's house slave. He kept the concubinage—an institutionally coercive practice prevalent in the South—hidden from his white wife and family, according to historian Kenneth Robert Jenken. Until his death in 1872, Ware financially supported Marie Harrison and her children. Madeline Harrison, his daughter with Marie, attended Clark University in Atlanta and taught school. Madeline's son, Walter Francis White, became a prominent civil rights activist and the executive secretary of the National Association for the Advancement of Colored People.

Senator Benjamin Harvey Hill returned to Bellevue from Richmond expecting to find his mansion destroyed. Astonished by its survival, he detailed in his memoirs his quest to solve the mystery of why Colonel LaGrange did not put his home to the torch. Today, visitors to LaGrange can tour Bellevue, the nearby Ferrell Gardens, and the small Confederate Stonewall cemetery.

In 1866, Sallie Fannie Reid married Captain William D. Grant, who founded a railroad company with his father and moved his family to Atlanta. Their daughter, also named Sallie Fannie, wedded John Slaton, a future governor of Georgia. Sallie's white-columned mansion on the Sunny Villa plantation in West Point fell to ruin, but a replica of the home—now a registered historic house called Whitehall—sits on the original site in a suburban tract on the east side of the Chattahoochee River. The town's defensive redoubt was reconstructed in

1998 by the Fort Tyler Association, a group of residents who hold an annual dinner to remember the men and boys who fell there.

The First Wisconsin Cavalry gained the distinction of helping capture Confederate President Jefferson Davis during his attempted escape across Georgia. General Joseph Wheeler was also arrested and briefly held at Conyers, but it is not recorded if Colonel LaGrange ever met again with his old rival. Wheeler was one of only four Confederate generals who received a Federal commission to fight for the United States during the Spanish-American War.

Colonel LaGrange declined the offer of a brigadier's commission and brought Lizzie Andrews north to marry her. After narrowly losing an election in 1865 for lieutenant-governor of Wisconsin, he moved to New York, studied law at the University of Albany, and gained admittance to that state's bar. Rendered penniless by a plunge in the cotton market, he took Lizzie to California and taught school for a year. In 1869, President Grant appointed him to the post of superintendent for the U.S. Mint in San Francisco. He later served as governor of the National Home for Disabled Volunteer Soldiers in Santa Monica. Lizzie died in 1880, and four years later, Colonel LaGrange married another Georgia plantation lady, Susie Bird, from Bibb County. They moved to New York City, lived in Manhattan until his death in 1915, and were buried in Woodlawn Cemetery in the Bronx.

Colonel LaGrange's mentor, Edward Daniels, became active in Reconstruction South politics. He purchased the Gunston Hall estate in Virginia and tried unsuccessfully to maintain a Utopian farming community there.

During the postwar years, Confederate veterans wrote with admiration and gratitude about Colonel LaGrange. Louis Burchette McFarland, one of the officers who defended Fort Tyler, became a justice on the Tennessee Supreme Court. He visited LaGrange while on a trip to California in 1910, and the two men spent a pleasant afternoon reminiscing. Describing the aftermath of the West Point fight in *Confederate Veteran* magazine, Justice McFarland confirmed that Hugh LaGrange "treated us well and was especially courteous to me." James Fannin, another Fort Tyler survivor, believed the Yankee officer saved his life. Posted at Andersonville prison during the war, Fannin was targeted by Union General Edward McCook for arrest when LaGrange intervened on his behalf.

Were the Nancy Harts ultimately successful in stooping to conquer? For an ardent Abolitionist Union officer from Wisconsin to wed a Georgia belle after spending so little time in the state might be dismissed as a happy coincidence. Marrying *two* such belles suggests the possibility, at least, that Colonel LaGrange's encounter with the Nancies left a profound and lasting impression. Perhaps he developed a deep emotional bond with those Southern women who, like him, had lost so much to the war.

Captain Nancy Colquitt Hill Morgan   Colonel Oscar Hugh LaGrange

Officers of the Nancy Hart Rifles

Lt. Jeremiah Brown Morgan

Sallie Fannie Reid

LaGrange Female College

Senator Benjamin Harvey Hill

Bellevue Mansion

Colonel Edward Daniels

General Joseph Wheeler

First Wisconsin Cavalry
Monument at Chickamauga

Lt. John Gay

General Robert Tyler

General William Hardee

Colonel LaGrange and the First Wisconsin Cavalry at Anderson's Crossroads

First Wisconsin Cavalry Reunion, 1900
(The author believes the man standing in front is Colonel LaGrange)

Sketch of the Battle of West Point by Private Robert Merrill
of the First Wisconsin Cavalry (Fort Tyler Association Collection)

ABOUT THE AUTHOR

A graduate of Indiana University School of Law and Columbia University Graduate School of Journalism, **Glen Craney** practiced trial law before joining the Washington, D.C. press corps to write about national politics and the Iran-contra trial for *Congressional Quarterly* magazine. In 1996, the Academy of Motion Pictures, Arts and Sciences awarded him the Nicholl Fellowship prize for best new screenwriting. His debut historical novel, *The Fire and the Light,* was named Best New Fiction by the National Indie Excellence Awards. He is a three-time Finalist/ Honorable Mention winner of *Foreword Magazine's* Book-of-the-Year and a Chaucer Award winner for Historical Fiction. His books have taken readers to Occitania during the Albigensian Crusade, the Scotland of Robert Bruce, Portugal during the Age of Discovery, the trenches of France during World War I, the battlefields of the Civil War, and the American Hoovervilles of the Great Depression. He lives in Malibu, California.

Learn more about Glen's books and subscribe to his newsletter for deals and new releases at **www.glencraney.com**.

Dear Reader:

If you feel this book is worthy, I would be grateful for a review on Amazon, Goodreads, Barnes&Noble, and other retail sites. Just a line or two can make all the difference in helping spread the word to fellow readers.

Thank you, Glen

Also by Glen Craney

The Fire and the Light
A Novel of the Cathars

As the 13th century dawns, Cathar heretics in southern France guard an ancient scroll that holds shattering revelations about Jesus Christ. Esclarmonde de Foix, a beloved Occitan countess, must defy Rome to preserve the true path to salvation. Christianity suffers its darkest hour in this epic saga of troubadour love, monastic intrigue, and esoteric mystery set during the first years of the French Inquisition.

The Spider and the Stone
A Novel of Scotland's Black Douglas

As the 14th century dawns, the brutal Edward Longshanks of England schemes to steal Scotland. But inspired by a headstrong lass, a frail, dark-skinned boy named James Douglas defies three Plantagenet kings and champions the cause of his wavering friend, Robert the Bruce, leading the armies to the bloody field of Bannockburn. Here is the thrilling saga of star-crossed love and heroic sacrifice that saved Scotland and set the stage for the founding of the United States.

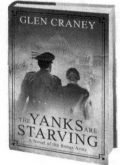

The Yanks Are Starving
A Novel of the Bonus Army

Mired in the Great Depression, the United States teeters on the brink of revolution. And as the summer of 1932 approaches, a charismatic hobo leads twenty thousand homeless World War I veterans into the nation's capital to demand their service compensation. Here is the epic story of political intrigue and betrayal that culminated in the only pitched battle ever fought between two American armies under the same flag.

The Virgin of the Wind Rose
A Christopher Columbus Mystery - Thriller

While investigating the murder of an American missionary in Ethiopia, State Department lawyer Jaqueline Quartermane discovers an ancient Latin palindrome embedded with a cryptographic time bomb. Separated by half a millennium, two espionage conspiracies dovetail in this breakneck thriller to expose the world's most explosive secret: The true identity of Christopher Columbus and the explorer's connection to those now trying to launch the Apocalypse.

More information at www.glencraney.com.

ACKNOWLEDGEMENTS

ThE author wishes to particularly thank John Jeter, a former Columbia University classmate and a great friend, for helping shape this book with the keen eye of a Southern gentleman who hails from an illustrious military family. Also thanks to the following for their invaluable assistance: Kathy Laughlin; Kristy Makanis; Shannon Gavin Johnson, Forrest Clark Johnston III, and Kay Minchew of the Troup County Museum and Archives; Rea Clark of the Fort Tyler Association; David Hyams of Luminaria Studio; Christopher and Josephine Holland Agricola; Julia R. Hardman, Margaret Frandsen, Michell Tucker, Kimberly Motteshard, and Sharon Tucker; Beau Burgess of the Fort Douglas Military Museum; the Wisconsin Historical Society; and the Wisconsin Veterans Museum.

The 1900 reunion photograph of the First Wisconsin Cavalry is included by permission of the Wisconsin Veterans Museum. The contemporary sketch of the Battle of West Point is by permission of the Fort Tyler Association.

REENACTRESS
A Documentary Film

The actor portraying Captain Nancy Morgan on the cover is **J.R. Hardman**, director of the upcoming feature-length documentary, *Reenactress.* At the intersection of history and modernity, the film tells the story of present-day women who crossdress as soldiers in American Civil War reenactments, commemorating the real women who disguised themselves as men to fight in the Civil War on both sides. Hardman embeds herself in the male-dominated world and progresses from novice spectator to expert military reenactor. Along the way, she battles harassment, gender discrimination, racism, yellow journalism, historical "fake news," and the internal conflict of how to accurately represent the complex and messy story of women's and transgender military history in the United States.

Hardman has been involved in the Civil War reenactment community for over eight years. She has participated in dozens of living history programs and also performs a first-person impression of the female Civil War soldier, Frances Clayton. Hardman currently serves as COVID-19 Training Specialist for Salt Lake County and has worked as Operations Manager for Sundance Institute Artist Programs in Park City, Utah, and Senior Tour Manager for Campus Movie Fest, the world's largest student film festival.

To learn more about the film, please visit **www.reenactress.com.**